"Please just tell me what it does," said Marisa.

"It bluescreens you," said Anja, shooing Omar from his chaise and sitting down in his spot. "An overwhelming sensory rush, an unbelievable high, and then boom. Crash to desktop. Your djinni goes down and takes your brain with it for, like, ten minutes. It's the best."

"Hang on—" said Marisa, but Anja grinned and popped the drive into her headjack.

"Play crazy," she said, and then her arms started to twitch. A wide, almost childish smile spread across her face, and her eyes rolled back before closing luxuriously. Anja started to hum, a long, sensual *mmmmm*, and her legs pressed together for just a moment before her whole head and torso started vibrating. Marisa jumped toward her, grabbing her by the arms and calling out in alarm, but in that moment Anja's body spasmed one last time and went completely still.

ALSO BY
DAN WELLS

BLUESCREEN

A MIRADOR NOVEL

DAN WELLS

BALZER + BRAY
An Imprint of HarperCollins*Publishers*

Balzer + Bray is an imprint of HarperCollins Publishers.

Bluescreen
Copyright © 2016 by Dan Wells

www.epicreads.com

Library of Congress Control Number: 2015943608
ISBN 978-0-06-234788-6

Typography by Torborg Davern
16 17 18 19 20   PC/LSCH   10 9 8 7 6 5 4 3 2 1

First paperback edition, 2017

This book is dedicated to Hedy Lamarr, an actress and mathematician who, in the 1930s, invented some of the Wi-Fi communications technology that make the internet age possible. She was brilliant and inventive, and the fact that most people remember her just for her looks says more about the world than a hundred books could hope to convey. Let's change that world.

BLUESCREEN

ONE

"Quicksand's down." Sahara's voiced hissed across Marisa's comm. "Fang, too. I made it out of the fight but only barely."

"They got Anja in a double blitz," said Marisa, crouching behind the lip of a shattered skylight. "I tried to save her but I was doing recon on the other side of the roof; I couldn't make it back in time." The battle had moved past her for the moment, distant gunfire echoing through the shattered ruins of the old industrial complex. The bulk of the fighting was down on ground level, leaving her hidden but desperate on the top of an old factory, gasping for breath. She checked her rifle: a long, black Saber-6 that fired pulses of microwave energy. There were only two charges left.

"Protecting Anja is your job," said Sahara harshly. "You were supposed to have her back. Now you and I are the only ones left."

Marisa winced. "I know, I'm sorry. I lost track of the battle, and you told me to recon the other side of the roof—"

"I also told you bring cameras on this run," Sahara snapped. "They could have reconned for you, and you could have stayed with your Sniper. Don't blame me when you— Damn, they found me." Sharp staccato gunfire crackled through Marisa's headset from two directions: the distant pops from the actual battle, and the louder, closer barks transmitted directly from Sahara's comm. Marisa muted the sound and checked her visor display, watching Sahara's embattled icon move across the wireframe map of the factory complex. She had a small group of bots to back her up, maybe six or seven, but there was a wave of enemies swarming toward her, and more icons popped up on Marisa's display as Sahara identified them: two, three, four . . .

"You've got all five enemy agents on you," said Marisa.

"Then get off your ass and help me!" roared Sahara.

Marisa jumped up and sprinted across the rooftop, her black bodysuit nearly invisible in the starlight—though with all five of the enemy focused on Sahara, Marisa had little fear of being spotted now. There were guard drones on the rooftops with her, but her optic armor made her undetectable to their sensors—they wouldn't bother her unless she bothered them first. As she ran, she cataloged her assets, racking her brain for any advantage that might help save Sahara and salvage the mission. Sahara's words still stung: it *was* Marisa's job to protect Anja, and that made it Marisa's fault that Anja was dead. Sahara had told her to bring cam drones, but she'd insisted on trying a new loadout for this run. She should have stuck with what she knew. The drone kit would have given her not only cameras but gun drones, mobile weapon turrets she could have locked onto Anja, sniping anything that got too close. Those same guns could be down there right now saving Sahara, too.

Marisa shook her head. It didn't do her any good to whine about it now. She'd brought what she'd brought, and she'd have to make do. She couldn't win the battle, but maybe she could . . . what? She had nothing that would be useful in a firefight: a stealth kit, and some new tech, just released, that she'd wanted to try out: force projectors. It had been fun using the gloves to knock enemy agents off the top of the factory, but what now? Even if she could get to the battle in time, the projectors didn't have the range to hit anything on the ground from up here, and she didn't have the armor to get in close. And a couple of force wave shoves weren't going to save the day in a five-on-two gunfight anyway.

She leaped over a short gap between buildings and kept running. Her visor showed her the specs of her new gloves, detailing exactly what they could generate: a force wave to knock people back, a force wall that could block a door or an alley, and a force field she could throw out as a temporary defense. It was crowd control and protection—all things that might have saved Anja, if Marisa hadn't left her, but wouldn't provide enough to help Sahara now that she was cornered and outnumbered. The enemy agents were going to kill her, and with most of Sahara's defensive turrets already destroyed, they'd roll right through the factory to Marisa's base and destroy it. The mission was lost, and the Cherry Dogs were dead.

Sahara's voice screamed across the comm, using Marisa's call sign instead of her name, "Heartbeat, help me!" Hearing her name refocused Marisa on the task at hand—she was an Agent, and she had a job to do; dead or not, her team was counting on her. She would have to improvise.

She checked her visor again, zeroing in on the scene of the battle, and angled toward the corner of the roof. The ledge gave a perfect view of the ground below, which made it an ideal sniping spot; it was guarded by one of the biggest attack drones in the complex, a massive Mark-IX, but Marisa slipped past it in her optic armor and dropped to one knee, leveling her rifle and looking through the scope. Sahara was pinned down in a dead-end alcove, kneeling behind a heavy cement wall—probably the corner of an old fusion reactor. She only had a few bots left, crouched in the rubble and firing blindly at the enemy swarm. The five enemy agents had taken up positions in the street, surrounded by their own army of bots, using old delivery trucks as cover and concentrating their fire on Sahara's position. It was a perfect kill zone.

"I'm right over you," Marisa whispered.

"Do you have a shot?"

"Not a great one." She looked up at the Mark-IX towering over her—a humanoid model bristling with blades and armor and a belt-fed chain gun on its shoulder. "I've got two charges in the rifle, but I'm right underneath an attack drone. As soon as I take the first shot he'll spot me, so I'm not going to get a second."

"Then make it count," said Sahara grimly.

Marisa nodded, scanning her targets and drawing a careful bead on the enemy Sniper. She breathed carefully, calculating the angle, aiming just a little high to account for the distance—

—and then she got an idea.

"Heartbeat, are you going to shoot or not?"

Marisa backed up, slinging the rifle over her shoulder and looking more closely at the attack drone. "You've got the laser kit, right?"

"Of course: *I* actually brought what I was supposed to."

Marisa held in a sigh. "Can you paint a target for me?"

Sahara was growing more frustrated. "Can't you pick your own target? How many times have you practiced with that rifle?"

"I'm not using the rifle," said Marisa. She planted her feet wide, bending her knees and bracing herself against the coming shock wave. She raised her hands, palms forward, keeping her eyes on the drone.

"What are you doing?"

Marisa turned on the projectors, building up a charge. "Just paint me a target, right in the middle of their group."

Sahara grumbled, but her icon moved on the wireframe map, and a moment later a pillar of light shot up from the center of the factory floor. "That's the enemy General," said Sahara. "The rest of his team is within ten feet of him, but one bullet isn't going to be able to take them all out."

"That's why I'm not using bullets. Now stay out of sight." Marisa moved slightly to the left, putting the attack drone in a direct line between her and the pillar of light. "Catch this, chango."

She fired the force projectors with all the juice they had, a blast that would have sent a human target flying across the map. The drone, far bigger and heavier, flew backward only a little before it started to fall, arcing perfectly down toward the enemy General. The drone's AI was basic: if it saw something that wasn't a fellow drone, it killed it. Marisa's attack had dropped the stealth mode on her armor, and the drone swiveled its gun toward her as it fell, sending a stream of bright white tracers buzzing toward her through the night; she was too close to avoid them, and staggered back as the rounds slammed into her armor. Then the Mark-IX landed, right in the center of the firefight, and with Marisa out of sight it swiveled again, acquired new targets, loosed a devastating hail of fire on the enemy agents.

"Great Holy Hand Grenades," said Sahara. "Can you even *do* that?"

"Probably not a second time," said Marisa, dragging herself to the edge and looking down at the chaos. The chain gun burst had nearly killed her, and she blinked to activate a healing pack. "They always patch the good toys as soon as we exploit them."

"Respawned," said Anja. "Quicksand and Fang are right behind me."

"Just in time," said Sahara. "Let's hit them fast, before they recover. Tap into the drone and focus fire on its targets. Go!"

Marisa watched as Sahara and her soldiers popped up from behind their cover, firing forward at the enemy while the attack drone rampaged through their battle line. Marisa lined up her rifle and fired its last two shots, dropping the enemy Sniper as he fled from the Mark-IX, and then she watched as her respawned teammates caught up and decimated the rest of the enemy team. Marisa blinked on the comm.

"Sorry I got you killed, Anja."

"Are you kidding?" Anja was flitting around the field with her jump pack, picking off stragglers while Sahara and the others mowed through the center of the enemy bots. "If we hadn't been desperate, we never would have got to see that drone launch move. You come up with that?"

Marisa grinned. "Surprised?"

"Expect to see it all over the net by the weekend," said Quicksand. "Another viral Cherry Dogs vid."

"And another kit nerfed," said Fang. "I was looking forward to trying the Force Projectors, but noooo. They'll nerf the hell out of it now. It's like Marisa specializes in breaking the game balance."

"It's what we do," said Anja. "When all else fails, play crazy."

A new wave of bots arrived to reinforce them, and together they finished off the drone and pushed forward to the enemy base. It had been a close game, and the enemy towers were already destroyed, so with all five enemy agents dead, the Cherry Dogs had an open lane to blaze in and pour all their damage onto the last few turrets. The enemy team respawned right as Marisa reached the base, but it was too late: the turrets went down, and the vault exploded.

"Cherry Dogs win!" The voice-over rolled through the factory, and the bots broke into their dance animation as triumphant music filled the comm. Marisa cheered, stretched her neck, and blinked out of the simulation. The factory disappeared, and she floated in nothingness for a second before the stat room materialized around her: a wide, round room full of benches and ringed with consoles, the walls covered with data from the battle. Marisa was still in her Overworld avatar: a skintight stealth suit—far skinnier than she was in real life—made of sleek black leather, with thin tracings of metal gadgets and exoskeleton. A basic design, but she was proud of it. The other team, Salted Batteries, was already in the lobby, laughing in shock at the sudden turn that lost them the game. That was a good sign. Not everybody could laugh off a loss like that. Sahara blinked in just as Marisa did, and strode forward to shake hands with the enemy General.

"Good game, guys," she said. She was also in her avatar, though it was mostly just a digital copy of herself, maintaining her branding as a vidcaster; she didn't even use a call sign, just her real name. The avatar matched Sahara's dark brown skin to perfection, and wore a rich, red dress so tight she'd barely be able to walk if this wasn't a video game. She smiled. "I really thought you had us there."

"So did I," said the General. His call sign was Tr0nik. They were all still in their game avatars as well, so Marisa didn't know what he really looked like; his voice was male, and his accent Chinese, with the stilted vocabulary that marked him as learning most of his English on the net. "We didn't think about giant killer robots falling out of the sky."

"Hong Kong," said Fang, blinking in to whisper in Marisa's ear.

"How can you tell?"

"How can you tell when an American's from Boston?" she asked. "He sounds like it. You need to practice your Chinese." Fang was a Chinese native, living somewhere in Beijing; Marisa had never met her or Quicksand in real life, but they were some of her closest friends in the world.

"I know, I know," said Marisa. Her mom was always telling her to study her Chinese, too. Marisa put on a smile and stepped forward to shake Tr0nik's hand. "Good game."

"Great game," he said happily, and the rest of the team crowded around to offer similar congratulations. "That was a good tactic, to throw the Mark-IX. Have you done that before?"

"That was spur of the moment," said Sahara, reinserting herself as the center of attention. She put her hand on Marisa's back, smiling broadly. "Nobody thinks on their feet like the Cherry Dogs."

"Play crazy!" said one of the other Salted Batteries. Anja's catchphrase had been gaining notoriety almost as fast as their team had.

"You guys did a great job, and this was a great match," said Sahara. She talked like she was in a beauty pageant. "Thanks for the game; we need the practice."

"You'd better believe we want a rematch," said Tr0nik. "Friend request sent."

"Received and approved," said Sahara with a smile. "Now: I hate to play and run, but we've got to go over these stats and get ready for the next one. Big tournament coming up."

"Us too," said Tr0nik. "Play crazy!"

"Play crazy!" Sahara smiled again, the perfect ambassador, and one by one the Cherry Dogs blinked out to their private lobby. Out of the public eye, Sahara's cheerful persona dropped, and she rolled her eyes. "Play crazy. We almost lost that stupid game playing crazy."

"I'm sorry I left Anja," said Marisa. "I'm so used to playing with the cam drones, I just wasn't keeping an eye on the map without them, and the other team got behind me."

"With Fang and me down you couldn't have done anything

anyway," said Quicksand. Her real name was Jaya, and she lived in Mumbai, but her English was flawless—better, Marisa admitted, than her own pocho blend of American and Mexican.

"I know we don't have a real coach yet," said Sahara, "but I do my best, and I told you to bring those . . ." Her voice trailed off, and her eyes had the slightly vacant look of someone watching a separate video feed. Marisa braced herself for another chastising tirade—Sahara was her best friend, but she could get angry when they played this sloppy. After a long pause Sahara shook her head. "You know what? Don't worry about it. Yes, there was some bad play, and that win was way too lucky to rely on in a real match, but wow." She smiled, and Marisa couldn't help but smile with her. "There's going to be replays of that drone launch all over the net for weeks, and in a practice game like this that's worth more than a win." She put a hand on Marisa's shoulder, her eyes refocusing on her face. "And we have plenty of time to practice before the tourney, so don't beat yourself up."

Marisa cringed at the reminder, and couldn't help feeling bad all over again.

"You up for another match?" asked Fang. "We ought to play with the Force Projectors a little more before word gets around, see what else they can do that no one's thought of yet."

"What time is it over there?" asked Marisa. "Like, one in the morning?"

"Sleep is for the weak," said Fang. "Let's do this."

"It's only half ten here," said Jaya. "I can do another game or two tonight."

"Only two?" asked Fang. "Weeeeeeak."

"Ten a.m. in LA," said Jaya. "Sahara, you and Marisa and Anja should be good for a few more hours of practice at least, right?"

"I haven't slept since yesterday," said Anja. She shrugged. "No sense sleeping now."

"No. No more practice today," said Sahara. "We've got to leverage this drone launch clip if we want to really get the word out." She was growing audibly excited. "We haven't had a really great exploit since Mari min-maxed the avatar builder, and that's what put us on the map in the first place; something like this could take our reputation into the major leagues. I've got to spend a few hours at least cutting good angles out of the replay and submitting this to broadcasters."

"Tomorrow, then," said Fang. "Or tonight, depending on your time zone. I'll run a few solo games with the new kit and see if I can get some good footage for you."

"I'll join you," said Jaya. "Maybe we can play catch with a Mark-III."

The two of them blinked out, and Marisa looked at Anja and Sahara. "I'll see you around, then. The restaurant'll be opening soon, see you there?"

"If I get a chance," said Sahara. "I'll ping you."

"Dinner, then."

"You ladies can come to my place," said Anja. "Pool's installed now."

"A pool party at a mansion in Brentwood," said Sahara with a smile. "That'll play great on the feed." She raised her eyebrows mischievously. "Let's do it. Eight o'clock. Wear something revealing."

Marisa faked a smile. "Anything for eyeballs?"

"Anything for eyeballs," said Sahara. "See you tonight. Cherry Dogs forever."

"Cherry Dogs forever," said Marisa. Sahara blinked away, and Marisa stared for a moment at the spot she used to be in.

"I've got something great for the eyeballs," said Anja. "You're going to love it."

"It's the internet, Anja; they've seen boobs before."

"Nothing that biological," said Anja, and grinned wickedly. "See you tonight."

"Tonight," said Marisa. Anja blinked away, and a few seconds later Marisa did the same. She opened her eyes in her bedroom, cluttered and cramped, lying flat on her bed. Above her on the ceiling was an Overworld poster, the limited edition she'd bought at last year's regional championship; it made the transition easier, she thought, to see a piece of that world as she entered the real one. She rubbed her eyes and sat up, looking around at the unfolded laundry and scraps of half-built computer equipment scattered haphazardly around the room.

Home.

She reached back for the cord, lightly touching the jack where it plugged into her skull. She never felt anything physical when she disconnected it—not even a tug, now that she'd upgraded her djinni to the Ganika 7. The new cord only connected with a weak magnetic link, so it could pull away freely if someone knocked it.

Even without a physical sensation, though, she always seemed to feel something else, something . . . psychological, she supposed.

She yanked gently on the cord and it came away, severing her hard line to the net.

The real world. She hadn't been here in a while.

The colors were so much duller.

TWO

Marisa Carneseca blinked, calling up her mail list. The djinni implanted in her head switched modes smoothly, projecting the words on her Ganika-brand corneas so that they seemed to float in the air in front of her, filling the room with dimly glowing letters. The icon for her spam folder was red and pulsing, and she dumped it without even bothering to look at what was inside. Her inbox showed two emails from her mother and five from Overworld—most of those probably ads, but there might be a few from Cherry Dog fans. She'd look through them later. Two emails from Olaya, the house computer; Marisa opened the folder and saw two repeats of the same passive demand for laundry access. She sighed and looked around; it had been a while, she had to admit. She saw a half bottle of Lift on the nightstand, and took a long drink.

She'd met a cute boy at a club a couple of nights ago, but his djinni had been so filled with adware she hadn't accepted his ID link; instead she'd written it down, like in the old days, and the paper was buried somewhere in this pile of clothes—she couldn't let the drone in until she'd checked all her pockets.

She blinked the house folder closed and scrolled down, rolling some of the stiffness out of her shoulders as she did. Her neck was pulling on the left again, where her natural muscles connected to her Jeon prosthetic. She lifted the artificial arm, splaying the fingers in front of her—it was her seventeenth birthday present, just a few months old. Obviously mechanical, but slender and elegant. Definitely a step up from the old SuperYu.

At the bottom of the mail list was a message from Bao, reminding her to ping him when she finished practice. She blinked on his number—no ID, because he didn't have a djinni, just an old-style handheld phone with an old-style number. It made her laugh every time, like he was her abuela. She kept the video turned off while she stood up and looked around for pants.

Bao didn't answer for almost thirty seconds. "Hey, Mari."

"Hey. You in school?"

"Took me a minute to get out of class."

Marisa smiled, sifting through a pile of old clothes. "If you'd get a djinni like a normal person you wouldn't have to get out of class."

"I need the break anyway. You're done with practice already?"

Marisa examined a shirt, but discarded it. Too wrinkly. "Sahara ended it early on account of me being a genius."

"I saw her post. Apparently you've broken the game again."

"She's already posted?" Marisa smiled.

"Just a sentence, says there's a big video coming later. What'd you do, another costume exploit?"

"Powerset exploit," said Marisa, finding a pair of black jeans and pulling them on as she talked. "Though I'm not even sure it's an exploit, just a lucky play. For all I know they *wanted* us to start throwing the sentry drones around."

"Throwing drones? This I've got to see."

Marisa split her vision, calling up the live feed from Sahara's vidcast. Sahara was sitting at her immaculate desk, the camera nuli watching from over her shoulder as her fingers flew across the touch screen, editing and sculpting the replay into a highlight video. She was wearing yoga pants and a T-shirt, her thick hair pulled up in a ponytail—a far cry from her evening gown avatar, but still impossibly adorable. Marisa shook her head. "How does she always look so good? We've been plugged in and lying down for three hours, and asleep all night before that, and she looks like she just got her hair done."

"I'm sure you look great," said Bao.

Marisa looked down at her own oversized nightshirt, and glanced at the mirror with a pained grimace. "I look like I'm hiding from the government." Her dark brown hair was a squirrel's nest of knots and tangles; the tips were dyed red, about four inches deep, which looked pretty cool when it was straight, but now it only added to the wispy chaos. She ran her hand through it, trying to smooth it down, and winced as she hit a snarl. She gave up for the moment and started hunting for a clean shirt. "You know what I think it is?" she told Bao. "I think she does it all before we practice. Nobody gets that cute, just-rolled-out-of-bed look by just . . . rolling out of bed."

"You coming to school today?" asked Bao.

Marisa shrugged. "Probably not. I can do most of it online, and the rest of it . . . technically also online."

"You can't just hack all your grades."

"Sure I can," said Marisa with a grin, "unless you're saying I *shouldn't* just hack all my grades, in which case you might have a point." She found a black blouse, fancier than she needed but the only presentable thing in the room. She really needed to let the laundry nuli in here. "You hungry?"

"I could eat."

Marisa blinked back to Olaya while she buttoned her shirt, looking at her family list: her parents were both at the restaurant, and her three younger siblings were all at school. Or at least they were checked in at school; Marisa had learned how to spoof the GPS on her djinni when she was thirteen, and her siblings might have figured out the same trick. None of them really seemed like the type, though. Sandro, maybe—he was a genius with hardware, but he'd never dare to actually do it.

Marisa finished with her clothes and looked at the bottle of Lift. "I haven't had anything today but a few sips of soda. Meet me for an early lunch?"

"Give me twenty minutes," said Bao.

"I'll need at least that long to wrestle with this hair before giving up and shaving it off."

"Your mom'd kill you."

"My dad'd kill me first."

"Thirty minutes, then," said Bao. "Saint Johnny?"

"Exactamente," said Marisa. "See you there." She ended the

call and attacked her hair again, with a brush this time, grumbling curse words in three languages as she pulled on the knots. She slipped her feet into a pair of flats as she brushed, and took a last look at the room. Did she need anything else? The boy's ID from the club was somewhere in this mess, if she could remember which pants she'd been wearing. Or had she been wearing a skirt? She tried to recall, and realized she couldn't even think of the boy's name. She shrugged and opened the door, laughing as the Arora laundry nuli burst in and started picking up clothes, rushing from pile to pile like an overstimulated robot puppy. She didn't need the boy's ID anyway. If he didn't even know how to keep adware off his djinni, how interesting could he really be?

The wheeled nuli almost looked like it could think for itself: picking up each shirt and bra and pair of tights, considering it, and sorting it efficiently into one of several onboard baskets. But it was all an illusion of efficient programming. Each piece of clothing in the house was marked with an RF chip, and it was these the drone was reading; they carried instructions on exactly how to wash the clothes, how to fold them, and where to put them away. It was a good system, when it worked. Last year their cat, Tigre, had clawed a sweater to pieces, getting the tiny RF chip stuck in her fur. They didn't have a cat anymore.

Marisa worked on her hair for another five minutes, linking her djinni to the bathroom mirror so she could read the Overworld forums in HD. People were already talking about the drone launch, including a video clip the Salted Batteries had posted, but it was still a relatively minor story. Much bigger news was the regional championship that had just wrapped in Oceana, with

Xx_Scorcho_xX taking the cup. No surprise there. Apparently Flankers were ruling the meta, which Fang had been saying for a couple of weeks now, so that was something to think about. The American championships were coming up in just two weeks, but the Cherry Dogs weren't on that level yet; someday, she told herself, but not yet. They had, however, landed a slot in the Jack-rabbit Tourney, a kind of minor-league invitational showcase. If they did well there, they'd have a shot at a major tournament in the second half of the year. Marisa scanned through the Oceana tourney results until her hair was more or less fit for public display, and then blinked the forum back from the mirror to her djinni so she could read while she walked.

The hallway smelled like fresh tortillas and cigarette smoke, a combination of fair and foul so familiar Marisa couldn't help but smile. It was her abuela, who hadn't appeared on the house computer because she didn't have a djinni; that was just as well, Marisa supposed, because she never left the house. They always knew exactly where she was: cooking in the kitchen. Marisa longed to slip in and grab a hot tortilla, fresh off the griddle, but she knew her abue would slap her with a chore or three if she saw her. Marisa slid out the back door instead—the old woman could barely see, and her hearing was worse. Marisa got away clean and stepped outside.

Los Angeles in 2050 was a hectic blend of past and future; it was one of the last great centers of business left in the US, and usually more interested in building new things than refurbishing old ones. The roads teemed with autocabs and rolling lounges, with a crisscross web of maglev trains and hypertubes bringing commuters in from all over the country. Steel and concrete and biowall buildings covered the hills and valleys like a carpet, bristling with solar trees that glittered green and black across the rooftops. Above them all the sky was thick with nulis, buzzing through the air in a million directions, so that the entire city looked like a hive of polymer bees in every possible shape and size.

Marisa lived in El Mirador, a midsize barrio that baked in the hot sun just east of downtown—not rich like Anja's neighborhood, but not destitute, either. Vast swaths of LA were practically shantytowns these days, but Mirador was holding on.

One of the reasons for Mirador's tenacity zoomed past on the road, a dark phantom in Marisa's peripheral vision: the distinctive black outline of a Dynasty Falcon. Don Francisco Maldonado was the richest man in Mirador, and he helped keep the peace with his small army of private enforcers in Dynasty autocars. With most police work handled by remote drone, the Maldonado enforcers were almost as fast as, and certainly more attentive than, the actual law—though even the law was in Maldonado's pocket, thanks to his eldest son working for the local precinct. The Falcon didn't slow down as it passed Marisa, but she knew the man inside was giving her a long, hard look. There was no one in the world Don Francisco hated more than her father.

Marisa rubbed her prosthetic arm and kept walking.

Her family's restaurant was barely a mile from their house, and an easy walk even in the scorching heat. Up until two years ago they'd lived behind the restaurant in a connected apartment, but her father had scrimped and saved and moved them to their new house the instant he could afford it. Sahara had moved in to the old apartment soon after; she'd never said why she left her parents' place, and Marisa had never asked. Marisa's parents hadn't pried either, and Marisa figured they saw it as an opportunity to be a good influence on their daughter's friend. Sahara paid her bills and kept her grades up, so it all worked out. Marisa didn't imagine Sahara would make it to lunch, being too busy with the video and her various media contacts, but that was just as well. Sahara's life was a twenty-four-hour vidcast, and Marisa wanted more time with her hair before the entire internet saw her in it.

Marisa's djinni pinged with a call from her mom; she blinked to answer. "Hey, Mami."

"Oye, chulita. Olaya told me you left; are you going to school?"

"I'm about halfway to you, actually. You got chilaquiles?"

"For breakfast? Ay, muchacha, this is why you don't have a boyfriend. Who wants to kiss that breath?"

Marisa rolled her eyes. "Ay, Mami . . ."

"You'll get your homework done online?"

"Of course."

"I'll tell Papi to start some chilaquiles. What does Bao want?"

"How'd you know Bao was coming?"

"I'm your mother, Marisita. I know everything."

"Then you know better than I do what he wants," said Marisa with a laugh. "See you in a few." She closed the call and waited at a busy corner, watching the autocars weave through traffic in their intricate hive mind dance.

Each storefront she passed read Marisa's ID from her djinni, checked it against her commerce profile, and filled its window with personalized ads. Most people would be getting pop-ups directly to their djinni, but Marisa had firewalled those out years ago. The last thing she needed was a two-for-one hairstyling coupon blocking her vision. The wide front window of a clothing store pulled a picture of Marisa from somewhere on the net, shopped their latest sundress onto her, and displayed it in HD for the entire street to see: *On Sale! Only ¥20/$123!* She stopped to look and the 3D image rotated; Marisa was pretty sure the automated photo alteration had slimmed her waist a bit as well, just to make the dress look more appealing. Clever, but rude. She considered hacking in through their Wi-Fi and displaying some incendiary political figure in the same dress, just for revenge, but laughed and walked away. It wasn't worth the time.

The family's restaurant was called San Juanito, named for the Mexican logging town where her father had lived as a boy. It was still early for lunch, not quite eleven, but the lights were on and the ad board was already grabbing the IDs of passersby to offer them the daily specials. It read Marisa's as soon as she got close, identified her as a regular, and greeted her by name.

"Welcome back to San Juanito, Marisa Carneseca! Would you like a free horchata today?"

She walked inside, and caught her mother halfway to a table, a tray of waters balanced carefully on her hand. "Buenos días, Mami." She kissed her on the cheek. "Is Bao here yet?"

"Table twelve." Guadalupe de Carneseca was a tall, broad woman, fair-skinned, and with her hair dyed a faint reddish blond. "How was practice?"

"Better every game. Just you today?"

"Everyone else is in school," said her mother, "unless you want to put on an apron and help wait tables."

Marisa stuck out her tongue and made a gagging noise. Her mom used the kids as cheap waitstaff when she could, and Marisa hated it. "Just buy a nuli already—you're, like, the only restaurant in the world that still uses live waiters."

"And our customers appreciate the personal touch," said her mother. "Go sit down. I'll be there in a bit." She bustled off, delivering waters to a table in the back, and Marisa tried to remember which was table twelve. Even this early, the restaurant was filling up, and Bao was just skilled enough—and just mischievous enough—to be impossible to find in a crowd. A handy skill when you fed your family by picking tourists' pockets in downtown Hollywood. After a moment she gave up, checked the diagram on the restaurant computer, and walked straight to him.

"Well done," said Bao with a grin. He was half-Chinese and half-Russian, and looked just enough like each to blend perfectly into either crowd. He was wearing all black, like Marisa, but whereas her clothes were designed to be noticed, his were designed to disappear. If he didn't catch you with his deep, piercing eyes, you might never notice him at all.

"I cheated," said Marisa.

"I'm shocked."

She took a drink of water, the ice so cold that the glass was drenched in condensation. The shock in her mouth made her shiver. "You didn't get caught leaving school?"

"You insult me."

"I never understand how you do that. Security's so tight in that place; it's like a prison."

"Their *digital* security is tight," said Bao. "Try to walk through any door in that building with an implant and fifty different security guards will know about it instantly. But when you're the only kid in school without a djinni, they tend to forget that sometimes plain old eyes are better."

Marisa nodded, taking another sip of ice water. How many times had they had this conversation? "Seriously: what kind of weirdo doesn't have a djinni? That's like not having . . . feet."

"Some people don't have feet."

"Not by choice. A djinni is a phone, a computer, a scanner, a credit card, it's my . . . key to my house. It's everything. You and my abue are the only ones left in LA without one."

"I've never felt the lack."

"It will change your life, Bao, I'm serious."

"Speaking of," he said, "you see the news?"

Marisa nodded. "Scorcher won the Oceana Regional."

"No, the real news. The Foundation is protesting the new Ganika Tech plant they're building in Westminster."

"I suppose we should have seen that coming. The biggest djinni company in the world and a militant anticybernetics group? It's like a match made in heaven."

"Not so much a 'group' as a 'terrorist organization,'" said Bao. "And they're right here in LA. This doesn't freak you out?"

"It's all the way down in Westminster," said Marisa, and held up a finger. "Note that this is not me being cavalier about them blowing people up just because they're far away. I sincerely hope that they don't, and that, if they do, they get caught. But I reserve the right not to be shocked when terrorists commit acts of terror.

That's exactly what they want; that's like playing their side of a lane."

"I'm going to guess that's an Overworld metaphor."

"Exacto. If we let the Foundation dictate the terms of—"

"Hold up," said Bao quickly, his voice low, and Marisa could tell instantly that something was wrong. "That looks like trouble."

Marisa followed his gaze back over her shoulder toward the front of the restaurant, seeing three young men in long, untucked dress shirts, their hair pulled back in tight ponytails. Two of them had bionic arms, Detroit Steel by the ostentatious look of them, one on the left side and one on the right. The third man, standing between them, was almost impossibly skinny, his face covered in ornate, skull-like tattoos.

"La Sesenta," said Marisa, identifying the gangsters immediately. La Sesenta was Mirador's resident street gang, and seeing them here was even more trouble than Bao suspected. "Mierda."

"You recognize any of them?"

"The skinny one's called Calaca," Marisa whispered. "He's pretty high up in the gang." The three cholos were standing in the entryway, surveying the restaurant like they were thinking about buying it. The look sent shivers down her spine.

"No gangs allowed," said Guadalupe loudly, bustling fearlessly toward them from the side room. Marisa felt her heart skip a beat at her mother's brazen disregard for the danger; the other customers had noticed the cholos now as well, and a nervous wave rippled through the restaurant. "No gang colors, no weapons. We don't want any trouble here."

"Si, señora," said Calaca. He smiled, and half his teeth were steel. "That's exactly why we're here—we don't want any trouble either." His accent was thick, but his diction was almost humorously overeducated. "The problem is, the man you rely on to keep you out of trouble is doing a very poor job, as our presence here might indicate."

"What's he talking about?" whispered Bao.

"My parents pay protection money to the Maldonados," Marisa whispered back.

"Seriously?"

"Everybody does," said Marisa. "It's the only reason this neighborhood isn't a smoking crater run by these chundos." Marisa stood up. "I gotta go talk my mom down before she gets herself shot."

"Sit," said her father sternly, appearing behind Marisa as he stormed out from the kitchen.

Carlo Magno was shorter than his wife, and wider—not fat, but thick and muscled. He must have been chopping meat, for his apron was streaked with blood; he looked fierce and imposing, but Marisa was grateful he'd left the knife in the kitchen. He pushed her firmly back into her chair without breaking stride, and stormed toward the gangsters with fire in his eyes. "Get out of my restaurant!"

Marisa linked to the police and sent a message pleading for help.

"As I've explained to your woman," said Calaca, "we're only here to—"

"I've called the Maldonados," said Carlo Magno.

"That seems like a very poor decision on your part," said

Calaca. "They don't like us very much, and my associates don't like them. If the enforcers show up and start making unreasonable demands, one side might—and I say might, because it is very uncertain—open fire on the other, and with your fine establishment caught in the middle that will—and this time I say will, because if we get to this point it will be an inescapable outcome—be very bad for your business."

"We pay them for protection," said Marisa's father fiercely, "and they pay you to stay away from us."

"They 'pay' us," said Calaca, looking at the thugs behind him. He turned back to Carlo Magno. "You'll have to excuse my English, as it's only a second language. *Pay* is the present tense, implying that the Maldonados currently, on an ongoing basis, pay us money to leave you alone. Is that what you're saying? Because I suspect the past progressive tense: they *used to pay* us to leave you alone. The brutal truth, which your statement did not allow for, is that they are not paying us anymore, which means that you're not being protected anymore, which is why my friends and I have come here today to magnanimously offer to pick up the slack where the Maldonados have dropped it—"

"Did my son put you up to this?" Marisa's father demanded.

"Is he talking about Sandro?" whispered Bao.

"No," said Marisa, shushing him with her hand. "I'll tell you later." She could barely breathe, watching the showdown, praying the police would come soon to scare them off. She glanced quickly at the other customers, seeing the fear etched into their faces. If the cholos weren't blocking the door, the customers would have already run.

"You mean Chuy?" asked Calaca. "He's a good man, but if you think he calls the shots in La Sesenta you have a poor under-standing of his role—he occupies more of a clerical position—"

"Are you trying to impress me by praising him?" Carlo Magno stepped forward, glaring at the gangsters. "He means less to me than you do, and if you or him or anybody else in your gang comes in here again, I'll give you a beating like you haven't seen since your own mothers put—"

The two bionic thugs pulled guns from under their shirts—massive silver pistols with magnetic accelerators blinking ominously in the barrels. Marisa stood, taking half a step toward the confron-tation before Bao caught her and held her back. "It's too dangerous," he whispered.

"They're going to kill them," Marisa hissed.

"Just stay cool," said Bao. "They're only trying to scare us, not hurt us."

The front door opened, and a pair of Maldonado's enforcers stepped in; they saw the drawn weapons, but stayed calm.

"Calaca," said the first enforcer. "Is there a problem?"

"We have no problems with anything," said Calaca, not tak-ing his eyes off of Marisa's father. "No problems or worries of any kind. But Señor Carneseca has certain issues with the quality of the protection he's been receiving lately. We were only showing him our weapons, in case he wants to arm himself similarly, as is his constitutional right in this great nation." He signaled with his finger, and the Sesenta thugs put their guns back under their shirts. Calaca turned around to face the enforcers. "If, on the other hand, you want to have a discussion with him and his mujer about how the quality of their protection might improve through other means, that could save us all a great deal of trouble."

The lead enforcer looked as if he was about explode, but he said nothing. Calaca gave a satisfied grin. "Señor, señora." He nodded politely to Marisa's parents, then shot a lecherous grin at Marisa. "Señorita."

Marisa's father stepped forward, his fists clenched, but Calaca and the two thugs stepped around the enforcers and out the door. The entire restaurant seemed to breathe a sigh of relief, and more than a few patrons started hurriedly gathering their things to leave. Marisa pulled away from Bao and stormed toward the enforcers.

"Do you want to explain that?" Carlo Magno demanded.

"We're sorry we couldn't get here sooner," said the lead enforcer.

"It shouldn't have happened at all," said Marisa. "They said you're not paying them off anymore?"

The enforcer sighed. "You'll have to talk to Don Francisco."

"What's going on with our money?" asked Guadalupe.

"You'll have to talk to Don Francisco," said the enforcer again. "We don't know any more than you do, but this is not the first business this has happened to today. I'm sorry." They turned and left, followed by a stream of terrified customers.

"Don't leave now," Guadalupe called desperately to the fleeing patrons. "They've left!"

"We've gotta talk to the Maldonados," said Marisa. "We can't let this—"

"You stay away from them," said Carlo Magno firmly, "and you stay away from this, too—from the enforcers, from La Sesenta, from all of it. And you go back to school, *now*."

"School, are you kidding? We need to—"

"You need to go to school and stay out of this!" he shouted.

Marisa stepped back, shocked at the heat of his outburst. His face softened when he saw her fear, and he shook his head sadly.

She stepped forward to hug him. "I love you, Papi."

"I love you, too, Mari." He hugged her tightly. "I love you, too. I don't know what's going on, but . . . I won't lose you like I lost Chuy. Promise me you'll be careful."

Marisa nodded. "I promise."

THREE

That evening, Sahara Cowan stepped out of her front door like a movie star, flanked by a pair of cam nulis hovering in the air around her—one in front to get a good shot of her face, and one on the side to catch Marisa in the background. Marisa had helped her program the AI that guided their camera angles; Sahara could control them with her djinni, but most of the time the algorithm was surprisingly good at capturing the best shots on its own. The small pink bow glued to the lead nuli identified it as Camilla, and its mustached companion was Cameron. Of course Sahara had named them.

Sahara strutted toward them like a runway model, and Marisa clapped politely.

"Gorgeous," she said.

"Thanks." Sahara twirled, showing off her dress: a short, layered skirt, almost like flower petals reaching down around her thighs, coming together at a tight waist only partially connected to a broad-shouldered top that left most of her midriff bare. No cleavage, but it hugged her curves enticingly. The whole thing was some kind of tie-dyed pattern, dark purples and bright yellows, probably hiding whatever shocking string bikini she had on underneath it, prepared for a dramatic reveal at the pool. Sahara's hair was curled into thick tendrils that bounced slightly as she moved, and Marisa couldn't help but envy the look.

"Sounds like I missed some excitement earlier," said Sahara.

Marisa glanced at the nulis dryly; privacy was a joke around Sahara, and there were certain parts of this conversation she didn't want to have in front of the entire internet. Sahara's vidcast wasn't world-renowned or anything, but it was still popular enough to get Sahara—and sometimes Marisa—recognized on an LA street. Marisa said nothing, and Sahara didn't press any further.

"You look amazing," said Sahara. "We going clubbing after?"

Marisa smiled. "Who knows? I came prepared for anything." She'd worn one of her favorite clubbing outfits—a dark green dress with a knee-length skirt, a high neck, and long sleeves extending halfway past her elbows. It glittered faintly in the early phase of the sunset, and would sparkle like crazy under the multicolored lights of a good dance floor. The subtle green was a great complement to her dark skin, and the red tips in her hair made a perfect accent. She'd always used to wear a glove on her left hand as well, covering the clumsy SuperYu prosthetic, but her new Jeon looked so good that she loved showing it off—faintly tan, with light blue highlights, like water over sand. She could even make the blue parts glow. In a dance club especially, it always turned heads. She smiled back at Sahara conspiratorially. "Remember the guy from the other night?"

"With the ID on the paper?"

"I lost the paper." Marisa shrugged helplessly, as if there was nothing she could do. "Obviously I don't *want* to go clubbing, but how else am I going to meet another guy?"

Bao appeared beside them, emerging like a ghost from the early twilight. "You never know where we might appear."

"Stop doing that," said Sahara, putting her hand on her chest in mock anger. "Can't you just walk up to someone like a normal person?"

"It's my gift to your audience," said Bao, pointing to Cameron. "Twenty bucks says at least one of them saw me before you did; it's a whole thing on the forums."

"So, did you call us an autocab?" asked Marisa.

"Tonight we travel in style," said Sahara, subtly avoiding Marisa's eyes. "I figured since we're all going to the same party, we may as well get a ride. . . ."

Marisa's jaw fell open. "You didn't."

"Obviously *she* invited him," said Sahara, "so don't blame me for that. All I did was ask him for a ride. Have you seen his car?"

Bao looked at each girl in turn, filling in the unspoken gaps in the conversation. "Omar's coming?"

Marisa stuck out her tongue. "I think I just remembered about seventy-eight different things I have to do at home."

"If you didn't want Anja to start dating a Mirador boy, you shouldn't have kept bringing her here," said Sahara. "Just be grateful she's dating one with a Futura."

"Are you kidding me?" asked Marisa. "This is Omar *Maldonado*, Sahara. As in, the people who practically shook down my parents for protection money not seven hours ago. He only has a Futura because his father's a crime boss." She looked right at Cameron, pointing dramatically. "Go ahead and sue me for libel, chundo, I dare you."

"Slander," said Bao, glancing at the nuli. "You can't sue her for libel unless she writes it down."

"Let me log in to the forums then," said Marisa, blinking one open, but Sahara spoke in her most soothing voice.

"Whatever his father's done," said Sahara, "Omar's our friend."

"Exactly," said Bao. "I like Omar."

"I like him too," said Marisa. "The boy is charming, but do you trust him?"

Neither answered immediately, and Marisa laughed in triumph.

"Regardless," said Sahara, "now that Anja's dating him, we see him almost every day."

"And it's problematic *every day*," said Marisa. "I was hoping tonight could be the one night we wouldn't have to deal with it—especially after what happened this morning. If my father ever found out I was hanging around with Omar, it would melt his processor; ojalá he doesn't watch your feed."

"And as if on cue," said Bao, looking down the street as a jet-black autocar rolled slowly to the curb. The Dynasty Falcons that the Maldonado enforcers drove were rugged muscle cars designed for utility and intimidation; Don Maldonado's youngest son, however, had a Futura Noble, designed purely for showing off how expensive it was. Marisa couldn't even see the outline of the door until it slid open silently, exposing the familiar thump of nortec music from within.

"Ladies and gentleman," said Omar smoothly. "Your carriage has arrived."

"Gorgeous!" Sahara's nulis swirled around, catching the best views of the luxury autocar as Sahara climbed in. The interior was more of a lounge than a car: lush seats around a central table, with a well-stocked bar against the far wall. The ceiling danced with abstract holograms, pulsing in time with the music.

Bao stepped in, but Marisa hung back on the sidewalk. Omar, seeming to sense her hesitation, stepped smoothly out of the Futura. He was tall and dark, clean-shaven and fiendishly handsome. Tonight he wore white slacks and a white tuxedo vest over a deep purple shirt and matching purple tie. The lack of jacket made him look like he'd just come from a fancy gala, through with the important stuff and ready to party; the calculated casualness of it made Marisa fume.

"Marisa," he said, bowing his head slightly in respect. "I heard about what happened today at your family's restaurant. I'm deeply sorry."

Marisa wanted to throw the apology back in his face, demanding to know what his family was trying to pull, but Bao was right: even if Omar's father was behind the gangster's veiled threats, Omar himself was probably blameless. He was barely eighteen years old.

"Come on, Mari," said Sahara. "It'll be fun."

Marisa thought a moment, holding in the sigh she so desperately wanted to release. She could slap the boy and storm off in a rage—give Sahara's viewers something to talk about for days—but that seemed so harsh, and Omar didn't deserve harsh. At least, not yet. No one in their group was completely innocent, legally speaking. Bao was an accomplished pickpocket, and Marisa had raided more private databases than she cared to admit. If it turned out that Omar had a hand in what was happening to her family, she'd hurt him in ways he'd never see coming, but for now . . . well, for now the Futura Noble looked inviting as hell. Her dress fit perfectly, her hair looked great, and she was out on the town with her friends. Why let their fathers' feud spoil the fun?

Omar offered his hand, and she let him guide her into the autocar. Marisa sat by Bao—the seats were even more comfortable than they looked—and Omar stepped in and settled across from her, next to Sahara. Cameron and Camilla were perched on opposite sides of the ceiling, catching perfect views of all four faces. Marisa had seen Omar's car but never ridden in it; in a neighborhood like Mirador, where most people couldn't afford a car at all, it was a shocking display of opulence.

"I miss anything good on your show?" asked Omar, pointing at the drones.

"Marisa called you a chundo," said Bao. "I don't know what it means, but she sounded angry when she said it."

Marisa faked a smile. "Thanks, Bao."

"After what happened at the restaurant, I'm glad to hear that's all she said," replied Omar. "But I really don't want to think about any of my dad's business crap tonight. Let's go have some fun.

Pedro! Close the door and take us to Anja's house." The door closed just as silently as it had opened, and the autocar pulled into the street with an almost eager purr from the engine.

"You have the most expensive car in Mirador," said Sahara, "and you call it Pedro?"

"Pedro's a powerful name," said Omar. "Pedro was the first apostle."

Bao smiled. "So now the first apostle's driving you around. This went from self-effacing to a power trip in, like, one second."

Omar laughed. "Honestly? I named it Pedro because that's what my grandfather called his first car, some tiny little Ford, like a Festiva I think. He drove that thing everywhere; that's how the family fortune started, hauling newspapers through some little pueblo in Texas."

"He was a paperboy?" asked Sahara, laughing gleefully at the idea. "When was this, a hundred years ago? I don't think I've ever even *seen* a paper newspaper."

"The last one closed distribution ten years ago," said Marisa, calling up the search on her djinni. "In Idaho, of all places. Most of them closed ten or twenty years before that, but some small towns just really wanted to keep the tradition alive, I guess?"

"As long as you're looking stuff up," said Bao, "how long has it been since anyone had to drive their own car? Was the Festiva the last one?"

Marisa caught Omar's eye, an unintentional moment of shared . . . what? Experience? Pain?

Bao didn't know what he was asking.

"You can actually still engage manual drive on cars today,"

said Omar. Marisa was surprised he didn't change the subject. "You could probably drive this one if you had a license."

"People still have licenses?" asked Sahara. "I mean, obviously motorcycles, but cars, too?" She looked around in obvious enthusiasm. "Where's the . . . handles? Or joystick? How do we do it?"

"I really don't recommend it," said Omar. "Cars can drive themselves more efficiently and more safely than any human operator." He recited the line as if he were reading a marketing report, and for all Marisa knew that's exactly what he was doing through his djinni. That, or he'd memorized all the reasons why his own personal tragedy should never have happened. "Since the move to autocars thirty years ago, fuel economy's increased a hundredfold, and traffic jams and collisions have dropped virtually to zero."

"I've heard about car accidents," said Sahara. "I just always figured they were due to autodrive malfunctions."

"Sometimes they are," said Omar. "Other times it's people, thinking they're . . . I don't know. Something. Smarter than a computer."

"Have you ever tried it?" asked Sahara, still oblivious to the tension slowly mounting in the car.

"What are we going to eat tonight?" asked Bao, abruptly trying to change the subject. "Order in, or pick something up on the way?"

Had he noticed something in Marisa's face? She blinked her djinni over to Sahara's vidcast, watching herself as she sat in the plush leather seats of the rolling party lounge. She looked haunted. She glanced at Omar again, wondering what he was feeling. If he was feeling anything. The silence dragged on, until finally Marisa stretched her robotic left arm across the table.

"Yes," said Marisa calmly, "sometimes people still drive their own cars."

Sahara raised her eyebrow. "That's how you lost your arm?"

Marisa nodded, tapping her fake fingers on the table. "I was two years old."

Bao's voice was soft. "Who was driving?"

"My mother," said Omar. "She died."

"Whoa," said Sahara, glancing almost involuntarily at the cam nulis to make sure they were catching this. Marisa could tell she was concerned—there was a good friend buried under all that media savvy—but sometimes Sahara's vidcasting obsession made Marisa want to grind her teeth in frustration. Sahara looked back at her intently. "You never told me this."

Marisa shrugged, bothered more by Sahara's attitude than by the story itself. She wiggled her fingers and watched the metal and ceramic joints as they moved up and down in sequence. "It's not a secret, it's just . . . not the kind of thing that comes up in conversation."

"Why were you in a car with Omar's mom?" asked Sahara.

"We don't know," said Marisa.

"Why did she shut off the autodrive?"

"We don't know," said Omar.

"Why was . . . ?" Sahara trailed off. "Well. I guess we don't know. But that certainly sheds some light on the family feud."

Marisa laughed dryly. "Does it?"

"I was in the car, too," said Omar impassively. "And my brother Jacinto; he got the worst of it, after my mother. He's more bionic at this point than human."

"I had no idea," said Sahara.

Omar shrugged. "That's because he hasn't left our house in seven years."

"I'm so sorry," said Sahara.

"Don't be," said Omar, and shook his head dismissively. "There's nothing keeping him in there but his own insecurities. Or laziness, I suppose. And *I* was fine—completely unscathed." He looked up suddenly, the old charm back in his face, and flashed Marisa a wide, devilish grin. It was like he'd turned the pain off with a switch. "Just like always, right?"

Sahara and Bao were too shocked, or too polite, to press any further, and Omar's abrupt change of attitude signaled the end of the discussion. He poured them each a glass of Lift, calling for an official beginning to the night's festivities, and asked what they wanted to eat. Marisa suggested her favorite noodle place downtown, and Omar laughed but ordered some anyway, buying way too much because it was so "cheap." Marisa couldn't help but feel a surge of anger—she had saved all week just to be able to afford a dinner out, but to him the money was meaningless. She looked out the window, watching the city roll past: slums and shanty-towns and decadent resorts. A few minutes later the delivery nuli arrived, bringing the hot white noodle boxes directly to the car as they drove. Omar insisted on paying, linking to the nuli's credit reader with barely a glance.

Anja lived in Brentwood with her father—not just the rich part of town, but the rich part of the rich part of town. Her father was a chief executive with Abendroth, a German nuli company that was still competing evenly with the Chinese. The nuli that brought their noodles was probably an Abendroth, Marisa realized, and the thought made her laugh. The Futura Noble carried them up the winding streets to the higher hillsides, and they watched out the windows as the trees opened up and the city stretched out before them—an endless field of buildings and lights and nulis, as far as the eye could see.

The autocar pulled to a stop in front of Anja's house, about twenty yards from a similar vehicle—not a Noble, Marisa thought, as it was far too small, but still some kind of Futura. Omar would know, but she didn't want to ask him. She snapped an image with her djinni and ran it through an image search: the car was a Daimyo, a two-seater Futura built for speed. Very expensive.

Omar frowned. "Did Anja invite someone I didn't know about?"

"Do you have to know about everyone she invites?" asked Marisa. She stepped out of the car just in time to see a young man walking away from Anja's door; he wore a simple pair of gray slacks and a red silk shirt, with the cuffs folded back to reveal a turbulent pattern on the underside of the fabric. Marisa guessed he was about twenty years old, probably Indian, and shockingly good looking. Sahara stepped out behind her and nudged Marisa slyly.

"Weren't you looking to pick somebody up tonight?"

Marisa was thinking the same thing, but the opportunity had appeared so suddenly, and in such an unexpected place, that she couldn't think of anything to say. The boy looked her way and smiled in a way that made her toes curl, but walked straight to his car, not even pausing as he said, "Have fun tonight." His accent was close enough to Jaya's that Marisa confirmed her earlier guess about his Indian heritage. In town for business, maybe? Or another child of an executive, like Anja. She couldn't seem to form any words, and managed only to blink a quick photo before he dropped into his car and drove away.

"Thank heaven I got that on camera," said Sahara, barely stifling her laughter. "Marisa Carneseca, Queen High Flirt of Flirtania, completely tongue-tied by the hottie in the silk shirt. Let's play that clip again." She paused, her eyes making tiny movements across her djinni interface. "Oh yeah." She laughed again, and Marisa rolled her eyes, grabbing her purse and walking toward Anja's door.

"He looked like a blowhole," said Marisa. "Another rich kid spending daddy's money while the rest of LA starves to death."

"Kind of like Anja?" whispered Sahara.

Marisa grimaced. "Anja's different."

"How?"

Marisa struggled to find an answer.

"What was he doing here?" Omar mumbled behind them, slowly standing up as the Daimyo turned a corner and disappeared.

"Jealous, Omar?" asked Bao.

"Ándale, gringos!" shouted Anja from her doorway. The waifish blonde was dressed eclectically, as usual: instead of a club dress she wore a pair of slim vinyl pants, black with a dark blue stripe on each leg and bright metal rivets running down each side; her shirt was gray and loose and sleeveless, an almost shapeless bag that somehow worked perfectly to accentuate the figure it looked like it was hiding. Her boots were patent leather, with platforms at least two inches high. She wore two metal chains around her neck, but whatever was hanging from them was tucked inside her shirt.

"I've told you before," said Marisa. Up close she could see Anja's fake eye—not a cybernetic enhancement, like Marisa's, but a full replacement, just different enough to freak you out if you weren't expecting it. And Anja loved getting close to people who weren't expecting it. Marisa gave her a quick hug and a kiss on the cheek. "You're completely misusing that word."

"You're a fourth-generation American, gringo," said Anja, shaking her head sadly. "It's time to face the truth."

"Second-generation on my father's side. That still counts as Mexican."

"Whatever. Get in here already. Willkommen a mi casa."

Marisa stepped into the opulent foyer, trying not to feel overwhelmed by the profound sense of wealth. Sahara and the boys followed her in; Anja wrapped herself around Omar and tried to pull him into a kiss, but he politely pecked her on the cheek and nodded to Anja's father on the couch in the living room.

"Good evening, Mr. Litz."

The man looked up, surveyed them, and nodded curtly before turning back to his tablet; he wasn't rude, Marisa knew, just very . . . efficient. Anja laughed and grabbed Omar's face.

"He doesn't care, baby, come on; give it up."

Omar gave her a longer kiss this time, full on the mouth, and Marisa turned away with a faux gag. "This is going to be a wonderful night," she said, "I can tell already."

"Let's head out back," said Bao, holding up the noodle boxes and gesturing toward the wide picture windows at the other end of the room. Beyond them was the back patio, the pool glowing blue in the fading light, and beyond that an intoxicating view of LA. Marisa followed him out, finding the side table already stocked with drinks—most of them alcoholic, as Mr. Litz never seemed to care what his daughter drank—and an array of snacks, mostly Chinese and Korean. Marisa picked through the bottles until she found a Lift, preferring caffeine to alcohol, and popped off the bottle cap on the corner of the table. Bao tried to do the same, and Marisa let him fail a few times before laughing, taking the bottle from his hands, and expertly levering off the cap.

"Thanks," said Bao, taking a swig. "I'm glad we got my inevitable emasculation out of the way early tonight." They walked around the pool and sat down, sipping softly from their bottles and staring out over the city.

"This house," mused Bao, "all by itself, is worth more than . . . any given house you can point to down there. I mean honestly, right? Pick a point of light down there in the valley and the odds are this house is worth at least twice what that one is."

"So I could pick two points of light," said Marisa.

"Okay, you just made this more interesting," said Bao. "Two is definitely too low, now that I'm really thinking about it. Taken as a unit of currency—one average lifestyle per light in the city—how many lights is this house worth? I think we're talking double digits."

Marisa looked out, watching the city come to bright, electric life as the sky faded to a deep blue-black. The color of Anja's pants, she thought, and the rivets on the sides were the stars. "Are we averaging everything together?" she asked. "The high-rises and the beach homes and the shantytowns?"

"All of it," said Bao. "From Bel Air to . . . well, as far as the eye can see, I guess. Mexico."

The city of Los Angeles had grown wildly over the decades, urbanizing every scrap of land until the street lights and pavement stretched in an unbroken tide from the beach to Moreno Valley, from Santa Clarita to the southern fringes of Tijuana. If you ignored the US-Mexican border—and most people did—the city was bigger than some entire states. Marisa didn't know who made the official measurements, but some of the craziest clubs had held a party when LA passed Connecticut in landmass.

A party, she realized, that most of the city's residents couldn't even afford to attend.

"This house was bought with nuli money," she said softly. "Abendroth makes industrial nulis—shipping, manufacturing, construction. If you've lost your job to a nuli in the last five years, you've probably lost it to an Abendroth. Maybe a Zhang." She twirled her finger in a spiral, encompassing the entire property in one abstract gesture. "So not only is this house worth, what, twenty lights? Forty? It's personally responsible for putting half of them out of work."

"And here we sit," said Bao. She waited for more, but he only watched the city.

Marisa tried to pick out the tiny light of her parents' restaurant. She couldn't be sure she could even see it from here.

"There you are," said Anja. Marisa put on her happiest face, hoping her friends could work their magic and raise her out of this sudden emotional slump. Anja sat down on the grass in front of her, heedless of stains on her designer pants; Marisa could just barely see a tattoo on her back, peeking above the hem of her shirt—a wing of some kind, but Marisa couldn't tell what exactly. Anja changed it almost every day. Dangling past it was a djinni cable, a slim white cord plugged into her headjack and braided in with her hair. Most people kept their djinni port empty and discreet, only inserting a cable when they needed to, but Anja liked the statement. She peeled open a box of noodles. "You want to see the new toys?"

"Is this the eye-catching mystery you promised me?" asked Marisa.

"Part one of two," said Anja, "though eye-*catching* is not necessarily the best word." Anja held up her right hand, displaying a flexible metal mesh across her palm, like a fingerless glove. "It's an EM field calibrated to interface with the sensory feeds on a Ganika 4 djinni. The settings are controlled on the back: one click for vision signals, one more for hearing, one more to turn it off." She demonstrated by pressing a touch sensor on the back of the glove, though it made no visible change. "I made it yesterday."

"How can you tell it's on?"

"I can feel when the field goes on and off, it's like a tingle in my hand. I might add a light, but I like the look now—very stealthy, no one knows that it can do anything."

"So it interfaces with the sensory feeds and . . . ?"

"Turns them off," said Anja with a smile. "*If* they have a Ganika 4, and *if* they haven't changed the factory settings. I had to sacrifice variability for speed, but I'm still refining it. Check this out . . . Omar!"

Bao cast a sidelong glance at Marisa. "Omar has a Ganika 4."

Omar arrived with a drink in hand. "I am at your command, Anyita."

Anja set down her noodles, jumped up, and put her right hand on Omar's cheek. "Boom."

"What?" asked Omar.

"He can't hear a thing," said Anja, grinning wildly at the others. "Djinnis tap into your brain's sensory centers, which is how they can do things like the VR in Overworld—they tell you you're seeing a city, hearing gunfire, or whatever. This little beauty simply tells you that you're not hearing anything."

"Damn it, Anja, what did you do to me?" Omar was roaring now, and Marisa couldn't help but laugh. "Mari, are you in on this too? What's going on?"

Anja looked over Marisa's shoulder, back at the house, and Marisa turned to see Sahara still talking to Anja's father, giving Cameron and Camilla a lengthy tour of the house. Even a dramatic bikini reveal could wait, it seemed, in the face of such a poshly furnished home.

"No word about this when Sahara comes out," said Anja. "Not that I want to hide it from her or anything. I just don't want the whole internet to know, you know?"

"Smart," said Marisa. Anja spent a lot of time on darknets, delving into body hacks most people knew nothing about. Getting an idea like this perception-denier into the mainstream could be dangerous, and a showcase appearance on Sahara's vidcast would be the first step to a potentially massive audience.

"Anja," said Omar, his voice impassive. "I want you to fix this now, please." Marisa wondered if his anger was really gone, or if he was simply very good at hiding it.

"Lie down," said Anja, clicking off her EM glove and guiding Omar to a nearby chaise. "There you go, this'll just take me a minute."

"You can't reverse it with another touch?" asked Bao.

"Turning the settings back on is way more complicated," said Anja, trying to wrangle Omar into the chair. "I can do a full reboot of the sensory package, which takes forever, or I can just tweak the settings if he'll freaking hold still." She finally got him down, then reached up into her hair and pulled out one end of her cord, plugging it into the headjack on the back of Omar's skull. Anja's eyes began moving across an interface only she could see, and Marisa leaned forward.

"While his hearing's still out," said Marisa, "I have to ask you: how serious is this thing with Omar?"

"I told you," said Anja, her eyes twitching, "I can just tweak the settings and he's as good as new."

"No," said Marisa, "I mean this relationship. Is this long term?"

Anja laughed. "I hope not."

"You don't like him?"

"Of course I like him, I just don't want to make this into something it isn't. Just because I'm eating lo mein tonight doesn't mean I want to eat lo mein every night."

"That's different."

Anja laughed again. "Come on, Marisa, you fall in love with half the boys you meet, and then the next day you're over them and ready to fall in love with someone else. I do the same thing, just . . . without the illusions." She refocused her eyes on her djinni interface. "All I'm saying is, you gotta keep your options open. There's too many things on the menu to just order the same one every time, right? And you never know what your favorite is until you've tried them all."

"That could be a very dangerous life philosophy," said Marisa.

"Play crazy," said Anja. She blinked, and Omar sat up suddenly, rubbing his ears.

"Ándale, flaca, what did you do to me?"

"She was demonstrating why I don't have a djinni," said Bao, and pointed to Anja's right hand. "Just stay away from that glove thingy and you'll be fine."

"Pobre Omarcito," said Marisa.

"Why Omarcito?" asked Anja, unplugging the cord from his headjack. "Isn't it just Omar? And for that matter, what's flaca? I don't speak Spanish, so I don't know if I'm supposed to hit him or not when he calls me that."

"Don't even try it," said Omar.

"Sorry," said Marisa. "We're Mexican; we have, like, seven nicknames for everything. You're Anja, and you're Anyita, which means 'little Anja' just like Omarcito means 'little Omar.' Flaca means 'skinny girl,' huera means 'white girl,' and loca means 'crazy girl,' so get used to that one because you're probably going to hear it a lot."

"I can handle *skinny girl*," said Anja, giving Omar a kiss on the cheek. "Though obviously I'd prefer *brilliant girl*; let's get our priorities straight."

"Everyone in my family has at least three names," said Marisa. "I'm Marisa, and Mari, and Marisita, and that's not even counting all the little chulitas and morenas and things my mother calls me. My grandmother is abue, abuelita, and sometimes la Bruja when we know she can't hear us. Patricia is Pati, Gabriela is Gabi, Sandro is Lechuga—don't ask me where that came from—"

"What about Chuy?" asked Bao.

Marisa glared at him.

"Everybody knows that one," said Anja. "It's short for Chewbacca."

"No," said Bao, looking straight into Marisa's glare without backing down. "She's got a brother named Chuy; she mentioned him today at lunch. She told me she'd tell me later, and now is later." He shrugged. "I'm curious."

Marisa looked at Omar, who knew the whole story, but he said nothing. She sighed and looked back at Bao. "Chuy's my older brother."

"I thought you were the oldest."

"We don't talk about him much," said Marisa.

"Because he's a wookie," said Anja.

"It's not Chewie, it's Chuy," said Marisa. "It's a nickname for Jesús."

"Jesús as in Jesus?" Anja could barely contain her laughter. "So Jesus is a wookie?"

"Or Chewbacca was a cholo named Jesús," said Omar, "and we just never knew it. Probably not, though, because they don't make hairnets that big."

Marisa shook her head, trying not to laugh. "My brother

Chuy joined a gang called La Sesenta about six years ago, and my father disowned him. He won't let him visit, he won't let us talk to him; today at the restaurant was the first time I've heard him say Chuy's name in . . . forever."

"Your father carries a lot of grudges," said Sahara. Marisa hadn't noticed her come up, and wondered how much of the conversation Cameron and Camilla had recorded. She didn't talk to Chuy often, but she knew he sometimes watched Sahara's vidcast. She found Cameron, looked right at the lens, and blew a kiss. "I love you, Chuy."

"You're here!" said Anja, jumping to her feet to hug Sahara. "This is why I brought you all here tonight. Time for part two: check it out." Anja pulled at the cheap metal chains around her neck, drawing a pair of small black headjack drives out of her shirt.

Marisa smirked, uncertain what the drives might hold. "Sensovids?"

"Better," said Anja. "Sensovids trigger your neural pathways in little doses, making you smell things or feel things or whatever; it's the same code I futzed with in Omar's head a few minutes ago. But it's only little bits to help tell a story—Bluescreen triggers them all at once, in one big rush."

Sahara looked incredulous. "What's the point of that?"

"The point is," said Anja, "the buzz is *amazeballs*. I've got a bunch more inside—I had Saif bring one for everybody. Bao excluded, of course, because he's a caveman."

Bao nodded politely. "I'll wait to get a djinni until after I finally figure out that 'wheel' contraption."

"So, it's a drug?" asked Marisa. "Like, a digital drug?"

Anja's eyes lit up. "Fully digital, so there's no medical side effects and no risk of addiction. It's the best; I found it last night."

"And that guy we saw leaving is your dealer?" asked Sahara.

"There's still a medical impact, though," said Marisa. "I mean, if it gives you a buzz that means it's releasing endorphins—that's a physiological response, not a digital one."

"Everything awesome releases endorphins," said Anja. "This isn't any more dangerous than . . . skydiving, or having sex."

"Both of which can be very dangerous," said Marisa. "Are you seriously going to plug some random dude's flash drive into your djinni? That . . . sounded a lot dirtier than I expected it to."

"Do you realize how much malware they could store in that thing?" asked Sahara.

"Relax," said Anja, "I've got my djinni wrapped in the thickest antiviral firewall digital security condom you can imagine. This morning a store tried to send me a coupon and their router caught fire—trust me, I'm protected. Here, I'll show you." She pulled her hair aside, exposing her headjack, and unplugged the cord she'd used earlier.

"Wait," said Omar. "You—" He glanced at the house. "Your father will see."

Anja furrowed her brow. "He saw me drinking your beer, too."

"He's asleep on the couch," said Sahara. "Said he was going to nod off while we were out here talking."

"Why are you so worried about my dad, anyway?" asked Anja.

"I want to know what it does," said Marisa. "Before you use it. I'm just . . . I don't want you to get hurt."

"I've already done it twice," said Anja. "That's why I had to get Saif to bring me new ones."

"Please just tell me what it does," said Marisa.

"It bluescreens you," said Anja, shooing Omar from his chaise and sitting down in his spot. "An overwhelming sensory rush, an unbelievable high, and then boom. Crash to desktop. Your djinni goes down and takes your brain with it for, like, ten minutes. It's the best."

"Hang on—" said Marisa, but Anja grinned and popped the drive into her headjack.

"Play crazy," she said, and then her arms started to twitch. A wide, almost childish smile spread across her face, and her eyes rolled back before closing luxuriously. Anja started to hum, a long, sensual *mmmmm*, and her legs pressed together for just a moment before her whole head and torso started vibrating. Marisa jumped toward her, grabbing her by the arms and calling out in alarm, but in that moment Anja's body spasmed one last time and went completely still.

"Anja." Marisa shook her slightly, touching her cheek; Anja's head lolled limply to the side. "Anja!"

"She's out," said Omar. He stared at her darkly. "Ten minutes or so, like she said."

Sahara turned to him. "You've seen this before?"

Omar's frowned deepened. "I've seen it around. It's new."

"And you let her use it?" asked Marisa.

"I've never even heard of it," said Bao.

"It's a rich-kid drug," said Omar. "Just forget about it; she'll be fine."

Marisa checked Anja's pulse, which seemed strong enough.

"Is she gonna be okay?"

"She'll be fine," Omar insisted, "she's just going to lie there and—"

Anja's head straightened, and she sat up. Her eyes were unfocused, her expression blank, like she was in a trance. Marisa said her name again, but Anja only stood, turned toward the house, and started walking.

"What?" asked Sahara.

"She's sleepwalking," said Bao. "That's . . . weird."

Marisa turned to Omar. "Does that happen often?"

"How am I supposed to know?" he growled.

"She's gonna fall in the pool," said Sahara, jogging after her as quickly as she could in her heels, but Anja navigated the backyard flawlessly. Marisa shucked off her own heels and ran to catch up, the boys trailing behind, everyone burning with curiosity to see what the sleepwalker would do. Anja opened the door, walked inside, and pulled the second Bluescreen drive up out of her shirt. She yanked on it to snap the chain, all the while walking straight toward the couch and her napping father.

"She's going to plug it into her dad," said Sahara, covering her mouth in shocked disbelief. "That's the funniest damn thing I've ever seen."

Anja reached her father, turned his sleeping head, and lined up the drive with his headjack.

"Anja, don't!" yelled Omar. The sleepwalking girl faltered, just for a second, and in that moment her father woke with a start.

"Nein?" he asked, looking at them in confusion. "What are you doing?"

Anja lunged for him again, but by now Omar had reached her, grabbing her wrist before she could plug him in.

"What is going on?" Anja's father demanded, standing up with a frown. "What is wrong with Anja?"

"She's been drugged," said Omar. He wrested the Bluescreen from her hand and threw it to the other side of the room. "We need to get her to a bed; I don't know how long this sleepwalking trip is going to last."

"Drugs?" asked Mr. Litz. He looked at Marisa angrily. "You brought her drugs?"

"It was the guy who came right before us," said Marisa. "We didn't know anything about it."

"I told her not to spend time with . . . street kids." Mr. Litz spit the words out like they disgusted him. Anja collapsed again in Omar's arms, her body going just as limp as the first time she'd crashed. Litz pointed at the door with a snarl. "Get out."

"But we didn't—"

"Get out!" Litz roared, and turned to Omar. "You, help me take her upstairs."

"We can help," said Marisa, but Bao pushed her gently toward the door.

"They can take care of her," said Bao. "If we hang around, we'll only start a fight; that's not going to help anyone."

"I'll call us a cab home," said Sahara, her voice somber. They walked to the front door and out into the yard, and Marisa watched over her shoulder as Litz and Omar carried Anja's body upstairs.

She looked as lifeless as a doll.

FOUR

"I'm not leaving until I know she's okay." Marisa folded her arms and leaned against Omar's car. "End of subject."

"She'll be fine," said Sahara. "You heard what she said—she's done it before and nothing happened. Even Omar said it was safe."

"Este pinche pirujo tan chin—"

"That much Spanish in a row means you're really pissed off," said Bao, "and I know you're mad at Omar, but he's seen this before—"

Marisa snorted. "So he should never have let her take it."

"But he did," said Bao calmly, "because he's seen it before, and he knows that it's safe."

"Taxi's here," said Sahara.

"I'm not leaving until I hear from her," Marisa repeated. "You can go if you want, but I'm—" She stopped abruptly, as a small flashing icon popped up in the corner of her vision. "Wait, I just got a message—" She stopped again, frozen in surprise at the name on the icon.

"Is she okay?" asked Sahara.

"It's not her," said Marisa. She looked up. "It's from Chuy."

Bao's eyes widened. "Mysterious brother Chuy?"

Marisa glanced at Cameron and Camilla, still hovering over them. She nodded wordlessly, and blinked on the icon. The message opened and expanded, four tiny words glowing softly in the center of her djinni display:

We need to talk.

Marisa hadn't talked to Chuy in months—they'd been friends for most of her childhood, even after their father had kicked him out, but then he'd had a kid, and Cherry Dogs had started trying to go pro, and with one thing or another she hadn't heard from him in . . . well, not since Christmas, and not for nearly a whole year before that. To hear from him now, though, after everything that had happened in the restaurant . . . it wasn't a conversation she wanted to have in public.

Sahara took a step toward the waiting autocab. "We're losing money on this taxi."

"I can't—"

Another icon popped up, from Anja this time, and Marisa blinked on it immediately:

I'm fine, get out of here before my dad calls the cops.

"Anja says she's fine," said Sahara.

"I think she sent it to all three of us," said Bao, looking down at his handheld phone. He looked up uncertainly. "You think he'd really call the police? I've got a record I can't afford any more marks on."

"It doesn't matter, because we're leaving," said Sahara. She put a hand on Marisa's shoulder. "You gonna be okay?"

"I'm not the one who—" Marisa took a deep breath, glancing at Anja's house, then back to the brief, ominous message from her brother. She didn't want to leave, but she had to answer him, and not just with another text. She shot one last look at the house, and nodded. "Yeah, let's go."

They climbed into the autocab, and Marisa sent Chuy a quick message:

Sure thing. Call you in an hour.

Bao gave the autocab their addresses and it rolled away smoothly; an adlink popped up in the corner of Marisa's vision, the cab offering to connect her music library to its onboard sound system, but she blinked it away. Sahara had apparently accepted the invitation, as one of her current favorite singers started crooning in the background. Ever the entertainer, Sahara faced her camera nulis directly and started talking, recapping the day in a bubbly final-thoughts speech. If it were any other friend, Marisa would have been hurt, but she knew Sahara was being kind; she was keeping the cameras and the attention on herself, giving Marisa a chance to think in relative privacy. Bao also seemed to sense her need for silence, or was lost in a reverie of his own.

Marisa couldn't help but fear the worst from her older brother's message. Maybe what her father said had angered Calaca, and he'd gone to take it out on Chuy? Maybe La Sesenta was overstepping their bounds because of pressure from another gang, and Chuy had been caught in the crossfire? Or maybe it wasn't Chuy, but his girlfriend or their baby?

Marisa worried herself into a panic, and when she couldn't stand it anymore she blinked into her djinni's message history, searching for Chuy's ID code, and traced it backward to find where the call had initiated. The GPS coordinates placed him in Mirador, within a hundred yards of his apartment—she could narrow it down even closer if she was willing to break a few laws, but the equipment she needed to cover her tracks was at home, and this was enough for now. He was likely calling from home, or close to it, so he was probably safe. Maybe it was nothing. Maybe he'd just seen her talking about him on Sahara's vidcast, and wanted to say hi. She took a slow, deep breath, and waited.

The autocab dropped her off first, and she gave Bao a hug and Sahara a quick kiss good-bye before stepping out onto the sidewalk. She waved as they drove away, promising to ping them later, and was so preoccupied with thoughts of Chuy that she opened her front door without remembering to engage her "sneak in quietly" protocol; Olaya instantly registered her entrance, updated the family list, and Marisa sighed as she heard a high-pitched "Mari!" from the back of the house. Her youngest sister, Pati, came squealing down the hall and tackled her with a high-speed hug.

"Mari, you're home so early! Did you have fun? Did you kiss any boys? Was Bao there? Please tell me you didn't kiss Bao because I love him and he's mine and you can't have him." She was dressed in old jeans—hand-me-downs from Marisa—and a faded Overworld T-shirt.

Marisa sighed, and hugged Pati back before turning toward the stairs. "I didn't kiss anyone." Pati hung on tight, making it hard to walk, clutching Marisa tightly around the waist and babbling on without a pause for breath.

"I thought you weren't going to be home until really late but you came home so soon it's not even my bedtime yet so we can hang out and I can do your hair and you can teach me how to do my makeup because I always put on too much but you never do you're gorgeous and I got a new program on my djinni do you want to see it it takes pictures and I can animate them and leave them on shop windows so everyone can see them—"

"You know I'd love to, kiddo, but tonight's not going to work." She maneuvered up the stairs as best she could with her sister still wrapped around her, pausing halfway through to kick off her heels. One of the nulis would get them later. "I've got some calls to make."

"Hey, Mari," said Sandro, leaning against the wall at the top of the stairs. His bedroom was next to hers, and he'd apparently been doing homework when he heard the commotion. At sixteen years old he was nearly Mari's age, and far more studious and organized than she'd ever been; even now, hours after school was over, he was still in his collared shirt and slacks, arms folded like a younger, male version of their mother. "I heard about La Sesenta and the restaurant, but Mom and Dad won't tell me anything. You were there?"

Marisa stepped around him, trying to shift Pati to her other side to keep from falling. "Yep. Can't talk right now—"

"Are you going to practice Overworld?" asked Pati. "I played a little after school but Mami found out and made me unplug right in the middle of a match because I hadn't done my homework yet. I was trying the new Force Pulse powerset but I couldn't launch any robots like you did because every time I get close they kill me so I got a ton of deaths but I launched Keldy off a mountain—"

"I'm not playing Overworld," said Mari, looking back firmly at Sandro's disapproving glare. "I need to call someone, and it's kind of urgent—"

"More urgent than what happened today?" asked Sandro. "You shouldn't even have gone out tonight. Mom's on some kind of red alert, practically barricading the windows, and Dad's downstairs calling every other business owner in Mirador trying to figure out what's going on, and meanwhile you're off screwing around with your friends like nothing happened."

Marisa's mouth fell open, and she gestured around at the hall-way. "I'm right here, at home, literally two feet away from you."

"Are you calling a boy?" asked Pati. "Is it the boy you met at school because I looked him up on your school database like you taught me and he's really cute and he has pretty good grades but there was another one even cuter and I can show you who it is hang on while I look him up."

"Gabi didn't even go to ballet today," said Sandro. "Dad wouldn't let her. When she found out you'd already left with your friends she almost blew a fuse—I thought she was going to break a window."

Marisa raised her eyebrows. "Gabi got *mad*?"

Sandro nodded. "Gabi got mad."

"Mier—" Marisa started to swear, caught herself, and looked

down at Pati with a wide, fake smile. "—coles. I will do makeup with you on miércoles."

"Today *is* Wednesday!" Pati protested. "Does that mean I have to wait a whole week?"

"Friday, then," said Marisa, finally prying the girl's arms apart and stepping out of the hug. "But only if you let me make this call, because it's really important."

"Fine," said Pati sullenly, then brightened and ran back down the stairs, her eyes unfocusing slightly as she watched something on her djinni.

"Tell me what happened today," said Sandro. With Pati gone the hall was suddenly quiet, and Marisa shook her head.

"Let me make this call first."

"What call could possibly be so important that you—"

"I'm calling Chuy."

Sandro fell silent.

Marisa leaned in close, keeping her voice low. "He sent me a message about an hour ago. That's why I came home early." It wasn't the whole truth, but it would keep him off her back. "Don't tell Papi."

Sandro hesitated a moment before answering. "Mari, Chuy is dangerous."

"He's our brother."

"He's dangerous," Sandro insisted. "Whatever's going on, he's mixed up in it. Those guys who came in to the restaurant today were his friends: his friends pointed guns at our mother, and now you're taking his side?"

"I'm not taking anyone's *side*," said Marisa. "He contacted me, and that means he has something to say, okay? Maybe he can tell us what's really going on, with La Sesenta and the Maldonados and . . . who knows what else. You want answers? Chuy might have them."

Sandro sighed, a resigned, frustrated snarl. "Fine. But be careful."

"I promise."

"And come talk to me as soon as you're done."

"I will." Marisa opened her door. "Thanks for warning me about Gabi."

Sandro nodded, and Marisa closed her door and locked it behind her. The nulis had been busy: her piles of laundry had been cleaned, sorted, folded, and stacked neatly in her drawers and hung carefully in her closet. The dishes had been taken away, the floor vacuumed, and her desk straightened—which meant she wouldn't be able to find anything, she realized with a sigh, and some of her smaller computer components might be missing altogether. She made a mental note to look into the nuli programming, to see what she could do to keep them away from her desk, then rolled her eyes and made an actual note in her djinni's reminder list. She hadn't used the list in ages, and it was already full of other reminders: old tasks she'd finished weeks ago, and some she'd forgotten completely. She grimaced, and promised to start using the reminder function better, then shook her head and closed the list. She could think about all of that later.

She opened Chuy's message, blinked on his ID, and called him.

It took Chuy nearly thirteen seconds to answer; an eternity for someone with a djinni. His voice was rough but familiar. "Marisa."

Not Mari anymore, Marisa thought silently. *Have we really grown that far apart?* Or is it just because I'm older now? She cleared her throat. "Hey, Chuy."

"Thanks for calling," he said. "I just wanted to say I'm sorry about what happened at Saint Johnny's today."

Marisa exhaled a soft sigh of relief. If that's all this call was about, it was a load off her mind. She wanted to say *It was nothing, don't worry about it*, except that it wasn't nothing, and the whole family was worried, and she didn't want to make light of it. She opened her mouth to talk, and realized she didn't know what to say that didn't either absolve him of blame or accuse him of being part of it. She grimaced, and skipped the small talk completely.

"What's going on?"

Chuy ignored the question, continuing to apologize—or to protest his innocence. Marisa wasn't sure which. "If I'd known Calaca was going to the restaurant, I'd have stopped him; you know that."

"I know."

"This is . . ." His voice slowed, and she could hear him breathing, like he was trying to figure out what to say. "You asked what's going on, and I don't know for sure, but I know it's going to get a lot worse before it gets better."

Marisa closed her eyes. So there was more. "What do you know? Even if you don't know everything, you've got to know more than I do. Calaca said something about the Maldonados not paying off the gang anymore?"

"That's the root of it, yeah. Those idiotas Maldonado uses to boss everybody around, about a month ago they just . . . stopped paying us."

"The enforcers?"

"Maldonado's thugs, yeah. We tried to figure out why the money wasn't coming, but they just keep saying the same thing: it's coming soon, be patient, don't do anything crazy. But it's been a month, so Calaca and his boys started shaking down some of the places around the neighborhood, just a little here and there, you know? But I didn't know they were going to you guys, you gotta believe me."

"So that's all it takes?" asked Marisa, feeling her anger rise. "La Sesenta is literally just holding us hostage, and as soon as the money stops you whip out the guns and start robbing old ladies?"

"I have a family now, Marisa." His voice was raw and earnest; he was taking this conversation very seriously. "Junior's almost one year old now, and I gotta feed him something. You know what I mean? I gotta feed Adriana. I don't like this any more than—"

"You could get a job," said Marisa harshly.

"Are you kidding me?"

She heard some muffled cursing, and the sound of things being moved.

"I'm gonna show you something," he said, and turned on a video feed. She saw him for the first time in months—shaved bald, his eyebrows pierced, his neck and arms covered with dark black tattoos. He was wearing a sleeveless white T-shirt with a slim silver necklace tucked inside of it; the wall behind him had once been bright blue, but the paint had faded and the plaster was cracking, and there were more than a few stains, either from water or . . .

something worse. Chuy swirled his finger, and whatever nuli was taking the video turned slowly around, giving Marisa a full view of the room: a kitchen, barely ten feet wide, with a metal sink and mismatched dishes stacked in a doorless cupboard. Everything was clean, and Adriana had obviously made some efforts to dress it up—a flower-print tablecloth, some photos on the wall, a cross and a rosary dangling forlornly from a hook—but it was small, and old, and falling apart. As the camera turned Marisa caught a brief glimpse down the short hall, seeing Adriana in a threadbare dress; she stepped out of view behind a doorframe when she saw the camera, but her eyes seemed to hang in Marisa's mind, soft and sad and desperate.

"This is how we live," said Chuy, his voice rising slightly. "This is how I'm raising my son, in this tiny little hole our landlord calls an apartment. You think I don't want more for them? You think I wouldn't get a job if there was any way to get one? You live in a palace compared to this—you have everything you ever want, and parents who pay for it, and my girlfriend is dressed in rags. So don't tell me to get a job, because you know there are no jobs for humans in LA anymore, and nowhere else for us to go. Maldonado's payoffs put food on the table, and now that they've stopped we have to get money from somewhere—or we have to remind Maldonado why he pays us. I don't like it, but that's the world we live in."

"I had no idea," said Marisa, wincing in sympathy. She put a hand on her own dress, bright and glittery and expensive, and felt a ball of guilt grow heavily in her stomach. Should she offer some clothes to Adriana? Would she be grateful, or offended? Marisa barely knew her, though she was only one year older. They'd gone to school together. "I had no idea," she said again, and realized that she couldn't bear not to offer them something, offense or no. "Chuy, you've got to let me help you—"

He refocused the camera on his face. "I didn't call to ask for charity."

"Some food at least," said Marisa. "I can sneak you the extras from the restaurant, rice and beans at least—"

"I don't want your help," he said fiercely. "I'm not a beggar, and I can earn my own living. That's not why I called, and that's not why I showed you where I live. I called to tell you that I'm sorry, and I'll do everything I can to keep them off you, but this is what you're up against, okay?" He gestured at the poverty around him. "Sixty other guys, living just like me, with wives and girlfriends and kids of their own, and no way to feed them. You think we're just diablos out here making trouble for no good reason? We've got to do something, whether we like it or not."

Marisa saw the pain in his eyes, could hear the regret in his voice, and she felt her fingers curl involuntarily around the sheets on her bed, clutching them with tight, white knuckles. She didn't want to ask, but she had to. "So . . . what are you doing?"

"Marisa . . ."

"You said you've got to do something, and I know you're talking about more than just shaking down some shops and taco stands. I know you, Chuy, and there's something you're not telling me."

He paused, then nodded. "Goyo started it last week."

"Who's Goyo?"

"The boss. If you think Calaca's scary . . ." He paused again, gritting his teeth. "We're selling, Marisa."

Marisa closed her eyes, her worst fears confirmed. "Drugs? Is it Bluescreen?"

"What's Bluescreen?"

"It's a new digital drug," she said quickly, "plugs right into your djinni. One of my friends did some tonight."

"Here in Mirador?"

"No, it was . . ." She didn't want to say *Brentwood*, feeling too guilty to even mention that she spent time with someone who has a home there. "The other side of town."

"Never heard of it," said Chuy. "Goyo's got us selling Hoot."

"Húluàn?"

"Exacto."

"Chuy—"

"I know."

"Hoot practically eats you alive! Have you seen the pictures? And it's, like, twice as addictive as normal meth."

"I know!" Chuy repeated. "I'm not saying I'm down with this, and that's why I wanted to warn you. I tried to talk to Calaca, but do you know how much authority I have in La Sesenta? Just barely enough to not get shot when I say that maybe we don't want to bring flesh-eating heroin into our neighborhood. So now I'm warning you that you need to be careful, and watch the little girls, and . . . be careful."

"I will," said Marisa, "but you've got to get out."

"I've told you, I don't have anywhere to go."

"Go to Mexico," said Marisa. "They have jobs there—"

"Mirador is my home," he said. "I was born here; my son was born here. My family is here—not you and Dad, the family that kicked me out, but La Sesenta, mis carnales, true blood brothers united not by some hereditary accident, but by choice. By pride. I would take a bullet for them, and any one of them would take one from me. We put food on each other's tables, and money in each other's pockets, and I'm not going to leave that just because the food isn't very much and the money doesn't go very far."

"So you'd rather sell Hoot on the playgrounds?"

"Why are you attacking me? I'm trying to help you."

"Then stop dealing drugs."

"Damn it, Marisa—"

"Then come home," she said.

He shook his head, looking suddenly exhausted. "You know that's not an option."

"You can patch things up with Papi—he misses you, I know he'd take you back."

"You were too young when I left," he said. "You didn't understand then, but I thought you'd have figured it out by now. He will never take me back, and I will never take him. I can't live with him. I can't *be* him. I have my own family now, my own woman, my own child, and I have to stand up and be the man they need me to be—if you don't agree with my methods, that's your problem and not mine."

"Is a little pride worth more than their safety?"

"Their safety is why I'm here," he said fiercely. "You think people just leave gangs, as easy as . . . logging out of a game? This is the real world. I swore an oath to Goyo, and to everyone else, and if I break that oath everything I have is in danger." He laughed—a short, disbelieving bark. "How sheltered are you, Mari?"

"I love you, Chuy." She faced one the computers on her desk and turned on the camera feed, wanting him to look her in the eyes. "I love you, and you know that, and I know you love us too. I'm glad you called, and I'm grateful for your help, but . . . for Junior's sake at least, and for Adriana's. For Mami's sake, so she never has to hear about you getting shot somewhere. You've got to get out. If not here, then Mexico—they won't chase you that far."

Chuy took a deep breath, and the pause seemed to drag on forever. "I'll think about it."

"Thank you."

"I love you, too, Mari. Be careful."

"I will."

She blinked, and ended the call.

FIVE

"Agents missing from the city," said Sahara on the comlink.

Marisa scanned the rooftop quickly, with a quick glance at her camera feeds to make sure. She'd brought the recon drones this time. "Nothing up here; they must be in the sewers."

"You hear that, Fang?"

"Kù," said Fang. "Think I know where they are. Hide in the rubble of that old laundry place, and drop down the hole on my signal."

"On it," said Sahara. Jaya echoed her, and Marisa watched on her map display as their icons moved across the battlefield. This match was in a ruined city, full of collapsed buildings and overturned cars. Marisa was perched on top of a bombed-out gymnasium, working as Spotter to Anja's Sniper.

"That leaves us alone for a while," said Anja. "Want to try something weird?"

"No, she doesn't," said Sahara. "We're trying to practice for the Jackrabbit, not screw around making blooper reels for some weekender's gamecast."

Anja was already up and running, sprinting across the rooftop as fast as she could move. Marisa smirked and followed her; as Spotter it was her job to keep Anja alive, and even Sahara couldn't argue with that. "How weird are we talking?"

"All the key spots to take out the turrets are guarded by attack drones, right? So the normal way to disable them is to kill the drones, move into place, and pour as much damage into the turret as we can before the drones respawn." She was moving forward as she spoke, headed for one of the standard sniping positions, but stopped a full rooftop short. "Today I brought every range enhancer I could pack in—my DPS sucks, but I can hit from way, way back, where there are no drones. Cover me."

Marisa caught up to her just as she started firing; Anja's avatar today was some kind of fairy princess, pink tutu and all, which looked hilarious crouched on the edge of a rooftop holding a six-foot Arlechino sniper rifle. She folded down her tripod, lined up her shot, and fired. The enemy turret was far down the road, only barely visible from this vantage point, and Marisa didn't expect any of the Overworld weapons to have that kind of reach . . . but the shot hit.

"You can attack turrets from all the way back here?"

"I saw it on a Korean gamecast." Anja fired again, more rapidly now that she'd set everything up. "It'll take me twice as long to kill it with these damage values, but I can do it."

"Spend that long in one spot and you're dead," said Marisa.

"The enemy Sniper's going to know exactly where you are."

"Which is why I waited for their whole team to go underground," said Anja, firing freely. Her shots left bright afterimages in the air: tracers designed to help a Sniper walk their shots, but which an enemy Sniper could just as easily follow back to the source. Marisa crouched low, trying to spot any threats before they could counter.

"Now!" shouted Fang, and the comm channel filled with the sounds of gunfire, swooshing magical effects, and the sharp clangs of the Katana powerset. Marisa watched her teammates' health bars move wildly up and down, while still keeping a wary eye on the rooftops.

"Enemy down!" roared the announcer.

"Ally down!"

"Enemy down!"

"Tā mā de!" yelled Fang, her icon transforming to a pale skull. "I almost got away."

"We're lucky you're the only one who died," said Sahara, regrouping with Jaya as the enemy icons retreated out of view. "They had all five agents down here."

"A two-for-one trade isn't bad," said Jaya. "Heartbeat, Happy, we scared them back up to you."

"Roger that," said Marisa. "Time to stop shooting, Anja."

Anja kept firing. "But I didn't kill it yet."

"But now they're all back, and they'll see you."

Anja grinned wickedly, still staring through her scope and firing shot after shot into the enemy turret. "Good thing I have a Spotter."

Marisa saw the three remaining enemy agents run past one of her recon drones. "You have a Spotter who isn't designed for melee. We're about to get crushed."

"Pull back," said Sahara, "we can't get to you in time to defend you."

"Keep shooting," said Anja sternly, in a broad parody of Sahara's voice.

"Incoming," said Marisa softly, and pulled out her handguns. She'd paired the Control Tech powerset with Ranged Light, giving her a pair of Stahri laser pistols with a handful of variable settings; she set them to Armor Piercing, braced herself for the onslaught, and started firing as soon as the first enemy agent appeared on the opposite roof. She landed a few clear shots when suddenly her recon drone sounded a proximity alarm, and she barely had time to turn around before she was hit by an attack from behind. The agent on the other roof had been a decoy, drawing her attention while the two other agents flanked her. Marisa screamed a war cry, dodging and firing with every ounce of skill she could muster, but it was too much. She whittled one of the agents almost all the way to zero before finally succumbing to their attack, and Anja was dead soon after.

Marisa appeared in the lobby room, waiting for her respawn timer to hit zero. Fang was already there, dressed in a steampunk avatar she'd been refining for the last few weeks; she was laughing uncontrollably.

Marisa raised her eyebrow. "You think that's funny?"

Anja appeared beside them, grinning from ear to ear. "That was awesome! I got it down almost seventy-five percent, completely on my own, from so far away their defenses were useless. They couldn't do anything about it!"

Fang nodded toward Anja, keeping her eyes on Marisa. "Yeah, I think that's pretty funny."

Marisa rolled her eyes at Anja. "You realize we died, right?"

"We died because we were unprepared," said Anja eagerly. "Imagine if you were built for defense, like with the force shield or something, or maybe crowd control to lock them down so they couldn't hurt me. I could probably drop a whole turret and still get away! Maybe!"

"This is why I work alone," said Fang with a smirk. "I don't know how you ever keep her alive."

"It's harder than usual these days," said Marisa. "You hear about last night?"

Anja's excitement didn't even dim. "Yes! Last night was awesome, too!"

Marisa ignored her. "You've heard of Bluescreen?"

Fang shook her head.

"Some new digital thing, like a sensovid but super intense. Seems to be LA only." Marisa gestured at Anja. "HappyFluffy-SparkleTime here took a dose and passed out."

"You're supposed to pass out," said Anja. "That's the point."

"Why would anyone want to pass out?" asked Fang.

Anja twisted her face into a mask of confusion. "What, do I have to defend the entire concept of recreational drugs now?"

"Yes, actually," said Marisa, "except don't, because that's crazy."

"Funny," said Anja, "because 'that's crazy' was pretty much

my whole defense." She looked at Fang. "It did suck, though, because I got grounded."

"Speaking of which," said Fang, "my respawn timer's almost up. Cherry Dogs forever."

"Cherry Dogs forever," said Marisa and Anja. Fang disappeared back into the game.

"Okay," said Anja. "I know I kind of scared you last night, so I want to make it up to you. Let's go dancing."

"I thought you were grounded."

Anja dismissed the concern with a wave. "Please. My dad's in meetings all night, and if I can't trick my way past the house computer, I don't deserve to go dancing."

Marisa grinned slyly. "I've got a new trick for that: instead of cycling your ID in your room, spoof it to a laundry nuli; that way if he checks it on GPS it'll look like you're moving around. Much more convincing."

"Ooh, I like that."

Marisa glanced at her respawn timer; it was almost done. "You got a specific club in mind?"

"It's called Ripcord; I'll send you the address after practice. Cherry Dogs forever."

"Cherry Dogs forever."

Marisa's parents were still nervous about La Sesenta, telling all their children to stay safely at home, but they couldn't afford to keep the restaurant closed forever. With them gone it was easy to sneak out, and Marisa took the extra time to help Gabi sneak out to catch a make-up ballet class, turning her younger sister's bitter rage almost instantly to undying gratitude. Marisa ordered her a prepaid autocab to get home, the address already programmed in, and made her way downtown to meet her friends.

Ripcord turned out to be a tall brick building near USC, wedged between two office buildings and partly covered with ivy; someone had carefully groomed the ivy to reach up in a reverse lightning pattern, which probably looked cool during the day, but at night it was completely upstaged by the four rows of narrow windows, each flashing a different bright color in patterns that alternated between cascades, starbursts, and utter chaos. The line to get in was long, and the enormous bouncer watching the door had replaced both of his arms with heavy-duty bionics—the kind with massive hydraulic pistons that made his arms look like a pair of gleaming motorcycle engines. He looked like he could crush boulders with his hands, and he stood tall enough that Marisa suspected his legs were bionic as well. She stepped out of the autocab and smoothed her dress—the same glittery green one she'd worn last night, since she'd never had the chance to show it off properly. Every business on the street immediately offered her discounts and adlinks, flashing on the periphery of her djinni display, but she brushed them off and changed her settings to keep her display clear of offers. She searched for Sahara's cameras, but the air was so full of nulis it was impossible to tell in the dark which ones were which. Marisa figured most of the nulis were probably from neighboring businesses, and as if to prove her point she was instantly swarmed by three of them: two hovering screens, each advertising some exciting new clothing store, and a waiter drone from a yakitori place offering her a free sample of spicy roast chicken. The pungent smell filled her nostrils enticingly, but she waved them all off. It wouldn't do to start the evening with a soy sauce stain on her dress.

Marisa opened the friends list on her djinni and found Sahara and Anja's names glowing brighter than the rest; they were close. She blinked on the track function, and a line appeared in her vision, shooting off through the crowd—she followed it to a point about halfway through the line, and joined the girls with a smile. Cameron and Camilla hovered nearby, but Bao was nowhere in sight. "No boys?" she asked.

"Bao had to work," said Sahara. She was wearing a short pink dress with a loose neckline that plunged almost to her navel. It looked as if any fast movements would make it downright scandalous, which was undoubtedly the purpose. The men waiting in line were only barely concealing their stares, but Sahara only had eyes for the women. "Omar said he had something, too," Sahara continued, scanning the crowd as she talked, "but he was kind of vague about it. He always is." She caught another girl's eye and smiled.

"He's probably hanging out with my father," said Anja, rolling her eyes. "They're getting along even better since he 'saved' me last night." She was dressed in what looked like a long black T-shirt with a giant white wolf on the front, buried under several layers of sheer black mesh that extended down into a puffy skirt, and up into a see-through hood framing her blond hair. She looked like a goth Red Riding Hood, with a rattan basket-weave purse to complete the image.

Marisa nodded, looking around at the crowd. Omar could be

anywhere, but if Bao was "working" that meant he was downtown somewhere, probably in a crowd like this one, skimming micro-payments from tourists' credit accounts. His mother had a job, but his stepfather had been out of work for over a year, and the only way to feed all five of them—Bao, his parents, and his twin stepsisters—was to supplement his mom's wages with whatever he could lift on the side. Marisa had offered to help him before, but just like Chuy he'd been too proud to accept it.

Marisa thought again about Chuy and his tiny apartment, and looked at the people in line self-consciously. Even this street, now that she took the time to look at anything other than the glowing, ostentatious building, was littered with garbage, and she could see here and there silhouettes of the homeless in the shad-ows. Watching. She wanted to give them something, but what? She hadn't carried cash in years. Did they have djinnis and credit accounts?

How did they even live?

Deep bass music shook the pavement, and Marisa closed her eyes.

"Now that you're here," said Anja, "let me see if I can get us in early." She pushed herself to the front of the line and chat-ted with the half-tech bouncer; Marisa took a moment to admire the boys in line with them, and smiled to herself. The pickings looked good. A minute later Marisa and Sahara both got a ping from Anja, telling them to come forward, and the bionic bouncer stepped aside to pass them through.

"Welcome to Ripcord, ladies."

Cameron swirled around to get a shot of the bouncer as the

girls passed, and they walked through the door into a neon volcano of bodies and sound.

"How much did you have to pay him?" asked Marisa, practically shouting to be heard over the pounding music.

"Pay him?" asked Anja with a laugh. "I just pointed at Sahara's dress and let his business sense do the talking. Those guys in line outside will wait hours to get in and try to pick us up."

The club was packed with people, dancing on the open floors or crowded around the circular bars that rose up like glowing blue trees. The ceiling rippled with a pattern of dark blue circles, shifting and interlocking like unpoppable bubbles, and here and there a thick oval pillar shimmered with a coruscation of otherworldly green. Even the floor seemed to glow, faint lights tracing waves under their feet, and as the girls pushed their way through the crowd Marisa couldn't tell if the lines were moving, or if it was just an optical illusion.

A raised stage bulged out from one wall, the same bulbous shape as the glowing bars, and an Aidoru band was projected there in full 3D, playing a variety of impossible instruments synced almost flawlessly to the music. It was Kopo music, of course, a kind of Korean/African fusion that had gripped the LA scene for nearly three months, drums and bass and synthesizers creating a seamless wall of dance-hall techno; Marisa started moving in time to the familiar rhythms, dancing almost unconsciously as they made their way across the floor. Her dress glittered, catching the blue and purple lights from the ceiling and refracting it into a riot of rainbow colors. A tall Chinese boy caught her eye and danced toward her, dressed in black jeans and a cowboy shirt that seemed to shimmer in the light. Marisa smiled back slyly, signaling a quick *I'll catch up with you later* to Anja and Sahara. She danced with the boy for a moment before moving deeper into the crowd, eager to explore all her options before spending too much time with any one guy. They were barely into the second song of the night when Sahara pinged her with a single, wordless photo: Sahara and Anja, on a plush red couch, sitting with the man they'd glimpsed leaving Anja's house the night before. He was even more gorgeous than Marisa remembered, but she couldn't help but scowl. Hadn't Anja said that was her dealer? There was no way Marisa was letting her buy more Bluescreen.

Marisa left the dance floor immediately, wiggling her fingers in a flirty farewell to the muscly Mexican boy she'd been dancing with. She blinked her tracker back on, and followed the ethereal line through the dancing crowd to a small cluster of furniture in the corner. The handsome stranger sat between the two girls, dressed in cream-colored pants and a red jodhpuri suit accented with burnished brass buttons. He looked maybe twenty years old, his hair a dark brown mess of calculated chaos, his stubbled chin strong and narrow, his slim nose as sharp as an axe. He smiled up at Marisa as she approached, the corner of his mouth wrinkling in a kind of boundless confidence. *Rich trash*, thought Marisa. It was people like him that were bleeding the rest of the city dry. She smoothed her dress and sat demurely on a plush red chair opposite the couch, crossing her legs and smiling back with a nonchalance she'd spent hours perfecting in her bedroom mirror.

"Saif," said Anja, "this is our friend Marisa. Marisa, this is Saif."

Cameron buzzed idly overhead, probably looking for a good vantage point to perch on, but Camilla was resting silently on the Synestheme table between them, soaking up as much of the conversation as her speakers could pick up in the noisy club.

"It's a pleasure to meet you," said Saif, nodding politely. He smiled again. "Didn't I see you last night at Anja's house?"

A message from Sahara popped up in the corner of Marisa's eye: **He didn't say that to me.**

Marisa faked a smile. "Was that you? I wasn't really paying attention." She stole a glance at his cheekbone, trying not to stare, then hid the glance by tracking her eyes all the way down to the Synestheme, touching the screen to call up the drink menu. She knew she should stay polite, but couldn't stop herself from making at least one subtle jab. "You had the car, right? The Daimyo? I hope it didn't drive you here—a car that expensive makes a tempting target in a neighborhood like this."

"You have a good eye for cars. Don't worry, though—a Daimyo can defend itself pretty well." He grinned. "Any of those bums outside try to mess with it, they'll get a surprise."

Marisa wanted to smack him, but instead laughed as fakely as she could. "Ha, ha! Stupid poor people."

Another message from Sahara popped up in Marisa's vision: **What the what? I thought you liked this guy.**

Not as much as I like laughing at poor people, Marisa sent back. **Ha ha!**

Saif looked at her a moment, like he was trying to decipher her attitude. After a moment he smiled again, and gestured at the menu screen with as much authority as if he owned the club.

"Where are my manners? Please, ladies, have a drink, it's all on me."

"Just Lift for me," said Sahara.

"Order a real drink if you want one," said Saif with a laugh, "I'm not going to narc on you."

Sahara smiled warmly, as if this was the nicest thing anyone had ever said to her. "Maybe later."

"Bubble tea," said Anja. "Lychee if they've got it."

Marisa looked at the menu. "Looks like strawberry, honey-dew, mango, rose, and taro." She tapped one. "Mango for me."

"Rose, then," said Anja, and tapped Saif lightly on the knee. Marisa looked at the gesture, lingering just slightly longer than necessary on the boy's leg, and wondered if Anja was . . . perusing the menu, to use her own metaphor.

Marisa sent her a quick message: **Are you after him or his drugs?**

He's all yours, Anja sent back.

That's not what I meant, sent Marisa. Why did everyone think she was chasing this bastard?

This gorgeous, gorgeous bastard.

Saif smiled, a kind of self-deprecating smirk that said *I should be embarrassed, but I'm too damn proud of myself.* The sheer confidence of it made Marisa want to gag. "You're going to laugh at me," he said, already chuckling at himself. "I've got a sweet tooth like you wouldn't believe, and that prompts some, shall we say, rather childish drink orders." He jerked his chin at the menu screen. "Order me a Candy Apple."

Marisa raised her eyebrow as she searched the menu. "I've

never even heard of a Candy Apple."

"Apple juice and butterscotch schnapps," said Saif. "It's every bit as thick and sugary as it sounds, and if they had it I'd add caramel syrup."

"You weren't kidding about the sweet tooth." Marisa sent the order, and a payment icon popped up on each of their djinnis; Saif grabbed it first, paying for the drinks with a single blink before leaning back into the curved red couch. Marisa forced herself to stay cool, looking anywhere but at Saif, and sent Anja another quick message: **Please don't buy any more Bluescreen**.

Anja didn't respond to that one.

"So what's up with the nulis?" asked Saif, and Sahara began to explain her vidcast. Marisa watched his polite responses, eager and charming, and idly scanned his ID: Saif Roshan, living in LA on a student visa from India, studying business at USC. There was an odd glitch in the data, probably from an aftermarket edit. She'd done similar work on IDs herself, including Bao's sisters, hiding certain legal information that they didn't want public. Knowing that Saif had something to hide made him even more interesting than before, like a drop shadow on an image that made it pop out from the background. She wondered idly what it might be—a juvenile record? Unpaid fines somewhere? Nothing serious, or he couldn't have gotten into USC.

I need to stop thinking about him, she told herself, and focused on the Synestheme again. She unspooled a long, white cord from the housing in the table, and when she plugged it into her head-jack the music seemed to come to life around her, pulsing visibly in the air as the Synestheme interfaced with her djinni to blend all five senses together. She blinked up a few enhancements, feeling almost as if her body itself was merging with the music, and watched Saif as he smiled and murmured politely to Sahara's ongoing monologue. A waiter nuli floated down to the table and deposited their drinks, and Marisa took a long, slow sip from her bubble tea; the mango was delicious, and the Synestheme interpreted the taste visually with a burst of subtle sparkles.

"So," said Anja, stirring her own tea with its oversized straw. "You carrying tonight?"

"Every night," said Saif. "You buying?"

"Buying what?" asked Marisa innocently, simultaneously sending another message to Anja: **You've got to be kidding me**.

Saif pulled a pair of black thumb drives from the pocket of his shirt. "Bluescreen. You girls try it last night?"

Sahara's message popped up in Marisa's vision: **Is that why she brought us here?**

"They didn't," said Anja, "because my father freaked out." The Synestheme turned her voice into a pale pink cloud the same color as her tea, and she winked with an audible *ding*. "But he's not here, so pass 'em out."

"Wait a minute," said Marisa, leaning forward. Her own voice came out like a cloud of shifting shapes. "He freaked out because something legitimately freaky happened." She looked at Saif. "You want to explain that?"

Saif's brow furrowed in genuine concern. "What happened?"

"She started sleepwalking during her trip," said Sahara. "I've got the clip saved if you want to see it."

"No, that's fine," said Saif. "I've . . . I've heard of that, but only rarely. It comes from the crash, I think: your brain gives up so much control that sometimes your body just does whatever. It's not dangerous, though; I mean, it's just sleepwalking, people do that all the time." He looked at Anja. "You didn't break anything, right?"

"I almost wish I had," said Anja. "Then they could worry about something real."

"We just don't want anyone to get hurt," said Marisa.

"Bluescreen is completely safe," said Saif, settling into the explanation like it was old, familiar territory. "It's no different than any other sensory program—like the Synestheme, for example, and you obviously have no problem with that."

Marisa frowned and unplugged herself, suppressing a shudder as the real world seemed to solidify around her. The music dulled into the background, seemingly on the edge of her awareness despite its volume. "Synesthemes don't cause blackouts."

"Not as a rule, no," said Saif, "but they can, like any sensory interface, and when they do it's completely harmless."

Anja grabbed the drives from his hand. "Stop focusing on the blackout," she said. "The buzz is the whole point. The blackout just means it's time for another dose." She dropped one drive in her purse and slipped the other up under her hair and behind her neck, and Marisa thought she could see in the girl's eyes the exact moment the drive clicked into her headjack. Anja leaned back against the couch, clenching her hands into tight fists, and Saif pulled another pair of drives from his pocket.

"Care to join her?" He grinned, flashing a brief glimpse of perfect, white teeth between his lips. "On the house. I'll stay here the whole time you're out—keep these khotas away from you." He gestured around at the crowd in the club.

Marisa looked at the obvious ecstasy on Anja's face, feeling more than a little envious, but before she could answer, another message from Sahara popped up in her vision: **Here comes the Princess.**

Marisa's eyes went wide, a combination of surprise and disgust, and she managed to recover just before La Princesa stepped into view: Francisca Maldonado, Omar's only sister and the unbearable, unofficial royalty of El Mirador. She wore a bright white dress that opened at the top like a flower, with unzipped petals of fabric folded down past her shoulders. Marisa thought it made her look like a spoiled banana in a colorless peel. She had long white sleeves that came all the way down into gloves, and the hem of the dress was almost exactly the same length, coming just to her fingertips, with nothing but fishnets on her long legs below. Her face was pretty enough, slender and smooth with proud, arching eyebrows and jet-black eyes, but tinged with such arrogance Marisa could hardly look at her. She was flanked by a pair of pretty yet nameless attendants.

"Mira, que bárbaras," said Francisca, eyeing Marisa and Sahara with unveiled scorn. "Playing 'rich girls' today, Marisita? Didn't they tell you at the door? Any clothes you bought on layaway aren't allowed inside."

Marisa fumed, but Sahara looked back coolly. "Is that why you bought your dress at a grocery store?"

La Princesa was unfazed. "Is this who you're selling to these days, Saif?" She affected a look of innocent sadness. "I thought you had better taste."

"Franca," said Saif, his voice smooth and diplomatic, "so good to see you. Would you like to join us?"

"I wish I could," said La Princesa, "but I can't imagine I'll stay long. This used to be such a classy place, but I simply don't feel safe here anymore." She glanced out at the dance floor, her eyes settling for a moment on the tight-shirted Mexican boy Marisa had been dancing with earlier. She looked back at Saif with a conspiratorial whisper. "Too much barrio trash."

Marisa sent Sahara a message: **You think we'll get kicked out if I knock this girl's teeth into the back of her skull?**

"I won't keep you then," said Saif, his voice unreadably formal. "Bluescreen?"

"Four," said Francisca, and smiled seductively. "Five if you'd like to come with us."

Keep it subtle, Sahara messaged back. **What's that nickname she hates?**

Marisa suppressed a grin; Francisca's father called her Pancha, but the girl despised it. Pulling that out here would be the perfect way to put her in her place . . . and then she noticed that La Princesa was watching Saif with obvious interest, her eyes roaming over his body as he reached inside his jodhpuri coat for more Bluescreen drives. The nickname was good, but if this entitled little brat was after Saif, there were much better ways of hurting her. Marisa glanced around, looking for something she could use, and her eyes lit on Saif's Candy Apple, held out in his right hand while he searched in his pockets with his left. The drink was so close she could practically touch it, and in a sudden fit of courage she did.

"Let me hold that for you, babe." She gently plucked the drink from his hand and took a small sip; it caught in her throat like a mouthful of syrup, even thicker and sweeter than she'd imagined, but she hid her hesitation expertly, and swallowed the cloying liquid as if it had cleared her throat refreshingly. "Thanks for stopping by, Pancha, it was great to see you."

The dark look that came over Francisca's face was like a thunderstorm of rage, incensed at the idea that Marisa and Saif were together. Marisa wondered for a moment if she'd gone too far, and La Princesa was about to attack her. Instead Francisca took a calming breath, visibly restraining herself as she prepared what was sure to be a brutal verbal counterattack.

"Where's Anja?" asked Sahara suddenly.

Marisa looked at the couch, but the girl was gone. "What?"

"She was right here," said Saif.

"The door," said Sahara, her eyes unfocused as she checked something on her djinni. "She's headed outside."

She's sleepwalking again, thought Marisa, jumping up to follow Sahara as they wove through the pulsing crowd, Saif and Francisca forgotten behind them. She caught a glimpse of Anja's hair as she disappeared out the door, and ran to catch up. Trancing out in her own home was one thing, but here in the middle of the city there was no telling what kind of danger she could be in. Sahara took the lead, shoving her way through the press of dancers with more fierce authority than Marisa could ever muster, and the two girls burst out onto the sidewalk, looking around wildly. Marisa saw Anja nearly a block away, walking—no, flat-out running—straight toward the entrance to Highway 110.

"Anja!" shouted Marisa, and tore off her shoes, breaking

into a sprint to try to catch her. Sahara kept the same desperate pace beside her. "We're lucky you noticed she was gone," Marisa panted. They reached the corner and spared only a tiny glance at the lone oncoming car, trusting its navigation software to avoid them as they bolted past it and across the street. "I thought she was still passed out."

"It wasn't me," said Sahara, arms pumping as she ran, "it was someone named FakeJakeHooper."

"The movie star?"

"No, some guy who watches the vidcast. The angle from Cameron's feed showed her standing up behind us and walking away, and he pinged the chatroom with a comment." They were gaining on Anja, but only slightly; she'd already turned up onto the slow incline of the freeway on-ramp, and Marisa didn't think they could reach her before she got to the freeway. "Saif said this never happened! When we get back I'm going to feed that blowhole his own testicles in a sandwich."

A car roared past them, headed for the same freeway, and Marisa felt the fear grow thicker in her chest, like a twisted lump of cold iron. Traffic accidents were rare, as the network of self-driving sensors could keep up with almost anything, rerouting at lightning speed around any obstacle, but no system was perfect, and mistakes still happened; it didn't matter how fast your processor was if your tires couldn't respond in time. A freeway like this would have thousands of cars, moving at hundreds of miles an hour, and Anja was running straight toward them.

What was going on?

Another car roared by, its horn blaring a warning, and then

another, and then two more, and suddenly the girls were standing at the top of the on-ramp, the freeway rushing past them like a river of light and steel. Autocars sped by up the ramp, merging seamlessly into the freeway traffic. Marisa searched for Anja, finding her all too easy to spot—she was in a narrow gap in the third lane over, like a rock in a stream, the cars swerving deftly around her. On the street that led to the on-ramp the cars had honked, their onboard computers blaring a warning to anyone who got too close, but here in the freeway there was no such courtesy—the cars were moving too fast, their control programs hurtling them along at two hundred miles an hour. Passenger cars mingled with larger trucks and delivery vans, all barreling down the tightly packed road like bullets through a gun, each vehicle warning the others of the frail, fleshy obstacle in their path, giving them just barely enough time to move around it.

"She might be safe," said Sahara, but she sounded completely unconvinced. "The cars can avoid her, and in a couple of minutes the emergency nulis will airlift her right out of the road."

"Except she's moving," said Marisa, pointing. "She's running against the traffic, and swerving back and forth between lanes. It's almost like she's . . ." Marisa scowled. "Like she's trying to get hit." She shook her head. "The cars can't dodge that forever."

Sahara grimaced. "Can't you . . . hack it, or something?"

"The entire freeway?"

"I don't know! I'm just trying to think of something we can do."

"There's no central AI for the road system," said Marisa, "it's a swarm intelligence, like a flock of birds, with all the cars communicating with each other in real time. There's nothing for me to hack!"

"Even just one car?" asked Sahara. "It's better than nothing."

Marisa growled in frustration. "Maybe if I had time to study the algorithm they use for collision avoidance I might find a way to . . . nudge it or something. Trying it now I'd be blind—as likely to kill her as anything else."

A car missed Anja by inches, and Sahara cringed. "Well, we can't just stand here doing nothing. Think the swarm can handle two extra bodies to avoid?"

"If we stick together, we'll count as one," said Marisa, and grabbed her hand. She swallowed her fear, and looked into Sahara's wide, terrified eyes. "Cherry Dogs forever."

They ran into the freeway.

The first lane of cars saw them coming, the swarm intelligence registering their presence and passing it along to the cars behind. Trajectories were calculated and courses were corrected, and the cars moved to avoid the girls before the passengers even knew anyone was there. Marisa ran along the edge of the freeway, trying to catch up to Anja's position, gripping Sahara's hand as the giant metal monsters rushed past, buffeting them with wind and noise. She saw each vehicle's passengers in a strobe-like slide show, smiling and laughing, oblivious to anything out of the ordinary. Their headlights caught the desperate girls, lighting them up in an almost subliminal flicker of leg and face and glittering mini-dress, but by the time the speeding passengers' eyes had relayed the information, and their brains had processed the sight and its deadly implications, the cars would already be half a mile down the freeway, restored to their place in the lane and the danger now safely behind them. For Marisa, stuck in the middle, the danger seemed to blot out the entire world, leaving her blind and disoriented.

"Follow Cameron!" Sahara shouted. "He's right above her!"

Marisa blinked open Sahara's feed. Camilla was inert, still back in the club, but Cameron was hovering unsteadily in the turbulent air above the freeway. Anja was visible only by the disruption she caused in the traffic, but the disruption was still moving, and Marisa took that as a sign that her friend was, for the moment, still alive. Anja had been running so erratically, weaving back and forth among the cars, that they'd almost managed to catch up to her, separated now by just three lanes of speeding traffic.

Three lanes of high-speed death.

Marisa took a breath and stepped out into the first lane.

The swarm algorithm had already started shifting the cars away from the edge of the road, and as Marisa and Sahara walked farther the lane emptied almost instantly, merging those cars with the ones next to them, funneling seven lanes of traffic into six. Marisa gasped, shocked by the sudden space, chilled to the bone by the violent air currents from the hurtling vehicles—the only way to fit the same number of cars through an abruptly smaller space was to increase their speed, and the added movement whipped her hair wildly across her face. The girls bent their knees, bracing themselves against the wind, and walked toward Anja: one step, five steps, pushing the traffic farther to the side, until suddenly the freeway network detected enough empty space behind them and rerouted cars to fill it, trapping them in a narrow tunnel of screaming metal.

Marisa checked Cameron's feed, seeing Anja now just one lane away, still weaving chaotically. A massive shipping rig appeared on the feed, and Marisa looked up in terror to see it barreling toward them down the center of the freeway. Anja threw herself in front of it, the swarm network struggled to react in time, and the truck was shunted into the only free space available: Marisa and Sahara's gap. They screamed and stepped back, turning their heads and trying to make themselves as flat as possible, and the truck roared past mere inches from Marisa's face, so close it clipped her Jeon prosthetic—only barely, but with enough force that it seemed to rattle her entire skeleton. She froze in place, not daring to open her eyes, but Sahara pulled her forward with a hand on her shoulder. The truck was gone, and they were still alive.

Anja was one lane away.

They ran forward, Mari's cybernetic arm dangling limply, their eyes catching strobed glimpses of Anja between the speeding vehicles. They kept moving forward, and the swarm recalculated again, rerouting another lane of cars; Marisa gasped as the screaming metal river seemed to melt away and reappear behind them. Anja was weaving erratically, apparently still in her trance but occasionally stopping to stare in awe at the sheer speed and power that surrounded her. She started to run again, but Sahara dove forward and grabbed her.

"Anja! Wake up!"

Anja's eyes were blank and unfocused. "They've got her," she said, her voice inexplicably calm, "I'm— Oh, shi—" She collapsed back into unconsciousness, as suddenly as if someone had flipped a switch. Marisa clutched her broken arm and huddled close to her friends, holding as still as they could. When the emergency nulis finally came for them, she sobbed in relief.

SIX

"Hello, this is Saif—"

"Shut up and listen to me, pendejo," Marisa snarled over the phone line. "You told me Bluescreen was safe—you promised me—and then Anja practically—"

"Marisa! I've been looking everywhere for you."

"You almost got Anja killed with that stuff!"

"Is she okay?" asked Saif. His voice sounding concerned. "After you left the club—"

"After we left the club," said Marisa, and touched her Jeon arm, probing the dents and ruptures with her fingers. It was completely unresponsive, and she worried that it was broken irreparably. "After we left the club Anja wasn't just sleepwalking; she was sleepjumping in front of semis on the freeway."

"What?"

"We barely caught her in time, and then spent the next three hours talking to every cop and doctor in the city—and thanks to you I had alcohol in my bloodstream, too, which made those conversations even better than I'd ever imagined. You're a real gem, you know that?"

"It was one sip of schnapps—"

"If you were so damned concerned, why didn't you come after us?" Marisa was fed up with him, too rich and oblivious to care about anyone but himself—she was fed up with everyone like him, with the whole damn system, and he was going to face the full force of her anger like the stream from a fire hose. "Why weren't you out there dodging autocars on the 110? What kind of blowhole sits in a nightclub sipping a maldicho Candy Apple while we're out getting plastadas por las camionetas en la calle?" She was so angry she could barely think in English anymore.

"Marisa," said Saif, "you have to believe me—I had no idea about any of that. I didn't follow you out of the club because I thought you were mad about whatsername, Francisca; I didn't know Anja was on the freeway, or even sleepwalking again. Please tell me she's okay now."

Marisa touched her broken Jeon arm again. "Anja's home," she said sharply. "And you're not going to sell to her anymore, okay? There is no amount of defensive tech in your pinche Daimyo to protect you from me." Marisa was home as well, locked in her room and grounded by her parents, but that wouldn't stop her from hunting him down.

"I promise you," said Saif again, "I had no idea that Bluescreen could be dangerous. I've been using sensory interfaces for years—Synesthemes, Sensovids, even VR games—and I've never had a problem with any of them. My supplier swore to me that Bluescreen was the same thing. But after this . . . I don't know. I've got a lot friends I have to warn."

"You have to stop selling it," said Marisa.

"Of course," said Saif. "I just—" He paused, and his voice became softer. "I, um, I'm really glad you called me. I'm a little surprised, especially because we didn't have time to exchange IDs, but . . . I'm glad."

Marisa smiled, just slightly, not because he'd wanted to talk to her—she was still furious at him—but because she'd impressed him. "I scanned your ID at the club," she said, "and then when I decided to yell at you I . . ." She paused, debating whether or not to tell him, but decided that impressing him a little more couldn't hurt. "You get your djinni service through Johara, so I cracked their network and got your full contact info, and your usage records, and your . . . current location." He was in an apartment near USC. A surprisingly cheap one, in fact, which Marisa wasn't sure how to interpret. Maybe he was spending the night with some cheap bimbo from the club? She ran a quick check; the apartment was in his name.

"Whoa." Saif laughed. "You can do that?"

"In seconds," said Marisa, turning her boast into a threat. "Hurt Anja again and you will not be able to hide from me."

Saif hesitated before speaking. "Listen, maybe you can help me, then."

"After this? Not fracking likely."

"If this stuff's really this dangerous," he said, "it's not enough for just me to stop selling it. There are dealers all over the city. We have to get the word out to them as well."

Marisa's scowl disappeared, and she sat up straighter in her chair. "Are you serious?"

"Of course I'm serious, I just don't know how to start. I can talk to my supplier, but there's no way he's going to put me in touch with his people, and what are the odds he and his bosses shut down their operation because one person had a bad trip? Tatti. . . . I thought I was just selling another djinni app, but this is a legit drug."

"Of course it's a drug."

"But you found me," said Saif, ignoring the ice in her voice. "That means you can find the other dealers too, right?"

Marisa said nothing, stunned by the plea for help. Was he serious? Did he really want to make this better? He had to be playing an angle—maybe he just wanted to learn her methods so he could teach the others how to hide better. There was no way he was sincere. She hesitated, torn between hanging up forever and actually saying yes, digging into the mystery to see what kind of trick he was trying to pull. After a moment she whispered, "Probably."

"Okay," he said, his voice eager. "This is a big operation, with a lot of dealers. We're going to have to find them one by one. Let's get together and figure out—"

"What's your plan?" Marisa asked. "Find each one and just . . . talk them out of it? Appeal to the better nature of a city full of drug dealers?"

"If I can change my mind, so can they."

"And if they don't, what then? Scare them? Kill them? And

if by some miracle they do change their minds, how do we stop the suppliers from just finding new dealers to replace them? How do we stop whoever's making the drug from just finding new suppliers?"

"I don't know the answers to any of these questions," said Saif. "But with my contacts and your skills, we can at least make a start—we can learn about them, and then come up with a plan from there."

"You're crazy."

"Well," he said, "if you really don't care about this—"

"Of course I care about this," she snapped. "Do you?" Maybe he wasn't as rich as she'd thought he was, but he obviously wanted to be. Selling Bluescreen had given him money, and instead of saving it he'd bought the most expensive car he could—he didn't care about helping people, he wanted luxury and prestige. Maybe that was the difference Sahara had asked about, why Marisa could be friends with Anja but hate all of the others. Anja didn't care about the wealth. Saif did. Bluescreen was his chance to get rich, and somehow he thought that lying to her was going to help it happen.

"I know you're still mad at me," he said, "so you pick the place. Anywhere you feel comfortable meeting me."

She closed her eyes, asking herself what she was getting into, but she still she didn't say no. Maybe she could play him, like he was playing her. Find out what he was trying to pull. He wouldn't be hard to fool: he thought everybody loved him, so it wouldn't be hard to convince him that she did, too. Another girl blinded by his charm. She thought about his face, his dark eyes, his devious smile. It wouldn't be hard to pretend to fall for him.

But it might be hard to stop.

She blinked open the map on her djinni, searching through the USC area. "You said you play VR games?"

"Now and then."

"There's a VR parlor on Thirty-Fifth," she said, finding one on the map. "Brown-Eyed Girl."

"I think I know it. You play?"

Marisa grinned wickedly. "A little. Tomorrow night?"

"Tomorrow."

She paused again, waiting for . . . she didn't know. She felt mad and tired and guilty all at once, and so desperate for . . . a way out? Revenge? She wasn't sure. Both, maybe. Someone had hurt her friend, and now she had the chance to not only protect Anja, but to hurt the bad guys back. She opened her mouth to speak again, but shook her head and closed the call without saying good-bye.

She touched her arm again, running her fingers along the broken prosthetic. It was an elegant, curving surface, plastic and metal and ceramic, once smooth and comforting but now scratched and dented, beaten out of shape by the force of the speeding truck. She'd wanted a Jeon all her life, saving every cent, pulling extra shifts in San Juanito, and now it was all gone. Without the servos and motors to move it around, it hung on her shoulder like an anchor. She rapped it with her knuckles, listening to the useless thud, and finally stood up off her bed, letting the dead arm swing free as she walked to her closet. Most of her old computer parts were on her work desk—a thick, wooden table covered with screens and devices of every shape and size—but the one she needed was in the back of her closet, high on a back shelf, in a box she'd hoped to never open again. She stood on the tips of her toes, pulled it out, and opened it.

Her old, crappy arm, a SuperYu 920. It was the only thing they could afford two years ago, but the stiff, robotic limb was so out-of-date today it made her wince just to look at it. Why did anyone ever think it would be cool to look like a Terminator in real life? She sighed. What other options did she have?

She blinked her djinni and tapped into Olaya, pulling up the full list of family members. Everyone was in the house, with the doors locked at her father's maximum security level—the outside doors, and her bedroom door. When they grounded someone, they meant it. Marisa blinked on Sandro's name and started a private call.

"Hey, Mari." His voice was almost maddeningly calm—how did he do that?

"Hey. Can you help me out with something?"

"You want to become a Super You?" he asked, repeating the company's sales slogan.

Marisa rolled her eyes. "I've got the stupid thing right here, can you help me out?"

"Not with your door locked."

"Come on, Lechuga, what do you think I am? Helpless?" She'd hacked Olaya's AI three years ago, and kept a backdoor program hidden in the code for situations just like this. She blinked into it now, and prepared to pop the lock, but realized suddenly that she was still wearing her green dress from the club. Where before it had made her feel sexy and independent, now it just felt itchy and uncomfortable, tight and loose in all the wrong ways and places. Worse, its long sleeves would make switching the prosthetic impossible—not to mention, the sleeve over the damaged arm was pretty damaged itself. "Score one more point for the giant truck."

"What?" asked Sandro.

"Just looking at my dress," said Marisa. "Give me a second to change out of it."

"I need to gather my tools anyway," said Sandro. "And don't call me Lechuga."

"Bueno," said Marisa, and ended the call. She wriggled out of the dress, doing her best with only one good hand. The broken outer plates on the Jeon arm kept catching in the holes in the ripped sleeve, ripping it farther, until finally Marisa growled in frustration and tore the dress off in one long pull, tearing a gash down the sleeve from elbow to hem. She threw the dress at her closet with a grunt of rage and pulled on a Pinecone Neko T-shirt that was so long it hung past her knees. She kicked the dress into the corner, much harder than she had to, letting it stand in for everything else that had gone wrong all night. She waited a moment, wondering where Sandro was, and realized with a wince that she'd forgotten to unlock the door. She opened it with a blink, and collapsed facedown onto her bed.

"Wow," said Sandro. "You look worse than I expected."

"Shut up."

"I mean your arm," he said. She felt the bed move as he sat next to her. "Did you really get hit by a truck in the middle of the freeway?"

"You should see the truck," said Marisa, trying to sound tougher than she felt. She kept her eyes buried in her pillow. "I gave as good as I got."

"Really?"

"No." Marisa sighed and peered out. "Sandro." She paused. "Am I a bad person?"

Sandro raised his eyebrow. He somehow looked just as tidy and professional in his pajamas as he did in his school clothes. "Do I actually get to say I told you so?"

"No," said Marisa. "Because I was trying to do the right thing—I wasn't the one doing drugs, you know, I was saving Anja's life."

"You were also the one who sneaked out and went to a place where people were doing drugs," said Sandro. "What did you think was going to happen?"

Marisa flopped back down on the pillow. "How do you make that sound so reasonable?" she asked. "I wanted to punch Dad when he said the same thing." She peeked out again, sitting all the way up. "I ought to punch you for it," she said, but she didn't feel it. Her rage had all bled away, leaving nothing but guilt and sadness. And fear: just a centimeter more, and that broken arm could have been her entire body.

"I'm not trying to make you feel bad," said Sandro, examining the damaged arm more closely. Marisa could feel the movement in her shoulder, the only part of the arm that was still flesh and bone, but with the prosthetic's sensors offline that was all she could feel. The arm was inert and useless, like a pirate's peg leg. Marisa pulled up her floppy T-shirt sleeve, exposing the full arm and shoulder, and then sat still, letting him work.

"I should be recording this," said Sandro. "I could probably convince Ms. Threlkeld to give me extra credit in robotics."

"Don't," said Marisa.

He nodded and grabbed his socket drill.

Most cybernetic limbs came in two pieces, and Marisa's were no different: the arm itself, which was removable, and the dock, which was grafted directly into her body and laced into her nervous system. Sandro worked silently on the point of attachment between the Jeon and the dock, undoing a series of precise bolts, until finally he unplugged it with a click and laid it on the bed. Marisa felt the sudden loss of weight, like someone had taken an iron chain from around her neck. She stretched her shoulders, the cone-shaped dock turning tiny circles in the air. It was barely three inches long. They wouldn't be able to get all the SuperYu's sensors and perks working with the Jeon dock—every company had its own proprietary hardware—but it would work well enough for the time being.

"Anja made some modifications when I had it replaced," said Marisa, handing Sandro the SuperYu. "The sensor ports aren't in the same places, or even the same shape, so you'll have to plug in some wires."

"Great," said Sandro dryly, grimacing at the tangled connectors on the end of the arm. "An Anja project."

"She does good work," Marisa protested.

"She does great work," said Sandro, shaking his head and

diving into the process of hooking up the wires. "I just wish she wasn't so messy about it. Half of these aren't even labeled. Move your fingers."

Marisa flexed her fingers—or, more accurately, she thought about flexing the fingers she didn't have—and watched as, instead of a finger, the SuperYu wrist rotated. It was bare chrome, smooth but weathered from use.

"That's not good," said Sandro, and switched one of the tiny wires. "Try it again."

The metal thumb moved, and Marisa smirked. "That was supposed to be my pointer finger." Sandro switched a few more plugs, sorting out which wire corresponded with which rotor, and they set about the process of lining them all up correctly. They were almost done when Marisa spoke again.

"I don't understand you," she said.

"I asked you to move your thumb."

"I mean I don't understand how you think," said Marisa. "How are you happy all the time?"

Sandro looked at her with his typically simple pragmatism. "What's not to be happy about? The restaurant is successful, we have food and a place to live, we all get along—occasional fights between you and Dad excepted."

"Is that how you define happiness?" asked Marisa. "Just . . . existing? In a situation that makes existence easy?"

Sandro plugged the last wire into place, and looked at her with a frown. "I've never thought about it, but I guess I define happiness as having the right opportunities. To be able to achieve things."

"To get what you want," said Marisa.

"That's the worst possible characterization of what I said," said Sandro. "It's not the getting, it's the doing. Achieving things makes people happy."

"It figures you'd pick work as something that makes you happy."

Sandro fit one of the bolts into place and secured it with his socket drill. "What about you?"

"Honestly?" asked Marisa. "The same as you, really. I like doing things—achieving things, like you said. But I like choosing what I want to achieve. I don't think I could ever be happy dedicating my life to someone else's ideas—to making somebody else's product, or telling someone else's story. You're going to grow up and get a job with Ganika or Zhang or whoever, and you're going to make a zillion dollars, and that's what everyone does, I guess—everyone who can get a job. They work for someone else. Even if you have your own business, like Mom and Dad, you still end up slaving away for people like the Maldonados. I don't know how you can do it."

"Unless you're planning to be homeless, your options are pretty similar," said Sandro. "Try the elbow."

Marisa flexed her mental elbow, and the SuperYu moved in perfect sync. Sandro nodded, obviously pleased but too serious to smile. He finished bolting the arm to her shoulder dock, and when he was done she flexed it, testing the feel and the weight. It wasn't as smooth as the Jeon, but it worked. She smiled.

"Thanks, Lechuga."

He rolled his eyes, shaking his head as if she were a child. She grinned and stood up, hugging him tightly. "You're brilliant, Sandro, but don't forget I'm a whole year older than you."

"Ten years ago that meant something," he said solemnly. "The difference between six and seven was everything in the world. Ten years from now, though, the difference between twenty-six and twenty-seven isn't going to matter at all." He stepped toward the door, but paused and looked back. "Promise me you'll live that long."

Marisa froze, shocked by the plea. It was the same sentiment, the same tone of voice, that she'd used on Chuy the night before. But Chuy was selling drugs and running guns and who knew what else. He was a gangbanger in thrall to an organized crime boss. She wasn't anything like that.

Was she?

Sandro left, and Marisa relocked the door, altering the log to make it look like it had never been opened. Her father might ask some questions when he saw her replaced arm, but he'd almost certainly leave the house before she even woke up in the morning, so she'd have plenty of room to concoct an excuse. She sat at her desk, tapping her clunky metal fingers on the plastic, thinking. She got why her family was upset, but they were wrong. She wasn't Chuy, and going to a club wasn't the same thing as running with a gang. Helping a friend who'd taken a drug wasn't the same as taking one.

She found her purse, discarded on the floor, and dug inside of it for the tiny plastic drive: the second dose of Bluescreen Saif had sold Anja at the club. Marisa had taken it from Anja on the freeway, waiting for the emergency nulis, because she didn't trust

Anja not to use it, even after everything that had happened—she was the one Sandro should be worried about, not her. Now that Marisa had it, she couldn't help but think: what was it, really? How did it work? The blackouts were an intentional effect of the code, obviously, but what about the sleepwalking? Was that an unintended error, like Saif insisted, or was it something they had written into the program? Saif didn't know anything about the code, he was just a dealer. Who made these things, and how? Were they just in it for the money, or was something else going on here?

She knew how to find out.

She looked at the clock: nearly one a.m. She should be asleep, or practicing in Overworld with Fang and Jaya. Anything but looking deeper into the drug that almost killed her friend.

She tapped the Bluescreen drive on the desk. She didn't want to put it down.

"Screw it."

She reached across the desk and dug her hotbox out of the back corner. It was an old computer, the kind of desktop model that was obsolete outside of the most traditional corporate offices, but she'd kept it upgraded, and it was every bit as fast as the newer, fancier machines that littered the desk around it. Most importantly, the hotbox was completely isolated, with no wired or wireless connections to any other computers or networks. It was the ideal environment for observing a suspicious piece of software without the threat of that software infecting any other systems. She used it often to examine various viruses she ran across in the wild. She connected a monitor and dug up her djinni adaptor, finding the short black cord that would allow a headjack drive to interface with a larger computer. She turned on the hotbox, let it boot, and plugged in the Bluescreen.

Marisa had designed the hotbox to watch everything that happened on itself, and report on it in real time. She tapped the screen, and watched the Bluescreen's small downloader program reach out, searching for a djinni operating system, eventually settling for the hotbox's own shell program. It offered to connect, and when the hotbox answered, the downloader responded with a massive dump of data—a hundred petabytes or more, all within the space of a few seconds. The hotbox hadn't even agreed to a download, just the digital equivalent of a handshake, but instead of a friendly hand, it found itself holding, metaphorically, a thousand tons of unprocessed ore. The data poured through the connection protocol in an overwhelming flood, and Marisa's fingers raced across the screen as she struggled to understand it.

Anja had said the Bluescreen was mostly junk data, and what Marisa was seeing seemed to be exactly that. None of it was organized or shaped in any way—no clips or fragments of larger data. It was the digital equivalent of gravel. The Bluescreen wasn't even trying to store it, just shove it in the hotbox's active memory. She wondered if maybe the speed was part of the purpose—a slower trickle probably wouldn't overload a djinni properly, which explained why they had to sell the program in thumb drives instead of pushing it across the internet. She pored through the downloader code, looking for anything she might have missed—

—and then her monitor blinked off, just for a second, and came back on.

She tapped the screen, frowning. She'd built this hotbox

herself, and knew it like the back of her own hand. She kept it scrubbed and ready for flawless performance in situations just like this. This sort of glitch could only have come from the Bluescreen. Was this the overload from the massive dump of junk data—what Anja said happened with human users—or was it something more? She disconnected the Bluescreen drive, and started a deep-level diagnostic of the hotbox operating files. After nearly an hour she found a possible culprit—a handful of unknown files in the root directory that she had never seen before. They didn't seem to have altered the hotbox in any way she could detect, aside from just copying themselves onto the drive in the first place. How had they gotten there? How had they gotten past the firewall? The hotbox was equipped with some of the best antivirus software in the world; there was no way the Bluescreen could have gotten these files in. Yet there they sat.

Completely inert and, as near as she could tell, useless.

She isolated the Bluescreen files and tinkered with them a bit, trying to see if she could understand them, but they were written in Piller, a programming language she was only passingly familiar with. She could follow some of it, but not enough to really figure anything out. After another hour of study, just past three in the morning, she decided to ask for help. It was time to take this to the darknet.

Marisa locked the files down as securely as she could, going so far as to chop the more suspicious-looking ones in half, just to be sure, and copied some representative samples into a plain text file. Then she scrubbed the hotbox as thoroughly as possible, connected a clean drive, and copied the text file over. Working with malware like this always made her feel like she needed a hazmat suit, like in a contagious disease lab, and when she pulled out the thumb drive to transfer the files to her main computer she felt a fleeting, irrational urge to handle it with gloves. She connected to the internet and queried Lemnisca.te, a closed network of semi-legal servers that was only accessible by direct link; it was like a separate internet, invitation-only, where the required invitation was being smart enough to find it in the first place. The dark-nets were the uncharted underbelly of the internet age, equal parts freeing and terrifying, and Marisa always treaded carefully when she ventured into them. There were monsters in the deep, and you never knew who you were going to find.

She opened one of the virus message boards and tapped out a post.

Cantina>>Forum>>Malware>>General

Heartbeat: Weird Djinni Code

Heartbeat: Anybody run across this before, or any-
thing like it? It was trying to interface with my
hotbox, but it's designed for djinnis. I *think*
that's why the files weren't recognized, but I'm
not sure, because I can't even tell what they do.
Any ideas?

Heartbeat: FileAttach>>detoxdump

She posted the file, disconnected her computer, and finally went to sleep at nearly four in the morning. When she awoke, she found a handful of answers, most of them in English, most of them some variant of *Learn Piller N00b!* One response stood out, however, poorly translated from Portuguese:

Cantina>>Forum>>Malware>>General>>WeirdDjinni-Code

Sobredoxis: Re:Re:Re:Weird Djinni Code

Sobredoxis: stop deleting my posts!! if you do not like, go to screw!! this remembers me of something I saw in Japan one time have you heard Dolly Girls??

Marisa refreshed the page, hoping to find something more recent, but when the page came back the response had disappeared. Someone was deleting Sobredoxis's answers.

She wondered how many times it had been deleted, and who had done it.

What was really going on here?

SEVEN

You going in to school today?

Sahara's message popped up in Marisa's vision while she was downstairs eating breakfast: hot corn tortillas with salt and avocado. Marisa glanced at her abuela, bustling through the kitchen making more tortillas, not paying any attention. Sandro and Gabi and Pati were seated around the table as well, but they were all checking their own djinnis and ignoring her. Sandro looked neatly pressed, like he'd just ironed his shirt a few minutes ago; Gabi wore sweatpants and a T-shirt, almost certainly covering her leotard for first-period ballet. Pati was dressed like Marisa, in a ratty black T-shirt and ripped jeans; Marisa looked closer, seeing something familiar in the clothes, and realized that they didn't just look like hers, they *were* hers: old stuff Marisa had worn when she was twelve, pulled out of a storage box somewhere in a back room. Had their mom given those clothes to her, or had Pati simply found them on her own? Marisa suppressed a laugh, and focused back on the message. She blinked once to start a message response to Sahara.

Not our school, she sent. **You up for a trip?**

You're killing me, Mari, Sahara sent back. **I'm failing three classes.**

Marisa took another bite of hot tortilla, and blinked into Sahara's video feed: she was wearing a pleated skirt and matching jacket in yellow plaid, with a white blouse and knee-high bobby socks—pure traditional, and as immaculate as always. She was sitting in front of a mirror, adding the final touches to her hair and makeup.

I analyzed that Bluescreen drive last night, Marisa wrote back. **I think there's a piece of malware in it, which means this is more than just a VR drug. I want to go see Anja.**

Sahara took a while to respond; Marisa watched on the feed as Sahara carefully finished her eyeliner, then set down the pencil and blinked. **If Anja knew anything else, she'd have told us by now. That run through the freeway scared her, and I don't think I've ever seen Anja scared of anything.**

It's not what she knows, wrote Marisa, **it's what she's got in her head—hang on, this is her.**

A new message popped up in Marisa's vision, in a second column next to the conversation with Sahara. **Guten morgen.**

Marisa blinked over to it. **I'm on with Sahara right now. Patch you in?**

Do it to it.

Marisa glanced at her abuela, needlessly worried that she'd

somehow get suspicious of all the secret plotting, but all the old woman did was plop another stack of steaming hot tortillas on the table.

"Gracias, Abue," said Pati brightly.

Their abuela's headphones were in, and Marisa could hear the buzz from the blaring music—some old rock something from the turn of the century. Old people listened to weird stuff. Marisa waited for her to turn away, and sent a new message to the group.

I analyzed some Bluescreen in the hotbox last night, and it's definitely malware. But it can't interface with a regular computer, so it's not doing whatever it normally does, and I'm not going to risk it in my djinni. I want to see what it's doing in Anja's.

There's no way I've got a virus, sent Anja. **I've got anti-virus software for my antivirus software. You know some of the places I go online, there's no way I'd leave myself open to malware.**

Look for this, sent Marisa, and copied her a sample of the neutered malware code.

I've got to go to school, sent Sahara. **My Chinese test is next week, and I'm not remotely ready for it. On the plus side, my school visits are one of my most popular segments.**

Schoolgirl fetishists, sent Marisa.

How in the bright blue hell? sent Anja. **That code you sent was part of a new file in my djinni's main system folder. How'd that get in there?**

Still working on that, sent Marisa. **Current theory: the**

Bluescreen overloads your system, causes the shutdown, and this file slips through the cracks while you're trying to reboot your security.

Then come help me get it out! sent Anja.

"That's my bus," said Pati, jumping up from the table at a sound only she could hear. Marisa looked up, murmured her good-bye along with the rest of the siblings, and blinked into Olaya's shared schedule. The elementary was the only one with a bus, so Marisa and Sandro walked Gabi to junior high on their way to high school. Olaya's schedule said they were due to leave in a minute and a half.

Can you look at her virus over the net? asked Sahara. **I know you have a remote diagnostic program because I saw you use it on a boy you liked last month.**

The Bluescreen file dump is too big, sent Marisa. **That's why they distribute it in thumb drives. The virus is small, but I don't know what it's going to do when I start poking it. I'd rather be there in person.**

I'm sending you a cab, wrote Anja. **It'll bring you to my school. Tracking info on its way.** An alert glowed yellow in the corner of Marisa's eye, and when she accepted it the icon transformed into a small counter. Three minutes to pickup.

I'm out, sent Sahara. **Keep me patched in, though, I want to hear what's going on.**

Another message appeared, from Fang this time. **Anyone up for a game?**

Sahara must have gotten the same message, because she merged it with the general conversation. **Looks like we're being** responsible this morning, sorry.

Americans are so boring, sent Fang.

Bite your tongue, sent Anja, **I'm German.**

Same thing, said Fang. **Come on, girls, we have a tournament to prepare for!**

Practice is tonight, sent Sahara. **Six p.m. our time, ten a.m. your time.**

Hey Fang, sent Marisa, remembering a snippet of the mysterious message board post from the night before, **have you ever heard of something called Dolly Girls? I think it's a band or something; it's from Japan.**

So naturally the Chinese girl has heard of some obscure Japanese band, sent Fang, **because all those Asian countries are pretty much the same anyway, right?**

That's not what I'm saying, sent Marisa, trying to decide if Fang was joking or actually offended. It was so hard to tell with her in writing.

Wait, said Anja, **you just equated America and Germany, like, two seconds ago.**

Your combined populations could fit in my apartment building, sent Fang. **And on a slow day we might actually notice you.**

I asked you because you're way more into music than any of us are, sent Marisa. **I didn't mean to offend you.**

I'm just screwing with you, sent Fang. **Laolao, you know I love you. But no, I've never heard of them, why do you ask?**

You heard about Anja? asked Marisa.

I told her, sent Sahara.

Sahara told me, sent Fang, half a second later. **You need to lay off the creepy djinni drugs, girl.**

Is that a real phrase? asked Anja. **"Lay off"? That sounds super weird.**

I dug through a sample of the drug and found a virus, sent Marisa. **I can't tell what it does, though, so I posted it on Lemnisca.te and a guy said he'd seen it before, and asked if I'd heard "Dolly Girls." I have no idea what it means.**

Maybe it's an Aidoru band, sent Anja. **Their hologram code might look similar to the way Bluescreen interfaces with a djinni's sensory system.**

"Time to go," said Gabi, taking a final sip of orange juice as she stood up.

"Hasta luego, Abue," said Marisa, jumping out of her seat. She grabbed her backpack, practically ripping one of the seams with her clumsy SuperYu hand—she'd gotten used to the lighter touch of the Jeon, and still made mistakes as she tried to adjust back to the older prosthetic. She kissed her abuela good-bye and followed Gabi out the door, with Sandro close behind.

Aidorus don't really use a lot of sensory interfaces, sent Fang, **just holograms. There might be a connection, but I doubt it.**

Marisa waited on the curb while her siblings walked away; they only got a few steps before they noticed she wasn't with them, and stopped to look back. Marisa smiled. "I'll catch up with you later."

Sandro rolled his eyes.

"Be safe," said Gabi.

"Don't worry about me," said Marisa, "I'm just going to school with Anja today."

They hesitated a moment, then turned and walked away. Marisa ran a quick net search for Dolly Girls while she waited for Anja's cab, but the top links were either toys or porn. She closed the search in disgust—had that Brazilian dude really posted all those messages just to trick her onto a porn site? It wouldn't be the weirdest thing that'd ever happened to her on the internet.

A message appeared from Bao. **See you in history today?** It was the only class they shared; she was two years ahead of him in math, and of course he was already fluent in Chinese. She told him about her plans with Anja. **Be careful,** he sent.

The cab arrived and Marisa climbed in, pursing her lips and thinking. Everyone kept telling her to be careful, but what was she really getting into? If the file she'd found in her hotbox actually was a virus, what were the people who made Bluescreen trying to do? What would she find when she studied the same file in Anja's djinni?

"Good morning!" said the cab. Its voice was cheerful but hollow. "I have your destination already programmed. Would you like to visit a Starbucks on the way for a refreshing iced coffee?"

"No thanks," said Marisa, "just go."

"Starbucks has five convenient locations along our route, and the most modern fleet of nulis in Los Angeles. We won't even have to stop."

"No more ads," said Marisa.

"Then let's go!" said the cab, and pulled away from the curb. As soon as it got up to speed a message popped up from Anja;

she'd probably been tracking the cab's GPS. **Now that you're en route and stuck I can tell you: Omar's here. He says hi.** The message ended with a giant winking smiley face. Marisa rolled her eyes.

The cab pulled up at Anja's private high school, and Marisa felt like she could feel the pretension rolling off the place in waves. Anja and Omar were waiting by the front gate; Omar climbed into the cab first, and Anja followed him in and sat in his lap. He was dressed as usual, in smart slacks and a dress shirt that seemed to hug the contours of his chest; Marisa wondered if he wore a size too small on purpose, just to show off his pecs. She tore her eyes away to look at Anja, who was wearing what looked like two halves of two different biking outfits: tight gray lycra pants crisscrossed with red lines and triangles, under a black-and-yellow jacket of slick, stippled leather. Against all odds, it looked pretty good.

"Good morning, Mari," said Omar. His expression was darker than usual, his typical smarmy humor replaced by a grim resolve. "Thank you for saving Anja last night."

"Holy crap yes," said Anja. "And now you're going to save me again!"

"Maybe," said Marisa. She opened her backpack and pulled out a MoGan tablet and a djinni cable. "Plug in and we'll take a look."

"Whoa," said Anja, grabbing Marisa's metal wrist. "Back to the old SuperYu, huh?"

"The Jeon was thrashed."

"I'm so sorry," said Anja, and her eyes looked so sad Marisa couldn't help but think of a guilty puppy, pleading for forgiveness. Marisa couldn't think of anything to say, and after a moment Anja fished a slim white cable out of her cascade of blond hair. She pulled the cord around and offered it to Marisa, who clicked it into the port on her tablet and opened the file manager. Anja twisted her face into a guilty smirk. "Sorry I got you grounded too."

Marisa shrugged, her fingers tapping the tablet's screen. "Meh. As long as they think I'm in school right now there's no real harm done. Sahara duped my ID signal for the day, so unless they do a visual check I should be fine." She glanced at Omar, expecting some crack about "kids" getting grounded—as a college freshman he had much greater freedom, and never missed an opportunity to tease them about it. Today he said nothing.

Got your back, honey, wrote Sahara, the message bobbing lightly in Marisa's peripheral vision. She was listening to everything they said, through the audio link in Marisa's djinni, but couldn't respond with voice while she was sitting in class. Marisa sent back a quick **thanks**.

Finally Marisa found the mystery file, buried in the system folder of Anja's djinni, and pointed eagerly at the screen. "There it is, but I don't see it doing anything weird . . . wait. Your version is bigger than mine, almost double the size." She peered closer, tapping out a few commands to ask the file manager for more information. "It's connected to two peripheral programs that I didn't have in my system: one in your sensor files, and one in . . . nowhere. A new folder it created. Obviously the first program is interfacing with your vision and hearing and whatever, but I have no idea what that second one is interfacing with."

"Let me see," said Anja, and Marisa handed her the screen. "This is . . ." Her fingers tapped out a few commands, opening the file to study it in detail. "This almost looks like Overworld code."

"Why would you have Overworld code in your djinni?"

"It's not actually Overworld," said Anja. "It's just similar. Something to do with the sensory feeds?"

"What exactly are the differences?" asked Omar.

"Why are you so interested in code all of a sudden?" asked Marisa, though she felt bad for saying it almost immediately.

"Because this thing tried to kill her last night," said Omar. "I want to know exactly why, and then I want to know how to stop it."

"Well," said Marisa, taking back the screen, "welcome to the club."

"It's not that my version of the file is bigger," said Anja, "I'll bet you anything that this is its normal size—what's really happening is that Marisa's version of the file was smaller than normal, because the hotbox lacked the target applications. When this thing gets into a djinni, though, it finds a system folder to start unpacking itself in and sets up shop. Typical virus behavior. But it's designed for djinnis, so the one in the laptop couldn't finish unpacking."

Omar nodded. "Like a plant in bad soil."

"I'm glad you found a metaphor you can understand," said Marisa, and instantly closed her eyes, sucking in a slow, guilty breath. "I'm sorry, I shouldn't be treating you like this. I'm just . . . it's been a rough couple of days."

"Just get rid of that virus," said Omar, "and all is forgotten."

"I can try to delete this root file," said Marisa, "but what are the odds that'll actually work?"

"Almost zero," said Anja. "Most of these things are designed to rebuild themselves when you attack them. But let's try it anyway—maybe we get lucky."

"Bombs away," said Marisa, and deleted all three files. *Tap, tap, tap,* gone.

They waited, watching the file manager.

What happened? asked Sahara.

Marisa stared at the screen. "Nothing yet."

And then the first file popped up again.

"Scheiss," said Anja.

"Your antivirals should be catching this," said Marisa, watching in confusion as all three files reappeared in the system. "Why isn't it working? Have you run a scan?"

"As soon as you pointed out the files this morning," said Anja, and tapped her forehead. "This frigging thing doesn't even recognize them as malware."

"Then let's teach it," said Marisa. "You use Yosae Cybersecurity, right?"

"All intelligent people do."

"What's Yosae?" asked Omar.

Anja gave him a patronizing pat on the head. "Don't worry, baby, I'm only interested in your body anyway."

"Yosae is a third-party antivirus system," said Marisa, her fingers flying across the screen of the tablet. "Just like McCarthy or Putin or whatever you use."

"Pushkin," said Omar. "It's the best you can buy." He frowned. "Isn't it?"

Omar uses Pushkin? wrote Sahara. **Trying so hard not to laugh in class.**

"Pushkin is okay for most things," said Marisa, nodding kindly. "The average user is going to be fine with it, if you keep it updated and . . . pay through the nose for upgrades. Yosae's just a little more high-level."

"A ton more high-level," said Anja. "You get better virus definitions, faster response time, a wider sweep, better control over your databases, full cortex customization—"

"It's all awesome stuff that you're probably not going to need," said Marisa. She shrugged, feeling guilty for saying the next part out loud. "Or know how to use. It's expert stuff; you have to be a coder to even understand most of it, let alone need it."

"So you're going to send Yosae a virus report?" asked Anja. "I know one of the guys in R&D, if you need an ID to send it to."

"Better than that," said Marisa with a grin, "I'm just going to update their definitions myself."

What? wrote Sahara.

"There's no way you hacked into Yosae," said Anja, smacking Marisa lightly in the shoulder. She bent forward, twisting around to get a better look at the tablet screen, stepping on Omar's toe in the process.

"Ow! Triste flaca—"

"Not Yosae itself," said Marisa, "just your local definition file. One of the benefits of user-driven security software. They update so quick we've never had to do it before, but you totally can." She typed in a few more commands and hit Enter. "Boom. I'm in." She smiled triumphantly, dropping in the Bluescreen virus code and setting up the admin flags. "Now, just run a scan, and it will recognize these files as dangerous and scrub them out of your brain, with what I respectfully call 'extreme digital prejudice.'"

"Awesome," said Anja. She blinked, and her eyes refocused on her djinni interface. Marisa watched on her tablet as Anja's Yosae Cybersecurity program began running a scan, searching each file and folder.

"And this will kill it, right?" asked Omar.

"That's what 'extreme digital prejudice' means," said Marisa.

Hey Mari! A message popped up in Marisa's vision, from Pati this time. **I'm home from school, where are you? Want to play Overworld?** Marisa deleted the message without responding; she'd get back to Pati later.

The antivirus program raced through the files, one by one by one, faster than Marisa could follow.

And then it finished. The Bluescreen files hadn't even been touched.

"That doesn't make sense," said Anja.

What happened? wrote Sahara.

"Yosae didn't find the files," said Marisa, frowning at her tablet. She checked the virus definitions again: the Bluescreen files were right there in the database, flagged as dangerous, ready to be destroyed as soon as the scanner found anything that resembled them. And yet it hadn't touched them. "Why didn't it find them? They're right there."

Maybe they're undetectable? wrote Sahara.

"There's no way they're detectable to a file manager but hidden from Yosae Cybersecurity," said Marisa. "There has to be something we missed."

"We're just asking one program to delete another," said Anja, "there's nothing to miss. The only reason it's not working is . . . the file system is literally not functioning like a normal file system is supposed to."

Omar grunted and punched the side of the autocab, hard enough that Marisa could feel it rocking from the impact.

Is he just super pissed off today? wrote Sahara.

Anja did almost die, Marisa wrote back.

I'm starting to like him for more than just his car, wrote Sahara.

"Hang on," said Anja, and her eyes unfocused again, wobbling back and forth in her head as she started moving files through her djinni interface. "If the file system doesn't look like it's working, maybe it's really not working. Maybe the virus rewrites the file system to make itself partially invisible—that could be what that other piece was for, the one you couldn't find a purpose for."

"Maybe," said Marisa, watching the tablet helplessly, "I just—"

We need to talk. The message appeared in Marisa's vision abruptly, not part of any other conversation, and without any ID tag. Marisa started in surprise, and couldn't help but glance out at the street. Rich kids were lounging on the high school lawn; others walked aimlessly in conversation. No one seemed to be paying them any attention.

"Did any of you get that message?" she asked.

Another message appeared. **I saw your post on Lemnisca.te. I have information you've been looking for.**

What message? wrote Sahara.

Anja shook her head. "What message?"

The words floated in Marisa's vision like lost spirits. **My name is Grendel. Meet me in NeverMind.**

EIGHT

"Marisa, you look sick," said Anja. "Did something happen?"

"I just got a message from someone named Grendel," said Marisa. "Do any of you know who that is?"

"Some old monster," said Omar. "Like a viking legend or something."

Never heard of it, wrote Sahara. **Where'd you meet him?**

"I didn't meet him anywhere," said Marisa, probing the message in her djinni. "Looks like he hid his ID—santa vaca, he even hid the route his message took to get here. It's like it just . . . appeared, out of nowhere."

"That's some high-level hacking," said Anja. "What'd he say?"

"He says he has information about the Bluescreen code," said Marisa. "He saw my post on Lemnisca.te."

He's from the darknet?!?!?! wrote Sahara.

"Double scheiss," said Anja, "with a cherry on top."

Marisa's djinni display lit up, showing a voice call from Sahara. Marisa blinked on it, patching her into the autocab speakers, and Sahara practically screamed in their ears.

"Don't talk to him, Mari; this is scary."

"Some shadow from a hacker forum on the darknet just messaged you directly," said Anja, her voice more serious than Marisa had ever heard it. "Without permission, without access, without even you telling him who you were. Scrub your ID and run."

"Don't you think that's an overreaction?" asked Marisa. "We don't even know what's going on yet."

"What's Lemnisca.te?" asked Omar.

"It's like a central hub for cyber criminals," said Anja. "They all have their own little hidey-holes, but when they want to talk to each other they go to a darknet message board called Lemnisca.te. Marisa and I use it sometimes for stuff like this, just information gathering, but we've never messed with anything big enough to attract real attention. You steal one gold piece from the dragon's lair, the dragon doesn't wake up; when the dragon talks to you directly, though, you drop what you're holding and run."

"It's not gold we're carrying," said Marisa, "it's a monster. And it's in *your head*. If he can help get rid of it, I think we've got to talk to him."

"Don't even think about it," said Sahara. "This is not a game, Mari."

"I know that," said Marisa, trying to sound braver than she was and accidentally sounding angry instead. "What else are we supposed to do? Best case scenario, following your suggestion: I scrub my ID and hide from this guy and we never hear from him again, but Anja's still got this crap in her head. We lose everything and we have nothing to show for it." She tried to say more, but she was shaking and lost her voice.

"It sounds dangerous," said Omar.

"Of course it's dangerous," said Marisa, swallowing nervously. She clenched her hands into fists, drawing strength from the pain of her fingernails in her palms. "That's why we have to do it. You don't get experience points sitting on your butt, right? You gotta go out and kill monsters." She sucked in a breath and glanced at Anja. "Play crazy, right?"

A slow grin spread across Anja's face. "Play crazy."

"You're insane," said Omar.

"That's what she just said," said Sahara, and Marisa felt a surge of confidence at the sudden power in her voice. It was time to get to work, and Sahara was all business. "If we're going to do this, we do it right," said Sahara. "How does he want to meet?"

"NeverMind," said Marisa, and shivered involuntarily. She'd never used NeverMind before, and it terrified her.

"Spooky," said Sahara, "but probably the safest. Anja, do you have a tablet?"

"Just Marisa's MoGan," said Anja, shaking her head to disconnect it, "but it's been plugged into my djinni, and we don't want to use it till we've had a chance to scrub it."

"I've got a MoGan," said Omar, pulling one of the six-inch miniscreens from his pants pocket. "I don't know if it's got the software you need; I really just use it for the speaker."

"This is why we have rich friends," said Sahara. "Marisa, plug it in and let Anja monitor your firewall. I assume *you're* using Yosae?"

Marisa clipped her adaptor cord into the port at the base of her skull. "Of course."

"Good," said Sahara. "Anja's an expert in it."

"Alles klar," said Anja, clipping Omar's minitablet to the other end of the cord.

"Watch her like a hawk," said Sahara. "If this blowhole tries to upload anything, you kill the connection immediately, okay? No waiting, no trying to contain it."

"You can't upload over NeverMind," said Marisa, "that's what makes it so safe."

"What's NeverMind?" asked Omar.

"It's a direct VR connection," said Marisa. "Brain to brain. Normal VR invites the user into a shared space and controls your djinni's sensory feeds, telling your eyes what to see and your ears what to hear, and so on. Really paranoid hackers—like Grendel, apparently—don't trust that method, because that gives a third party access to your djinni. NeverMind bypasses that by skipping the VR and going straight into the feeds. The only thing giving it commands are the two brains connected to it."

"Whoa," said Omar, looking deeply suspicious. "You're going to . . . That's like stepping inside another person's mind."

Marisa shivered again, and grimaced. "Yeah."

"That's a VR program built out of some creep's subconscious," said Omar. "Some creep who named himself after a half-human viking cannibal." He shook his head. "You're not going to do this."

"It's freaky as hell," said Anja, "but it's safe. There's no bad code in there, because there's no code at all—there's nothing but what you take with you. He can't upload anything into Marisa's djinni, just like she can't upload anything into his. We can't even monitor their conversation. I've done it before, and it's fine—it's the only way some of these weirdos can trust each other enough to communicate."

"Anja's going to watch the incoming data," said Sahara, "just in case this guy's found a loophole. And I've already got Marisa's ID copied, so I can start tracing the signal back toward him, just to keep him occupied. If he's busy trying to jam my trace, he won't be able to mess with Mari."

"I thought you were in class," said Marisa.

"And abandon my best friend?" asked Sahara. "I stepped out—I'm hiding in a custodial closet."

"I can't wait to watch the replays of that," said Anja.

"This is starting to freak me out," said Marisa. She felt small and vulnerable. "What if he's . . . got some sort of control over NeverMind? What if this is a trap?"

"It's three-on-one," said Sahara. "We've got you."

"Four," said Omar. "What can I do?"

"Hold her," said Anja. Marisa and Omar both looked at her in shock, and Anja laughed. "What? She's about to go into VR—her real body will be completely limp."

Marisa looked at Omar, their knees practically touching in the small cab, and rolled her eyes. "Oh, please no."

Omar sighed. "What am I going to do? I'm not the bad guy here." He stood up, awkwardly, and moved across to Marisa's bench. She moved her SuperYu arm self-consciously, as if it were too gross for him to touch. Omar tried to maneuver his arms around her, eventually just leaving them in the air like he didn't know what to do with them. "Maybe lean on the door?"

"Oh, for crying out loud," said Sahara, "just put your arm around her. Mari, lean on his chest. Omar, hold her upright, and know that if you do anything you shouldn't, I'll publish video of it to the entire city."

"I'm not going to do anything," Omar growled. "What do you think I am?"

"I think you're sexy," said Anja with a wicked grin. "Marisa, don't get any ideas."

"I'm going to be unconscious," said Marisa dryly. She paused for a moment, then settled into the crook of Omar's arm, propped up by him and the door. He smelled wonderful, and she rolled her eyes at herself. She took a breath. "We can do this."

"Yes we can," said Sahara. "Everybody ready?"

"Check," said Marisa.

"Check," said Anja.

"Let's do it," said Omar.

Sahara's voice was firm. "Go."

Marisa read the message again: **My name is Grendel. Meet me in NeverMind.** The last word was hyperlinked, and when she opened it she found a NeverMind portal, with the simple tag xNeeLO. She'd seen such portals a dozen times, and never dared to follow them—too often they were tricks, used to force people to experience something horrible: porn or snuff or worse. Once she was in, how did she get back out again? Would it be obvious? Would she be trapped?

She was doing this for her friend, and her friends were watching out for her.

She opened the portal, and the world disappeared.

Darkness.

Marisa panicked, feeling her body come into existence only as she thought about it: she reached with her arms, and suddenly her arms were there, and as she grasped with her fingers they appeared as well, curling out from her hands in a desperate need for—something. Anything. There was nothing anywhere. She looked down, seeing her chest, waist, hips, legs, feet, unfurling like smoke, wearing the same clothes she'd put on that morning. She felt her face, and it was solid; her hair moved around her shoulders like it always did. Almost. Everything felt familiar and distant at once, like a memory.

She was standing, but on what? It was too dark to see. *But no*, she thought. *It's not dark—my mind is interpreting it as darkness because there isn't any other input. I can see myself just fine. The reason I can't see anything else is because there's nothing else to see.*

In the instant she realized she wasn't standing on anything, she felt herself falling, plummeting through the nothingness at breakneck speed. She screamed, and the sound seemed to fill the world—the only sound this world had ever known. She flailed wildly, terrified at the sheer vastness that surrounded her—she could fall forever, never landing, because there was nothing for her to land on. She could grow old and die and still be falling, a tattered skeleton in ragged clothes. *But no,* she thought again. *It's only limitless because that's how I've imagined it. NeverMind is a reflection of my own thoughts. Anja said there's nothing here but what I put here.*

So she put something there.

She imagined the autocab, and suddenly there she was, sitting inside of it, with Omar holding her side and Anja studying the tablet screen intently.

"Are you real?" Marisa asked.

"We're manifestations of your subconscious," said Anja, "but you know that already, or I wouldn't be able to say it." By the end of the sentence it was Marisa speaking, not Anja, and Marisa couldn't help but shudder at the sensation—these were her own thoughts, reflected back at her through an Anja she had imagined out of nothing. Marisa looked out the windows and saw Anja's high school, but only in vague outline—it wasn't a building she knew well, so her mind filled in the gaps as best it could, extrapolating the specific shape into a broad generalization of other buildings pulled from Marisa's memory—red bricks, wide windows, and tiled roof covered in solar trees. She studied it, looking for pieces she recognized, and saw bits of her own school: a corner here, a lawn there, and suddenly it *was* her school, more familiar than Anja's and thus more clearly rendered, as solid in NeverMind as it was in the real world. She focused on the school, unnerved by the fluid way the world kept redefining itself, willing it to stay here, to stay one thing just for a moment. The wind blew in the trees; the sun glinted from the glass in the windows. She smelled flowers.

"Not bad for a first-timer," said a voice. Marisa spun, searching for whoever had said it, feeling the whole of reality seem to lurch with the realization that the speaker was Someone Else. A brain that was not hers had entered NeverMind, and with that sense of invasion her control shattered, the school physically splintering like a cracked mirror, bright shards of a false reality spinning off into the void. She felt herself falling again, only to be caught by a soft leather couch, black and smooth and gleaming faintly from a light source she couldn't identify. The rest of a dark red room seemed to fly at her from all sides, walls and floor and ceiling and a low black table assembling themselves into a simple box with her in the middle. A glass bowl appeared on the table, filled with white stones, and the voice spoke again. "Not bad at all. I always thought that table needed something on it."

"Are you Grendel?" asked Marisa. Her voice was coarse, like she was out of breath, and she tried to force herself to calm down. Her body wasn't even here—she could sound like whatever she wanted. Her heart rate—her imaginary heart rate—seemed to slow, and she breathed deeply, filling her lungs.

"I am."

Marisa nodded. "What are you doing?"

"I'm building a room," said Grendel. "It's the same room I always use for these meetings, but the bowl is new. You added that. I like it."

"We're creating this reality together," said Marisa, trying to sound more sure than she really was. She almost said *That makes sense*, but stopped herself. She needed to look more certain than that, more experienced. She crossed her legs with what she hoped was a stylish flair. "What makes you think I'm a first-timer?"

"Because you fell," said Grendel, and she could feel his amusement rippling through NeverMind. "Everyone falls the first time."

Marisa winced. "How long have you been here? I thought I was alone."

"I've been here ever since I sent the invitation," said Grendel's voice. "You just didn't see me because I'm . . . very good at not existing."

"Do I get to see you?"

"Trust me," said Grendel, "I'm the last thing you want to see," and as his voice grew angry the room grew dark, the red walls seeming to fester into the dark purple color of a bruise. The stones in the glass bowl hatched into maggots. Marisa clutched the arm of the couch, but even that was fake, another construct of this warped mind, and the armrest shrunk beneath her hands as if shying back from her touch. She stood up just before the couch shriveled in on itself and disappeared completely. She felt her skin crawling, and desperately started counting, concentrating on the numbers, *one-two-three-four-five*, praying that the single-minded focus would help her regain control before her subconscious mind converted the skin-crawling feeling into actual insects wriggling through her clothes. She breathed deeply, ignoring the stranger's angry voice, the twisted images that oozed out of his mind, the fierce unreality of everything around her. Soon the numbers gave way to computer code, and she recited the commands in her head, calmed by the familiar words and cadences of programming. She opened her eyes and the room had returned to normal.

"You said you had information about that code," said Marisa. Her voice wavered, but didn't crack. "Do you know what it is? Do you know who made it?"

"I've seen that code twice before," said Grendel. "The first time was in Japan, in a Dolly Girls program."

"That's what the guy on Lemnisca.te said," said Marisa, leaning forward.

"Sobredoxis," said Grendel. "His English isn't the best."

Marisa tried to build a wall in her mind, keeping her thoughts private. Someone had been deleting Sobredoxis's messages almost as quickly as they were posted, and yet somehow Grendel had seen them. Had he just gotten lucky, catching one of the posts during that tiny window before it disappeared? Or was he the one who'd been deleting them?

"If I was the one trying to hide his posts," said Grendel, "why would I be coming to you now?"

"You're reading my mind," Marisa accused. She gritted her teeth, as if that would help to keep him out. The disembodied voice chuckled softly.

"And you're reading mine," said Grendel. "That's what Never-Mind is. Don't worry—the more you practice, the better you get at controlling what other people see and hear."

"So what are the Dolly Girls?" asked Marisa. "Is it a band?"

"It's not a group," said Grendel, "it's a technology. Djinni software that can sever a mind's conscious control of its body, allowing someone else to control the body like a puppet. I'll leave it to your imagination what they tend to use it for."

Marisa felt a wave of disgust roll over her, rippling through the walls of the room like the slow, lazy flick of a tentacle. "That's horrible."

"And highly illegal," said Grendel. "They circumvent a few laws by only installing it in paid, consenting hosts, but even then there's still a ton of laws they're breaking. That's why most people have never heard of it."

Marisa closed her eyes, trying not to think of those poor human puppets, dancing on the end of some sick bastard's digital string, and then her eyes flew open. "Anja!"

"Who's Anja?"

"Nobody," said Marisa fiercely, mentally kicking herself for saying the name out loud. She felt a sharp pain in her thigh, and as she staggered away she turned to see a copy of herself standing behind her, her foot raised in a kick. She wished the copy away, and felt an uncomfortable shiver as she watched herself disintegrate, turning to dust and blowing away in an intangible wind. She turned around slowly, peering into every corner of the room, expecting to see Grendel hiding in a shadow, but she was alone. The shadows grew deeper as she probed them, until she found herself at the center of a tiny circle of light. She wasn't even sure if the walls were still there.

Grendel's voice seemed almost unnaturally calm in the darkness. "I want to stress that the code you showed me is not the same as the Dolly Girls code. Just similar."

"It's a truncated version," said Marisa. "It wasn't growing in the right environment so it couldn't—"

"You're missing my point—it's *more* sophisticated," said Grendel. "Not less." He paused for a moment, letting that sink in. Marisa felt the ramifications settle on her heavily—if the truncated code she'd found in the Bluescreen was somehow more powerful—

"So somebody found it in Japan and brought it here," she said.

"And then they . . . improved upon it."

"You didn't say on the message board where you found the code," said Grendel, and then he paused just a fraction of a second before adding, "or where you are. I can only assume from your statement that you're not in Japan?"

Marisa grimaced again, angry at how easily she was letting so much information slip out. "I'm not," she said, "and I'm not going to tell you any more than that."

"Let me take a wild guess," said Grendel. "Los Angeles?"

Marisa glared at the darkness. "How in the hell did you—"

"I told you I've seen that code twice," said Grendel. "The first was in the Dolly Girls, and the second was about three months ago. A hacker named eLiza posted on Lemnisca.te, just like you did. I recently learned that she lived in Los Angeles."

"Lived?" asked Marisa. "Past tense?" She felt her chest tighten with fear.

"I wasn't planning to contact you at all," said Grendel, "but then I saw the news and decided I should warn you. eLiza was found murdered in her Los Angeles apartment not two hours ago."

"Ay, que no," said Marisa, shaking her head. NeverMind grew darker as the light slowly faded away.

"Be careful, Marisa Carneseca," said Grendel, and Marisa felt her heart freeze. *He knows my name.* "Don't go poking around where you don't belong. Whoever knows this secret *really* doesn't want it to get out." The light disappeared, and Marisa sat up with a desperate cry, gasping for air in the back of the autocab. She felt like she'd just surfaced from a deep dive. Omar steadied her, and Anja grabbed her hands.

"Easy," said Anja, "you're back."

"What happened?" asked Sahara from the speakers. "Is everything okay? Somebody talk to me!"

"We're screwed," said Marisa.

"He didn't upload anything," said Anja, "I was watching the whole time. We're safe."

"We're not even close to safe," said Marisa, shaking her head and panting. "We're back to plan A: run."

NINE

"What happened?" Sahara demanded. "Did you get hurt?"

"Doxed at the very least," said Marisa. "He knew my name, and if he knows that, he knows everything." She took a deep breath and pulled away from Omar. "But he's not what we need to worry about—he was warning me. Autocab, start driving."

"Where would you like to go?" asked the cab. Its voice was friendly, but there was no real personality behind it.

"I don't care," said Marisa, "just drive."

"Let's take a tour of the city," said the autocab. "Would you like me to point out landmarks as we drive?"

"Just shut up and let her talk," said Anja.

"Marisa," said Sahara, "calm down. Take a breath, and tell us what happened."

"A hacker was found dead," said Marisa. "Have either of you ever heard of someone named eLiza?"

"Of course not," said Omar.

"She means Anja and me," said Sahara. "And no, I haven't."

"I think maybe?" said Anja. "Nothing big—I probably just saw her name on Lemnisca.te somewhere."

"That's where Grendel found her," said Marisa with a nod. "She was asking about the same Bluescreen code we found, and now she's dead." She grabbed Anja's hands. "She died the same night Bluescreen made you run into traffic, and the same night I posted the code on the darknet. This is not a coincidence."

"I'm looking her up now," said Sahara. "Sharing the link to your djinnis."

An alert from Sahara appeared in Marisa's vision, and she blinked to open it. The cab seemed to fill with small white squares, each containing a news story or blog post. Marisa blinked on the nearest one, and it unfolded into a small, hovering video screen that only she could see and hear.

"A USC student was found dead in her Jefferson Park apartment early Friday morning," said the reporter. "Authorities are holding five fellow students for questioning. Officials say that Elizabeth Swaim, twenty-one, was found on the living room floor of her apartment just before six a.m. The woman suffered several stab wounds to her chest and arms, and was pronounced dead on the scene. Neighbor Christopher Lodge told this reporter that Swaim was always a quiet resident, keeping to herself. . . ." Marisa closed the article.

"Elizabeth Swaim?" she asked. "We're sure that's the right one?"

"The link I watched said she was a computer science student," said Anja. "And her death matches what Grendel told you—it sounds like she's our hacker."

"Who killed her?" asked Omar. "These links keep saying 'five fellow college students,' but we don't know if they're suspects or witnesses or what."

"It's too early to find that kind of information," said Sahara. "The police probably haven't even released it."

"But they've collected it," said Marisa, sitting up straighter, "and that means we can find it."

"Jeez, Mari," said Sahara. "You can't hack the LAPD."

"You can *absolutely* hack the LAPD," said Omar. "I go to the same school as all these people; I want to know who did this."

"Saif's a student there, too," said Marisa, opening the LAPD website. "Business college or something. Everything keeps tying back to USC."

"Who's Saif?" asked Omar.

"My dealer," said Anja. "You've never met him."

Omar glowered. "I don't want you to meet him anymore, either."

"Shut up," said Marisa. "I'm bringing out the Goblins." She needed to concentrate; she'd never hacked a government website before, but there was a first time for everything. She opened one of the hidden folders and activated her Goblins—a suite of programs she'd written specifically to help with hacking. Each one of them performed a specialized, automated function to make the process faster and harder to trace.

The first Goblin was a distraction—it went out into the internet, grabbed whatever unprotected computers it could find, and told them all to access the target website over and over again, all at the same time. It didn't help the hacking process, but it made it easier to cover her tracks later. The second Goblin went to work on the website's link map, building a visual reference of exactly what the site contained, and how the different sections were connected to each other. This showed her quickly where the login points were, and what security system they used to manage their passwords. "They're using Longhorn," she said out loud. "That's tough, but at least it's basic."

"How can it be hard and easy at the same time?" asked Omar.

"It's like a really tall wall," said Anja. "It might be hard to climb, but there's no flying crocodiles to fight off while you do it."

"Let her work," said Sahara.

"We call those dragons," said Omar.

"I know the word for dragon," Anja snorted. "I said flying crocodiles on purpose."

Marisa activated the third Goblin, which went to work on her own connection to the target server—not breaking the connection, or even hiding it, just resetting it over and over. Then she pointed the fourth Goblin at the login page and set it loose, trying every password it could think of, starting with the most common. Usually a blunt-force attack like this would raise a red flag, and Longhorn would block the connection completely, but with the third Goblin constantly resetting the connection Longhorn would get confused, and the attack could proceed unhindered. She waited, holding her breath, and then a sad goblin face appeared in her djinni display, shaking its head.

"Crap," said Marisa. "We're locked out."

"Another security layer?" asked Anja.

Marisa closed her eyes, feeling overwhelmed. "Biometric."

"Those have got to be hard to hack," said Omar.

"They're *impossible* to hack," said Sahara. "It's probably a fingerprint or a retina scan or something—the only way to get through the second layer is to literally be the person in charge of the account. You can't even cut off the person's finger, like in the vids, because it checks for blood flow—not that I'm into severing fingers, I'm just saying."

"This is ridiculous," said Omar. "Give me sixty seconds, max." He leaned back in his seat and blinked, holding up his finger for silence. He started a call on his djinni, and when he spoke his voice was pure honey. "Hi, can you connect me with Brooklyn Grace? This is Angel Vasquez, personal assistant for Francisco Maldonado. Thank you." He winked at Marisa, and whispered conspiratorially. "LAPD financial administrator. They're transferring me." He looked up suddenly, smiling brightly even though it wasn't a video call. "Good morning, Ms. Grace, this is Angel Vasquez, personal assistant for Francisco Maldonado. How are you this morning?" Pause. "Yes, he got your gift, thank you very much for sending it." Pause. "No, please, it's *we* who thank *you*. Mr. Maldonado considers it a privilege to donate to the department." Pause. "Well, as it happens, Mr. Maldonado is very concerned about the news this morning. It's always a tragedy to lose someone so young, especially a promising student like Ms. Swaim. As you know, Mr. Maldonado's son Omar attends USC, and—oh no, don't worry, Omar's fine—but we would like very much to know the names of the students being held by the police, so that we could help the families with anything they might need." Pause. "I understand the rules, but Mr. Maldonado was hoping that you might be able to bend them, just a little, out of respect for his long history of extremely generous financial support." Pause. "Thank you very much. I'll let Mr. Maldonado know how helpful you've been. Thank you. I'll talk to you soon."

He closed the call, and spread his arms in a gesture of triumphant humility. "That, ladies, is how you hack. Forget the software, and go straight for the user."

"I take back what I said earlier," said Sahara. "*This* is why we have rich friends."

"How worried should I be that you have the police in your pocket?" asked Marisa.

"Just spill it already," said Anja.

Omar sent them the list, and Marisa blinked to open it—it wasn't just a list, it was the full police report. "James Bennett, Angela Dietz-Hanson, Jared Garrett, Cyrus Hayes, and Eliyanna Kaiser," she read out loud. "All being held for the murder of Elizabeth Swaim. Do you know any of them?"

"I've met *a* James Bennett," said Omar, "I don't know if it's the same one. Rich kid, lives in Anja's neighborhood, studies engineering—mechanical or digital or something. He built a synthetic last month."

"Not exactly the kind of guy you'd expect to find murdering a woman in Jefferson Park," said Marisa.

"I'm doing quick searches on all five names," said Sahara, "looks like they're all from wealthy families."

Marisa read deeper into the police report, and found the

attached forensic file listing everything in the suspects' possession at the time of arrest: lychee gum, breath mints, a couple of tampons, and . . .

"Oh, crap," said Marisa. "All five of them had Bluescreen drives in their pockets." She saw the pieces fall into place, and felt her heart sink. "Rich kids," said Marisa. "Anja's rich, too, and so is La Princesa."

"What do we have to do with this?" asked Anja.

"It's the Bluescreen," said Marisa. "Even Omar said it was a rich-kid drug."

"My sister's using it?" said Omar. He punched the cab door again. "Me cago en todo lo que se menea!"

"That sounded nasty," said Anja.

"Anja," said Marisa suddenly. "Disconnect right now."

Anja frowned, confused. "From what?"

"From the net," said Marisa, "from everything. Cut yourself off—don't let any signal in or out or anywhere at all."

"Why?" asked Anja.

"That's the other thing Grendel told me," said Marisa, rushing through the words as fast as she could. "I should have said it earlier, but I was scared by the murder and I didn't figure out the connection until just now. You know the Dolly Girls thing I asked about? It's an illegal djinni technology from Japan, and it uses the same code as Bluescreen. It turns you into a puppet, so somebody else can tap in and take control of your body."

"Holy mother," said Sahara.

"Those five students aren't dealers," said Marisa, "they're users. eLiza was getting too close, poking around where she didn't belong, and the dealers—whoever they are—used their puppet program to take control of James Bennett and the others. They controlled their bodies remotely, and they used them to kill a girl."

Anja's icons disappeared from Marisa's djinni display.

"I just lost Anja," said Sahara. "Is she okay?"

"I'm fine," said Anja, "I cut myself off. Can you hear me through Mari's connection?"

"You're faint," said Sahara, "but yeah."

Anja shuddered. "I haven't been disconnected since . . ." She winced. "I don't even remember. This is so weird—I feel like I lost three or four senses and half of my brain. There should be alerts popping up, and they're not there. Nothing's there." She laughed nervously. "How do I check my email?"

"Through this," said Omar, handing her the MoGan tablet. "Whatever you do, do not reconnect your djinni to anything online until we can figure out how to clean it."

"Forget cleaning it," said Anja, "I'm going to buy a new one. If I get my dad to pull some strings, I can have it installed in the next . . . three days, max?"

"That's expensive," said Marisa.

"And it's brain surgery," said Sahara. "At least give us a chance to solve this from the software side first."

"You have three days," said Anja. "Then I'm getting this Trojan horse out of my head if I have to cut it out myself."

"I'll keep working on the Yosae thing," said Sahara, "see if I can figure out why the antivirus program isn't working."

"And I'll start with Saif," said Marisa. "He's our only link to whoever's behind this—we might be able to learn something."

"Forget learning from him," said Sahara coldly. "I'm going to break that blowhole's legs in seven places."

"I'll help," said Omar.

"She's not exaggerating," said Anja. "Sahara's been taking Jeet Kune Do for, like, ten years."

"I'm meeting Saif tonight," said Marisa. "He claims he doesn't know anything about this, and says he wants my help getting Bluescreen off the streets. I don't believe him, obviously, but if I pretend to I think I can maybe learn something that can help us."

"Maybe's not enough," said Sahara. "We have to be sure about everything we do."

"At least let me talk to him before we start breaking legs," said Marisa. "Please? He could be the only hope we have to save Anja."

"You're thinking too small," said Anja, leaning forward. There was an odd light in her eyes, like she'd just peeked behind a hidden curtain. "This isn't about me, and it isn't about the other victims. What would you do if you had this technology?"

"The Dolly Girls are basically sex slaves," said Marisa.

"Too small," said Anja, shaking her head. "Every country has an underground sex trade, but what's the difference between Dolly Girls and Bluescreen?" She tapped her head. "My fracking firewall. Whoever's making this didn't just bring a creepy technology over from Japan, they weaponized it. They found a way to override security systems and get their code into heads that don't even know it's there. Rich kid heads, specifically. And what do rich kids have?"

"Money?" said Sahara.

"Rich parents," said Omar, looking at the ceiling. "Este cabrón.

Anja's right." He looked at Marisa. "What was the first thing Anja did when she started sleepwalking the other night?"

Marisa tried to remember the details. "She . . . stood up, she walked inside, she—holy crap." Her jaw dropped, and she looked at Anja. "You went straight for your father, with an extra dose of Bluescreen, and tried to plug it into his djinni. Then whoever was controlling you would get control of him, and that'd give them access to—"

"Billions of dollars," said Sahara. "No more nickel and dime stuff selling djinni drives in dance clubs—his bank account's got to be enormous, and if you control his body the bank's biometric security means nothing. You just hacked the unhackable, like what Omar did—skip the software and go for the user."

"Too small," Anja repeated, firmly. "Think about it. My father isn't just a bank account, he's the vice president of one of the largest nuli companies in the world. Control him and you control Abendroth. Control some of these other kids' parents, and you control half the major industries on earth." Her voice was solemn. "This isn't a drug ring, and it isn't a bank robbery—it's a hostile takeover of the world's economy."

TEN

As Marisa waited outside the VR parlor, she nervously adjusted her clothes—a black T-shirt with subtle gold tracings in the style of a circuit board, finished with a sleeveless jacket of dark velvet, and a pair of black harem pants tied at the waist with a pale blue cord. It was flirtier than she'd intended—her meeting with Saif wasn't a date, it was a temporary truce with a dangerous enemy. And yet here she was, wearing one of her most casually flattering outfits. Even her makeup had been a battle of will with herself: she didn't want to overdo it, but the last time Saif had seen her she'd been done up for a night at a dance club. If that's how he thought she looked, and she showed up in old jeans and a bare face, what would he do? She didn't want to dress up for him, but she didn't want to see the disappointment on his face, either. So she'd dressed up, and now she felt stupid, like she'd somehow betrayed herself.

"It's okay," she muttered. "I'm trying to make him think I like him, right? I might be underdressed for that. I don't know."

Marisa looked down the street again, not seeing Saif anywhere, and abruptly decided that it was stupid to wait for him here, on the sidewalk, like some kind of lovesick puppy. She went inside and paid for two VR chairs, side by side—a solid week's wages at the restaurant. The hostess pointed to a pair of chairs by the side wall, a massive panel of blue that shifted slowly from light to dark and back again. Marisa sat down but didn't plug in, tapping the console restlessly with her metal fingers, listening to the clink. On a sudden whim she sent a message to Jaya.

You there?

A moment later the response came back: **You sent that message to a computer inside my brain—how could I not be here?**

I mean, are you free to talk?

I can't play right now, sent Jaya. **Some of us have jobs, you know.**

Marisa glanced at the time on her djinni display: eight fifteen at night, which meant Jaya would be at nine forty-five in the morning. She winced. **Sorry, I wasn't thinking.**

You okay?

Just nervous, sent Marisa. **I'm meeting a guy, but it's not a date.**

Then what are you nervous about?

Marisa sent her the photo she'd snapped at Anja's the other night.

Damn, said Jaya. **Why is it not a date? He's gorgeous.**

Marisa saw movement in the corner of her eye and glanced

at the door. Saif was there, dressed in a simple collared shirt and slacks—far simpler than what Marisa had worn, and somehow completely perfect. She fiddled with the knot on her belt, seized by the sudden urge to hide, but told herself to calm down. She placed her hands on her legs, palms flat, resting instead of fidgeting, but it felt wrong, and she realized that she had no idea what to do with her hands. Did it look stupid to have them resting there like that? Should she move them? At last she simply stood up, resting one hand on the back of the VR chair, trying to look confident and effortless at the same time.

You still there? sent Jaya.

He's here, she sent back. He saw her and smiled, walking toward her with a cocky spring in his step that made her feel weak in the knees.

I'll leave you alone, then, sent Jaya.

No! sent Mari. **I need you!**

I'm working, Mari. I'll ping you at lunch.

Marisa ran through her list of options, watching Saif get closer; Anja and Sahara were busy trying to root the Bluescreen virus out of Anja's head, and Fang had no patience for social situations. Bao? Even without a djinni, he could talk to her through his phone. But would he? He'd be more likely to just come in person, and she didn't want her friends actually *with* her, she just wanted their support.

Saif stopped in front of her, smiling. "You look great—I feel a little out of place."

"You look great too," said Marisa. "Don't worry about it." But as soon as she said it she wished she'd turned it into a joke: *just don't let it happen again*, or something like that. Something a little more self-assured, to match his confidence with some of her own. She tightened her grip on the VR chair, and thinking about the game she couldn't help but smile. She'd show him confidence.

Saif slapped the chair cushion. "So—you play?"

"A little." She gestured to his. "Sit down." She lowered her voice. "We can talk more freely once we're in."

"Good idea." They sat down and plugged the cords into the jacks at the base of their skulls. Marisa adjusted her vest, making sure it was straight—there was no sense in her body looking sloppy while her mind was in the game. Saif pulled up the list of games on their shared screen. "What are you in the mood for? Highway 1? Muffin Top?"

"You play Muffin Top?"

He grinned. "There's nothing wrong with Muffin Top; those things are delicious."

Marisa laughed. "Are you seven years old and forgot to tell me?"

"Is that a problem?" Saif made a look of mock concern. "Wait, how old are you? Nine? The other seven-year-olds are going to be so jealous."

"Overworld," said Marisa, tapping the screen. The entry button for Overworld expanded to fill the monitor.

"So you're an athlete," said Saif. "This one's tough—are you sure you can handle it?"

Marisa debated whether to tell him now, or make it a surprise. "You follow the game?" she asked.

"Not really, I'm more of a movie guy than a sports guy."

"Let's give it a try," she said.

"Okay. But you'd better bring your A game."

She tapped the button again and lay back in her chair. The real world disappeared, and the Overworld lobby appeared around her with a subtle frisson of shifting sensory inputs.

It was similar to NeverMind, but more stable—more solid, though she knew that it was just as illusory. Everything she saw and touched was a construct put into her mind by the virtual reality program, but at least she could rely on it staying the same from moment to moment. She looked down at her body, seeing the same stealth suit avatar she'd been wearing the last time she played. It was one of her favorites, and she'd set it as her default; the body style wasn't a perfect match for her physical body, because there were parts of her physical body she didn't like. Why had she worried so much about what she looked like in the real world, if they were going to spend all their time in this perfected one? A moment later Saif appeared beside her, though of course he didn't look like Saif; he wore one of the game's starter avatars, a random assemblage of face and body options, under a mostly featureless jumpsuit. He looked around in surprise, and Marisa wondered if he'd ever played Overworld at all.

"Okay," he said, taking a moment to study the lobby. "This is about what I expected, but . . . why do you look so much more awesome than I do?"

Marisa laughed, all the confidence she hadn't felt in real life flooding into her now that they were safe in the virtual realm. "I can't help it," she said, "I'm awesome in every version of reality."

"My skin is blue," he said. "Not even a cool blue, I'm like a robin's-egg blue." He felt his face. "And kind of . . . doggish? Am I a baby blue dog man?"

Marisa laughed again. "The game randomizes all the variables when you enter without a defined avatar. You can design your own, or I can just give you one of mine."

"I'm getting the impression you play this a lot. This interface says your name is Heartbeat? That's your username?"

"We call it a call sign in Overworld, but yeah. You can set yours to whatever you want—if it's not taken."

"I've tried ten different ones already—everything's taken. How'd you get Heartbeat?"

"There . . . may have been some slight hacking involved," she said. "The previous owner of the username canceled their account."

"On purpose?"

She shrugged innocently. "Who can say? They started a new one the next day, so maybe not."

"I think this one works," said Saif. "Bh4s4d. I had to go Hindi *and* Leet just to find something that no one else had used before."

"I like it," said Marisa. "I've heard Jaya say *bhasad* before, but I don't know what it means."

"There's no good translation," said Saif. "Kind of like a big mess?"

Marisa laughed. "That's what you chose?"

"Well, I mean it more like *chaos*, which is on the more awesome side of its spectrum of definitions."

"Whatever helps you sleep at night." She opened her inventory menu. "So: for your avatar. You want to be a man or a woman?"

He grinned slyly. "Are those my only options?"

Marisa raised her eyebrow. "You want to go nuts? I've got a dragon, a snake—though that one's tricky to get used to, because there's no arms—a zombie, a statue—"

"Ooh," said Saif, "let's try statue. I've always thought there should be a statue of me."

"Of course," said Marisa, and had to struggle not to roll her eyes. No matter how charming he tried to be, that rich arrogance was still in there. She hid her disgust and scrolled through the menu to find the statue. She used female avatars almost exclusively, but she loved designing new ones, and she couldn't help but collect an assortment of male looks over the years. She pulled up the statue design and linked it to his account; he accepted, and suddenly the baby blue dog man was replaced with an eight-foot marble statue, sculpted into an image of ancient Roman perfection. Saif looked at himself again, and the marble face smiled as proudly as if he'd designed it himself.

"This is incredible," he said. He looked at her. "Do you . . . buy these?"

"I make them."

"Yourself?"

"Of course." She said it casually, but inside she was beaming with pride. She looked back at her menu and opened the list of arenas. They were all functionally identical, but with different skins—a blasted city, a nuli factory, a pirate ship, a jungle island, and more. She found the one that looked best with the statue, a kind of Mediterranean ruin called the Colosseum, and opened it up. The lobby announcer declared that the game was loading, and a moment later they were standing on the crest of windswept hill, looking out at fallen pillars and cracked flagstones, nestled amid tufts of grass. Instead of military robots, the drones on this map were lions and manticores and other mythic beasts; Marisa could see them prowling in the distance.

"This game looks way cooler than Muffin Top," said Saif.

"We haven't even started playing yet," said Marisa. "Each team has five agents, and you can customize your powers. . . ." She paused. The VR game was just a pretense, really—they weren't here to play; they were here to talk about Bluescreen. She wanted to find out what he knew about the people who made it . . . she *needed* to find out. Anja was in trouble, and how many other people? eLiza was dead, and five innocents were in prison for it. What she learned from Saif might save them.

Or it might implicate Saif. Despite herself, she suddenly didn't want that to happen.

Marisa looked across the Colosseum, watching a manticore pace across a high stone platform. "You know what?" she said. "Forget the rules, I don't really want to play."

Saif's statue looked at her. "You just want to talk?"

"Eventually." She felt the sudden urge to stall, to delay as long as possible the confirmation that he was lying to her. She opened the power menu, scrolling through the various abilities. "But if you've never played, there's something you've got to try first." She blinked on a power package, and copied it to him. "Flight."

The powers engaged, and Marisa felt herself float up, just a centimeter off the ground. She flexed some imaginary muscle and flew off into the sky, the ground falling away beneath her in a rush. The wind on her face wasn't real, but the exhilaration was; she pulled to a brief stop, high above the Colosseum, and plunged into a power dive, forgetting everything else, just for a moment, whooping with joy as she aimed for a fallen arch and rocketed through the gap, dodging the vine-wrapped pillars and skimming the tops of the grass with her fingertips. She soared back into the sky again, looking around for Saif, and saw him sailing toward her with a grin.

"That was amazing," he said. "You're good at this."

"The flashy stuff is easy," she said. "It's the fine control that takes a lot of skill—hovering in one place to line up a sniper shot, or making fast turns through the sewer stairways."

He smirked. "There's a sewer in a Roman ruin? Big enough to have stairs?"

"We just call them sewers, no matter what the map looks like—the part underground is the sewer, and the player who fights there is called the Jungler. I don't know why."

"So there's something about this game you're *not* an expert in?"

She grinned at him. "Maybe a couple of things. The terminology is old, full of weird holdovers from games so old my abuela used to play them. But"—she flew back a little, spreading her arms—"when it comes to actually playing the game, I'm almost pro."

The marble statue raised its eyebrow. "Want to prove it?"

She studied his face. "You don't believe me?"

"Of course I believe you," he said, and the corner of his lips curled into a mischievous grin. "But how many times am I going to have a one-on-one with a semipro Overworld player?"

She nodded her head; he wasn't doubting her skills, he was testing them. She eyed the field, looking for a suitable challenge. "We can't go head-to-head, because you've never played—even a novice could beat a total noob. But maybe . . . okay, here we go. You see that manticore on the roof?"

"I'm a big manticore fan," said Saif. "I'm a fanticore."

She stopped and blinked.

"Sorry," said Saif. "I'm usually cooler than this. Maybe I should go back to the baby blue dog boy outfit."

"Don't worry about it," said Marisa, trying not to smile. It was endearing, she realized, to see some cracks in his perfectly groomed facade. "But: here we go. You've got your flight controls down? You know what you're doing?"

He moved back and forth in the air. "I think I've got the hang of it."

"Then we're doing an obstacle course: straight out, touch the manticore, do a loop under him through that old window arch, touch him again, and then back here."

"I'm going to guess that touching the monster is the hard part of this race."

"Touching a monster is easy," said Marisa. "The hard part's getting away from it alive."

"Well, yeah—"

"But you've got to do it with attitude," she said. "You don't just fly right at it, you look the monster in the eye and say, 'Tenemos un pollito que comernos.'"

"Tenemuh . . . what?"

Marisa laughed. "Try it in English: 'We have a little chicken to eat together.'"

"That is . . . the worst threat I've ever heard."

"What, like you've got a better one? The English phrase is 'I have a bone to pick with you.' How is that more menacing?"

"Maybe it's the other guy's bone, and you're going to pick it, like, out of his body or something."

"That's not what it says."

"At least it doesn't say you're going to serve him dinner." He looked at the manticore. "Hey buddy, watch out, in a minute I'm going to come over there and give you some chicken; I thought we could eat it together, maybe catch up on some stuff."

"Fine, then," said Marisa, trying to control her laughter. "Excuse me for trying to inject some style into this competition. If all you want to do is race, we'll race. Three." She leaned forward, preparing herself to launch.

"Wait," said Saif, "we're going now?"

"Two," said Marisa, not waiting for him. Saif copied her pose. "One." They both launched toward the manticore at full speed, and Marisa laughed at the thrill of it. Halfway there she swerved sideways, bumping Saif with her hip, but he corrected his course almost immediately, and bumped her back with a grin.

They reached the manticore at the same time, but with two different strategies. Marisa aimed for the center of its mass, knowing that it would be the easiest to hit at high speed; Saif went high, trying to slap the monster's head as he flew past, but he'd overestimated his flying skills and missed it by more than a foot. The manticore attacked, lashing out at Marisa with its thick scorpion tail, and she barely managed to **dodge** out of the way. She pulled herself almost to a stop, and dropped below the roof to circle through the window and back; Saif was coming in for another pass to touch the monster and aimed for its center this time. The manticore was still focused on Marisa and ignored him. She ducked through the ruined arch and popped up again on the other side, slapping the thing on the tail before zooming back toward the starting point, but checked herself halfway to look back at Saif. He was struggling with the small gap in the stone window, giving the manticore just enough time to refocus on him. The scorpion tail shot out and stung him, and a damage meter popped up in Marisa's vision: he'd been poisoned, and his life started dropping tick by tick. Saif cleared the window and came up the other side, only to be stung again, and when he flew away the manticore followed with a roar. Marisa gauged the distance, staying just outside the point where the monster would lose interest and return to its post; when Saif came in range she targeted him with a healing boost, and he limped to safety with just a few points of health left. The poison effect ended, and the manticore flew away.

"Ouch," said Saif, but he was laughing as he hovered in the air. "That's harder than it looks."

Marisa grinned. "Satisfied?"

"You're definitely good. I figure it wouldn't take me much practice to do that and live through it, but to do that, live through it, *and* heal the doofus who couldn't figure out how windows work? You have my respect, madam, and my thanks."

His health was regenerating now, and she watched the numbers tick up. She was having fun—not the satisfaction of a successful race, but real, can't-stop-smiling fun. She didn't want it to end, but the poison icon seemed to burn in her memory, and she thought about Anja. She flew a small loop, more of a flip than any real movement, and kept her eyes on the ground, or the sky, or the manticore; anywhere but Saif's face.

"Saif?"

"Yeah?" He seemed to sense that her demeanor had changed, for his voice became serious. "What's up?"

"Saif, I need to know if you're a part of this. I need you to tell me the truth: Did you know what Bluescreen does? Did you help make it?" She raised her eyes and found his; pale marble orbs laced with rippling bands of quartz and color. She held his gaze, and he held hers. After a long moment, he spoke.

"Do you know how it works?"

"Saif, tell me—"

"I don't know anything," he said. "I'm telling you the truth, Mari. I know it gives you a buzz, I know your friend had a weird reaction to it, and that's it. I haven't sold a single drive since you called me last night. But you're talking like you know how it works."

"It's not enough to stop selling it," said Marisa. "Everyone who's ever bought from you is in danger, in real, life-threatening danger, and you have to warn them."

"What danger are they in?" he asked. "What do you know, and . . . how do you know it?"

"What do *you* know?" she asked again. "Do you know how it works? Do you know what it does to their minds, all the people who use it and turn into . . . puppets?"

"Puppets?"

She couldn't tell if he was shocked at the information, or at the word she'd used to describe it. "It takes over their bodies, and turns them into . . . well, nulis, I guess. Mindless slaves that someone—whoever's in charge of all this—can move around like robots."

"That's impossible."

"No it's not," said Marisa. "Anja and everyone else who's ever used this is a puppet, remotely controlled, and they've already used them to kill, and that's just one of the crimes they're capable of."

She watched him, waiting for a response, trying to see something—anything—in his sculpted stone face. An Overworld avatar was tied directly to the brain, and detailed enough to convey the player's emotions. She watched his eyes for a sign of care, of concern, of horror at the truth.

He didn't even blink.

"Saif?"

He said nothing. She touched him, and he bobbed in the air like a buoy, anchored but uncontrolled. She frowned; this happened sometimes in online matches, when someone's link to the game was interrupted, but how could that happen here? How could you go link-dead when there was no online link, just a direct cable from the console to the djinni?

Unless the djinni itself had gone offline, but what could—

Bluescreen.

Marisa blinked out of the game as fast as she could, exiting the menu, exiting the lobby, tearing through the layers of virtual reality until she jerked upright in the parlor chair, blinking in pain as she opened her eyes too quickly in the real-world light. Saif was standing straight up, walking away from his VR chair, the djinni cable stretching out behind him like a thin white umbilical cord; it reached its limit, went taut, and snagged him for a moment before finally slipping free of his headjack and falling to the ground.

He moved in the same strange trance that Anja had, sure-footed but mechanical, with none of his usual smooth grace. He was headed for the door. Marisa ripped out her own cable and ran after him, grabbing his shoulder. He pulled away from her easily.

"Saif!"

He didn't seem to hear her. Someone was controlling him.

Outside the street was full of speeding cars and autocabs, not moving straight like they had on the highway, but weaving in and out of each other in a far more delicate pattern. How easy would it be to have him jump in front of a bus—or had they learned their lesson with Anja, and they'd devised a new, surer way to get him killed? She grabbed him again, calling for help; the VR parlor receptionist looked up, doing something to his nails, but didn't offer any assistance.

"Quiet down," he said, irritated. "We don't want to disturb the other guests."

"He's . . ." She paused, straining against Saif's relentless walk, not knowing what to say, or how much of it to describe. "He's OD'd on something," she said at last. "Close your door so he can't get outside; he could be killed."

The receptionist frowned, his irritation bleeding halfway into confusion. "The door is glass, though, what if he breaks it?"

Marisa grunted in frustration. Saif was almost to the door.

The only reason to try to kill him now, at this precise moment, was if they'd been monitoring his sensory feeds and heard their conversation, and wanted to get rid of him before he told her anything else. One more loose end cut off, like eLiza. And if they were monitoring his senses before, they were definitely monitoring them now—anything he saw, they'd see, which is why she didn't dare to get in front where they could see her.

Except . . . they'd already seen enough. They'd heard him say her first name, they'd seen her character information in the game system, and they'd heard her talk about Anja; if they were smart enough to code this drug in the first place, they were smart enough to trace that information backward and find who and where she was. Nothing was secret anymore. All she could do was save his life.

She stepped in front of Saif, blocking the door with her body, staring into his eyes. "Let go of him. I won't let you kill him."

"Who do you think you are?" said Saif, only it wasn't him; the voice wasn't right, and the eyes weren't focusing on her. It was the puppetmaster, speaking through his toy.

"My name is—"

"We know your name, Marisa," said Saif. "We just don't understand why you think that matters. Why you think *you* matter. You can't stop this."

"I don't have to stop the whole—"

"Just kill her, too, and get it over with," said Saif's mouth, as if whoever was controlling him was talking to someone else— another mastermind, far away in their secret lair. They didn't even take her seriously enough to address her directly. Saif grabbed her by the shoulders and slammed her against the door, rattling her bones and cracking the safety glass; it fractured into a spider's web of brittle shards. Another slam would shatter it completely, and he adjusted his grip to do it.

"I'm sorry, Saif," she said, gritting her teeth. She raised her SuperYu arm, curled her stainless steel fingers into a fist, and hammered it into his face. He staggered backward, twitched once like he'd touched a live circuit, and dropped to the floor.

Hey girl! said Jaya, the message bouncing cheerfully in Marisa's djinni. **How's the date going?**

ELEVEN

"Don't call the police," said Marisa, shooting a quick glance at the receptionist. He leaned over the counter, looking down at Saif's unconscious body like it was a frog he'd been told to dissect. "We'll clear out; we were never here." The police would call her parents again, and the hell she'd catch for getting in trouble with the cops two days in a row would make being grounded look like a vacation. There were worse things than being sent to your room—if they wanted to get serious, they could shut off her djinni service altogether.

"Is he going to be okay?" asked the receptionist.

"He'll be fine," she said, and right on cue Saif moved his head. "See?"

"Buuuuuuuh," said Saif, struggling painfully back into consciousness. His lip was split, and his face was bloody. Marisa grabbed the front door and pulled it open, propping it with her foot so she could drag Saif out onto the sidewalk—she needed to get him into hiding before the Bluescreen puppeteers could reestablish their link.

Mari, sent Jaya, **you there?**

Call everyone, Marisa sent back, grabbing Saif under the arms. **Especially Bao—I need Bao.**

What happened?

I punched a drug dealer in the face, said Marisa. **Call Bao!**

"Urrrrrr," moaned Saif.

"Just hang on," said Marisa. She pulled his feet clear of the door, and it swung shut behind them. "We're going somewhere safe." The sidewalk was empty, but the street was full of cars, their lights just beginning to come on as daylight gave way to a pale half-darkness. She looked at the passing autocabs, knowing they would make a great place to hide, but she didn't want to pay with her own ID for fear of being tracked, and her fake account didn't have enough money. Where else could she go?

Sahara's voice icon popped up in Marisa's vision, and she blinked on it to accept the call. "Mari, honey, what happened?"

Marisa grunted as she dragged Saif away from the busy intersection. "The good news is, Saif's on our side."

"Are you okay?"

"For now," said Marisa. "The bad news is, the genius used his own drug. He's got the puppet program, same as Anja, and they tried to kill him with it. He's unconscious for now, but I don't know what to do."

"How'd they knock him out?"

"They didn't," said Marisa, straining to keep her grip as Saif started to squirm. "I became a Super Me. Triste chango, he's starting to wake up."

"Knock him out again," said Sahara, and then Jaya and Fang both entered the call.

"Jaya filled me in," said Fang. "What the hell have you gotten yourself into?"

"You have to go dark," said Jaya. "Turn off your ID and your net connection completely."

"They don't have my ID code," said Marisa. "They can't track it through GPS."

"They don't need GPS," said Jaya. "I'm in marketing, and this is what we do: as long as you're in a business district, every storefront you pass is going to read your ID. If the Bluescreen dealers know who you are, they can track you through that."

Marisa glanced up at a pawn shop as she dragged Saif past it; she'd set her djinni to automatically filter out any coupons and ads, so she'd forgotten, but of course they were still scanning her. She swore.

"That's brilliant," Marisa growled. "Remind me to try that trick sometime when I'm not running for my life."

"Hey lady," said a man in the doorway of a branding hall. "You okay?" He was covered with several brands. Tattoos were so easy to do and undo, the only way to stand out was to destroy your skin, either with chemicals or a red-hot branding iron. This guy had several examples of both, by the look of it. Marisa looked back down, trying not to make eye contact.

"He's my boyfriend," she said quickly, "he got in a bar fight. We'll be fine."

"Dump the loser and get with a real man," he said, stepping out into the sidewalk.

"Mari," said Sahara, "you need to get out of there."

Saif stirred again, his eyes half opening; one of them was rapidly swelling. "Mrrrr," he said. The man on the street stepped closer, and Marisa let go of Saif to stand up straight, ready to defend herself. The approaching man only smiled.

"Mrrrrisa," Saif slurred. "Did you punch me in the face?"

A passing car ran its headlights across them, causing the blood on her SuperYu fingers to glisten. The man saw it, paused, and backed off with a smile.

"No problem here, sister, you do what you gotta do." He laughed. "Hit him once for me."

"Mrrrrisa, I think you broke my face bone."

"He's kind of stupid when he's unconscious, isn't he?" said Fang.

"I've got Bao," said Sahara. "What's the message?"

"Tell him to meet me . . . by the USC campus, southeast corner. And then tell him to turn his phone off. We're going dark."

"Be safe," said Sahara, and Fang and Jaya echoed the same. Anja was already offline. Marisa took a deep breath and shut off her djinni.

The world seemed to shrink.

The first sensation was, fittingly, blindness. It was still only twilight, and the street was still lit by neon signs and speeding headlights, but Marisa had become so accustomed to the djinni's heads-up display lights that the whole world seemed darker with them off. Gone were the chat alerts, the news feed icons, the subtle navigational cues that were so much a part of her existence she didn't even think about them anymore. Her peripheral vision had been filled with information overlaying the world, and now it was gone. She felt the darkness like a tangible object, smothering her like a cloak.

With the darkness came a sense of isolation—she was surrounded by people, but they were strangers, and the people she actually relied on were cut off and unreachable. Sahara and Anja were only a few miles away, but without that constant link they might as well have been in China with Fang. She couldn't send messages, she couldn't make calls, she couldn't even blink the police or an ambulance if something went wrong. She had no one to rely on but herself.

It terrified her.

She almost turned her djinni back on, but it wasn't safe. Even if they couldn't control Saif, they could control others, like the five college students who'd killed eLiza. The only way to be safe was to hide. She stopped dragging Saif and stooped down, gently trying to shake him the rest of the way into consciousness.

"Saif, wake up. Come on, cuate, let's stand up. Come on." She pulled on his arm, urging him to his feet, and he stood up gingerly.

"My face hurts."

"You're lucky that's all that happened," she said softly. "I need you to turn your djinni off."

"Did you punch me?"

"And I'll do it again if I have to," said Marisa, "but it's better to just turn off your djinni."

"Why do I have to turn off my djinni?"

"Because you're an idiot drug dealer who uses his own drug."

He seemed to freeze for a moment, then deflated slightly, his head drooping. "You said they could . . . control people," he said. "Is that why I can't remember the last ten minutes?"

"That and my fist," said Marisa. "It was the only way to break their control. Now turn off your fracking djinni before they take control again."

He nodded, and after a pause he seemed to cringe. "Oh, this is freaky."

"Tell me about it," said Marisa, and pulled him forward. "Now, let's get walking. The people who did this were trying to silence you, because of something you know, and that means two things: first, they're going to keep coming, so we have to stay offline and we have to get away from this spot, which is the last place they knew you were. Second, you need to tell me whatever it is they don't want you to tell me."

"I don't know what they don't want me to tell you."

"Think," she said, stopping at a curb while the traffic roared by. "Start at the top: do you know who programmed Bluescreen?"

"Of course not."

"Do you know who manufactures it?"

"No."

"Do you know . . ." She covered her eyes with her palm, trying to think, then looked up again as he pulled her forward; the traffic had stopped, and they crossed the street. "Do you know where to find them? Where their warehouse is, where they operate from, anything like that?"

"I don't know anything," Saif insisted. "I'm a low-level dealer, Marisa. I get the drives from a supplier, and the next time I see him I give him the money I made and he gives me more drives."

"The supplier, then," said Marisa. "He's our first link in the chain. What's his—" She stopped shaking her head in frustration. "I was about to ask for his name, so I could look him up and try to track his djinni, but that's obviously out of the question right now. I hate being disconnected like this; it's like someone . . . chopped my brain in half."

"Tell me about it." Saif thought for a moment. "I don't even know his name, honestly, just some street handle he uses: Kindred."

"Do you know where to find him?"

"Confronting him is not a good idea," said Saif.

"Obviously we don't confront him," said Marisa, "but we can watch him. He meets with other street dealers besides you, right? So we can watch a handoff, and maybe follow him back to who-ever *he* reports to."

"This is getting way too dangerous," said Saif. They crossed another street, arriving at the corner of the university campus. "These are hardened criminals," he said. "Do you know what they'll do if they see us?"

"A little too well," said Marisa. "That's why we make sure they don't. There's Bao."

"Marisa!" Bao ran toward her, wrapping her in a bear hug and then stepping back awkwardly, as if the display of emotion had embarrassed him. He was dressed in a black jacket, faux leather, with intentional gaps at the shoulders held together by safety pins—the effect was ragged, but one of studied banality. Half the tourists in Hollywood wore safety pin jackets these days, and with his plain brown T-shirt and blue jeans he was perfectly dressed to blend into a crowd. "You're safe. And you . . ." He looked at Saif. "Well, you're safe-ish. Unless whatever did that to your face is still following us?"

"You're looking at her," said Saif.

Bao's eyes widened. "Ouch, Mari. Sahara told me you punched a guy, I didn't realize it was this one."

"She probably saved my life." Saif narrowed his eyes. "And you are . . . ?"

"I'm sorry," said Marisa. "Saif, this is Bao, he's one of my best friends in the world, and a professional . . ." She didn't want to say *thief*, even though it was essentially true. "Sneak," she said at last. "He's the guy best qualified to help us disappear. Bao, this is Saif, a former Bluescreen dealer. They're trying to kill him."

"Oh, this is *that* Saif," said Bao. "I thought we didn't trust him?"

"I'm standing right here," said Saif.

"We didn't," said Marisa, and shot Saif an apologetic grimace. "No offense, but you were kind of a . . ." She paused, rephrasing to something more polite than *arrogant asshat*. "You're the one who got Anja in trouble, and up until ten minutes ago you had a lot more in common with the enemy than with us."

"Glad I convinced you," said Saif.

"You didn't," said Marisa. "They did, when they tried to kill you." She looked back at Bao. "Speaking of which, we've got to hide."

"I can't stash you anywhere long-term," said Bao, "but I can at least get you off the streets for the night. Sahara kind of filled me in—your djinnis are off?"

"We're completely disconnected," said Mari. "Honestly, I can't believe you live like this; this is utter hell."

"You lived like this for twelve years," said Bao. "And the human race survived like this for thousands of years, if you can believe it." He led them to the side, away from the streetlights. "But the upside is, this city is just as dependent on djinnis as you are. As long as you stay turned off, ninety-five percent of the ways anyone's going to use to find you will be completely useless. Now, step two is even simpler—get off the roads, get out of sight, lay low. If you don't feel safe at your place, you're welcome to crash at mine—"

"I know how to hide in my own house," said Marisa. "I need you to show us how to hide here, in the middle of the city. We're going after Saif's supplier."

Bao looked at Saif, then back at Marisa. "Oh, this seems incredibly stupid." He pointed at Saif. "Your plan?"

"Hers," said Saif. "I'm with you, though, this is way too big for us to be messing around with."

"This was your idea!" said Marisa. "This is what you asked for: to meet me so we could figure out a plan. Well, now we have a plan."

"Honestly?" said Saif. "I didn't think you'd take it this far."

"But then . . ." Marisa stared at him, her face screwed into a look of confusion. "Then why did you want to meet me?"

"Why do you think he wanted to meet you?" asked Bao.

"Please," said Saif, with a look of disdain. "Like I have to play superspy to get girls? If this was just about getting into her pants, the deal would already be done."

"Oh, for the love," said Marisa, slapping her hand over her eyes. "You are a bigger blowhole than I ever imagined—and that's saying a lot."

"I have my own plans for these dealers," said Saif. "Plans that do not involve chasing them around until they shoot me. But first I need to know what you know."

"You know what I know," said Marisa, practically shouting. "Bluescreen takes over your mind. They can control people like nulis. They can control you too, apparently, and they're willing to kill you to keep you from talking, so why are you chickening out when I talk about stopping them? This is your life we're talking about."

"I told you, I have a plan," said Saif. "I'm going to go to the police."

"The police are useless," said Marisa. "Not ten hours ago I watched Omar talk a police chief into a felony; with as much money as Bluescreen is making, they're sure to have some cops in their pocket as well, assuming they don't control a few outright with the puppet program. We can't rely on the police for anything."

Saif clenched his jaw, and shook his head slowly.

"She's right," said Bao, "but she's also talking crazy. Knowing that the cops can't protect us is all the more reason to run screaming in the other direction. Going after the Bluescreen dealers by ourselves is suicide."

"Only if we get caught," said Marisa. "Which we won't, if you help us. So that gives you three options: help me, or I go by myself, or you knock me unconscious and drag me home."

"Why is this so important to you?" asked Saif. "Why are you willing to risk your life for it? You don't even have the virus."

Marisa looked at him, a thousand answers rattling through her head, each one some angry variation of *because it's important.* But she knew he was right—it had to be more than that. There were plenty of important issues she never did anything about, drifting through the internet and plugging herself into Overworld and forgetting her real life as much and as often as possible. This was different. This was personal. Was it the threat to Anja? Or was it even closer to home?

"Because I want to trust someone," she said at last. "Look around—do you know any of these people? Do they know us? Do any of them even care? Most of them are on their djinnis, their minds half a world away. We're in the middle of a crowd and yet we're isolated from everyone but our closest friends and our strictest authorities, and we can't trust the authorities: the government is corrupt, the cops are paid off, and the megacorps that run the world just look at us like walking bank accounts. And now with Bluescreen we can't even trust our friends anymore. We have no security, no privacy, we have nothing we can rely on. I want to rely on something again, because I can't do this anymore."

Bao sighed. "Fine. Let's track these guys down."

"And find what?" asked Saif. "More people you can't trust?

Even if I take you to my supplier, and by some miracle we find a way to spy on him without being seen, what then? They'll keep selling Bluescreen, the cops will keep taking bribes, the whole world will go on exactly like it always has. The people with the power will still have it, and you won't have anything."

"I'll have information," said Marisa.

Saif nodded. "What will you do with it?"

"I'll figure out how to get more," said Marisa. "Sooner or later, we'll have enough to do something."

Saif studied her, his eyes dark, his face lit by the dim yellow of a streetlight. After a long silence he glanced at Bao, then back at Marisa. "I'll help you, but only tonight. I'll show you my supplier, and then you're on your own."

"Thank you," said Marisa.

"Then let's go," said Bao, "but we go carefully, and you do what I say, and if I see anything suspicious we cut and run. Deal?"

"Deal," said Marisa. "Saif, where's Kindred?"

"An industrial park a few zones south of here," said Saif. "We're going to need a car."

"I'm guessing neither of you can pay for one without your djinnis?" asked Bao. Marisa and Saif shook their heads, and Bao pulled out a slim piece of plastic. "This is untraceable credit, representing a full day's work and my family's food. You'll pay me back?"

"Absolutely," said Marisa.

"Come on." He walked to the curb, hit a few buttons on his phone, and an autocab rolled to a stop. It slid its doors open with a cheerful welcome.

"Good evening!" said the cab. "Where can I take you today?"

Saif gave it the address and helped Marisa in. Bao followed, tapping his plastic card on a small flat panel.

"We should be there in about thirty minutes," said the cab, sliding the doors closed behind them. "Would you like a—"

"No ads or offers," said Marisa. "Ay, I hate these things."

"Tell me about where we're going," said Bao.

"It's called the Donato Center." Saif kept his voice low. "It sounds swankier than it is—mostly just rentable warehouses and office space, maybe ten or twelve buildings with a little web of roads between them. But we're not going right there—I didn't want there to be a cab on the grid heading to that address, in case these people are monitoring. Instead the cab's taking us to a little strip mall nearby: taco stands and dry cleaners and that kind of stuff. We can walk the rest of the way, and most of it in the dark."

"That's smart," said Bao. "Does the Kindred guy use one of the offices?"

Saif shook his head. "Just one of the parking lots. The place is empty after hours."

"Even better," said Bao. "Any security cameras that see us won't belong to anyone who cares. We should be prepared for private surveillance nulis, though—a guy selling drugs is going to have at least a couple of those to watch his back."

"And they'll be doing more than just scanning for djinni IDs," said Marisa. "Even Cameron and Camilla have nightvision. And infrared. We can't let them see us."

"That's why you have me," said Bao, smiling for the first time that night. "This is how I make my living, remember? Item number one." He opened his jacket and pulled something from an inner pocket: a short black stick with a foam cone on one end. "Directional microphone," he said. The end opposite the foam had a small earbud, which Bao pulled out on a taut, retractable cord. He let go and the earbud zipped back into its housing. "The first rule of sneaking in somewhere is that the less 'in' you have to sneak, the better. This will let us hear everything they're saying from two hundred meters away. Item number two." He handed the microphone to Marisa and reached into a different pocket, pulling out a beige cloth cap, like a ball cap, rolled into a wad. He unfurled it to show the logo on the front, the stylized black bear of Monarch Studios, a movie company.

"How is a Monarch hat going to help us?" she asked.

Bao smiled, and reached his finger inside the hat up under the brim. He pressed a button and the logo vanished, replaced by the Cherry Dogs logo Marisa had designed.

Saif frowned. "That still won't help us."

Marisa smiled. "It's electric ink. He can make any logo he wants."

"The second rule of sneaking in," said Bao, "is that looking innocuous is more important than not being seen, because not being seen is impossible. The hat has a camera, so I can re-create any logo I see. Hold this." He handed the hat to Saif, then took off his black jacket and turned it inside out, revealing a second surface the same color and material as the hat. Even the safety pins were gone, replaced by a normal shoulder seam. Bao put the jacket on, then the hat, and looked for all the world like a uniformed employee of some generic company. He reached one more time into his pocket and pulled out what looked like a slim plastic block with a clip at one end; he unfolded the block into a single flat sheet, and Marisa saw that it was clipboard. "This is the costume I use for loitering; anytime I need to just hang around and listen to someone, or stand in a crowded street and snag bank numbers from passing tourists. People get suspicious if you just stand there, and now that nulis do all the menial jobs like groundskeeping and custodial, you can't just pretend to be picking up trash. But stand around with a clipboard, talking to yourself and making a mark every now and then, and people think you're official. Better yet, stand in a busy street with a clipboard and *try* to talk to people, and it's like you've just turned invisible."

"For a crowd, sure," said Saif, "but that's not going to work in an empty industrial park at night."

"That all depends on which logo I use," said Bao, and took the hat back from him, pressing the button inside it again. It flipped through a dozen or so logos, most of which Marisa recognized as local megacorps, and then stopped on Los Angeles Department of Water Conservation. "Ideally no one will approach me at all, but if anyone does I can tell them I'm checking the sprinkler system. Now, I only have one outfit, but your faces are anathema anyway, right? You stay by the taco stand; I'll go check it out and report back."

"You said your hat has a camera?" asked Marisa.

"Yeah, but this is the best logo for this situation—"

"I don't want you to change it, I want you to patch your camera to your phone, and send me the signal."

"But your djinni is off," said Saif.

"Crap," said Marisa, smacking her forhead. "I'm so used to having it; this is the worst."

"I have a tablet," said Saif, pulling a MoGan from his pocket. "Can we link it to this?"

Marisa took it, examining the slim rectangle. It was the same model as Omar's, and she couldn't help but shake her head. "Let me guess: you just use it for the speaker?"

"Yeah," said Saif, furrowing his brow. "How'd you know?"

"Because all you rich boys are the same," she said. "Bao, I can disable the ID on this MoGan and set up an ad hoc network with your phone. If we go a safe distance from the strip mall, there won't be any storefronts to track our signal, and we should be completely undetectable."

"We're almost there," said Bao, handing her the phone and hat. "Work quickly."

Marisa fiddled with the devices until she found a way to link them with a hard line; the hat seemed adamantly opposed to any form of wireless communication. For good measure she patched in the microphone as well, and then linked them all to Saif's tablet on a private, short-range network. The autocab let them out at the strip mall, a small stretch of busy shops and restaurants on the edge of a large industrial park. It looked like it contained many more complexes than just the Donato Center. They walked a quarter mile to find the right fence, hoping no one at the strip mall had paid enough attention to recognize them, and Bao set off to find the gate. Marisa hesitated a moment, staring at the tablet, then went online with it and created a dummy account in a chat program. She called the account Zora582, Sahara's first-ever account name in Overworld, and used it to send Sahara a message.

"What are you doing?" asked Saif.

"Building a backup plan while Bao gets into position," said Marisa. A response popped up from Sahara, and Marisa held up her finger. "Hang on a sec." She opened the message.

You're back online, wrote Sahara. **Are you crazy?**

My djinni's still off, Marisa typed back. **This is a tablet, far away from any ID readers. We're spying on Saif's supplier, and I need your help.**

For what?

I want a nuli to follow the supplier. Look for something called the Donato Center.

Okay, sent Sahara. **Aaaaaaaand . . . got it. And I've got Fang as well, I'll patch her in.**

Hey Mari, sent Fang. **You're having one hell of a day, aren't you?**

There's a strip mall nearby with a bunch of fast food places, sent Marisa. **I saw at least one that had delivery nulis. See if you can commandeer one of them for us to boss around.**

Heh, sent Sahara. **That's ironic.**

Don't remind me. Marisa sent the final message to Sahara and looked up at Saif. "You doing okay?"

He touched his face. "I've been hit harder that that, believe it or not."

"I don't mean that," said Marisa, though she couldn't help but feel a pang of guilt—not just for having hurt him, but for knowing that he'd been hurt before. She inched closer. "I mean Bluescreen," she said. "Being betrayed like that; being controlled. That's . . . got to hurt a lot more than just a punch."

Saif's eyes twinkled with mischief, barely visible in the darkness. "That was 'just a punch,' huh? I'd hate to see what happens when you really attack someone."

"I've got them," said Bao, his voice whispering from the mic connection on the table. Marisa connected the audio to the chat program, so Sahara and Fang could listen in as well. "I'm about three buildings away," said Bao. "Video feed coming now." They waited, and after a moment a grainy, black-and-white image appeared on the screen. She saw a small car, she couldn't tell what model, with a man leaning against it, but the image was so poor she couldn't see what he was wearing, let alone what he looked like.

Another car pulled up in front of it, head-to-head. Marisa heard a click and a moment of static, and the newcomer spoke.

"Kindred!"

"Gomez!" said the first man. They shook hands, and one of them said something Marisa couldn't quite make out.

"I missed that last part," she said.

"I'm trying to get closer," said Bao, and the image shook wildly as he walked forward.

That's going to make me seasick, sent Fang.

"Don't go too far," said Marisa, "the network on this tablet only reaches out a hundred meters or so."

I'm working on that nuli, sent Sahara. **Fang, can you run interference?**

On it, sent Fang.

Kindred opened his trunk and pulled out a bag. Gomez held up a bag of his own, and the two men traded.

Marisa nodded. "Bluescreen drives in exchange for . . . I have no idea. Dinner, maybe? What would you hand to a drug dealer?"

"It's cash," said Saif.

"You're kidding," said Marisa. "Who uses cash?"

"It's the only way to keep a transaction private," said Saif. "If we pay in credits, suddenly the banks know where the money came from, and where it's going, and even where we were standing when we exchanged it—digital currency has a trail you can never erase."

"Makes sense," said Marisa.

"I started hitting that new neighborhood today," said Gomez. "It worked out pretty well."

"Glad to hear it," said Kindred. "Lal says to make sure you lay low; we can't afford to attract any attention right now."

"What's going on?" asked Gomez.

"Don't worry about it," said Kindred. "Keep selling, but stay out of trouble."

"Who's Lal?" asked Marisa.

"Never heard of him," said Saif.

"They're expanding their territory," Marisa murmured. "Which new neighborhoods are they moving into? Beverly Hills?"

"Probably," said Saif.

"Wouldn't they already be there?" asked Marisa. "Why would they be in Brentwood and not Beverly Hills?"

"I . . . don't know. Look, they're leaving."

Gomez took the bag of drives and walked back to his car. Kindred went to his, and both vehicles started moving.

They're leaving, sent Marisa. **Do you have that nuli yet?**

We're working on it, sent Sahara.

We're going to lose him, sent Marisa.

"They're coming toward me," said Bao. "I'm going to hide and wait for both cars to leave the Center." His video and audio feeds shut off, and the tablet screen went blank.

Mari, sent Sahara, **we need the Goblins.**

I'm not on my djinni, sent Marisa. **I don't have them.**

"We've got to hide," said Saif.

We're not going to make it in time, sent Sahara.

"He's coming toward us," said Saif. "Come on!"

Go! sent Sahara. Saif grabbed Marisa's hand and sprinted back toward the strip mall. She turned off the tablet as she ran, just in case one of the storefronts managed to read a useful ID from it. They reached the first restaurant, a crowded neon diner called Taco Riendo, and Saif put his arm around her shoulders, pulling her close and hiding their faces from the road, facing the window as if they were reading a menu. Marisa longed to know what was happening—had they gotten away cleanly? Had Bao been seen? Had Sahara hacked the nuli in time, or had Kindred gotten away?

"Here he comes," said Saif, and he leaned in closer; she smelled his sweat from the run and his blood from the wound on his face; she felt the faint rasp of his stubbled chin on her cheek, like a thrill of electricity. Her breath caught in her throat, and suddenly it felt impossible to think about anything but the heat of his body. He pointed to the window, and Marisa forced herself to look at a reflection in the brightly lit glass: the street behind them, and the warped outline of Kindred's car as it slid by on the road. Marisa

189

waited, motionless in the curve of his arm, trying to concentrate on the car instead of him, and only when the car moved completely past them did she dare to turn her head and watch as it drove away, past the strip mall and into the city . . .

. . . and right then, in the final second, a small nuli flew out from the fast food place and followed the car, a tiny glowing dot in the neon sky.

"Got him," she breathed, and gripped Saif's arm in triumph.

Saif shook his head in disbelief. "You stole a nuli from a restaurant and tailed a drug dealer with it, all in . . . what was that, five minutes?"

"I think four," said Marisa, smiling from ear to ear. "I didn't think we'd make it." She made a fist and pumped it forcefully. "Cherry Dogs!"

"I didn't even think that was possible," said Saif. Marisa turned back from the street, looking at him, and found him staring at her, considering her with a face he hadn't used before. He was impressed, and . . . something else she couldn't pin down. It made her heart beat faster, and she looked away. He spoke again, softly. "What else can you do, Marisa Carneseca?"

She slowly turned back toward him, doing everything she could to maintain her cool. "Didn't I tell you? I'm amazing in every reality."

"I think . . ." He paused. "I think you're one of the only people I've ever met who could say that and not sound arrogant."

Marisa felt like she didn't know how to respond, though when she finally spoke it seemed obvious, and she didn't know what had seemed so complicated. "Thanks." She looked back at the restaurant window, on the verge of asking him to step inside for a drink, but her eyes lit on a clock and she cursed. "Ten thirty? I've got to go."

"This early?"

"My parents' restaurant closes in half an hour, and about a half hour after that they'll get home. If I'm not in my room dutifully doing homework, they're going to disassemble me one cybernetic implant at a time." She held up her SuperYu arm, and realized he'd never even mentioned the loss of the fancier Jeon he'd seen in the club. She licked her lips, trying to think of what to do next. "Do you have somewhere to go?"

"I'll be fine," he said, "but I'll also be disconnected. If we're going to meet again we have to plan it now."

"I thought you didn't want to meet again," she said, feeling the tiniest flutter in her stomach. "I thought it was tonight and then done."

"That was before I saw you in action," he said. "I can't help but think that . . . I want to ask you something."

"What?"

"Tomorrow," he said. "Give me some time to think this through."

She stepped closer, lowering her voice. "What is it? What's going on?"

"Tomorrow," he said again. "Somewhere new—we can't go back to that VR parlor."

"Tomorrow," she said slowly, then shook her head. "No—the day after. If I slip out like this too many days in a row, my parents are going to have an aneurysm."

Saif smiled. "Just one aneurysm between them?"

"They share everything."

"Sunday night, then."

Marisa nodded. "At the San Juanito restaurant in Mirador. It's the best food in the city, which I say with no bias whatsoever." She saw movement over his shoulder, and looked up to see Bao, now changed back into his black jacket, the clipboard and hat and microphone hidden in his pockets. She pulled away from Saif, not realizing how close they'd been standing, and called out to him. "You okay?"

"Happy and carefree," he said, though there was a look of concern in his eyes she couldn't quite place.

"Ready to go?" she asked.

Bao nodded. "I'm paying for the cab again?"

"I'll pay you back as soon as I get home," she said. "With interest." She looked at the clock again. "Now let's hurry, I'm down to fifty-five minutes before my parents go nuclear."

TWELVE

Marisa made it home in fifty-two minutes.

She'd spent the ride home using Bao's phone to coordinate a plan with Sahara, copying Marisa's ID to Cameron and then sending him out to sit on the back of a long-distance hauler and ride away across the country. If the Bluescreen dealers tried to track her, they'd think she was fleeing—it wouldn't fool them for long, but it would buy a few days at least. A camera nuli was a small price to pay. And if Marisa's parents happened to check her on GPS, well, she was at home now, right? She'd pass it off as a glitch.

Marisa tried her front door, but found it locked. She closed her eyes, sighing at herself for forgetting—without her djinni, the house didn't recognize her. It gave her a moment of sickening unease, imagining that all her devices were really only communicating with each other, and she was incidental; the house didn't let *her* in, it let her djinni in. If all the humans disappeared one day, would the city still go about its daily business, busy little nulis running around building and cleaning and repairing, without ever noticing that the people were gone?

She shook the thought away. She had more pressing concerns. Marisa looked down the street, as if expecting to see a black van lurking in a shadow, ready to attack, but of course there was nothing. She stared at the door again, sighed, and knocked.

"Like the caveman," she murmured.

"What on earth?" said someone inside. The voice was too muffled to identify. "Don't answer it, and call . . . the enforcers, maybe? The police?"

"It's me!" Marisa shouted. "It's Marisa!"

"Why are you knocking?" And why are you . . . on the highway to Albuquerque?"

Marisa recognized the voice now. "Just open the door, Gabi. My djinni's turned off, it's a long story."

Gabi opened the door, and stared at her with one eyebrow raised. "Do I want to ask?"

"Of course you do," said Marisa, stepping inside and closing the door firmly behind her. "You just don't want me to answer. Trust me."

"Mari!" shouted Pati, running toward her at full speed. She was still dressed in Marisa's old clothes from that morning. That seemed so long ago now. Pati checked herself at the last minute, merely grabbing Marisa's waist in a hug instead of slamming into her full-force. "I knew you were out doing something awesome. Did you go dancing? Did you kiss a boy?"

Marisa thought about Saif's chin on her cheek, and shook her head. "I did not kiss a boy."

Pati's eye's widened. "Did you kiss *two* boys?"

"I didn't kiss anyone," said Marisa, trying to push the twelve-year-old away. "I need to get up to my room, Pati. Mami and Papi are almost home."

Gabi looked at Marisa dryly. "Mami called me to ask where you were; apparently your calls weren't going through."

"Djinni off," said Marisa again, and cringed as she asked the next question. "What did you tell her?"

Gabi shrugged. "That you were on the rag, and turned off calling because you didn't want to talk to anyone."

Marisa practically melted with relief. "Thanks, Gabi, you're the best."

"Thanks for taking me to ballet last night," said Gabi. "Just don't . . . just be careful, okay? I don't want to be the one who lies to Mami the day someone finds you dead in an alley."

Marisa shook her head, not sure how to answer. "I'm doing my best."

"Mari never gets hurt," said Pati. "She's the coolest. She even has—mierda, Mari, is that blood on your hand?" Pati grabbed Mari's prosthetic hand and lifted it to her face, studying the blood still crusted on the metal knuckles.

Marisa pulled her hand away. "We don't say that word."

"Did you get in a fight?" asked Pati. "Did you win? Is that why your djinni was down?"

"I'm fine," said Marisa, pushing her away again and moving toward the stairs. "It wasn't a fight, I was . . . helping somebody.

It was like first aid." She started up the stairs, with Pati close on her heels.

"Did you get my message this morning?" asked Pati. "I have something to show you, I got it at school and it's the best thing ever."

"Not right now, Pati, I have to get to my room."

"That's fine, I'll meet you there!" Pati pushed past her on the narrow stairs and ran to her bedroom. Mari walked to her own room, waving at Sandro through his open door; he was sitting at his desk, as always, his eyes glued to a textbook.

"Hey, Sandro."

"Just in time," he said, without looking up. "They're on the front porch."

"Crap," said Marisa. "Can you open my door?"

Sandro shot her a concerned look, but rolled his eyes and bypassed their father's lock. Her door swung open; she ran inside and started desperately trying to wipe up the blood from her hand with an old T-shirt.

"Buenas noches!" called her father from below. "How are my beautiful children today?"

"It's eleven-thirty, Dad," said Sandro. "Don't shout."

"You're all awake," shouted Carlo Magno, even louder than before, "I know my own children!"

"Ay, Carlo," said Guadalupe, "we have neighbors, too, you know."

"Hello to them, too!" shouted Carlo Magno. Guadalupe laughed.

Marisa examined her knuckles for any visible blood, listening for the creak on the stairs that would announce one or both of her parents coming up. Instead she heard pounding footsteps in the hall, and looked up at her unlocked, open door just in time to see Pati come barreling through it, two dark blue headjack drives clutched in her hand.

"Miralos, Mari, they're called Bluescreen—"

Marisa dropped her T-shirt in shock. "No."

"My friend Paolo had some at school," said Pati, "and they're super awesome—big kids only, 'cuz they work with your djinni—"

"No!" Marisa shouted again, storming toward her and wrenching the drives out of Pati's hands. She was too horrified to even think. "Did you use them already?" She held them up to the light, studying them closely, though there was no outward sign of whether a dose was still valid or not. "Tell me you didn't use them!"

"I . . ." Pati looked shell-shocked. "I got one for each of us, I thought we could use them together."

"Absolutamente no!" shouted Marisa, gripping the drives tightly in her fist and shouting at Pati in a fury. "Do you have any idea what could have happened to you? What these things can do to you?"

Pati was nearly crying now. "I thought you'd think they were cool."

"Do you have any more?" Marisa demanded.

"What's going on?" said their father, stomping forcefully into the room. "Marisa, stop yelling at your sister."

"These are bad," Marisa continued, feeling the heat rise in her cheeks. "Tell me you didn't use any, Pati—stop crying and answer me!"

"Stop yelling!" shouted Carlo Magno; he planted himself between Marisa and Pati. Guadalupe came running into the room behind him, with Gabi and Sandro peering in from the hall.

"These are drugs," said Marisa, too angry to stop now. "We can't have them anywhere in the house."

Carlo Magno turned to Pati, his anger already hot. "You bought drugs?"

"Let her calm down," said Guadalupe, folding Pati into a hug. "She can barely breathe for crying, let alone talk with everyone shouting at her."

"You—" Pati was blubbering too much to speak, glaring at Marisa, conveying with every ounce of her twelve-year-old body the betrayal she felt. "You—told on—me."

"You think that's the worst thing going on right now?" yelled Marisa.

"Stop yelling!" her father roared. "Give them to me!"

"Who'd you get them from?" Marisa demanded, looking past him at Pati. If they were in the school—in the elementary school, no less—then they could be anywhere. But Pati had already told her where she'd gotten them; Marisa was so angry she wasn't thinking straight. "Where did Paolo get them? Who'd he get them from?"

"Give them to me," said Carlo Magno, his loud shout dropping down to a menacing growl, so deep and furious it stopped Marisa short. He was inches from her, his body tensed like a spring ready to pop. She argued with him a lot, but he'd never struck her; from the look of it now he was barely holding himself back. She swallowed, her breath suddenly ragged, and handed him the drives.

"These are dangerous," she said.

"It is not your job to yell at my daughter," Carlo Magno hissed. "I do not take kindly to people who yell at my daughters."

"I'm sorry."

"Don't tell me, tell her."

Marisa tried to look around him, but he moved to follow, his face still inches from hers. "I didn't tell you to look at her, I told you to apologize."

Almost instantly, Marisa's rage was back again. "I can't even look at her?"

"You don't deserve to look at her!" he roared.

"Calm down, Carlo!" shouted Guadalupe. "This isn't helping!"

"She has to obey!" shouted Carlo Magno. "She never does what she's told, and that ends now!"

"She bought drugs!" Marisa shouted. "Why am I the one in trouble?"

"I never said she wasn't," shouted Carlo Magno, "but I'm dealing with you first!"

"I didn't tell her to buy—"

"You showed her," said Carlo Magno. "Pati worships you, Marisa—she acts like you, she plays your stupid games, she even dresses like you! And she sees you running out at all hours, ditching school, ignoring curfew, breaking every rule I set for you, breaking every law that gets in the way of whatever stupid, dangerous thing pops into your head, and do you care about that example? Do you care what she learns from you when she sees the policia drop you off at one in the morning, dressed like a whore, your new arm broken and your breath reeking of alcohol?"

"It wasn't reeking," said Marisa.

"Do you think that makes a difference?" her father roared. "Do you think that a twelve-year-old child sees where your path is leading? Or does she simply see your footsteps, one at a time, as she follows them straight down to hell?"

Marisa stepped back, eyes wide, shocked by his accusation. He hadn't touched her, but she felt as if she'd been slapped in the face.

She was the good one here, wasn't she? Wasn't she trying to do the right thing?

Wasn't she trying to help?

"You're grounded," he said fiercely. "And not pretend-grounded, where I trust you to stay where you're told and not use all the little tricks and back doors you've built into Olaya. Yes, I know about them. Tomorrow's Saturday, so you don't have school, which means you're confined to the house for the entire weekend—no friends, no clubs, no Overworld. I'm deactivating your djinni."

Gabi gasped, and Marisa looked up through hot tears to see that even Abuela was there, standing in the hallway, the shouting loud enough that she could hear it.

"Everybody out," said Carlo Magno. "And straight to bed. Pati, you come with me—your Mami and I need to talk to you about this." They left the room, and Sandro closed it with a final, helpless look.

Marisa was alone.

She flung herself down on her bed, clutching her pillow to her face and sobbing. She'd been trying to do the right thing, but she'd been doing it all wrong. Of course Pati worshipped her—wasn't that obvious, now that she took the time to pay attention? Wasn't Marisa the cool older sister she couldn't stop talking to? And Marisa had done nothing but ignore her, and push her aside, and give her so little attention that of course she kept escalating her rebellions. *I play Overworld, just like you. I skip school, just like you. Aren't I cool now, just like you? Do you think I'm cool yet? What do I have to do to be cool?* Bluescreen's street dealers promoted it as the perfect drug—all the buzz with none of the consequences, a perfect rebellion for anyone looking to stand out. *Big kids only.* As if it were some kind of harmless toy.

"I'm right to be angry," Marisa told herself, "but not at Pati. She was only doing what everyone told her to do." And then she started crying again, because she knew she was just as guilty as anyone.

She sat up, holding her pillow tightly in her lap. She felt isolated, the same as she'd felt the first time she'd turned off her djinni—not just isolated, but abandoned. Even the house didn't recognize her. She hadn't seen her father punish anyone this severely since he'd thrown Chuy out of the house.

It surprised her, all over again, how much she relied on her djinni. When was the last time she'd been truly alone? She could talk to anyone she wanted, anywhere in the world, in a nanosecond or less. She could hear her friends' voices; she could see their faces. She could read the latest Overworld news, or even jump in a game and forget the real world completely. Now was she simply here, stuck in one place and one time and one small room. The seconds ticked on, with no new noises or photos or chats.

"I'm not completely cut off," she said, looking at her desk. The hotbox was isolated, but she had two other systems that were still connected to the network, systems with a mouse and a keyboard and a touch screen, for a better interface when designing avatars or doing a lot of heavy coding. She stood and walked to the desk, moving the broken Jeon arm gently to clear a space. She could talk to someone, but who?

Not her father. He was too angry; she needed to give him time to calm down. She'd gotten into far too many screaming matches over the years, and she knew how they played out. Her mami would be just as useless, at least tonight. Maybe Sahara or the others? What could they do? But Marisa had dragged them into far too much of this already—yes, it was Anja who'd gotten them all involved in the first place, but it was Marisa who'd poked her nose where it didn't belong, studying the code and attracting the notice of hackers like Grendel, and eventually the Bluescreen dealers themselves. Sahara and Anja and everyone else was busy enough tonight, protecting their IDs and searching for a way to scrub the Bluescreen code out of Anja's head. They didn't have time to dig Marisa out a hole she'd dug all by herself.

Marisa stared at the computers, wishing she could do something—needing, in some primal way, to make something better. To fix something, anything, since she couldn't fix herself. But the problems all seemed so big: Chuy and Adriana, jobless and half-starved. A whole city full of hungry, homeless nobodies, scraping out whatever existence they could in the shadow of people and companies so rich they seemed to live on different planets. But they were all right there, in the same big city. Maybe the Foundation was right to protest the new Ganika plant—it wasn't going to help anyone. It wasn't going to make any new jobs, it wasn't going to feed anyone, it wasn't going to do anything but make expensive new toys for people like Anja, so rich she could just replace her djinni at the drop of a hat.

It made Marisa feel uncomfortable, just for a moment, to sympathize so strongly with a terrorist group like the Foundation. The Ganika plant was just one building, just one more circuit in the giant machine that was LA, but it represented so much more. More people put out of work by nulis. More neighborhoods bulldozed to make room for a factory that none of the unemployed masses could ever hope to find a job in. For one brief, exhilarating moment, she thought that maybe Bluescreen was the best possible thing that could happen to this city: get everyone good and terrified of djinnis, force people to realize how much they depended on them, and how easily their technology could slip its leash and destroy them. How would the city react if they knew about a virus so powerful it could break through all your firewalls and control you like a marionette? How many people would turn their djinnis off, just like Marisa had, and go back to a world where people had to open their own doors, and do their own laundry, and build their own world? If Bluescreen was what it took to save the city . . . would that be worth it?

As soon as she thought it, though, she grew angry. Bluescreen in Brentwood was one thing, but they had brought it into Mirador. Into Pati's school. Into Marisa's home. Selling this drug to children was as unforgivable as it was inexplicable. Why make a drug that controlled people's minds, and give it to kids who had nothing? What could they possibly hope to gain? Certainly not money—how much could Paolo, whoever he was, possibly have paid for his handful of drives? It didn't make any sense.

But it did make her mad. If they were going to hurt her sister, Marisa was going to hurt them back.

She turned on her largest machine, a computer she called Huitzilopochtli—the Aztec god of war. It was time to follow up on that nuli they had sent to follow Kindred, and see what she could find.

Her father had already cut off her Wi-Fi access, but it only took her a few seconds to hop on the neighbor's network—she'd learned some of their access codes last year, planning ahead in case it ever came in handy. She felt a sharp stab of guilt as she did it, circumventing her father's rules not ten minutes after he'd accused her of betraying his trust. But what else could she do? It was either guilt about this, or guilt about not stopping the people behind Bluescreen. That didn't stop the sick feeling in her gut, but she pushed ahead anyway.

She started with a quick message to Sahara: **I'm fine. Papi freaking out. Send me the nuli feed.**

The answer came just a few seconds later: **Nothing yet. Still working on the malware. Still can't get Anja's security software to kill it.** At the end was a link to the nuli feed. Marisa clicked on it, and a camera window spiraled open on her second monitor.

Kindred was still cruising around the city, his car a sleek black shape that seemed to warp and glitter as it rolled past streetlights, headlights, and the multicolored reflections of passing nulis. She

clicked an icon in the corner and another window opened, showing her a GPS tracking map of everywhere the car had been: from
Compton to Pasadena to Beverly Hills, and currently heading
south on La Cienega—in the direction of Inglewood, though she
couldn't tell if that was his final destination. The route seemed to
meander, sometimes on the freeways, sometimes on the surface
streets, stopping here and there for what she assumed were more
drug handoffs. The nuli was doing a good job of staying discreet,
keeping the car in sight but skittering off every few minutes, dropping back or zooming ahead or slipping off to the side. Sahara
had probably fed it one of the tracking algorithms she'd written
for Cameron and Camilla. With the sky already full of nulis, one
more or less would be almost impossible to notice.

And then Kindred's car pulled off La Cienega and up a hill,
turning quickly from a dense city to a forest—one of the few left
inside the city borders. Marisa toggled the map labels: it was the
Kenneth Hahn State Recreation Area. A small lake, some hiking
trails, and a winding, scenic drive. And almost no nulis to blend
in with.

Marisa's hands flew across the keyboard, looking through the
nuli's admin controls to see if Sahara had left a back door for manual
control. Thankfully, she had. Marisa blew out a puff of air, realizing
that she'd been holding her breath. She found the hardware controls and turned off the nuli's running lights—that was a ticketable
offense, but so was stealing one in the first place. She hit a few more
keys and took control of the now-stealth nuli, and followed Kindred's car through the trees to a long parking lot, almost empty.

Almost.

Three cars waited at the end of the pavement, their headlights on, five or six figures standing beside them, silhouetted in the darkness. Marisa steered her nuli to the side, out of the line of headlights, and kept it low to prevent a similar silhouette effect. Kindred's car rolled forward, and Marisa's nuli flew along beside it, forty yards away, weaving behind tree trunks and picnic tables. She didn't have access to a microphone, so she couldn't tell what they said when Kindred stepped out. She circled far to the side and came in behind for a closer look, and gasped out loud when she saw the waiting men up close. They were four men and two women, each armed with a heavy rifle, their long magazines dotted with the glowing text that marked them as smart ammunition. The roof panels on the cars signified some pretty extensive upgrades in them as well, possible armor or some kind of advanced computer package. Maybe both. For what seemed like the fiftieth time in three days, Marisa realized just how far in over her head she was.

Kindred handed the lead man a roll of cash, and two of the thugs opened one of the cars and pulled out a case, hauling it across to Kindred's car. This was the next step up the chain, the link between the street suppliers and, she hoped, the manufacturers themselves. But what could she possibly do?

And yet she had to do something. The police weren't exactly reliable or trustworthy, but they were at least armed, and trained for dealing with this kind of thing. She swung the nuli farther toward the back and crept in closer, barely hovering above the ground, trying to get in close enough to read the license plates on the cars. She blinked on the numbers, trying to save them to her notepad, and when it didn't work she blinked again, only belatedly remembering that she didn't have a djinni. She grumbled at her stupidity and searched the desk for a pen, scrambling through the pile of old computer parts until she found one. She jotted down the numbers and backed the nuli away, hiding it under a picnic table to watch the drug dealers talk while she opened another window. She routed her connection through a string of straw-man proxies, and accessed the police server with a dummy account.

Drug deal in progress, she sent. **Kenneth Hahn State Recreation Area. Vehicle numbers 387GSH745, 574OBE056, and 238ACK782.** Then she sat back to wait.

The dealers kept talking, and suddenly Marisa's computer clanged an alert. One of the straw-man servers had been scanned—the police were tracing her. Why are they wasting time on me when they should be sending every car they have over there? She swore and killed the connection, frying each server as she pulled out of it, barely staying ahead of the trace. When she looked back at the screen the dealers were on the move, not running but searching the area, apparently aware that someone had been spying on them. How had they known? One of the women pointed at the picnic table where the nuli was hiding, and Marisa tried to fly it away, but it was too late; the woman raised her rifle, fired, and shot the nuli in midair. The camera feed died instantly, and Marisa scrubbed that connection as well, trashing every scrap of digital evidence of who had been connected to it. When she was finally sure she was safe, she collapsed back in her chair, breathing heavily.

They'd almost found her. Why had she been so stupid? Of course the people who'd programmed something as sophisticated as Bluescreen would be able to protect themselves from digital threats. She looked at the handwritten license plate numbers in frustration—that was probably what had set them off. Reporting those numbers must have triggered an alert somewhere, cluing them in that someone was on to them. What other explanation could there be, unless they had a double agent inside the police—

—but of course they did. With Bluescreen they could control anybody, and access anything, and hide enough security to cover their own tracks and follow everyone else's. She couldn't go after them directly, and now she couldn't go after them them online, either. Her only remaining weapon was gone.

What other resources did she have? How could she protect Pati, and everyone else in Mirador? She had already caused too much trouble—she didn't want to be responsible for any more. But she had to protect her sister; she knew that now, more clearly than anything else. She'd try to be a better role model, but that was only part of it. A dealer was selling drugs in Pati's school, and she had to stop them. But how could she possibly fight a drug cartel?

"With another cartel," she said out loud. The answer was there the moment she'd thought of the question. La Sesenta was into drugs now, and if she told them another dealer was moving in on their territory . . . But, no. She'd told Chuy to be careful, she had no right to throw him into a gang war.

"Except that the gang war is coming anyway, right?" She stared at her reflection in the monitor, willing herself to see someone who helped, instead of someone who only made things worse. "La Sesenta is going to find out about Bluescreen sooner or later, right? If I tell them now, I can protect a few extra kids. It's not like they're going to start murdering each other in the streets. They'll just beat their chests a little, whatever guys do to chase each other off their territory."

She wanted to believe it. It made so much sense. It might turn into a gang war, but . . . it didn't have to. And if it did, it wouldn't be her fault.

She had to protect Pati.

Marisa opened the computer's phone program, and typed in Chuy's ID. It rang twice.

"Marisa?" Chuy sounded concerned. "Two calls in one week; this can't be good news."

"It isn't," said Marisa. "I need to talk to Goyo."

"Goyo's the leader of La Sesenta, Marisa, you can't just call and—"

"Pati got drugs at school," she said, clenching her fists below the desk, hating every word that came out of her mouth.

"I . . . Well . . ." Chuy stumbled over the words. "That wasn't us, I promise you, we would never sell to children—"

"I know it's not you," she said quickly. "It's a rival dealer, invading your turf. You drug dealers care about that, right? About keeping the other ones out?"

Chuy said nothing, but she could hear him groaning, a deep-throated growl like a restless lion. "Of course we care, but why do you? You told me to get out, not to start a war with a rival dealer."

"Better the devil you know," said Marisa. "You're from Mirador—everyone in La Sesenta is. You care about it as much as we do. Plus you just told me you would never sell to children,

209

to our children, to our families, but now somebody is. I want them gone."

Chuy growled again, and then all sound ceased; he'd muted her. She waited, biting her tongue, until another name popped up on the screen, requesting to join the call: *Gregorio Marquez.* Goyo. She clicked Yes.

"Señorita Carneseca," said Goyo. His face appeared on her screen, as scarred and craggy as the surface of an asteroid. His voice was deep and gravelly; his left cheekbone was pocked with a chemical brand. "You have something to tell me." He spoke with the confidence of someone people obeyed; his time was precious, and if you used it, you'd better be worth it.

"There's a new drug in LA called Bluescreen," said Marisa. "It's—"

"I know what it is," said Goyo. "Rich-kid drug. Not my problem."

"It is now," said Marisa. "My sister came home with some today, says she got it at school. She's in sixth grade at José Olvera Elementary."

Silence. She could hear background noise: faint music and indistinguishable voices. Goyo stared at her, and she swore she could feel her life draining away under his stare. She bit her lip, wondering what she'd gotten herself into. Finally Goyo spoke again. "Thank you. We'll take care of it. Your brother has a good sister."

"Don't hurt anyone," she said, hopelessly, "I don't want to start a war—"

"I said we'll take care of it," said Goyo. "We're done now."

The line went dead.

THIRTEEN

Marisa slept fitfully, dreaming of Chuy dead on the side of the road; of Pati walking stiff and zombie-like, creeping through the house, opening Marisa's door, reaching for her head, forcing a Bluescreen drive into her headjack—

Marisa bolted upright, wide awake and sweating. She didn't have a clock in her room—who needed one, when you had a djinni?—so she lifted the blackout curtain over her window, peeking out at the city beyond. It was still dark, but sparkling with the lights of a million streets and nulis, for Los Angeles never truly slept. Over it all the sky was a dead, slate gray. Dawn was still a few hours off. She walked back to her bed, shivering despite the warmth, and lay down on the sweat-soaked pillow. She lasted seven seconds before getting up again, too uncomfortable, too nervous.

She turned on Huitzilopochtli and checked the time: four in

the morning. Seventeen thirty in Mumbai; twenty in Beijing. She pinged Jaya and Fang with a chat, but got nothing. They were probably playing Overworld. In another two hours Sahara would be waking up to join them for Saturday practice, but with Anja and Marisa both gone . . .

What are we going to do about the Jackrabbit Tourney? she wondered. Barely a week and a half away now. Even if she got her djinni back in time to play, she was missing too many practices. She was holding back the team.

Instantly she felt bad for thinking it—putting her own troubles above Anja's. Marisa was just grounded. Anja had someone else's fingers in her brain, just waiting for the chance to strike.

"As long as I'm up," said Marisa, "I may as well make myself useful." She opened a net window and tried to log in to her bank to pay Bao back, but without her djinni to verify her ID she couldn't do it. The bank locked down her account, flagged it as suspicious, and emailed her a notification that someone was trying to log in under her identity. She shook her fists at the computer screen and tried the same thing in Yosae Cybersecurity, hoping she could upload the virus code to their user submissions board, but ran into the same problem. She grimaced at the screen, baring her teeth, and created a new account, hiding her connection behind another string of straw men.

New malware discovered in the wild, she wrote. **Street name: Bluescreen. Please add to virus definitions immediately.** She attached the code, just as she'd tried to do with Anja, and posted it to the message board.

A moment later she got a response from someone named SparkleTime: **Heartbeat?**

Marisa raised her eyebrows; Heartbeat was her Overworld call sign, and HappyFluffySparkleTime was Anja's. Was this Anja? She typed a response on the message board, saying something that Anja would recognize, but that wouldn't give away their real names to anyone reading along: **Brentwood?** Anja's neighborhood.

She waited just a few seconds before the next post popped up: **Seagate, Position000.** The name of a free chat program, and . . . Marisa wasn't sure what the second word was supposed to be. Anja's Seagate username? She downloaded a copy of Seagate, started to create an account, and froze. If they were really worried about somebody reading their conversation—and Marisa was really, really worried—then Anja wouldn't announce her username directly. The word had to be a clue, not an actual name. "Position000," said Marisa out loud. "What does Anja know that I know, but which someone trying to eavesdrop doesn't?" Her position on . . . politics? Overworld? The players on an Overworld team held specific positions, just like any other sport; Anja was telling her to base her new username around that. She created a chat account called Spotter000, and sent a request to Sniper000.

Marisa? asked Anja, accepting the request barely half a second later.

Anja? asked Marisa.

Awesome, sent Anja. **I thought that was you. Djinni still down?**

213

My dad shut it off, sent Marisa. **I could probably get it running again, if I go around the password in his admin account, but then the bad guys would be able to find me so . . . here we are.**

Irony is the worst, sent Anja.

Tell me about it.

Don't bother with Yosae, sent Anja. **I sent them the same code yesterday, right after you left, and they claim they added it, but I ran an update and a scan and . . . nothing. The Bluescreen code's still in there.**

Marisa was horrified. **You turned your djinni back on?**

How else was I supposed to run the test? I turned it off right after; nothing happened.

As far as you know, sent Marisa. She paused, thinking. **What does it feel like when they take over? Do you remember it?**

Not really, but after it's over I know that it's happened.

The first time they tried to use you against your father, said Marisa. **The second they tried to kill you—but why? You're more useful as a tool.**

You were talking about Bluescreen, said Anja. **Maybe they just wanted you to stop.**

Maybe, said Marisa, **if we'd been on the verge of revealing something secret. Or discovering it. But we still don't know anything—it doesn't make sense.** Marisa tapped the desk, trying to think. Why didn't the Yosae update work? She frowned, remembering her suspicions about the police. **Do you think they have someone inside of Yosae?**

214

Anything's possible at this point, wrote Anja, **but I don't think that's it. I had Omar call the police again, and got some technical specs on those five people that killed eLiza—none of them were using Yosae. Two Pushkins, two Harrisons, and a Washboard.**

Marisa almost laughed. **There's no way they bothered infiltrating Washboard. No one uses Washboard.**

I know, sent Anja. **It's a joke, but it gives us information. It lets us know that this malware can hit anything, regardless of the security system, which probably means that there's no inside man and there's no security exploits— it's just really, really . . . something.**

What, though? sent Marisa. **If we can figure out how it's getting around these antivirus programs, we can figure out how to stop it.**

Beats me, said Anja. **I'll keep working, though—what else am I going to do?**

Did you make an appointment to get it replaced?

Monday morning, said Anja. **First thing. But that doesn't help anyone else who's got the malware. Plus it's going to be a pain in the butt to reconfigure a new one the way I like it. You know how much bloatware they put on those things.**

Speaking of which, said Marisa, **I need to update some of the settings on this brick, I'm not getting any of my regular feeds.** She opened another browser window and started setting up news alerts; she didn't expect to be djinniless for long, but it was soothing, in a way, to set her concerns aside for a few minutes and just read about Overworld—the latest tournament news, the latest strategies. Sahara's *Throw the Drone* video had gone big, much bigger than she'd expected, even starting a meme: people had edited the video to make the drone say something annoying, and then Marisa's avatar would tell it to shut up, until finally she couldn't take it anymore and shoved him off the building. It was a funny meme, and Marisa laughed out loud at a few of them—something she hadn't done in far too long. The meme had lasted about a day, by the look of it, which wasn't bad, and then the boards flooded with people making their own drone-launching videos. It was a good bump of visibility for the Cherry Dogs, but without any time to sit down and follow it up with something awesome—like a Jackrabbit win—it wouldn't be as helpful for the team as Sahara had wanted. Marisa clicked on another meme video, watching the drone complain about nuli rights, when suddenly one of her new alerts pinged. She opened the link, read the headline, and immediately sent it to Anja.

Have you seen this? "The Foundation Claims the Elizabeth Swaim Killers Were Corrupted by Their Djinnis."

Great Holy Hand Grenades, sent Anja. **That's eLiza, right? And the protest group trying to picket the new Ganika plant?**

Exactly, sent Marisa. **Now we know for a fact that eLiza was killed by people with corrupted djinnis, but how does the Foundation know it?**

Who else has figured out what Bluescreen really does? asked Anja. **We haven't heard a whiff about it in the news, or from the police, and Omar's talked to them twice today.**

I don't think anyone's figured it out, sent Marisa.

Certainly not an antitech terrorist group. They use less tech than Bao does.

How could they have even heard of Bluescreen? asked Anja. Do antitech terrorists hang out in upper class Aidoru bars?

It's spreading, sent Marisa. Pati got some at school yesterday.

Nine hells . . . she didn't use it, did she?

She says she didn't, sent Marisa. She read the article again—no revealing details, just standard Foundation ranting about the evils of human augmentation. Maybe they don't know about Bluescreen at all, she wrote. Maybe it's just a coincidence? The Foundation hates djinnis—they talk crap about them every day. They're bound to get it right every once in a while.

Anja paused a long time before responding again. Does it mean something that eLiza was studying djinni software? She was literally majoring in what killed her—most people can't say that unless they're getting a degree in nuclear fusion. Or bears.

That's probably why she noticed it, sent Marisa. She saw the code, and could tell it was wonky because she knew enough about djinnis to see it for what it was.

No one in the Foundation would just stumble across the code like that, sent Anja. Plus, it doesn't look like they mention Bluescreen in their protests. If they knew where the code was coming from, wouldn't they have used it as an opportunity to link djinnis with drugs?

No, because it doesn't feed their story, sent Marisa. **If eLiza was killed by victims of a mind-control virus, the bad guy is the virus. If they leave out that detail and just say she was killed by people with messed-up djinnis—which is technically true, just incomplete—then the bad guy is the djinni.** She looked at her window, still covered with blackout curtains. What was out there, hiding in the city? She looked back at her screen. **You're right about them not finding the code themselves, though. If they know about Bluescreen, it's because somebody told them.** She opened a new browser window and started another fake server trail, hiding her connection even more fiercely than before. **I need to talk to Grendel again.**

Without a djinni? You think he'll meet you outside of NeverMind?

I guess we'll find out.

Play crazy, said Anja.

Marisa forced a smile, and logged in to Lemnisca.te.

Cantina>>Forum>>General

Heartbeat: Dolly Girls

Heartbeat: I need to talk again. NeverMind not an option.

She posted the message, and sat back to wait. Grendel was too careful for her to approach him directly: if she put his name on the post he might never respond at all, to maintain his anonymity. She had to hope he had some kind of alert system, though, that told him when someone was talking about Dolly Girls.

On the other hand, posting about Dolly Girls so blatantly

might be dangerous, especially with eLiza killed for looking into the mind-control code. But it was a chance Marisa was willing to—

WhiteStones: A lot of people having problems with their djinnis these days.

Marisa stared at the message. When she'd been in NeverMind there'd been a bowl of white stones on the table; her mind had put them there, and Grendel had said he was impressed. This had to be him, hiding behind a throwaway username. She sat up straight, composing her thoughts; she didn't know how long he'd stay in the message board. She had to be fast.

Heartbeat: Who else have you talked to?

WhiteStones: Why do you ask?

Heartbeat: Somebody knows. If you told them, that answers a lot of questions, but if you didn't, there's another player in the game.

She waited, holding her breath. What would he say? Would he say anything at all? Did he even know what she was talking about? The cursor blinked on the screen, never moving, on and off, on and off, on and—

WhiteStones: You've impressed me again. Not many people do.

WhiteStones: I tipped off the Foundation myself.

Marisa's fingers flew across the keyboard, trying to keep her words coherent as her thoughts went flying in every direction. She wrote and deleted a half dozen responses, some demanding more info, some theorizing, but all too pushy, all too wrong. He'd only answer if she asked the right question, and finally she wrote simply:

Heartbeat: Why?

She waited for hours, but when the sun came up, he still hadn't answered.

FOURTEEN

"Despiertate, mija, it's time to get up."

Marisa opened her eyes a tiny sliver, only to squeeze them shut again at the sudden burst of light. Her mother had turned on her lights and thrown open the curtains, and was now bustling through the room, picking things up as she went.

She's worse than a nuli, Marisa thought. She threw her arm over her eyes and croaked a retort: "I'm grounded, remember? I'm staying in bed all day."

"We've changed the parameters of your grounding," said Guadalupe. "You're helping us in the restaurant today."

"Ay, Mami."

"Get up." Guadalupe had crossed to the closet, and Marisa could hear her rattling through the hangers. "Here's your San Juanito shirt, all clean and ready to go."

"Papi grounded me to my room, you can't just change it."

"I don't think you understand how authority works," said Guadalupe, and kissed her on the forehead. Marisa rolled over. "Now come on, vámonos. The other kids are all asleep, so the shower's free. You've got fifteen minutes."

"No human being can shower in fifteen minutes," said Marisa. "It's quantifiably impossible."

"Sixteen, then," said Guadalupe. "Rápido, or I'll throw a bag of frozen carrots under your blanket."

She left the room, and Marisa lay in bed for another few minutes before finally sitting up with a groan. She blinked for her clock, remembered that her djinni was off, and swore. Just to be sure her parents had heard her, she swore again more loudly. Her eyes adjusted slowly to the light, and she saw that her mami had laid out clothes for her on the edge of the bed: a San Juanito T-shirt, a pair of khaki slacks that made her look like a cow, and the most boring set of bra and underwear she owned. She put the slacks back in her closet, grabbed some black jeans, and stomped to the bathroom with a grumble. She blinked on her nonexistent djinni three more times as she showered and dressed.

They walked to the restaurant together, Mami and Papi and Marisa; her parents chatted idly about various bits of news, and their plans for the special of the day—chiles rellenos—but Marisa ignored them. When they got to the restaurant and unlocked the back door, Marisa was tempted to ring Sahara's doorbell in the attached apartment, begging her to come and join in her pain, but she didn't go through with it. Why make someone else suffer? She swept the main room and wiped down the tables while her parents got started in the back, and her stomach growled in eager anticipation as the smell of roasting chiles drifted out from the kitchen. When her father brought out two steaming bowls of breakfast, she sat down with him gratefully.

"Chilaquiles," he said. "I know it's your favorite."

"Gracias, Papi." She took a bite, closing her eyes as the creaminess of the cheese and the heat of the chiles seemed to burn her mouth and cool it at the same time. "Ay, que rico."

"I'm sorry I yelled at you last night, Marisita."

"No, Papi, I'm sorry. I know I've been running out and doing crazy things, and I know Pati was watching me but I just wasn't thinking—"

"It's not because of Pati," he said. "I guess part of it is, but you're my daughter too. Te amo. You know that, right? I love you and I want you to be safe, not just because of the other kids, but because of you."

Marisa felt a tear forming in the corner of her eye, and took a huge bite of chiles, hoping she could hide her crying as a reaction to the spicy food. "Thungz."

"What?"

Marisa laughed, covering her mouth and trying to swallow. "I said thanks, but my mouth was full."

"Que grosera," said Carlo Magno, exaggerating his mock disgust. "Here I'm trying to pour my heart out to my oldest child, and she talks to me with her mouth full?"

Marisa laughed again, then looked up in surprise as someone banged loudly on their front door. It was still locked; they didn't open for another two hours. She looked at her father, then back at the door as whoever it was knocked again. She heard a voice, distant and feminine, shouting through the wall:

"Señora Carneseca! Please open up, I have to talk to you!"

Marisa frowned. "That sounds like . . ."

"It's Adriana," said Guadalupe, walking in from the kitchen.

"She's not welcome here," said Carlo Magno sternly. He had disowned her along with Chuy, guilty by association. Marisa cringed, remembering just a second ago that her father had called her his oldest child, not his oldest daughter. And she'd laughed.

"She sounds terrified," said Guadalupe, striding toward the door. "She might need our help." Marisa followed, with Carlo Magno right behind. Guadalupe opened the front door, and Adriana looked up in shock to see all three of them standing over her. She was young, just a year older than Marisa, pretty but thin, with eyes that looked bright red from lack of sleep. She clutched their son, Chito, tightly to her chest.

"Señora," said Adriana, nodding her head in deference. She looked at Carlo Magno, hesitating and scared, then did the same to him. "Señor."

"What do you want?" he snapped. Guadalupe pushed him backward.

"Cállate, Papi," said Guadalupe. She backed up to make room in the doorway. "Come in, you look terrified." Adriana stepped in, glancing nervously at the street behind her.

"Is everything okay?" asked Marisa.

"It's Chuy," said Adriana. "He . . ." She glanced at Carlo Magno again, then back at Guadalupe. "He's been shot."

"Este cabrón," growled Carlo Magno, throwing up his hands and turning away in disgust.

Marisa felt her heart drop, remembering her call to him last night. She couldn't find her voice, and Guadalupe spoke first.

"What happened?" she demanded. "Is he okay? Is he alive?"

"He's alive," said Adriana, nodding. Chito looked out at them with wide eyes, as silent as a photograph. "He's at our house now, with one of the others trying to treat him. I don't think it's serious, but—"

"What did you think would happen?" Carlo Magno demanded, turning back to face her. "We were stuck with him, but you *chose* this."

"He was protecting you!" shouted Adriana. Marisa leaned back in surprise; she'd never heard Adriana raise her voice, but it looked like she had a spine of solid iron when you riled her up. "Someone was selling drugs in your daughter's school, and Chuy and the others took care of it. Pati is safe today because Chuy took the bullet that could have hit her."

Marisa gasped again. "They attacked the Bluescreen dealer? I thought they were just going to—"

"Nobody asked him to go kill people," said Carlo Magno, "drug dealer or not. We have police for that—"

"Are you kidding me?" asked Guadalupe. "Carlito, we pay ten thousand dollars a month to Maldonado for protection, precisely because we can't trust the police to help with anything."

"Then Maldonado should have handled this," said Carlo Magno, "not La Sesenta. That's who we pay to be protected *from*—Chuy and Calaca and all those other rulachos they run with."

"And they're not doing their jobs," said Marisa. "Calaca told us, and then the Maldonado enforcers said the same thing not five minutes later. If we can't rely on them, La Sesenta's all we have left."

"Then we're packing up and moving to Mexico," said Carlo Magno, "where it's safe to walk around in your own damn neighborhood!"

"We need your help," said Adriana, looking at Guadalupe again. Chito started to fuss, scared by all the shouting, and Adriana switched him to her other hip. "That chundo they have treating Chuy isn't a real doctor, and he needs a real doctor. Chuy's too proud to ask, but we can't afford to go to the hospital, and you can."

"Absolutely not," said Carlo Magno.

"He's your son," said Guadalupe.

"He did this to himself!" Carlo Magno shouted back. "We can barely afford to pay our mortgage, and he's out playing cops and robbers in the barrio getting himself shot to pieces, and now we're supposed to pay for that, too?"

"So you want to let him die instead?" demanded Marisa.

"He's not going to die," said Carlo Magno. "She said it's a flesh wound—worst case he needs rehab—"

"And you're okay with that?" shouted Marisa.

"I tried for years to teach him this was dangerous," said Carlo Magno. "Gangs don't protect you, they get you shot. If this is the only way he learns that lesson—"

Chito started crying.

"Of course we can help," said Guadalupe, ignoring Carlo Magno and leading Adriana to a table. "Let me get some beans and rice for that baby; I'll put them in a box so we can take them with us." She went into the kitchen, and Carlo Magno followed her in. Marisa sat down with Adriana, hoping her parents' argument didn't get too heated.

Adriana looked at her without speaking. Did she blame her for tipping Chuy off about the rival dealer? Did she even know? Marisa swallowed nervously, staring back, until her curiosity overcame her fear. She leaned forward and spoke in a low tone, not wanting her parents to overhear. "Who was it?"

"You mean who shot him? How am I supposed to know?"

"Did he say anything?"

"It was a Chinese gang," said Adriana. "Ti Xu Dao—not one he's talked about before."

"My Chinese is terrible," said Marisa. "Something . . . mention . . ."

"I don't care what it means," said Adriana, that hidden steel coming through in her voice again. "They put a bullet in Chuy's shoulder, but Calaca killed one of them. They're going to be back for revenge."

"Ti Xu Dao," said Marisa, blinking on her djinni to run a search for the name. She growled and shook her head, standing up to walk to the hostess computer.

"Have you heard of them?" asked Adriana.

"No, I just need to run the search over here," said Marisa. She waved angrily toward the kitchen. "They turned off my djinni."

"Your father's pretty harsh."

"Yeah," said Marisa, tapping the screen to dismiss the restaurant management app and open a browser window. "In my case, though, he was right. I'm not exactly the best daughter in the world right now. Or sister." She searched the name, taking a few tries to get the spelling right. "Tì Xū Dāo: the Razors. Plenty of news articles pop up in the search, but no history of drugs. Violent little monsters, though."

"Why does this matter?" asked Adriana. "A gang is a gang—it was fun when we were kids, all flashy clothes and throwing money around, but we have our own kid now. We can't live like this, and if Chuy loses his arm he can't get a job doing anything else, either. It doesn't matter which gang shot him; he was shot, and he's all I have."

"I'm sorry," said Marisa. "I'm . . . I'm just trying to figure out what's going on here." She could hear her parents still arguing in the kitchen, and talked louder to drown out the sound. "This gang must have been working for a larger group—the drug they were mixed up in was way too sophisticated for some street gang to cook up. I'm trying to figure out if the payback will come from Tì Xū Dāo or from that larger group."

Adriana held Chito tighter. "Do you think they'd come for Chuy in the hospital? Calaca said it was better to hide him, but he's so sick, Marisa, you have no idea—"

"Attacking a hospital would be a pretty big risk just to kill one person," said Marisa, hoping it was true. But if there was one thing she knew about these people, it's that they weren't concerned with risk. They'd killed, or tried to kill, three people that Marisa knew about, two of them in public places. eLiza was the anomaly there. They struck hard, and they struck fast. . . .

"Wait a minute."

"What?" asked Adriana.

Marisa glanced at the kitchen door, then back at Adriana. "Three months," she muttered. Grendel said eLiza had posted the code on the darknet three months ago. She *was* an anomaly. Saif was targeted within moments of talking about Bluescreen, and they'd tried to kill Anja just one day after she failed to infect her father. But eLiza wasn't killed until three months after she'd started snooping.

"What if she was working for them?" Marisa said out loud.

"I don't know what you're talking about," said Adriana.

"What?" asked Marisa. "Oh—sorry. I was thinking out loud."

"Are you talking about me?" asked Adriana. "Because I would never work with La Sesenta—"

"No, no," said Marisa, "I was talking about the girl who was killed yesterday. Did you see that?"

Adriana raised her eyebrow. "Do you have any idea how many people were killed in LA yesterday?"

"This one was killed by the same dealers who hired Tì Xū Dāo. I thought she was killed for snooping around in their business, but why wait three months? They're not the kind that waits, which means she did something else to anger them, just a couple of days ago: she knew too much and started talking, or maybe she asked them for something they didn't want to give. Either way, the best explanation is that she was working with them—she studied djinni programming, hell, she might be one of the original programmers for all we know. Grendel said she was asking about the code, but he didn't say *what* she was asking. We assumed she wanted to know what it was, but it could just as easily be that she was working on it and needed advice. eLiza wasn't a snoop, she was a loose end."

"What does any of this have to do with Chuy?" asked Adriana.

"I'm sorry," said Marisa, turning toward her. "I'm being rude. Chuy's in danger, and I want to help him, but . . . I'd go and talk to my parents, but like I said I'm kind of on the outs right now. But this is something I can do—I can figure out how they did this, and I can make sure they don't get the chance to do it again." She paused, clutching Adriana's hand. "I want to get to know you better. I'm sorry we waited for something like this to make it happen."

Adriana squeezed her hand back. "I'm going to see if your mom is ready to go," she said, and stood up with Chito to walk back to the kitchen.

"Tell Chuy I love him," said Marisa. She returned to the touch screen and started another search, looking for everything she could find about eLiza. There was very little under that name— some posts on hacker boards here and there, but the hacker boards on the regular internet were mostly useless, and she couldn't check Lemnisca.te until she got home to her secure equipment. Instead she searched for eLiza's real name, Elizabeth Swaim, and found a deluge of info that would take her days to sort through.

"I need to narrow the search," she muttered. "What am I looking for, specifically? Where she was? Who she was with? Yes; who were her friends, who did she know. A hacker studying djinni programming at USC would know a lot of other programmers— maybe they built Bluescreen together." She found USC's public registration records, and quickly coded a search to look at all of eLiza's classes to see who else was in them, sorted by frequency.

The list of common classmates was surprisingly long—Marisa supposed that they had a limited number of djinni programming students at any given level, and they all took the same classes. She wrote another search code to compare that list against eLiza's social networks, to see which of her classmates showed up most often as friends. This search revealed a clear outlier: another programming student named Nils Eckert. It listed his specialty as cyber security.

"What's your story, Nils?" Marisa said, and started typing in another search, when suddenly she was interrupted by a loud bang. She looked up—it had come from the street somewhere. She looked at the front windows, then back toward the kitchen. Her father was standing there, looking toward the same windows. "What was that?" she asked.

"I don't know," he said, walking toward her, "let me take a look—"

More bangs sounded, and distant screams.

And suddenly the front windows exploded inward under a hail of bullets.

FIFTEEN

"Get down!"

Marisa couldn't tell who'd shouted, her or her father or both in unison. She dropped to the floor, ducking low and covering her head. She heard someone screaming, mixed with the crackle of falling glass, and realized it was Adriana, shouting Chuy's name over and over. Chito was wailing in terror.

"Get in the kitchen!" shouted Carlo Magno. Marisa peeked out through her fingers and saw that the attack was over—but no, she could hear more guns on the street. The attacker was still shooting. Either San Juanito wasn't the main target, or it wasn't a target at all, just caught in the crossfire.

Another swarm of bullets burst through the front door, showering the room with shards of glass and and a hurricane of splinters. Marisa screamed and ducked her head again, curled into a ball behind the narrow hostess podium. When the shooter moved on to other targets Marisa knocked the podium over and dragged it with her across the floor, heedless of the sharp debris, pulling it behind the nearest wall for cover.

"Get in the kitchen," her father hissed. "Now, before they shoot us again!"

Marisa looked at the wall above her, and saw it perforated with bullet holes. She shrank lower, lying flat on the floor. "We have cameras outside," she said, tapping the touch screen. "I want to see what's going on."

"Leave that and use your djinni!"

"You turned off my djinni!"

Marisa accessed the restaurant's exterior cameras. A delivery van was driving slowly up the street, the top removed, with four Chinese thugs, two men and two women, poking up out of the top, firing as they went. They seemed to be targeting everything, calmly spraying the streets with bullets like they were watering plants with a hose, pausing now and then to reload when their guns ran dry. One of them turned toward the camera, and Marisa shouted: "Everyone get down!" Bullets tore through the restaurant again, splintering tables and shattering decorations, digging long trenches in the walls. Somewhere in the back, Chito kept screaming. Marisa was just glad he was alive.

"Get off the road!" Guadalupe shouted. Marisa looked up, confused, wondering who she was talking to. She looked back at her screen: no one was outside but the Tì Xū Dāo gunners, and there was no way her mother was talking to them. When the bullets stopped again Marisa jumped up to a low crouch and ran toward the kitchen, grabbing her father as she went. They dashed

233

through the door and threw themselves on the floor; Marisa's mouth fell open in shock to see that the devastation had reached all the way back here—pots and ovens and thick metal cabinets were all pocked with bullet holes.

"They must be using accelerators," said Carlo Magno. "Same thing Calaca's idiotas were carrying when they came in the other day." He pulled a gun from behind his apron.

Marisa's jaw fell open. "You have a gun?"

"Those cholos came in the other day threatening my family, and I'm not going to get a gun?"

"Hide behind something," said Guadalupe. Marisa glanced at her and saw the telltale unfocused eyes of someone talking on their djinni.

"Who are you talking to?" Marisa demanded. "Who's out there?"

"The girls," said Guadalupe, her eyes refocusing on Marisa. "Gabi and Pati—they were on their way here. They say there are shooters everywhere!"

The back door opened and Sahara dove in, crouching near them on the floor. She was dressed in her pajamas: pink sweatpants and a loose camisole, her makeup half-on and her hair a disheveled mess. "Who the hell is tearing up Mirador? They're all over the barrio."

Chito's cries echoed through the kitchen like a primal scream. Adriana tried to hush him, but nothing seemed to work.

"They're called Tì Xū Dāo," said Marisa, "and my sisters are out there."

"Can they get somewhere safe?" asked Sahara. Two camera

nulis flew in behind her: Camilla and a new one.

"You brought your nulis?" asked Marisa. "Is this really the time?"

The new drone opened a small door on the side of its housing, revealing the sparking prongs of a stun gun. "This is Campbell, and he's the best self-defense drone the store had," said Sahara. "Now, let's get back outside—there's no sign of damage in the back, which means these appliances are stopping the bullets."

The group moved outside, staying low, Adriana clutching the wailing Chito tightly to her chest. The backyard was more of a loading zone than anything else—a long, narrow driveway came past the restaurant, ending in a small, paved courtyard with a spigot and a drain and just enough room for a delivery van or a garbage truck.

"Stay down," said Guadalupe, talking to the girls again. "I know it's scary, just—Pati, no! Gabi, grab her!"

Marisa couldn't hear the conversation, but she could guess what was happening—Pati had spooked, and was running. And the first place she'd think to run was toward the restaurant.

Straight into the line of fire.

Before she was even aware of what she was doing, Marisa was up and running as well, charging down the driveway to the street. Her father shouted after her, but Marisa didn't stop. She didn't even have a plan, she just had to save her sister.

"She's hit!" screamed Guadalupe.

"Get back!" shouted Sahara. Marisa ignored her, but a moment later Sahara grabbed her shoulder and yanked her back, just a few feet short of the building's front corner. The space Marisa had been just about to enter was suddenly raked with bullets, and Marisa backed up with a yelp.

"I tried to warn you," said Sahara, holding her tightly with both arms. "The cavalry just got here."

Marisa looked up to see Campbell and Camilla hovering above the street, giving Sahara a bird's-eye view. Half a second later a black car roared past the mouth of the driveway: a Dynasty Falcon. Maldonado's enforcers had arrived.

"Stay hidden," Carlo Magno whispered fiercely. He tugged the two girls farther back into the cover of the wall, keeping his gun up and ready.

"We have to get to Pati," said Marisa.

"I know," he said, "but we're going to do it smart." He looked at Sahara. "Tell us what you see."

They waited, Sahara's eyes moving across her video feed. "The enforcers stopped in front of the next shop over. The Tì Xū Dāo shooters are one door further down—ew, one of them just got hit."

"Are they leaving?" asked Carlo Magno.

"No," said Sahara, "they're coming toward us."

Carlo Magno nodded. "Tell me when they get right in front of the Maldonados—that's when we move."

Marisa turned to him. "When the shooting is worst?"

He shook his head. "When none of the bullets are coming in our direction."

"Now," said Sahara, already moving toward the street. "Go!"

The three of them sprinted out, turning sharply to the left, away from the battle and toward the two girls. The noise of the gunfire was deafening, and the street looked like a war zone: every building was riddled with holes, the windows shattered and the palm trees splintered and broken. The cars parked by the curb were devastated, some of them smoking where accelerated rounds had blown up their electric engines. Marisa saw her sisters huddled behind one of the burning wrecks, and dashed forward to reach them. "Is she okay?"

"No!" screamed Pati. Her eyes were closed, and she jerked back when Marisa tried to touch her.

"She's not hit," said Gabi, so agitated that her words came out in a ferocious jumble, almost too fast to decipher. "She just tripped, I think on the sidewalk, I didn't see, I didn't mean to freak out, but they're shooting at us. Who's shooting at us?"

"They're shooting at each other," said Marisa. "Just come with us and you'll be fine. We have to get out of here." She reached for Pati again, trying to pull her from the heat of the burning car, but the little girl screamed and lashed out with a kick. "It's okay!" said Marisa. "It's me, it's Mari, I'm here to help you."

Pati opened her eyes, wide and terrified, and latched on to Marisa as if the embrace alone would save her life. Carlo Magno helped her to her feet, and Sahara took Gabi's hand, and they ran for the corner, away from the battle, only to shriek as two more gangsters came around it, walking toward them. They wore denim jackets covered in glass and colored gems, a ridiculous image in the midst of the carnage. Marisa was too shocked to react, and as the woman in front raised her gun Marisa could only stumble backward, but Carlo Magno's gun was already up, and he fired two shots before the attacker could aim. The Tì Xū

Dāo shooter went down. The second gangster had more time, and fired his thick-barreled pistol with a sound that seemed to shake the earth, the deafening blast of a rail gun, and Carlo Magno fell with a gurgle of pain.

"Like hell you did," Sahara snarled, and suddenly the man was surrounded by Campbell and Camilla, darting back and forth, distracting the gangster while Sahara ran toward him. Marisa dropped to her father, rolling on the ground clutching his bloody leg.

"I'm fine," he grunted. "Just get the girls out of here."

The gangster screamed, and Marisa looked up to see him shaking as Campbell shot him with a stun dart. He staggered to the side, swinging his gun toward the nuli to fire, but Camilla swooped in behind and shocked him with a stunner of her own, cutting off the current just as Sahara reached the gangster and spun her foot in a whirlwind kick, knocking the weapon from his hand. He swung his fist and she ducked out of the way, slapping his side in a counterattack that didn't seem to hurt him at all; Marisa couldn't tell if Sahara had missed, or if the gangster had dodged just enough to take all the force out of the blow.

Marisa was surrounded, helpless in the street. The gangster pulled a blade from his back pocket and flicked it out of its housing with a menacing hum: it was heated, designed not just to wound but to scar. Sahara backed away, and Marisa pulled her sisters back as well, though the gun battle behind them continued to rage, and she knew there was no retreat—worse still, two of the three Maldonados were already dead, and the Tì Xū Dāo gang had only lost one of their four shooters. Marisa clutched Pati tightly with her metal arm, holding Gabi with the other, trying to think of a way out, when suddenly her mind seemed to expand and her vision lit up with icons and vectors, data filling her like a breath of life. Her djinni was back on.

"I reactivated your account," said her mother, calling in the instant the djinni booted up. "Get them out of there."

"Just leave me," Carlo Magno growled. "Get the girls to safety."

"Cállate," said Marisa. "We're not leaving without you." She glanced up and down the street, desperate to find some way of escaping, and her eyes fell on the front of the restaurant: the glowing San Juanito sign was broken and sparking, and the ad screen by the front door was flipping through a series of glitched ads, framing a shattered bullet hole in the center.

"We have to go!" said Gabi. "We're going to get shot!"

"There's no safe path off the street," said Marisa, "so I'm making one. Did you install those security upgrades I sent you a few months ago?"

Carlo Magno closed his eyes, trying to control his breathing as he put pressure on his bleeding leg wound. Gabi stared at Marisa in shock. "Is this really the time to be asking about that?"

"Yes or no?" Marisa demanded, blinking on her web interface to access San Juanito's website. She logged in to the admin area, and moved from there to the restaurant control panel: she had climate controls, lighting, and everything. Including the ad board.

"Yes," said Gabi, "I installed your security. Now can we get off the road before somebody murders us?"

"Yes we can," said Marisa. "Watch this." She opened the ad

board controls, blinked on the nearest daily special—a free tamarindo soda with any purchase—and raised the instigation value past its limit. The ad board would find every djinni within half a block and bombard them with the digital coupon, sending copy after copy until their processors couldn't handle the load, bypassing all but the most powerful anti-ad software. If the target had a good security system, it would slow them down for a bit; if they didn't, it would blind them completely with a flood of pop-ups that would take minutes to get rid of. She applied the settings, and watched as the shooters faltered, hesitated, and then ducked for cover as their own djinnis betrayed them.

Sahara's cyber security was flawless; she took the ads in stride, if she even noticed them at all, and pressed her sudden advantage with a devastating flurry of punches to the gangster's stomach, face, and throat. He dropped his knife and staggered back, and Sahara finished him off with a roundhouse kick to the side of the head. He fell, and she ran toward Marisa, helping the girls raise Carlo Magno back to his feet.

"Run!" said Marisa, "I don't know how long this will keep them distracted." Gabi and Sahara supported Carlo Magno, one on each side, and Marisa ran with Pati held tightly to her chest, bolting back to the restaurant for safety. They ran through the front door, weaving through the broken tables and other debris, hoping the attackers on the street hadn't seen where they'd gone. They reached the kitchen and fled into the back, where Guadalupe pulled them into a sobbing embrace. Adriana and Chito were still huddled by the wall.

"You're okay?" asked Guadalupe.

"Papi got shot," said Marisa, collapsing against the thick brick foundation. "The rest of us are okay."

"They're leaving," said Sahara, watching the feeds from her nulis. "They told the car to go, and they're gone."

"Sandro's still at home, and says he's fine," said Guadalupe, and glanced at Adriana. "Chuy, too."

Marisa nodded, stroking Pati's hair. "We're alive. Now let's get Chuy and Papi to the hospital."

SIXTEEN

The hospital was a desperate chaos of blood and shouting, as tense as the shooting had been. Doctors and nurses ran through the halls, pushing gurneys and IV stands as they rushed wounded bystanders from room to room, chased through the halls by nulis trying to catalog each patient's stats and vitals. Marisa had been hit by shrapnel from a shattering window—six pieces of glass had embedded in the skin of her abdomen, but she'd been so full of adrenaline she hadn't even felt it until an orderly had asked about her shredded shirt. She sat now in the hospital, the glass picked out but the adrenaline worn off, her stomach throbbing with pain, waiting her turn while the doctors dealt with the more serious cases first.

Like her father.

"I hated this waitress shirt anyway," she said to herself, gritting her teeth and trying to think about anything other than the burning pain. "Now maybe I won't have to work in the restaurant for a while."

Not that the restaurant would be in any condition to open for a while anyway. Could her family even afford to repair it? Especially with all the revenue they'd lose from being closed?

Marisa looked up and down the hall, wondering where Chuy and Adriana were. La Sesenta had told the ambulance medics he'd been hit in one of the dozen drive-by shootings, to cover their tracks from the gang fight the night before. They were somewhere in the building now, but Marisa hadn't seen them yet, and didn't dare to leave this hallway until she'd heard back about her father's condition. He was only hit in the leg, and it had apparently missed the bone, but she was worried. She was the only one from the family who'd come—Guadalupe had insisted on taking Chito and the girls home, dragging Sahara with her for safety. Marisa stayed connected to Olaya, monitoring their safety at a distance, terrified that Tì Xū Dāo would come back.

And even more terrified, the more she thought about it, of whatever had brought them in the first place. Her djinni was back on now; if they were looking for her, they'd find her. But it had been hours, and no one had come.

Her first thought was that Tì Xū Dāo had attacked Mirador in direct retaliation for La Sesenta's attack on them. Adriana's description of the attack had been incomplete, probably because Chuy hadn't told her the truth: according to the buzz Marisa could dig up on message boards, Calaca had found the Tì Xū Dāo dealer who'd been selling at Pati's school, and led more than a dozen gangsters in a midnight raid on his apartment, killing three people and destroying thousands of dollars' worth of Bluescreen. It was an aggressive move with a single message: stay out of Mirador. Some reports said that Calaca had gone so far as to leave a note, though a competing report said that he'd dictated the message to the sole survivor of the raid, and then shot off his hand. Either way, Marisa couldn't believe it had escalated so quickly. Was Goyo trying to start a war?

And then there was the Bluescreen connection. What if this wasn't a gang retaliation, but a direct order from the people behind Bluescreen? What if the suppliers, the programmers, the shadowy puppet masters behind the drug, were using their street-level pushers to send a message of their own?

Except that didn't make sense. Why would those people bother with a poor neighborhood like Mirador at all, let alone go to this insane length to protect their business in it? And why attract this kind of attention, when it seemed like they'd been trying so hard to stay underground? The attack had to come from Tì Xū Dāo, acting on their own—which meant that the Bluescreen cartel was losing control of their dealers. Just like Don Maldonado was losing control of La Sesenta. The dogs were biting the hands that fed them.

And the city would be eaten alive.

Marisa looked up as another gurney went by, surrounded by doctors shouting orders back and forth. She pulled her legs up to make more room for the hurried crowd, only to wince again as the movement sent a new surge of pain through her abdomen. She leaned back, gripping the armrests and sucking air through her clenched teeth.

"Marisa Carneseca?"

She opened her eyes and looked up. Francisca Maldonado was standing over her. La Princesa. Marisa closed her eyes again, trying to remain as still as possible. "I don't need this right now, Franca, okay?"

"I'm not Franca."

Marisa cracked her eyelids again, peering up at the girl. She looked disheveled, and her left shoulder showed a nasty scrape, still untreated and bloody. But it was definitely Franca—Marisa had known La Princesa her whole life, she wasn't going to mistake her now, no matter how much pain she was in.

"I told you I'm not in the mood for any crap, Franca, okay? My dad and and my brother got shot today, and I'm sorry you messed up your hair or whatever, but—"

"I'm not Franca," said Franca. "And I think you know what's going on here."

Marisa felt as if the heat had fled out of her body, rising up from her toes to her legs to her chest, until nothing was left but fear. Franca had used Bluescreen that night at the club, and that meant . . .

"Great Holy Hand Grenades," Marisa whispered. "You're one of the programmers. You made Bluescreen."

"I didn't want this," said Franca's voice. Now that Marisa knew what was happening, she could see the signs of it—a slackness in Franca's face, a stiffness in her posture. La Princesa wasn't standing the way she typically stood, elegant and haughty, like she was posing for a photo spread only she could see. Now she was standing like . . . Marisa couldn't quite put her finger on it. She'd taken off her heels, and her legs were braced widely, going for solidity instead of a look. She was standing like a man.

"All I wanted was the money," said Franca. "I knew that once people saw what it could do, the code would be worth millions. It was Lal who wanted us to use it ourselves."

Marisa had heard the name Lal before—through the drone last night, when she'd followed Kindred's car to a meeting in the park. "Who is Lal?" she asked.

"Quiet!" Franca hissed. Even her accent, that faint hint of Mexico, was gone when she talked. "Do you know what he'll do if he finds out I came to you?"

Marisa looked around at the madness in the hospital. "I've got a pretty good idea. So why risk it?"

"Because none of this was my idea," Franca's voice insisted. "Distributing it like a drug was fine when it was just us, but hiring gangs to sell it for us? Especially these psychopaths from Tee Shoo Whatever the hell they call themselves? I can't control this, and neither can Lal, no matter how tough he thinks he is." Franca's body leaned in. "I know you've been looking into him, and I don't know what you've found, but I need your help. I don't know who else to go to—he's got the cops in his pocket now, and half the city for all I can tell. I can feed you information, but even that much is risking my life—I can't do anything else. I don't want to go down like eLiza—"

"So she *was* working with you," said Marisa. "I knew it! And that makes you . . ." What was the name? She'd seen it on the screen at San Juanito right before the shooting started. Something German? "Nils," she said. "Nils Eckert."

In that moment, Franca's eyes rolled back, and she collapsed on the floor like a limp sack of beans.

"Help!" Marisa screamed. She got down from the bench, kneeling over La Princesa's unconscious body. "Somebody help! My friend just passed out, I think she's . . . in shock or something. Help!"

Nurses and orderlies rushed toward them, probing Franca's neck carefully before rolling her onto her back and laying her flat. A medical nuli swooped in from above, reading Franca's vital signs, and another nurse took Marisa by the shoulders, pulling her away.

"Give her room," said a nurse.

"That's my friend," said Marisa desperately, "you have to help her."

"We are," said the nurse, "just give them room."

"Stretcher!" shouted an EMT, and the nurses cleared room on the floor beside Franca's body; they laid it next to her, counted to sync their movements, and lifted her onto the stretcher.

"Make a hole!"

"Get me a room with a DORD; she needs an immediate brain scan."

The flurry moved away, melting into the rest of the chaos, and Marisa watched them go in stunned silence.

"This is crazy," she muttered. "This is completely crazy." She sat on the chair, suddenly shivering, wrapping her arms around herself to try to warm up, or keep still, or something. Anything. She felt like her brain wasn't working anymore.

"I think you're going into shock, too," said the nurse, and

pushed Marisa's head gently down, between her knees. "That will help with the blood flow," said the nurse. "Do you feel a little better?"

"Yes." Marisa breathed slowly, controlling each long exhalation, trying not to hyperventilate. The Bluescreen cartel had talked to her—not just anyone, but what sounded like the lead programmer. Someone who had worked with eLiza and a man named Lal, turning a few lines of code into a criminal threat so dangerous that it terrified even him. He was so afraid of his partner he couldn't even tell her his own name. He wanted her help, but what was she supposed to do?

"Marisa!" A man's voice this time. She looked up, wild-eyed, and saw Saif running through the crowd; she jumped up so fast she got light-headed again, and he caught her and held her for a moment before pulling back slightly, studying her face, looking over her body for signs of injury. "Are you okay?"

"I don't know," she said. He was dressed simply, in dark slacks and cowboy boots and a denim shirt so pale it was almost white. She felt herself crying, and shook her head, embarrassed. "I don't know."

He took her hand. "I came as soon as I heard—I've been looking everywhere for you."

"I'm okay," she said, and remembered the dull ache in her stomach. "At least until the adrenaline wears off again."

"Again?"

"I just had kind of a big scare," she said. She looked at the bustling hallway, wishing she could take him somewhere more private to talk, not wanting to let go of his hand. Instead she just lowered her voice and leaned in closer, whispering in his ear. "One of them talked to me. One of the Bluescreen people."

"What?"

"Through Franca Maldonado—he used her as a puppet to give me a message."

"Did he threaten you?"

"No," Marisa whispered, "he asked for help. He said it's gotten too big, and he can't control it anymore. They hired Tì Xū Dāo, and it sounded like some other gangs as well, but they've slipped their chains, and now they can't control it."

"Damn it," Saif growled. "The last thing we needed was a drug war. But . . ." He paused, his teeth clenched, staring into space. Finally he shook his head. "Why you?" He looked back at her. "Why would this traitor talk to you, of all people?"

"I don't know," said Marisa, shaking her head. "But I . . . They know who I am. They saw me through your eyes last night at the VR parlor. I've been keeping my djinni off because I was afraid they'd try to kill me, but it's been back on for hours now and I'm fine. This traitor—Nils, I think—he's protecting me. He knows that I know what's going on, and he doesn't have anyone else to turn to, so he's keeping the rest of them off my back so I can do . . . I don't know. He cut the connection as soon as I said his name."

"You can't trust him," said Saif. "It's too dangerous."

"Look around," said Marisa, pulling back. "It's already too dangerous. They have to be stopped. Do you have any better ideas?"

"If he talks to you again, just . . . everything he says will be a lie, okay? Don't believe anything . . ."

Marisa watched him struggle for the right words. "What? What do you—"

"Excuse me?" A doctor had walked up next to them. "Ma'am?"

Marisa saw the sadness in the doctor's eyes, and felt a sudden flurry of nerves. What had happened to her father? She gripped Saif's hand, warm and strong, and brushed the hair from her face. "Yes?"

"Are you the young lady whose friend collapsed here in the hall?"

"What? Yes, yes of course." She felt a rush of gratitude—the bad news wasn't about her father—but then almost immediately felt guilty. Something terrible had happened to Franca. "Is she okay?"

"Do you have contact information for her family? We can't read it off her djinni, it's . . . completely bricked. And we're reading essentially zero brain activity."

Marisa inhaled sharply. "Is she dead?"

"No," said the doctor. "But her brain might be."

SEVENTEEN

Marisa's father was released six hours later; they would have held him longer, but the family couldn't afford to keep two people in the hospital at once, and Chuy's injury was worse than Carlo Magno's. They cleaned the leg, stitched the wound closed, and prescribed a painkiller strong enough to get them mugged if anyone knew they had it. All Marisa got was an antibiotic ointment and a wide bandage, covering half her stomach. Saif called a cab, and the three of them rode to the restaurant.

San Juanito was in shambles. Marisa walked through the front door in silence, looking at the bullet holes lining the walls and the splintered wood of the plastic-coated tables. Broken glass crunched under her feet. Carlo Magno hopped behind her on his crutches, and she righted a fallen chair, dusting it off so he had somewhere to sit.

"This is terrible," said Carlo Magno, chuckling softly as he collapsed into the chair. "I built this place with my bare hands."

Saif eyed him strangely. "You don't sound too broken up about it."

"I'm high," said Carlo Magno. "Ask me again when these painkillers wear off."

"Sahara's on her way," said Marisa, reading the messages that had stacked up in her djinni. "And Bao. I don't know what they're going to do, just . . . stare in shock." She laughed, though it sounded thin and desperate, with none of the drugged goofiness of her father's chuckle. "Staring is all I can seem to do."

Saif walked alongside her through the rubble. "It's not too bad," he said. "The windows are gone, sure, and that's going to be trouble if it rains, but most of the tables are okay, and almost all the chairs. If we sweep this up and give it a good scrub, you can open for business tomorrow. Put up a big banner outside that says 'Drive-by special! Half-price entrees!' Make it a survival thing, like your neighbors should all be proud to eat here because the attack couldn't keep Mirador down. They'll come because of the bullet holes, not in spite of them."

"I like this cuate, Mari," said Carlo Magno. "Where'd you find him?"

"Drinking butterscotch in a dance club," said Marisa.

"I guess I can overlook that," said Carlo Magno. "He's got a good head for business."

"Two years of business school at USC," said Saif.

"I don't think I can overlook that," said Carlo Magno with a frown. "What are you, twenty-one?"

Marisa rolled her eyes, feeling her face flush with embarrassment. "Papi . . ."

"Twenty-two," said Saif. "I did some school in India before I came here."

"Ay, hombre," said Carlo Magno, "Marisita's barely seventeen years old."

"Por favor, Papi, can we stop talking about this?"

"If you sleep with her, I'll have you locked up for statutory rape," said Carlo Magno, his speech slurring from the drugs. "Or just shoot you. I dropped my gun in the fight, can you see it anywhere? Hey you, in the denim shirt, find my gun." His eyes started to close. "I need to shoot that guy who was in here with my daughter."

"He is exceptionally doped," Saif whispered.

Marisa nodded, too embarrassed to look at him.

"He's falling asleep."

"Gracias a Dios." Marisa dragged a table closer to her father's chair, propping him against it so he wouldn't fall and hurt himself as he slept. His leg was wrapped up like a mummy—not a hard cast, but layer upon layer of thick, cloth bandages. Blood was already seeping through the inner layers, darkening the surface without discoloring it. She'd have to change his bandages when they got him home.

"I'm really sorry about this," said Saif.

"Just forget he ever said it," said Marisa.

"No," said Saif, "I mean your restaurant. The attack. The . . . everything."

Marisa looked at him, somehow looking as comfortable here in the ruins of her family restaurant as he had in the dance club, or the VR parlor, or even the hospital. He fit perfectly, everywhere he went—and she couldn't help but think about how well he had fit around her, holding her, and how well she'd fit in his arms. He'd come halfway across the biggest city in the world just to find her, just to see if she was safe.

"I punched you in the face," she said suddenly.

"What?"

She took a step toward him, reaching for the bruise on his cheekbone, the cut in the center of it barely concealed by a bandage. "I'm just . . . so sorry that I punched you in the face. I thought you were just another rich idiot, but you're really trying to help. You're trying to help *me*." She brushed his skin with her fingertips, feeling the warmth of his skin, the smoothness of it. He touched her hand with his own, staring into her eyes.

"Marisa," he started, "I—"

"Andale, gringa!" It was Anja's voice, shouting from outside. Marisa tore her eyes away from Saif's, and looked toward the door in time to see Anja walk through, followed by Sahara and Bao. They ran toward her, and she met them in the middle of the room, catching both girls in a tight embrace. "I'm so glad you're okay," said Anja.

"Your family's fine," said Sahara. Camilla and Campbell hovered in the air behind her. "Don't worry, I'm not broadcasting."

"Hey," said Bao, waving at Saif. "The dude from last night. Sorry I forgot your name."

Saif nodded toward him. "Saif."

"Yeah, I know," said Bao. "I just don't like you."

Saif pressed his lips into a thin, humorless smile.

"I got your message about Nils," said Sahara. "That must have been freaky."

"You have no idea," said Marisa. "But what really worried me came at the end: I said Nils's name, and he cut off the connection—probably because he was scared, maybe because he was found, I don't know. Whatever the reason, he severed the link to La Princesa's mind while it was still live. And she didn't come back."

"What do you mean, she didn't come back?" asked Anja. "She hasn't talked to you again?"

"Her mind hasn't come back online," said Marisa. "She's in a brain-death coma in the hospital, because the way Nils severed the link caused a glitch in her neural circuits. Bluescreen took control of her body and then never gave it back again. She's a shell." She looked at Saif, because she couldn't bear to say the next part while looking at Anja. "If the link goes down while anyone else is being controlled, I think the same thing might happen to them, too."

"That's . . ." Bao shook his head. "I speak two languages, and I don't know any words bad enough to express how bad that is."

"How many people have the malware?" asked Sahara.

"Ask the dick who sells it," said Bao, and looked at Saif. "That word's not bad enough either, but I had to say something."

"Hundreds," said Saif, "maybe thousands. Look, Mari, can I talk to you in private?"

"Anything you have to say you can say in front of all of us," said Anja. The group looked at Saif, but he only growled and looked away. "Fine," said Anja. "That's more or less what I expected." She looked at the rest of the group. "Frankly, I don't think brain death is our primary concern here: before that ever becomes an issue we have mind control, gang warfare, and world domination to deal with first. We know we can't go to the police, so who? Some random programmer on the inside? That's a great resource if we can use it, but how do we contact him? He said he'd feed you information, right? I'm not volunteering to be the next speaker he talks through and then puts into a coma."

"We could follow Tì Xū Dāo," said Sahara. "They probably went back to whoever hired them, right? That might lead us straight to Bluescreen, and then . . . I don't know. Maybe we can get a message inside somehow."

"That's not going to help," said Saif. "Even if you could find them—which you can't because you don't have their djinni IDs—what are you going to—"

"We do have their IDs," said Marisa suddenly. Her father mumbled and shifted in his chair, not quite waking up, and Marisa lowered her voice, practically bubbling over with excitement. "San Juanito has them." She ran to the corner where she'd dragged the fallen podium that contained the hostess touch screen, and stood it up with a grunt. It powered on, and she brushed away the layer of drywall dust that had settled on it after the fight. "I used the restaurant's digital marketing system to flood their vision with ads during the firefight. That means it read their IDs, just like any other storefront. They should still be in the cache." She opened the file system, found the ad board history, and scrolled through it for the time of the attack. Six names appeared, none of which she'd ever seen before, in the same block as the Maldonado enforcers who'd come to fight them off. "That's them."

"Johara's the best way to track them," said Anja. "Do you still have that back door open?"

Saif raised his eyebrow. "You have a back door into Johara? The biggest ISP in the world?"

"Not full access," said Marisa, "but we can piggyback on their positioning system to find djinnis. I've been saving it for a rainy day, never using it because there's always a risk that they'll see what we're doing and plug the hole. I'd say this is the rainy day we've been waiting for." She blinked onto Johara's website, entered the message board, and flipped the preference switches that opened the back door—a security hole in their forum that gave a user limited access to the company's tech support tools. A few seconds later she was in. "Technically speaking, this is illegal," she said. "Not just the hacking, but tracking djinnis for private use. Sahara, I need you to cover my trail."

"Already working on it," said Sahara. "Find those blowholes fast, and let's get out of here."

Marisa copied the IDs over from San Juanito's computer, and started the search. The Johara system narrowed them down slowly, pinging satellites and data centers and relay towers, leaving in each one a tiny remnant of the search itself, all evidence that could be traced back to Marisa.

"Still searching . . . ," she said, flexing her metal fingers, barely daring to breathe.

"I'm burying your server trail as well as I can," said Sahara, "but if I do much more they'll be able to just follow mine and find us anyway."

"I need to help you," said Anja.

"Keep your djinni turned off," said Marisa. "We can do this, and we can't risk losing you to Bluescreen again."

The search narrowed to North America, and then California, and then Los Angeles. Marisa watched as it sectioned off each part of the city. Los Angeles had tens of millions of people, almost all of them with djinnis, which meant there were thousands of relays and repeaters to sort through—it took time, but it would allow a very specific result when they found the target. The Johara display highlighted areas on the map, drilling down to . . .

"Mirador," said Marisa.

"Your search found us instead?" asked Bao.

"No," said Marisa, "the map's not showing San Juanito, it's . . . south, maybe a mile or two. A warehouse." She looked at him. "But it's here. The Bluescreen headquarters is right here in Mirador."

EIGHTEEN

"What do we do?" asked Bao.

"We talk to the police," said Saif. "If they're not working with Tì Xū Dāo, maybe we can trust them—"

"You keep suggesting that," said Marisa. "You know we can't trust them. Even if they hadn't warned the dealers about the drone we were using, there was a barrio-wide shootout this morning and they still haven't followed up on it. The police are out."

"And we can't go to La Sesenta, either," said Sahara, falling into her standard role as the leader. "Not after what happened last time. We have to do this ourselves. Our way."

"You want to try to hack them?" asked Anja. "The programmers who figured out how to circumvent every cyber security system in the world?"

"Not a hack," Sahara said, and looked at Bao. "An infiltration."

Bao looked at her in surprise. "You want to go inside? In

person? Did you get shot in the brain this morning?"

"No, she's right," Marisa said, and blinked on the satellite display, saving the image and cutting the connection to Johara. She looked at Sahara. "We're still hidden?"

Sahara nodded. "They'll find your search history if they're paying attention, but they won't trace it to us."

"Thanks." Marisa looked around the restaurant for a large screen, and found an undamaged TV on a side wall. She sent the satellite image to it, and the five of them stared at the top-down view of the warehouse. It had a wide stretch of pavement around the building, with a fence around that, and the roof bristled with solar trees.

"What are you trying to do?" asked Saif. "Specifically. I assume you don't want to blow it up or murder everyone inside, so . . . what? What's your endgame?"

"First we need to cut their connection to the net," said Marisa. "And then trash their system, so they can't control anybody ever again."

"They're connecting over satellites," said Anja. "See the size of that antenna? The only way to shut them down will be to cut their power."

"But look at all the solar trees on that place," said Saif. "There's no way you're killing their power supply."

"You're not thinking about the kind of hardware they've got in there," said Marisa. "The VR is probably as simple as a chair, like we used in the parlor, but the server farm they'll need to run it has got to be massive. They almost certainly supplement with an outside power source."

"Right here," said Sahara, pointing to the image. "There's a cable running into the warehouse—we cut that and we drop them to emergency levels."

Bao nodded. "And don't forget, the solar trees don't connect to the server farm through magic. There's going to be one or two heavy cables right there in the server room that we could cut once we get inside."

"Okay then," said Saif. "How are you going to get inside?"

"These people have been working closely with a Chinese gang," said Bao. "I, as you may have noticed, am Chinese. What are the odds that any given security guard employed by the Bluescreen cartel knows every Tì Xū Dāo thug by sight? It's virtually impossible. If I can get my hands on one of those goofy, spangly jackets, I'm betting I can slip in."

"That . . . shouldn't work," said Saif. "Is this a live image?"

"It was two minutes ago," said Marisa.

"Then look," said Saif, pointing at the parking lot. "This entire fenced area is crawling with people and vehicles. That's got to be Tì Xū Dāo, and I guarantee they know each other. You're not getting past them."

"Not easily," said Bao. "I haven't figured that part out yet."

"This exterior power cable probably goes right to the server room," said Anja, pointing at the screen. "With only one angle, though, I can't tell exactly where that room is. Main floor? Second floor? How many floors does this place have?" She looked around at the rest of the devastated restaurant. "How many of these screens work? Let's get some street views of this place."

"On it," said Sahara, focusing on her djinni display. "Get the screens."

Anja and Marisa leaped into action, collecting every working screen in the building, and Bao helped arrange them into a make-shift command center: two wall screens, three table menus—one with a spidery crack across the center—and the small hostess screen from the podium. Sahara connected to the San Juanito net-work and sent each screen a different image: live feeds from traffic nulis, archived street photos from the net, and even a blueprint from the construction company that built the place. Put together, they could see the building from every angle.

"Perfect," said Marisa. "Okay, so this is where the power cable comes in, on the west wall." She tapped the image on one of the table menus. That's the top floor, and from the layout of the win-dows I'd say there's only two floors inside. So the server farm is probably here, in the northwest corner, and the nearest entrance is . . . this side door."

"Almost certainly locked," said Bao. "I'll have to go in the front and find my way from there."

"Which you can't do," said Saif, "because you'll never get past the Tì Xū Dāo."

"Maybe we could distract them," said Bao. "Find some way of pulling their attention, or just completely . . . scaring them away?"

"You want to scare an armed gang?" asked Sahara. "How good at this do you think you are?"

"They've only recently hooked up with the Bluescreen cartel," said Bao. "Maybe they have a headquarters of their own some-where else in the city—we could threaten it somehow, send out a fake fire alarm or something."

"Or light a real fire," said Anja. Marisa glared at her. "What?" asked Anja. "Everything else we're doing, and arson is where you draw the line?"

"What about these loading doors in the back?" asked Sahara. "Could you get in there?"

"Maybe if you had a delivery van and a convincing invoice," said Saif. "But there's no way you could get that."

"We'd have to steal a shipment that's already coming in," said Bao, "or hack their calendar so they think one's coming in."

"Hacking's not going to work," said Marisa, staring at the screen. "Which sucks." She tapped her teeth with her metal fore-finger. "I wish we could see inside—maybe there's something there that will tip us off—some awesome something that makes this all work."

"I might be able to get Camilla close enough to peek inside," said Sahara. "Even if they shoot her down, it might be worth it for a quick look."

"And then they'd know we're coming," said Marisa, shaking her head. "We need the element of surprise."

"How about another delivery nuli?" asked Anja. "Like the one you stole last night? A random cambot would raise questions, but one with a legit logo might be able to get in. Assuming these are the type of people who order delivery."

"That . . . ," Saif growled. "Damn it, that might work."

"You don't sound very pleased," said Marisa.

"Because I don't want you to do this," said Saif. "Marisa, can we please talk?"

"A dinner delivery will work great," said Sahara. "Everyone will assume it was someone else who ordered. No one will even question it."

"Let's try it," said Marisa. "What do you think: tacos?"

"Chinese," said Anja.

"I can't decide if that's racist or not," said Bao.

"Are you kidding?" asked Anja. "Take it from an outsider—you Los Angelinos eat Chinese, like, four meals a day. Even San Juanito serves lo mein."

Bao shrugged. "Fair enough."

Marisa called up a list of Chinese restaurants with good delivery options, and read one aloud: "Fung Noodle; it's about ten miles away, which gives us time to hack into the onboard systems of whatever nuli they send. Plus it's cheap—how much are we sending them?"

"These people shot up my neighborhood," said Sahara. "No way am I buying them dinner."

"You know what?" asked Saif. "I'll pay for it. I have to admit I'm dying to see how they react to this thing."

"Wait!" shouted Marisa. "Don't turn your djinni back on!"

Saif froze, staring at her with his mouth open. "Kutte ke tatte, I totally forgot. Sorry for cussing."

"I'll ask Jaya what that means later," said Marisa. "Are you on now?"

"Yeah," said Saif, "I'm halfway through the order, just let me finish and I'll turn it back off."

"How long have you been on?"

"I got on just now," said Saif. "It's okay, I'm fine." He blinked a few more times, and then his eyes refocused on Marisa. "Done. And . . . off."

"Be careful," said Marisa softly, feeling her heart slowly return to a normal speed. "That was close, and I . . . don't want . . ." She almost said *I don't want to lose you*, but stopped herself.

"They didn't take him over," said Anja. "Why did they not have an alert for when he popped up in their system?"

"I just barely logged in," said Saif. "Maybe it . . . takes a while for my profile to pop up? Or maybe they're not even watching anymore. Maybe it's safe to use our djinnis again."

"Too risky," said Marisa. "Stay offline."

"The order just entered Fung Noodle's tracking system," said Sahara. "I'm observing but don't have any admin controls. Break out the Goblins." Marisa blinked open her Goblin file and set them loose on Fung Noodle, helping Sahara break in. They cracked the main system by the time the food was ready, and hijacked the delivery nuli halfway to the Bluescreen warehouse. They mirrored its camera to the main screen on their wall, and watched as it flew across the city, houses and palm trees and uncountable autocars zooming away beneath it.

"This almost feels too easy," said Anja. "I'm suspicious."

"I bought dinner for four," said Saif. "Told them it was the techs on the top floor. How far in do you think the nuli can get before they stop it?"

"I'll be happy with a good look at the lobby," said Bao.

"Obviously more is better, and it is a warehouse—for all we know it's open inside like a barn."

"There it is," said Marisa. She grabbed Saif's hand without thinking, so nervous she rose up on her toes. "Work," she whispered. "Just show us something we can use, that's all I ask."

Anja frowned, watching the screen as the nuli dropped down over the crowd of Tì Xū Dāo, heading for the front door. "Is that . . . ?"

"Nine hells," said Marisa, so shocked she felt the world seem to spin away beneath her, crumbling into nothingness like she was back in NeverMind and reality had failed. Standing in the lobby was a tall blond man, agitated and scared, deep in conversation with a young Mexican man: well-dressed, devilishly handsome, and impossible to trust.

She found her voice again. "Omar."

NINETEEN

"What are they saying?" asked Bao.

"I'm going to kill him," said Sahara.

"You know him?" asked Saif.

"We—" Anja stammered, "we don't know if he's working with them. Maybe he's there representing the Maldonados, negotiating a truce . . . or something . . ."

"Alone and unarmed?" asked Sahara. "Are you kidding?"

"What are they saying?" asked Bao again. "Marisa, can you get sound?"

"I . . ." Marisa felt helpless, but Bao's question gave her focus; she couldn't fathom finding Omar in the headquarters of their enemy, but manipulating a nuli to broadcast sound was simple and technical, something she could wrap her head around. "I think so. Hang on." She blinked through the nuli's remote admin controls, searching for a microphone, but found nothing.

"The nuli doesn't have anything."

"Of course it does," said Sahara. "There's always a speaker you can use to talk to the restaurant."

"It doesn't have one," said Marisa.

"What kind of backward nuli did you hack?" asked Anja.

"What else do we have?" said Sahara. "Is there another nuli nearby? I could send Camilla, but it'd be ten minutes just to get it there."

"We don't have time," said Marisa. "Let's use the . . . the Johara network again. I have Omar's ID, we can activate his mic remotely."

"That's twice as illegal as the last thing we used their network for," said Bao.

"Then cover me," said Marisa, and blinked back into the Johara network.

Saif shook his head. "If Johara finds you snooping around in their system—"

"Already in," said Mari.

Sahara growled, blinking rapidly to follow her. "Damn it, Mari, wait for me."

"No time," said Marisa, She opened the back door again and started flipping through the tech support system, looking for a remote link. "You'll have to hide two connections—me to Johara, and Omar's djinni to San Juanito."

"I can't work that fast," said Sahara.

"Just get out!" yelled Saif. "You'll get us all arrested!"

"I'll help," Anja said, and powered up her djinni.

"Anja, don't!" Marisa shouted. "This is—"

"—too important to miss," said Anja. "Now go!"

Marisa found the link, entered Omar's ID, and routed it to the San Juanito wall screen. "Ready?"

Anja blinked a final time, and she and Sahara spoke almost in unison: "Go."

Marisa activated Omar's ambient mic, and connected the link.

"—and that's unacceptable," said the blond man. "Completely unacceptable." He had a German accent, thicker than Anja's but still easy to understand.

"That must be Nils," said Sahara.

"You were supposed to provide protection," said Nils. "That's why we came to this neighborhood in the first place—because you said the local gang was under your thumb—"

"It was," said Omar, answering just as angrily, "but the Maldonados can't control La Sesenta with all our money tied up in this damn operation."

"That's what Calaca was talking about when he shook down the restaurant," said Marisa. "That the Maldonado money had dried up—"

"That's where the money went?" shouted Anja. "They're helping make Bluescreen?"

"Can you all please be quiet?" said Bao. "We can freak out about this later, let's listen to it first."

"We can't pay you," said Nils. "Lal explained this before—you made an investment, and we won't have anything to give back to you until that investment pays off. That's what an investment is."

"Your business plan didn't say anything about shooting up the barrio!" shouted Omar. "I don't care what you have to liquidate to pay us back, but you do it now—you shut this down, you sell your equipment, you get us our money."

"I don't even know if that's possible," said Nils. "I'm not the money guy—you need to be talking to Lal."

"So where is he?"

"I don't know," said Nils, and seemed to notice the nuli for the first time. "Rosa, did you order food?"

A woman answered from across the room. "No, maybe it was Steve."

"Well, get it out of here."

"Stop changing the subject," said Omar. "Where is Murali-thar?"

Rosa came into view as they talked, collecting the food from the delivery nuli. Marisa thought she maybe recognized her, but she wasn't sure; the woman was definitely Hispanic, but so was half of Los Angeles.

"I don't know," said Nils, "out with that girl he keeps talking about, maybe—I'm not his secretary. I'm a programmer, and that's all I do here."

"You mean when you're not murdering college students?" asked Omar. Nils looked shocked, and then the nuli turned and flew away, and all they had left was the audio.

"What are you talking about?"

"I'm talking about eLiza," said Omar. "Or did you think we weren't going to figure that out?"

"That wasn't me," said Nils.

"But it was your organization," said Omar. "It was your pinche

Bluescreen—just like Tì Xū Dāo is your pinche muscle."

"I didn't hire them," said Nils.

"That's not how this works!" said Omar. "You're a partner in this; you need to take responsibility—"

"You're a partner, too," said Nils. "Or your father is. I do the code; Lal does the business; your father does the money—that was our agreement, and once we finally get into Ganika we can pay you back and you can be done."

"Oh, schiess," said Anja.

"Wait, what about Ganika?" asked Omar. "What's the plan for Ganika?"

"I shouldn't have said anything," said Nils, "I'm—I'm not the business guy—"

"Stop saying that, and tell me what you know!" Omar shouted. "What is Lal planning?"

"Do you know what he'll do to me if he even finds out we've been talking?" Nils shouted. "I don't even go home anymore—I couldn't sleep if I tried. It is a nightmare in here, and we're trapped in it, and anyone who crosses Lal gets—"

The audio cut off.

"Get it back," said Sahara.

"What was he saying about Ganika?" asked Anja.

"And who's Lal?" asked Marisa. "Saif, this is the third time I've heard them talk about someone named Lal—have you ever met—whoa, are you okay?"

Saif was leaning heavily against the wall, sweating. "I'm fine."

"Are you sure?" asked Marisa, stepping toward him. She put a hand on his cheek. "You're burning up."

"Just nerves," said Saif, "this is . . . bigger than we thought it was, we need to—"

"It's way bigger," said Anja. "I'll bet you anything they were talking about the new Ganika plant in LA. That's what their whole plan has been building toward."

"We already know they're going after major corporations," said Sahara. "Like your dad and Abendroth—if they get the right people they can bypass biometric security, they can control buying and selling decisions, manipulate the world economy—"

"No," said Marisa, "she's right. Control a few djinnis and you control Abendroth, but control Ganika and you control djinnis themselves."

"Oh, scheiss," said Bao. "I assume that's an appropriate curse word for this situation?"

"If they get access to the Ganika production floor, they can do anything they want," said Anja. "They can hardwire the Bluescreen code directly into every new djinni they make. They can add it to software updates and push it out to every customer in their system. People will upload the puppet virus directly into their own heads."

"Sixty-five percent," said Sahara. "Two-thirds of the world's population, completely under Bluescreen's control."

Marisa sat down. "Now *I'm* going to be sick."

"We don't know this for sure," said Saif. "This is all just speculation—"

Anja's arm flew up in the air.

"Whoa," said Bao. "You okay?"

"I don't know—" Anja's arm twitched again, up and then out

to the side. "I don't—" Her leg twitched, so sharply she almost fell. She grabbed the nearest table for support.

Marisa stood up. "Anja, did you turn your djinni back off?"

"I'm trying," said Anja, gritting her teeth. Her knuckles were turning white where she gripped the table. "I can't . . ." Her teeth were clenched tightly together. "Move."

"We have to cut her off from the net," said Sahara. "Kill the connection—don't worry about fighting the program, just kill the connection—"

"I'm trying," said Anja again. A tear rolled down her cheek. "This isn't like before—something's different."

"You couldn't fight it before," said Marisa, crossing to her. "You're getting better at it—"

"It's not a mind," said Anja. "I can feel the difference. I'm not . . . it's not another mind forcing me out. It's an—" She went limp, staying on her feet, but with all the tension flowing out of her muscles in a rush. She straightened up, and her head swiveled, surveying the room.

And then she attacked.

TWENTY

Anja went after Sahara first, lashing out with her elbow and smashing her in the side of the head. As Sahara reeled back, both from the blow and the surprise, Anja leaped forward, pulling away from Marisa's shocked grip to keep the pressure on Sahara, hitting her again in the head, keeping her unbalanced, and then, when the opportunity came, punching Sahara powerfully in the throat. Sahara staggered against a chair, tripping over it backward as she gasped for breath, and smacked her head against the floor. She was unconscious before the others could even react.

Marisa was next. Anja turned and ran back toward her, and Marisa put her arms up in front of her face just in time to block a flurry of blows. Anja's fists slammed into Marisa's forearms, shaking her entire body. Bao leaped in from the side, trying to grab Anja and pull her away, and Anja turned her attention to him, striking back viciously, driving him back against the wall. He was only trying to stop Anja from attacking; he wasn't prepared to actually hit her back. Marisa tried to gather her thoughts, looking for a good course of action. Should she tackle her? Could the three of them hold her down without hurting her? Sahara was the only one in their group with any combat training, and she was already down.

"Anja!" Marisa shouted, but shook her head immediately. There was no sense trying to talk to her, as it wasn't Anja doing it—it was someone controlling her, a Bluescreen puppet master. "Nils!" she said. "Or Lal! Stop this, please! Let her go, and let's talk!" Anja didn't even slow her assault, punching Bao until her knuckles bled. Marisa screamed: "Say something!"

Anja's attacks were fierce, but raw; even Marisa could tell that whoever was controlling her wasn't a real fighter, just a berserker trying to cause damage. Someone who could afford to swing too hard, to drop his defense too often, to leave himself open to injury because the body that got damaged could be discarded when he was done.

Bao dodged the next punch, and Anja's fist hit the screen behind him, so hard Marisa thought she could hear the hand break. The screen cracked and the image disappeared.

"Lal!" Marisa screamed. "You're going to kill her."

Whoever was controlling Anja didn't give any sign that they had heard her . . . but Anja had said it didn't feel like it had before. She'd felt something trying to take over, and she could tell it was somehow different from a human controller. What else was there? An AI? True AI didn't exist—nuli control programs, sure, but nothing that could think. Marisa shook her head. This was something simpler, something rudimentary. Something that could carry out a single command: attack.

Anja had been taken over by an algorithm.

"What's happening?" said Saif. His eyes were wide, his mouth hanging open in terror.

"Help me stop her," Marisa said, and dove back into the fight, grabbing Anja from behind, wrapping her arms around her to hold her still. Anja responded by slamming her head backward, smashing Marisa's face. Marisa lost her grip and staggered back, then launched herself forward again, too dazed to see clearly, knowing she had to move fast before Anja had a chance to move away. She caught her again, lower this time, and held on tight while Anja pummeled her mercilessly with her elbows. Marisa felt Anja's weight shift suddenly, and Bao shouted.

"I've got her legs," he said. "Drop her!"

Marisa let go, and Anja fell backward, landing heavily on her back. She groaned, a sound more painful than Marisa had ever heard, and Marisa backed away in horror at what she'd just done to her friend.

Anja slowly climbed back to her feet.

"Grab her again," said Bao, diving forward.

"We're going to kill her," said Marisa. "She's going to kill herself!"

"So grab her and stop her!" said Bao. "We need to tie her down so we can figure out how to—"

Anja landed a kick on his head, snapping his head back and dropping him to the ground. He didn't move.

"Please, Lal," said Marisa. "Please don't do this."

Anja walked toward her, limping, bleeding, so damaged she shouldn't even be walking, but the algorithm wouldn't let her stop.

"We have to trick it," said Marisa suddenly. "We have to make it think it's won—"

Anja punched her again, rocking Marisa's head to the side, and it was all too easy to slump to the side, falling to the ground, pretending that Anja had defeated her. Anja swayed in the middle of the room, surveying the destruction. Bodies lay in crumpled heaps in a chaos of broken walls and overturned chairs.

Stop now, Marisa thought. *It's over. Stop, and let go of Anja. Let her go to sleep. Let her turn off her djinni.*

Anja turned, and shuffled toward the door. Marisa's voice caught in her throat, terrified to let her go, even more terrified to call her back. Anja walked outside, and was gone.

"She'll get herself killed," Marisa sobbed. "We have to stop her."

"You can't stop them all," said Saif. He was shaking his head, staring at the floor. "They're everywhere. All over the city. Every Bluescreen user in Los Angeles—they're under control now." His eyes focused on Marisa. "The city is burning. They're an army, and they're destroying everything."

Marisa struggled to sit up, her head still reeling from the head-butt. It felt like Anja had broken her nose. "What are they doing?"

"I don't know!" said Saif. "I don't even know how they're doing it! There's nothing in the code that should allow for this."

"How do you know?"

Saif turned on her, and Marisa looked at him, her head slowly clearing, and the question grew more terrifying with every second.

How did he know? She could hear screams outside, screams and cries and shattering glass. Anja, and others; every Bluescreen user in the city.

Except one.

"I told you I needed to talk to you," said Saif. "Now I need you more than ever. I don't know code—you do. You can help us figure this out, and stop it."

Marisa's heart sank, and then seemed to stop altogether. She looked at Saif and forced out the question she could barely stand to think:

"You're connected to the net. You're reading the news—that's how you know all of this. But if every Bluescreen user in the city is affected, if they've all turned into puppets at once in one giant attack . . . why not you?"

"I thought you were just some kid," said Saif, "some party girl with more guts than sense, but you're brilliant, Mari. Do you realize what we could do if we worked together?"

"You lied to me," she said. "You're not infected with Bluescreen at all—you never were. You faked it to make me trust you, and then you gave me all this information and asked all these questions, and . . ." She shook her head. She could barely believe it. "You've been lying the whole time. Everything we've done together, everything we ever tried, they've adapted so quickly we couldn't keep up. We followed them with a drone, and they figured it out. We found their headquarters, and made a plan to get inside, and you listened to all of it, using us to find the holes in your security."

"Think about it, Mari!" His terrified desperation was giving way to anger, as if volume and force could convince her as effectively as reason. "The world is upside down—it's not even upside down anymore, it's shattered, it's unrecognizable. I was just as poor as you, a dead-end street rat with nothing to eat, and nowhere to go, and a hundred years ago we might have been part of a communist revolution, taking back the power from the oligarchs on top to the workingman who makes it all possible. But there isn't a working-man anymore. Machines make it possible, nulis and autocars and automated factories, and nobody has anything but the people on the top. Bluescreen was our ticket to change that. To take back the power and—"

"And what?" asked Marisa. "To become the new oligarchs? To rob from the rich and give to yourself and kill anyone who gets in your way?"

"Revolutions are bloody," said Saif. "As bad as this has been, it's still one of the cleanest in history."

"If you think—"

"If you want to add more compassion, bring more compassion!" He stepped toward her, eyes wide and pleading. "That's what I'm telling you—what I've been trying to tell you all day. You can help us, Marisa, you've more than proved it. Help me build a better world."

"What happened to Anja?" Marisa demanded.

"I have no idea—that's the first thing we can do together, solve that puzzle. But we have to do it now, they're all over the city and it's going to be ruined—"

"Anja didn't attack you," said Marisa. "Somehow she knew not to. It's part of the algorithm."

"There is no algorithm." Saif stood up. "You don't understand—"

"I understand everything," said Marisa, her voice quivering with despair. "You have a glitch in your ID. I saw it the very first night, and I didn't think anything about it, but you're . . ." Her voice was a heartbroken whisper. "You're Lal."

He turned and walked to the door, pausing before he opened it. "I have to stop this, with or without you." His shoulders straightened and he pushed open the door and walked away.

TWENTY-ONE

The world had gone mad.

Marisa could hear screaming outside—some from pain, some from terror, all of it helpless and desperate and confused. How many people had been taken over? Saif—no, Lal—said—

Marisa's breath caught again. She had trusted him.

He had only been using her.

If they wanted power, why kill Anja? It had never made sense. Now she knew it was just another way of using her. Running her through the streets hadn't been a murder attempt, but a . . . distraction, maybe? What had he been doing while they chased her? Marisa rubbed her eyes and blinked into Sahara's video archive. Camilla had stayed behind at the club, passively observing. She found the footage, opened it up, and watched.

Lal Muralithar, the man she had known as Saif, watched them go, gave a Bluescreen drive to La Princesa, and then plugged another one into the Synestheme. Dozens of people were connected throughout the club, and a few seconds later they all passed out, one at a time, slumping to the side in their chairs. He had risked Anja's life, and Sahara's and Marisa's, not to keep a secret or save his own life, but to gain a few extra puppets. She closed her eyes, feeling too broken to move.

Bao stirred.

"Oh my gosh," said Marisa. She wiped her face with the back of her hand, and crawled toward him through the rubble. "Bao, are you okay? I thought she broke your neck."

Bao groaned. "I kind of wish she had." He tried to sit up, winced, and lay back down. "My brain feels like a milk shake."

"He betrayed us," said Marisa, practically choking on the words.

"Saif?"

"Saif is Lal Muralithar," said Marisa. "The mastermind behind the whole thing."

"Good," said Bao, wincing. "Now I don't have to feel guilty about hating him."

"He killed eLiza," said Marisa, "but not until after he used her. He was using us the same way. I'm such an idiot, Bao, I've ruined everything."

"Don't," said Bao, suddenly serious. "Don't blame yourself for this."

"The whole time it was him, and I didn't—"

"There was no way you could have known," said Bao. "This is not your fault."

Marisa shook her head, wiping her eyes with the hem of her

tattered San Juanito T-shirt. Bao looked at her a moment longer, then groaned and rolled over, surveying the room more closely.

"What about Sahara?" He crawled toward her on his hands and knees, and Marisa followed numbly. He checked her pulse, and sighed in relief as he probed the back of her head. "She's got a big bump back here, but I think she's okay."

"We have to help Anja," said Marisa. "But I don't know how. Is she out there attacking more people? Is she dead?"

Bao shot her a worried glance. "What happened after I got knocked out?"

"I faked unconsciousness, and she left," said Marisa, sniffing and wiping her eyes again. "The thing that took her over was an algorithm, and I don't know what it's trying to do. Neither did Lal. Attack us, or everyone? Did she leave to find more victims, or is she going somewhere? I don't know what to—"

She froze, suddenly, hearing a noise by the door—not the screams that seemed to fill the air, but a scrape or a slide, closer than the voices. A footstep, maybe. It came again, and Bao's head shot up. They glanced at each other, then back at the door.

A step, and a long, dragging limp. Someone was coming.

"Get behind me," Marisa whispered.

Bao shook his head. "I'm not going to let you—"

"You're hurt," Marisa insisted, moving past him as quietly as she could. Was Anja back, or was this someone else? Lal? Tì Xū Dāo? A looter? Her father was still sitting by the door, slumped and unconscious from the drugs. Was he in danger? Maybe the intruder wasn't dangerous at all—maybe it was Sandro, or Gabi, coming from the house. But wouldn't they have called first, or at least sent a ping? What if they were—

A handgun barrel came through the door first, millimeter by millimeter, long and silver and lined with blinking lights, humming just loud enough to hear in the silent room. A rail gun, like the gangsters had used. Behind it came a hand, and then an arm, bronze and tattooed, and before the head and body even appeared the arm swiveled directly toward Marisa, the gun pointed at her chest. She planted herself in front of Bao, and stifled a gasp as Calaca, bleeding and haggard, limped the rest of the way through the door.

"Buenas noches, Marisita," said Calaca. His eerie demeanor was cracked and splintered, the menacing calmness barely concealing a fierce anger. "I apologize for any inconvenience I'm about to cause you, but you have information I need, and I don't have time to ask nicely."

"I don't know anything—"

Calaca fired his gun, the noise deafening in the enclosed room, the magnetically accelerated bullet tearing through the air so close to her head she could feel the heat of it. She fell to the side, clutching her ear, eyes wide with fear. Bao grabbed her shoulders, holding her tightly, but neither of them dared to speak again.

"You did not let me finish," said Calaca. His voice had the familiar cadence he always used—bizarrely calm and erudite—but with a raw, angry undercurrent breaking through. "I just had to beat up my own sister, and tie her to a chair to keep her from killing her own kids, so you'll excuse me if I am impatient. Before we begin I consider it prudent to establish some ground rules, so listen carefully. I'm going to ask a question, and you're going to answer it, and that's the only thing allowed in the room: you and me, questions and answers. Anything that comes out of your mouth that does not answer my question will get shot at. Here's the first question, as a trial run of this process: Is that clear?"

Marisa nodded.

"It's okay to say it out loud," said Calaca, "as that is the purpose of this exercise. Let's try again: Is that clear?"

"Yes," said Bao, "but we—"

Calaca fired again, and Marisa dropped to the floor, covering her head. As soon as she realized she wasn't hit she spun around, terrified to see Bao with a bullet in his forehead, but he was fine—cowering, like she was, but unhurt. Behind them, the last of the wall screens had gone black, the hole in the center of the fractured screen gently smoking. She turned slowly back to Calaca.

"You said two words that weren't part of an answer," said Calaca. "Count yourself lucky that I was able to shoot the screens without hitting you—despite my extensive training with firearms, I can't guarantee that I'll be so lucky in the future." He glanced at the broken windows, then back at Marisa. "Now. As mentioned previously I'm in something of a hurry. This is the second time today that our barrio's been attacked, and you know something about it. You're the one who tipped us off about Bluescreen, and we've been doing our due diligence with that information, and now every single person I know who's taken the drug—including my sister—is attacking people. Something's going on. Answer carefully: Do you know what it is?"

Marisa stared back, trying to think of how to answer. He wanted to know where the Bluescreen headquarters was, but if she told him he'd go there in force, with all of La Sesenta's gun's blazing, and they'd shut it down through violence. With thousands of puppets connected to the server, a sudden shock like that would put them all into the same, brain-dead coma as La Princesa—thousands and thousands of people. She couldn't let that happen. They'd start a fight with Tì Xū Dāo, and it would only get worse from there.

Is that what the algorithm was doing—protecting the programmers?

She realized with a start that some of the screens in the room were still showing the Bluescreen warehouse. She glanced at Bao. The wall screens were all broken, but if Calaca looked at one of the smaller ones . . .

"It appears you've found a loophole in my instructions," said Calaca. "Allow me to close it. If I ask a question and you say nothing, I'll shoot your father." He moved his handgun, pointing it at the sleeping Carlo Magno, and Marisa started talking desperately.

"I know some of it," she said quickly. While she talked, she blinked into the San Juanito network controls, trying to replace all the screen images before he saw them. There were four left, and she went to work while she talked. "Bluescreen is a drug that installs a control program in your djinni, allowing someone else to take control of your body, like a puppet. I don't know why all the puppets are attacking, or who's controlling them."

One screen down.

"But you see," said Calaca, gesturing with the rail gun, "I don't believe that you don't know who's behind it. You seem to know everything these days, and your brother Chuy can't stop talking about how brilliant his little sister is. So let me ask you specifically: who's controlling the puppets?"

"We don't know," said Bao. Calaca aimed the gun at Carlo Magno again.

"His name is Lal," said Marisa. "He works with a man named Nils, but we've only ever found them online—never in the real world—"

"Online is the real world," said Calaca. "Find them in one and you find them in the other." He pointed the gun back at her, taking two steps forward. "Or are you trying to tell me that our friendly neighborhood hacker girl couldn't find one little drug dealer?"

Two screens down.

"One little drug *programmer*," said Marisa. "I'm a hacker, but I'm small time—these are big fish, swimming in some very deep water, and they have fought back against every attempt I've ever made to try to find them. One time I followed them with a nuli, and not only did they kill the nuli, they traced my satellite connection and almost found me. I had to burn a whole server just to get away." She hadn't told him everything, but everything she'd told him had been true. She prayed that it would be enough.

Calaca stared at her a minute, the gun not even wavering. Marisa watched his eyes, waiting for the telltale twitch that he was about to pull the trigger. He stared back, practically boiling with fury, and abruptly flicked his eyes to the right, looking over her shoulder at Bao. "Is she telling the truth?"

"Yes," said Bao.

Three screens down.

Calaca roared in anger. "I need to know where they are! This is my pinche neighborhood, and I'm not going to stand by while some cabrón tears it apart. If what you say is true, all we have to do is find these people, and then it's game over for them. We cut off the connection, and everyone they control goes back to normal. Am I understanding the situation correctly?"

She changed the final screen, praying that she'd done it right, switching the satellite image of the warehouse with one so similar he wouldn't notice that she'd been trying to hide anything. All the screens were clear.

He took another step toward her. "You tell me how to save my sister, or I will drop you right where you are, and everyone else in this room with you."

"I don't know!" Marisa cried.

He stalked forward, pressing the rail gun barrel directly against her head. "You have to know! You—" And then he stopped, his mouth open, staring at the table behind her. "What's that?"

She'd missed a screen.

She turned. The menu screen on the table had been damaged, the surface splintered and cracked so much that the network couldn't even talk to it. She'd thought it was broken. But the image was still there, fractured but visible.

"Marisa Carneseca," said Calaca, staring at the surveillance image. "You've been lying to me. I'm honestly kind of impressed; that takes balls."

"I didn't mean to—"

He shot, and Marisa dropped to the floor in pain. Her eyes refused to focus, seeing a double image of Calaca saying something else; she couldn't hear what it was, her ears still ringing from the sound of the gunshot. Calaca turned and walked out, and Bao rushed to Marisa's side.

She tried to push him away, but only one of her arms worked. The bullet had destroyed her prosthetic arm. She looked down at her torso, expecting to see a pool of blood and viscera, but all she found was a bruise. The SuperYu had stopped the bullet.

"Are you okay?" asked Bao.

Marisa couldn't find the words to answer him. Her entire world seemed to be falling apart.

Bao touched the twisted arm gingerly; the force of the bullet had bent it to a hideous angle, slagging the circuits and crippling the motors. Her side felt like she'd fallen off a roof, but nothing had broken the skin. "This hunk of junk saved your life," said Bao. "That new Jeon you used to have never would have stopped a bullet like that."

"I can't do this," said Marisa, shaking her head. "This is too much. Calaca and Lal and Nils and Omar and Tì Xū Dāo and who knows how many thousands of puppets. They're better hackers than I am, they have more guns than I do, they have more everything." She shook her head, tears collecting in her eyes. "I can't do it."

"You have friends," said Bao. He tried to lift her, but she pushed him away again, so he simply slid down the wall to sit beside her. "You're one person, but together there's two of us. Wake up Sahara and there's three. Call in Jaya and Fang, and we're five. Cure Anja and we're six."

"I can't cure Anja."

289

"Not yet," said Bao, "but we can figure it out. We can do this."

Marisa shook her head. "No we can't! I'm a teenage girl, for crying out loud—I'm not a hero, I'm not a fighter, I'm barely even a hacker after the last few days. Everything I've touched has gone wrong. Everyone I've tried to help I've failed."

"I don't know who you're talking about," said Bao.

"I'm talking about me, la Reina Idiota—"

"I watch every one of your games," said Bao.

Marisa stopped, confused. "What?"

"Your Overworld games," said Bao. "I haven't missed one since you entered the league."

"You . . . don't even have a djinni."

"There's a bar downtown that shows them on a big screen," said Bao. "I even have one of those Cherry Dogs logo hats—not just my fake hat, but real branded merchandise."

"Okay," said Marisa, "but . . . what does that have to do with anything?"

"Your Overworld persona is a hero," said Bao. "Heartbeat is a hero. Calaca's a psychopath, but he was right about one thing— the internet is the real world. What you do there matters, and what you do here matters. I've seen you spend days nursing a sick sister back to health; I've seen you work triple shifts in this restaurant to pay your family's mortgage. You took Gabi to ballet when your parents were too scared to send her. Three nights ago you ran into the middle of a freeway to rescue your friend. You're not just a hero, Mari, you're my hero. If anyone can figure this out, it's you."

Marisa put her arm around him, a couple of tears rolling

down her face, though this time they didn't come from despair. "That's the cheesiest thing anyone's ever said to me," she said. He smirked, and she smiled back. "Thanks."

"I try," said Bao.

"Don't worry," said Marisa, pulling away to wipe at her eyes. "You've convinced me. But if we're going to do this, we need all the help we can get."

Sahara groaned, and rolled on her side.

"Just in time," Marisa said, and crawled to Sahara's side. Her broken arm dragged behind her, twisted and useless; if she was going to do this, she'd have to take it off. She smiled grimly at the image: a one-armed girl taking on two rabid gangs and a deadly cartel. She laughed.

Bao followed her to Sahara's side. "Is that a confident laugh, or a just-slipped-off-the-deep-end laugh?"

"I was just thinking," said Marisa, disconnecting the main coupling from her prosthetic. The tangled wires pulled taut, and she ripped them free with a final tug. "I'm literally going to beat them with one hand tied behind my back."

"So," said Bao. "Just-slipped-off-the-deep-end it is."

Sahara groaned again, her eyes fluttering behind her eyelids. Marisa took her hand and shook her gently by the shoulder.

"Wake up, babe," she said. "We've got a game to plan."

TWENTY-TWO

"Everybody here?" asked Marisa. She was upstairs in Sahara's bedroom, changing out of her tattered, bloody T-shirt while Sahara and Bao waited in the room beyond. All the Cherry Dogs were patched into a call, preparing for battle.

Jaya's voice was clear as crystal over the djinni. "Ready to go."

"Ready to tear Lal a new anus," said Fang.

"I'm ready too," said Bao, grouped into the call over his handheld phone. "But less graphically than Fang is."

"I think I'm still seeing double," said Sahara, "but I'm ready."

"We don't have a lot of time to plan," said Marisa, looking in Sahara's closet. Most of her clothes were too flashy, but the back of her closet held the perfect standby: black shirt, and a black leather jacket. She pulled them on as she talked, struggling with only one arm. "La Sesenta is headed for Bluescreen's headquarters, and Tì Xū Dào is already there, and that's going to be enough of a bloodbath even without Maldonado's enforcers, plus the news feeds are showing all the Bluescreen puppets converging on Mirador. This has to be where they're going—some kind of failsafe defense mechanism, I guess, to protect the programmers? I don't know why they're doing it, but if we don't find a way to stop it fast, thousands of people could die or be permanently catatonic, including Anja."

"The good news," said Bao, "is that all the plans we made before are pretty much screwed."

"How is that good news?" asked Jaya.

"Because Lal has no idea what we're going to do instead," said Marisa. "He was using us to identify holes in his security—we just have to hope we didn't find all of them."

"If La Sesenta and the Maldonados are heading there," mused Sahara, "we don't have to have to worry about being subtle anymore."

"She's right," said Jaya. "We've got the best distraction we could ever ask for, so let's take advantage of it."

"There has to be a back door to this place," said Fang.

"There is," Bao confirmed. "The side entrance we spotted when we were first surveying the warehouse. If we can ensure a big enough commotion out front, I'm sure we could slip in there without attracting too much attention, even if there are alarms."

Fang laughed. "If we're going that far, let's go all the way. Set off every alarm they have—even if they follow up on some of them, they can't handle all of them."

"That's perfect," said Marisa. "Especially if we can force them to follow up on one or two in particular—breach the front door so dramatically that they can't help but leave the back door for later."

"There's a gang war on their doorstep," said Sahara. "Do we really need to add more distractions?"

"If they're smart, the guards in the building aren't involved with the gang war—they're waiting for the building to be breached. As soon as we open the back door, they'll head straight to it, unless we can convince them that another breach is more important."

"I think we can pull that off," said Sahara. "We're going big, right? No pulling punches?"

"As big as we can make it," said Marisa. She finished changing, and stepped back into the main room with Bao and Sahara.

"Looking good," said Sahara. "So check this out: after our chase through the freeway the other night, I started studying autocar swarm algorithms, to see if there was any safer way we could have saved Anja. Like reviewing an Overworld mission—old habits die hard, I guess. I don't think we can mess with the swarm, because it has too many backups—that's the point of a swarm AI, to let each car support the others. But if we can cut a car off from the swarm, we could drive it right through the front door."

"I love you," said Fang.

Marisa felt suddenly short of breath, and she reached instinctively for her prosthetic arm. Her hand closed on the loose, empty leather of the jacket sleeve, which only made her feel more anxious. "You mean . . . drive a car? Manually?"

"Not in person," said Sahara. "The controls are all electronic, so we can reroute them to anywhere."

Fang was almost breathless. "Pick me pick me pick me!"

Marisa was still leery of the idea. "Those are dangerous."

"What's the worst that could happen?" asked Fang. "I'm *supposed* to crash it."

"What car are you planning to use?" asked Bao.

"I don't have time to reroute the controls *and* hack the access, so it has to be one I already have the codes for," said Sahara, and her face twisted into a malicious grin. "That leaves Marisa's dad's . . . or Omar's."

"Did I tell you I love you?" said Fang. "Because I love you."

Marisa couldn't help but mirror Sahara's grin. "That is the first step of a very long and painful reckoning for that boy. I love it. But Fang, don't hurt anyone—our goal is to reduce casualties, not add more."

"Got it."

"I just called the car," said Sahara. "Turns out he doesn't have it with him at the warehouse—he probably went in something less recognizable, trying to stay incognito. That means it'll be here in about two minutes, and then it'll be ten more minutes to get us to the warehouse. If I can work while it's driving, I can do most of this hack job on the way, and then hand control over to Fang when we get there."

"Twelve minutes might be too late," said Marisa, clenching her teeth. "But—" She looked up. "I doubt we can get started much earlier than that anyway. Let's do it."

"We still need more distractions," said Bao. "This plan only works if we overwhelm their security staff."

"They'll have plenty of online alarms," said Jaya. "I can work on those from here."

"You won't get in," said Marisa.

"I don't have to," said Jaya, "I just have to set off the alarms and distract them, right?"

"Protect yourself as much as you can," said Marisa. "False servers, decoy accounts, bounced signals—everything you can possibly think of. These are the best coders I've ever come up against, and if they trace you, it will hurt."

"Already working on it," said Jaya. "Let me know when to pull the trigger."

"What else?" asked Sahara. "I'm trying to remember the satellite images, and I'm pretty sure there were some proximity alarms around the fence."

"Trip them all with nulis," said Fang.

"No good," said Marisa. "We used a nuli to spy on the building before—Lal will be ready if we try it again."

"All the better to distract him," said Bao. "Show him exactly what he's expecting to see."

"Good enough for me," said Sahara. "If they're looking at an army of nulis swarming in, that makes it easier for us to reach the building without being recognized."

"Forget 'recognized,'" said Bao. "I want to get in there without even being seen."

"How?" asked Marisa. "It's barely twilight, and there are least two gangs between the gate and the building. That's a lot of people to see us."

"We could go through the back fence," said Sahara. "Or maybe over it."

Marisa shook her head. "Every side of the property that doesn't touch the street fronts against another industrial property. We don't have time to research those other places' security systems, let alone figure out how to break through them *and* Bluescreen's in the next twelve minutes."

"Eleven," said Sahara.

"So we go in the car," said Bao. "Instead of getting out when we reach the gate, we can stay inside while she circles the building. If everyone's in front fighting, we can get out in the back without anyone seeing."

"Especially if our army of nulis gets there first," said Sahara. "Maybe we can use them to take out the security cameras or something."

Marisa felt that wave of fear again, like a tightness in her chest. "Staying in the car while a human is driving it is *not safe*."

"Omar's car is bulletproof," said Bao. "Even on manual controls, it'll be safer to drive past a gunfight than run past one."

"You don't understand," said Marisa, her voice rising. "You don't know what happens to one of these things in an accident—"

"I know what you went through," said Sahara, putting her hand on Marisa's. "I know what you must be feeling to confront such a long-standing fear. But this is a good plan, and I'll be with you the whole time."

"I'll only be driving you for a hundred meters," said Fang. "Maybe a hundred and fifty. We'll pass the gangsters, you'll jump out in back, and then I'll circle back to the front. I'll hit the lobby the same time you hit the back door, causing enough damage that they're sure to come to me instead of you."

"We can do this," said Bao. "I know it's risky, but we can do it. We have to do it."

Marisa closed her eyes.

"You know I hate saying this," said Sahara, "but . . . play crazy."

Marisa felt the empty left sleeve of her jacket, imagining the human arm that she couldn't even remember anymore. She was only two years old when that car accident spun her world off its axis; her few remaining memories were fragmented and terrifying.

I can do this, she told herself. *It's just another game of Overworld.*

"Car's here," said Sahara. "We don't have time to wait."

"Let's go," said Marisa, standing up. She clenched her hand into a fist, and then put it into the middle of the room, palm down. "Cherry Dogs forever."

Sahara put her hand on Marisa's. "Cherry Dogs forever." Fang and Jaya echoed the phrase over their djinnis, and Bao hesitated just a moment before adding his hand to the stack.

"Cherry Dog for one evening," he said. "Let's go save Anja so she can have her spot back."

"You don't get out that easy," said Marisa, squeezing his fingers. "You're on the team for good now—an honorary member." She put her arm around him and started toward the door. "We'll be the only team in the league with six players."

"And the only team in the world with a player who doesn't have a djinni," said Sahara, following them down the stairs. "Five women and one caveman."

Omar's Futura Baron was waiting for them on the curb, as attentive to Omar's access code as it ever was to Omar. They got in, gave it an address a few blocks away from the warehouse, and told it to hurry. While Sahara plugged herself in to the command core, Marisa blinked online and got to work on the fleet of nulis.

"Can you hack that many nulis that fast?" asked Bao.

"Not a chance," said Marisa. "We're doing this the old-fashioned way—we're paying them." She searched for every window washing company she could find and started placing rush orders for the warehouse: get to this address right now and give it the full treatment. She bought the largest service packages they had, paid extra for immediate service, and sent them off, wave after wave, hundreds of window-washing robots converging on the cartel like a plague of locusts. It cost thousands of dollars—money Marisa didn't have—but she didn't care anymore. She'd deal with that later, and with Omar, and with everything else. She realized with a shock that they hadn't even planned an escape route—they were putting everything on the line. All that mattered was saving the people, and stopping the war.

They heard the gunshots long before they reached the warehouse. The streets looked like the world had ended; cars were stopped, windows and doors were broken, and bodies lay strewn across the parking lots and sidewalks like broken dolls. Marisa wondered if they were dead, or beaten unconscious by the Bluescreen puppets.

The puppets were the most terrifying part of the scene—hundreds of them, some running toward the warehouse fence, some walking stiffly, some only crawling on limbs too damaged to walk. Marisa looked for Anja, but couldn't see her in the crowd. Some of them chased the car, but only vaguely; most were marching toward the Bluescreen warehouse with a grim, mindless obsession.

"What are they doing?" asked Bao.

"This can't be about protection," said Fang. "The best protection Bluescreen had was secrecy, and they just blew that."

"Lal claimed he didn't know what was going on," said Marisa. "Maybe this is a glitch? A malfunction in the virus."

"Or another virus," said Bao, "infecting the first." The thought made Marisa shiver.

"Done," said Sahara. She looked up from her coding and grimaced. "Just in time for the apocalypse, apparently."

The Baron pulled to a smooth stop five blocks from the warehouse. More of the Bluescreen puppets took notice and started walking toward them.

"We didn't count on this many of them," said Bao. "Fang, are you going to be okay driving through this crowd? They might not jump out of the way like the others will."

"Ten more seconds and it's not going to matter," said Fang. "Hold on."

The car lurched forward and stopped abruptly. Sahara fell off the bench, and Marisa caught her, bracing herself in place with her feet.

"Sorry," said Fang. "I've never been a car before."

"*Been* one?" asked Marisa.

"That was the easiest way to fake the controls," said Sahara. "She's not using a control panel, she's literally jacked in, like a VR game."

A glassy-eyed teen beat his fist against the car window, a larger group right behind him, and the car lurched forward again, leaving them behind and weaving through the crowded street. "Just don't forget that this isn't a game," said Bao, gripping a cup holder for stability. "We're actually in this thing."

"I'm fine," said Fang, though her voice was strained. "Stop distracting me."

Marisa held Sahara's hand as tightly as she could, forcing herself to take slow, deep breaths as the car got faster and faster. "Jaya, you ready?"

"Ready enough."

"Hit it." Marisa couldn't see it, but she knew that the digital onslaught Jaya unleashed on the Bluescreen servers was working its way through their system now. The car sped up, swerving more wildly.

"You weren't kidding about these guys' cyber security," said Jaya. "This is crazy. I feel like I'm—holy crap—I feel like I'm being bombed."

"You okay?" asked Marisa.

"I'm hanging on," Jaya grunted. "You?"

"Stop talking!" said Fang. "This is harder than it looks—"

The gunfire grew louder, and the crowd thicker, and Fang accelerated suddenly, leaping the curb with a rattling bump, and roaring through the open gate. The space inside the fence was filled with gangsters, running and shooting and crouching for cover behind bullet-riddled cars, both sides retreating toward the building as the Bluescreen puppets advanced across the yard. Fang swung sharply to the left, hugging the outer edge of the compound as she angled a wide right turn toward the side of the building. Marisa hung on, pressing herself into the corner of the seat and praying the car wouldn't roll over. A bullet slammed into the window and she almost screamed, and then a barrage of alarms leaped up in her djinni, scaring her even worse. But they were just service alerts from the window washers: the nulis had arrived. She craned her neck to look up and saw the sky over the warehouse fill up with quadcopter robots, racing toward the windows and doors, spraying them with foam and water, attacking them with articulated rubber wipers. Fang zoomed around the first corner of the building and slowed slightly; the side door was there, waiting on the back of the west wall. The side of the car slid open, the noise of the battle suddenly growing louder and more terrifying. Marisa watched the asphalt speed by in a blur, and pressed herself against the seat, practically climbing up on the bench to get as far from the open door as possible.

"Slow down," said Sahara, "we can't jump at this speed."

Fang hit the brakes, a little too abruptly, and they tumbled to the floor of the car. "Hit the ground the same way," said Bao. "Rolling absorbs the impact."

"I'm not ready," said Marisa. Her muscles felt locked and rigid; she couldn't move if she wanted to. Sahara and Bao grabbed her together and pulled her out of the speeding car.

Marisa hit the ground with a scream, scraping and rolling and tumbling across the rough asphalt. She covered her head with her arm, and even when she stopped moving the world seemed to keep spinning around her. Her torso ached, the new bruise throbbing on one side and the jagged scab tearing with her movement on the other. She took a deep breath, clearing her head, and staggered to her feet. Bao was nearby, and she helped him stand up.

"Thanks," she said. "The door's there." Sahara caught up to them, Campbell and Camilla hovering over her, and together they ran toward the cloud of window nulis jockeying for position to wash the back door.

"There's like ten doors back here," said Fang. "I just passed them, on my way back around to the front."

"Mierda," said Marisa, panting as they ran. "I forgot about those—there's a whole row of loading doors back there."

"We have to breach every door we can," said Sahara. "If we only hit two they'll know exactly where to look."

"Can the nulis do it?" asked Bao.

"Not the window washers," said Marisa. They had almost reached the back door.

"Maybe one of the camera nulis," said Sahara, "but I don't know how, and we don't have a lot of time to figure it out."

"Take the gun," said Bao, handing it over to Sahara. "You two go through the side door, just like we planned; I'll head to the loading doors and . . . improvise. We have about thirty seconds." He flashed a split-second grin, then turned and sprinted toward the back of the building.

Marisa ran to the side door, but saw a movement from the corner of her eye. She looked toward the front of the building and saw three Tì Xū Dāo gangsters running toward them. "That's not good."

Sahara joined her by the wall, looking down at the gun in her hands and then back up at the thugs. "They must have followed the car."

"Maybe they're just running away from the fight," said Marisa.

One of them raised a gun and fired, barely missing them. "Okay then. Maybe we're just screwed."

"Hurry up, Fang," said Sahara. She reached the wall, Marisa right behind her, taking what shelter they could from the swarm of nulis trying to polish the door. The gangster fired again, and one of the nulis exploded in a shower of sparks and plastic fragments. "Any time you're ready."

"Not yet," said Marisa, "Bao needs more time."

A thundering crash echoed through the air.

"Niú bī!" yelled Fang. "I *can't wait* to do that again!"

"Time to get out of this kill zone," said Sahara. She stepped out from the wall, aimed, and fired one-two-three-four rounds into the doorknob. Carlo Magno's pistol wasn't a rail gun like Calaca had been packing, but at this range it blew an ample hole in the door, and the shattered remains of the bolt fell out onto the ground. Marisa threw it open and charged in, and Sahara emptied the rest of the magazine at the gangsters, trying to slow them down before following her in. The girls found themselves in a short hallway at the base of some metal stairs leading up to the second floor. Campbell and Camilla buzzed in behind them, and Sahara sent them ahead to see where the hall and stairs went, while she and Marisa pulled the door closed and dragged a garbage can in front of it. Marisa wished there was something more, but it was the best they could do.

"Up," said Sahara, and they clattered up toward the second floor. They'd barely reached the first landing when the door flew open below them, and the charging gangsters kicked the garbage can out of the way with a shout of rage. Marisa patched herself into the nulis' camera feeds as she ran; Campbell was in the first floor hallway, and turned around for a look at the Tì Xū Dào. All three were still there, and climbing the stairs. Camilla had already reached the top of the stairs, finding only a closed door.

"Miércoles," said Marisa. She sprinted up the last few steps and tried the handle. It was locked. "We're trapped."

Sahara put her back to the door, facing the oncoming thugs with grim determination. "Trapped isn't beaten," she said. "Stay behind me."

Marisa felt a sudden sense of vertigo, half of her vision showing Campbell's burst of speed as he zoomed down the hall, chasing the gangsters up the stairs. Camilla dove toward them at the same time, catching the Tì Xū Dào just as they reached the landing, pinning them between the two nulis.

The thug in the back was short, with a scar on the side of his face that cut off the top of his ear; Campbell shot him with a stun gun, and he fell back down the stairs, twitching as he went. Camilla did the same to the gangster in front—a woman with the right half of her head shaved. She was already on the landing when she fell, so she didn't roll away, but Sahara jumped down and kicked the gun out of her hand, using only the rubber sole of her shoe so the current from the stun gun didn't affect her. The man in the middle, more than six feet tall but with a boyish face, raised his gun and fired, but Camilla moved smoothly in front of the barrel and caught the bullet perfectly, falling to the stairs in a smoking pile.

Campbell shot a blob of pink foam at the gun, swallowing both the gun and the hand in a dense blob of goo, swelling and hardening in seconds. He tried to fire again, but the goo held his finger and the trigger firmly in place, stiff and immovable, so instead he swung the useless blob like a club. Sahara countered by catching the arm and levering it backward, popping the shoulder out of joint with an audible crack.

The tall man screamed and backed away, and Sahara turned to face the woman, now recovering from the stun gun. The woman pummeled Sahara with a tight, fast flurry of punches, and Sahara parried each one almost faster than Marisa could follow. The woman swung a wide roundhouse kick at Sahara's midsection, forcing her to change her stance to block it, and the woman used the opening to launch a devastating chop at Sahara's head, with no way for her to dodge in time. Campbell zoomed in and knocked the punch aside at the last second.

The woman faltered, surprised, and Sahara rammed her elbow into the side of the gangster's head, dropping her again to the floor. The tall man came back into the fray, favoring his wounded shoulder but showering Sahara with kicks so powerful it was all she could do to block them with her forearms, grunting in pain at each impact. She fell away from the onslaught, backing up until she was pressed up against the metal railing with nowhere to go. She blocked two more fierce kicks, then ducked away from the next one, dropping almost to the floor; the move left her exposed, but the tall man's kick had too much momentum, passing through the air where Sahara had just been and slamming into the railing instead.

Marisa heard the ankle snap. The man screamed, and Sahara lashed out with a kick of her own, knocking his other leg out from under him. The tall man toppled, and Sahara stood up with a grim smile.

"Now who's trapped?"

The door at the top of the stairs rattled, and the girls turned toward it wearily, bracing themselves for another attack. Sahara raised her fists, and the door swung open.

Omar stepped out, his gun raised. "You shouldn't be here."

Marisa yelped and ducked, but he fired over their heads, hitting the scar-faced gangster who'd crept up behind them. The gangster fell, dropping his rail gun, and Sahara fell into another fighting stance, ready to face Omar bare-handed.

Marisa clenched her fist. "You gonna kill us, you fracking bastard?"

"I just saved your lives," he said fiercely. "I saw you on the security cameras and came as fast as I could."

"You're part of this!" Marisa shouted. "You're helping them! Anja was your friend!"

"Anja wasn't supposed to take it," said Omar. "Neither was Franca—and Tì Xū Dāo was definitely not supposed to get involved."

"But everyone else can go screw themselves?" asked Sahara. "This is evil, and you know it."

"My father will be pissed when this all goes down," said Omar, not bothering to defend himself, "but I've seen enough. It's time to end this."

"How do you expect us to trust anything you say?" Marisa demanded. "You supported this—there's no reason for us to believe you've changed your mind now."

"Look around you," said Omar. "I supported this because it was a good business decision. Can you imagine what we could do if we got this into Ganika? Our control code in millions of heads, all over the world. Power and money become almost meaningless at that point—we'd control enough of the world to make no difference. But that's impossible now. We could have weathered the gang war, but not this zombie thing, whatever the hell glitch is turning them all into killers. Not only are we not getting into Ganika, but Ganika might take a huge hit—no one's going to trust their djinnis anymore once word of this gets out. It's no longer good business, so I'm pulling us out."

"You heartless, soulless bastard," said Marisa.

"I've already destroyed any evidence linking my family to this company," said Omar. "But I can't cut the power to the server without everyone out there ending up like Franca. Six thousand eight hundred and twenty-three people. I'm not a total monster, you know—I want to release them all safely, but I don't know how. We're locked out of the root software."

Marisa struggled for words, not knowing what to say, or how. Finally she walked toward him, opened her hand, and slapped him across the face as hard as she could.

Omar glowered, but didn't attack her back. "I deserved that," he said darkly.

"How many guards are in the server room?" she asked.

"None," said Omar. "They all went downstairs when my car flew into the lobby—I assume I have you to thank for that?"

"Thank Sahara," said Marisa. "My revenge is coming later. For now, get me to those servers."

He turned back through the open door, motioning for them to follow him down a long, dark hallway. "What happened to your arm?"

"Calaca," said Marisa. "He's going to catch hell, too, if I make it out of here alive."

Omar grunted. "Shut this place down and I'll make sure you do."

"Here it is." Omar stopped in front of a door and swung it open, revealing the room beyond. A bank of server towers stood against the west wall, drawing local and external power, just like they'd guessed. The south wall was lined with monitors, some showing lists of data, some showing security images, and some showing live feeds through the eyes of Bluescreener puppets locked in combat with the gangsters outside. In front of the monitors, set up on folding tables, were more screens and drives and keyboards, linked together with a vast tangle of cables. The most important feature, however, was the center of the room, which held a pillar of ad hoc computer parts, surrounded by five VR chairs, spaced around it like petals on an industrial flower. More cables snaked between them. The only person in the room was lying in a chair, jacked into the cylinder and oblivious to the rest of the world. Marisa stepped forward, looking at his face.

It was Lal.

TWENTY-THREE

"That's how they control them," said Omar. "Or at least that's how they're supposed to. They jump into your body just like jumping into a VR game."

"Or a Futura Baron," said Sahara. "Thanks for those access codes, by the way."

"I never gave you the access codes."

Sahara smirked. "Thanks anyway."

Marisa stepped closer to the VR setup, trying to decipher how their system was laid out. "What are they doing?"

"Active control can override whatever malware is turning the users into combat drones," said Omar. "Lal was hoping we could figure out how to reverse it permanently by looking at the infected djinnis in person, but so far they haven't found anything they can use."

"So it's malware?" asked Marisa.

"None of the programmers put anything like this into the code," said Omar, gesturing at the screens on the wall. The battle outside was a chaotic mess. "At least nothing they'll admit to. With Nils and eLiza dead, Rodriguez here is the only actual programmer left, so it's not like any of them profited from it."

"Nils is dead?" asked Sahara.

Omar gestured at Lal. "He found out Nils betrayed him—went to someone behind his back, trying to get out."

Sahara nodded. "That was us."

"Let's assume it is malware," said Marisa, "and not just a glitch. Who *would* profit from it?"

"None of us," said Omar. "None of the puppets. None of the megacorps we've been trying to infiltrate—a disaster like this is bad for all of them, especially the ones that make djinnis, like I said with Ganika. They're going to want this whole mess to disappear as quietly as possible, not burn the city down and kill seven thousand people."

"Right now it doesn't matter who did it," said Sahara. "We have to find a way to undo it." She walked to one of the chairs and picked up a djinni cable. "How do you select which mind you jump into?"

Omar shrugged. "A menu system, I guess? You're not going to use it, are you?"

Sahara lay down on the chair. "You're damn right I am. We've got to get Anja out of there before she gets herself killed." She plugged the cable into the jack at the base of her skull. "Okay, this makes sense. There's a rudimentary menu, but mostly it's just a list with a search function. I'm finding Anja . . . there she is. Going in." Sahara's body went inert, and one of the wall screens lit up with a new view: the view through Anja's eyes, in the middle of the battle. "It's the end of the fracking world out here," said Anja's voice from a speaker.

"Can you hear me?" asked Marisa.

"Barely," said Anja/Sahara. "Only if I try—it's crazy loud out here. I'm going to find cover. I think her wrist is broken, and—ow—maybe a couple of ribs."

Marisa pointed to Lal. "That means he can hear us, too, if he's paying attention. We need to find some way of incapacitating him so we can work." She looked around the room, saw a box full of blue headjack drives, and smiled maliciously. "Oh, that's perfect."

"What are you going to do?"

Marisa pulled out one of the drives—a dose of Bluescreen—and walked toward Lal. "I'm going to crash this blowhole's brain." She ripped the djinni cable out of his headjack, and his eyes popped open, disoriented and frightened.

"What? Marisa?"

"Hi, cutie," Marisa said, and jammed the Bluescreen dose into the jack.

"Wait," he said, "don't do that!" His eyes started to roll back, and his muscles clenched as the drug took effect. "Stupid . . . bitch . . ." He passed out, and Marisa unplugged the drive triumphantly.

"Call me a bitch?" She spit on his chest. "Help me tie him up, the crash only lasts a few minutes."

"There were easier ways of subduing him," said Omar. "Now he's going to wake up as a lunatic killer zombie, right here in the room with us."

Marisa pulled a long cable from a box in the corner. "That's why we tie him up," she said. "And believe me, this was way more satisfying." She lashed Lal's wrists together as tightly as she could, then his ankles, and finished by tying him firmly to the chair. "Now we can get down to business. If this is malware, we need to look at the code—but that'll take hours, maybe days to sift through it."

"I thought you were a computer genius," said Omar.

"This is the most complex program I've ever encountered," said Marisa, "and I'm completely unfamiliar with it. Finding the piece that doesn't belong is like . . . looking for a needle in a needle factory. There's no way to tell the piece I want from the zillion other pieces I don't. Maybe if we try it from another angle . . . do you have any idea how the malware got in?"

"I don't know code," said Omar. "You know that."

"Is it a targeted attack," Marisa asked, thinking out loud, "or some kind of mutant glitch? Maybe it got in through whatever back door you use to bypass the users' security systems. I've been trying for days to get Anja's antivirus software to delete Blue-screen, and nothing works. Did you just disable each target's software completely? How did you not expect something like this to happen?"

"Are you crazy?" asked Omar. "What good is a puppet with no antivirus software? A system with no security is useless; we'd lose control of the target within seconds."

Marisa nodded—she'd studied enough viruses on her hotbox to see how quickly they could destroy a system, turning the fanciest computer into a useless brick. So how did Bluescreen bypass everyone's security? The program broke past the security once by overloading it, which is how it installed itself, but then what? They needed the security disabled to protect their software, but enabled to protect the user. How did they do both . . . ?

"That's it," she whispered. "Why didn't I see it before?" She looked at Omar. "They add their own security software. It's kind of brilliant, actually: when Bluescreen installs itself it also installs a second antivirus program, over the top of the one you already have. It's just like Yosae or Pushkin or whatever you use, but run out of private databases on these servers." She gestured to the servers lining the south wall. "They keep your pre-existing system active, so you don't notice, but they disable it, so that all the actual antivirus work is being done by Bluescreen itself. That's why we could never get Anja's Yosae to kill it, even when we added it directly to the database." She nodded; this explained everything. "eLiza was studying VR, so she's the one who built the puppet code, but Nils was a security specialist. This was his job on the team—not cracking people's security, but maintaining it."

"That, well . . . ," Omar stammered. "That makes sense. But how does that help us find the malware inside of the malware?"

"We don't have to," said Marisa, looking at the servers. "Now that we know how it works, we can save everyone out there the same way we tried to save Anja outside of her school: we upload a copy of Bluescreen to the Bluescreen security database, and tell it to recognize itself as a virus. Then we run a system update and it will delete itself from every connected system that has a copy of the virus." She turned to look at him, feeling hope for the first time in days. "We can wipe Bluescreen off of every puppet out there, all at once, and then burn this place to the ground so it can never happen again."

"It might work," said Omar, "But that server is protected by biometric security. It's completely unhackable."

Marisa looked at Lal, still unconscious from his Bluescreen overload. "No it's not."

TWENTY-FOUR

Marisa lay down on a VR chair, fishing for the cable behind her. Just before she plugged it in she looked at Omar, eyeing him warily. "Don't do anything stupid while I'm in there."

"I'm on your side," said Omar.

"For the moment," said Marisa, glaring at him. "That doesn't mean we're friends."

She watched him a moment longer, then plugged the VR cable into her headjack. The world faded away, replaced by a simple menu: green glowing names on a plain black background, with a search function sitting dormant in the corner. She blinked on it, and entered the name *Lal Muralithar*.

That user is not found in the database.

"He's not in here," she said.

Omar's response seemed distant and tinny, like he was speaking through a ventilation duct: "Try again. He's starting to wake up, so maybe it's done installing."

She ran the search again, and there it was. Lal's name. She hesitated a minute, then blinked on it . . .

. . . and suddenly she was back in the room, but instead of lying in the chair she was tied tightly down to it.

"Omar," she shouted, "you triste mula! I'm gone for two seconds and you tie me up?"

Omar glanced at her, raising his eyebrow. "I'm assuming from the Spanish that you're Marisa?"

"Of course I'm Marisa," she said, "who else would I . . ." She trailed off, turning her head to look at the chair next to her. There was her body, limp and inert. She was in Lal. "Oh, that's freaky as hell."

Omar was watching her with a mixture of fascination and disgust. "You're telling me."

"Untie me," she said. "The less time I have to spend in here the better."

He knelt down, working the knots loose in the cables. Marisa shifted in the chair, trying to see her new body better. Everything felt different; her muscles moved differently than she was used to, and they felt more powerful. She looked down at her body, disoriented by the bizarre new shape of it: her waist wider, her thighs thicker, her breasts replaced by a smooth, flat chest. The sense of wrongness made her nauseated, and she looked away, closing her eyes.

"This is so weird."

"You use other bodies all the time in Overworld," said Omar. "This is no different."

"This is monstrously different."

"But it's the same skill set," said Omar. "All you have to do is walk across the room and access the DNA scanner—you can do everything else back in your own body."

Marisa sat up, swinging her legs over the edge of the chair. Lal's body was taller than hers, and balanced differently; most of his height was in his torso, which made his waist bend in a way she wasn't expecting. She stood up slowly. "They must have done this a lot to be so good at it," she said out loud. "The things they did in Anja's body, running through the streets like that—they must have practiced for months in other bodies, getting the technology right."

"Sahara's doing fine in Anja," said Omar.

"Their body types are similar," said Marisa. "Sahara's a little taller and fuller, but not by much. Going from me to Lal is just . . . way too much."

"Hurry," said Omar. "They're still fighting out there."

Marisa nodded and walked to the biometric scanner, finding that it was, as Omar had predicted, easier than she'd expected. She gave it a thumbprint, a retina scan, and a pinprick blood sample. The display rotated, processing the data, then turned green. "I'm in."

"Then get back into your body and finish this," said Omar.

"Tie me back up," said Marisa. "No, wait! One thing first."

Omar raised his eyebrow. "Are you going to punch yourself in his face?"

"Tempting," said Marisa, and blinked on Lal's djinni interface. "I've got something so much better in mind. Saif, tenemos un pollito que comernos." She sat back down on the chair, rearranging some of Lal's software while Omar retied the cables. When the ties were secure Marisa blinked out, appearing back in her own body. She felt a moment of vertigo from the sudden shift in reference frame, then shook herself out of it and stood up. "Get Sahara out of there," she said brusquely, walking to the computer equipment. "I don't know what will happen if she's in Anja's head when the software gets erased." Omar nodded, and Marisa went to work on the computers, using both her djinni and several of the keyboards at once—old mechanical models and standard touch screens, her one hand jumping back and forth in a dizzying pattern, working faster than she'd ever worked before. She found the antivirus database, dumped the Bluescreen code into it, and shouted behind her. "We clear?"

"Clear," said Sahara. "Hit it."

Marisa hit the button, initiating a full system update. The server contacted every Bluescreen user, told their djinnis to force a virus scan, and thus began methodically deleting itself from every user's head. Marisa watched the screens, holding her breath, praying it would work. Sahara stood next to her, holding her hand and watching with her.

"Where'd you leave Anja?" Marisa asked.

"In the back corner of the lot," said Sahara. "Bao's watching her."

"But she's free again," said Marisa. "The algorithm's in control, and she'll attack him again."

Sahara nodded. "So let's hope this—" She pointed at one of the screens. "It's working." The puppets were slowing, some of them stopping outright, or even falling over. The gangsters, practically allies at this point in the battle, protecting each other from the endless horde of puppets, stopped as well, watching in wonder as the mindless army went limp. The puppets blinked, stared, swooned; some of them lost their balance, while others screamed in horror at their sudden awareness of where they were, and what they were doing. Marisa called Anja, weeping in joy when she heard her voice.

"Mari," said Anja. She sounded exhausted—her voice raw and broken—but she was alive. "Did you do it?"

"We did it," said Marisa. "It's all over."

"Not all," said Sahara. "We need to destroy these servers—we need to make sure none of this can ever happen again."

"Drop the firewall and give me access," said Jaya. She sounded exhausted as well. "I just fought this gaandu system for thirty solid minutes—I'm going to do things to it that'll give my own computer nightmares."

"We can't risk it," said Marisa. "None of this can be allowed to hit the net, even in a cache somewhere. It has to die here, and physically."

"It will be my pleasure," said Omar, and fired a shot into each server in turn.

"No!" screamed Lal. Marisa turned, seeing Lal awake and struggling with his bonds. The cables held, and she turned back to the screens without a word.

"That's a good start," said Sahara, "but give me an hour with a fire axe and I can be gruesomely thorough."

"No time," said Marisa. "Anja, how are you doing?"

"I'm pretty broken up," said Anja. "I'm going to pass out now, and I sincerely hope I wake up in a hospital."

"We'll get you there," said Bao.

Marisa looked at the monitors again; the Tì Xū Dāo gangsters were leaving, and so were the enforcers, probably terrified that the momentary peace would end at any second. Calaca, barely walking, led the remnants of La Sesenta resolutely toward the building. "They're going to tear this place apart," said Marisa. "We don't want to be here when they get in."

"What do we do with him?" asked Omar, gesturing to Lal with his handgun.

"You've got to save me," said Lal. "You need your money back—I can get it for you, just don't destroy my servers, and don't leave me for the cops—"

"We're not just going to leave you," said Sahara, "we're going to leave you in pieces. Where's that fire axe?"

"We don't need to hurt him," said Marisa. "He's already hurt himself."

"Spare me the moralizing," Lal spat. "How have I hurt myself—by forgetting the power of friendship? By losing *you*? I thought you had more vision than this, Marisa, but you're a useless little girl. I have plenty of other thugs on the payroll, and when they get here—"

"Oh no!" Marisa formed her mouth into a perfect O, looking as falsely concerned as she could. "Did you go online?"

"Of course I went online, you stupid bi—"

"I told you not call me that," said Marisa. "Which is only one of the many, many reasons I took the liberty of deleting your security software."

"You—" he spluttered. "How?"

"I was in your head," said Marisa. "It's a pretty nasty place, but trust me, it's about to get a whole lot nastier." She looked at Sahara. "He's been online . . . ten seconds now? Twenty? How many computer viruses do you think he has by now?"

"Depends on his service provider," said Sahara, copying Marisa's tone of mock concern. "Johara, I assume?"

"Naturally," said Marisa.

"That's a very popular target," said Sahara. "Those satellite pathways are *crawling* with malware—none of it's all that dangerous if you've got a good security system, but . . ."

Lal blinked.

"Deleting a pop-up?" asked Marisa. Lal glared at her, then blinked again. "You're going to get a lot of those," she continued. "Ad loops, bloatware, free offers from porn sites. Free offers from *goat* porn sites." Lal was blinking almost constantly now, and Marisa looked at him coldly. "You're a monster, Lal, and I can't think of any better punishment than to throw you in with the biggest monsters on the net. If you're good, you can crawl out of that virus-infested hole in four, maybe even three months. You'll be in jail by then, though, so, you know: spoiler warning."

Lal fell back on the VR chair, his eyes twitching involuntarily, his brain lost under an avalanche of malware.

TWENTY-FIVE

"The Foundation is claiming responsibility," said Bao. "They said they built a virus to attack the djinnis, to show how easily they can be corrupted."

Bao, Marisa, and Sahara were sitting in the hospital, watching the chaos, waiting to hear from the doctors about Anja's condition. Omar had come as well, but the friends had refused to talk to him, and he'd left the waiting room almost as soon as he arrived. Marisa didn't know where he'd gone, and frankly hoped she'd never have to see him again.

"How can the Foundation build a virus?" asked Sahara. "They hate technology."

"That doesn't mean they don't use it," said Bao.

"I don't like it," said Sahara, folding her arms. "It's too easy."

"Nothing about this has been easy," said Marisa, tapping the empty prosthetic dock on her shoulder. The hospital was even more crowded and desperate than it had been that morning—was it really still the same day? Even with most of the Bluescreen victims shuttled off to other hospitals, the Mirador facility was ground zero for the worst of the worst cases. It made Marisa cringe to think that Anja was among them.

Sahara nodded. "So the explanation shouldn't be easy, either. There has to be more to this than some big, obvious villain. It's too . . . well, obvious."

"Just be grateful we got out clean," said Bao. They'd left out the back of the building just as La Sesenta entered from the front, and from the sounds they heard Calaca was every bit as thorough in his destruction as he'd promised.

"I just wish any of my nulis had survived," said Sahara. "This is the kind of stuff my show needs—not the secret, criminal stuff that could get me arrested, but the dramatic aftermath is awesome. I could be raking in the blinks right now."

Marisa heard a voice cutting through the chaos—Mr. Litz had arrived. Anja's father. She jumped to her feet, bracing herself for another rant about her bad influence on his daughter, but her heart plummeted when she saw that he was talking gratefully to Omar. That sneaky rat had been waiting for him by the front door. . . .

"Here they are," said Omar, pointing toward Marisa and the others. "They won't admit it, but it's true."

"What is he doing?" asked Sahara, scowling at Omar as she stood up. Bao stood as well, and Mr. Litz walked toward them. He shook their hands firmly.

"Omar has told me everything," said Mr. Litz. "Thank you for saving Anja's life."

Marisa stammered, caught by surprise. "We . . . uh . . ."

"She's our best friend," said Sahara, handling the surprise far more effectively. "We'd do anything for her."

"And some people would do anything to hurt her," said Mr. Litz. "The news has been telling stories about Bluescreen's ability to control people, and Omar has filled in some frightening details for me. Do you really think they were targeting me, as well? Targeting Abendroth?"

"You're one of the most powerful men in Los Angeles," said Marisa. "If they'd been able to corrupt you, all of that power would have been theirs."

"It's good to know we have such capable allies," said Mr. Litz. "Thank you again. Now, if you'll excuse me, I'm going to see Anja—father's privilege." He shook their hands again, then left them in the waiting room.

Marisa looked at Omar. "Somehow, this makes me like you even less."

"Consider it a peace offering," said Omar. "You hack computers, I hack people. He likes me because I always show him exactly the kind of young man he wants to see."

"One day he'll see the real you," said Marisa.

"*You* he sees as a bunch of club-hopping losers," said Omar. "Horrible influences on his only daughter. After this he'd never have let you see her again, but I vouched for you. I'm calling us even now."

"Not even close," said Sahara. "People died today because of you, and Anja is never going back to you."

"I don't expect her to," said Omar. "It was never serious anyway."

"What a douchebag," said Marisa, shaking her head. "Just using her for her body?"

"For her father," said Bao. "He is, like you said, one of the most powerful men in Los Angeles. And now he thinks Omar saved his daughter's life—that's a pretty big foot in some very important doors."

"You got your best friend back," said Omar, ignoring Bao's accusation. "We're even."

"And the Maldonado mafia?" asked Marisa. "You don't think your family's going to prison for their part in this?"

"I told you," said Omar, "all of that evidence was destroyed. And the police aren't likely to look for any more. Now if you'll excuse me, I'm going to visit my sister. She's still in her coma." He turned and walked away through the crowd.

An alert popped up in Marisa's vision: a "friend of a patient" contact, updating her on Anja's condition. She glanced at Sahara and Bao, seeing that they'd received the same thing; Bao's, of course, had appeared on his phone. Marisa scanned through the message quickly, read that Anja was stable but sleeping, and sighed in relief.

"Good," said Sahara. "Now I can go home and get some sleep."

"Me too," said Bao. "If I start walking now I can be home by midnight."

"We'll split an autocab," said Sahara. "Marisa, you coming?"

"I'm going to visit Chuy first," said Marisa. "See you tomorrow."

"We'll skip a few more days of practice," said Sahara. "Rest up."

"You're still going to the tournament?" asked Bao.

"We're going to lose," said Marisa, "but we're definitely going."

"Winning isn't everything," Sahara said, and winked at Marisa. "I mean, winning is still *most* things, but the occasional awesome video is good, too, right?" She smiled. "Play crazy."

"Play crazy," said Marisa. "See you later."

She left them in the waiting room, and walked through the halls toward the long-term care ward. Chuy was alone in his hospital bed, watching something on his djinni, and Marisa knocked on the open door to get his attention.

"Hello?" His eyes focused on her, and he smiled. "Mari, come in." He was wrapped in bandages and tubes and wires, simultaneously treating and collecting data on his abdominal wound. "I'd get you a chair, but—"

"I can get my own chair," she said, laughing at his helpless chivalry. She pulled a small seat to the side of his bed. "You okay?"

"It's healing pretty quick," he said. "Some minor organ damage, but this gene-bath they've got pumping through me is regrowing everything bien machin. They say I might be out in two days, and I promise I will pay Papi back—"

"Forget the money," said Marisa. "Go to Mexico, get a real job, and that's all the payment we need."

"I . . ." He grimaced, looking guilty, and Marisa felt her heart sink. He spoke softly. "I'm not going to Mexico."

"But you promised—"

327

"Do you know how many of my friends died today?" asked Chuy.

Marisa hardened her face, trying to look serious instead of heartbroken. "That's why you need to leave."

"Goyo was one of them," said Chuy. "His little brother Memo is taking over. Do you know how I got shot last night?"

"By running with La Sesenta."

"By jumping in front of Memo," said Chuy, "and taking the bullet that was meant for him. The entire power structure is shaking up, and I saved the new leader's life. I'm almost at the top now—I'll be getting more money, and with less danger, than ever before. I can't walk away from that."

"Yes you can."

"These are my brothers," said Chuy, repeating his argument from before. "I won't just walk away from them when life gets rough—that's when we need to pull together even more."

"But your family?" asked Marisa. "Who provides for them the next time you take a bullet for someone?"

"We're looking out for all the widows," said Chuy. "We take care of our own. And someday, god forbid, if I go down, they'll take care of Adriana as well."

"So what am I supposed to do?" asked Marisa. "Just . . . wonder all the time? Wonder if you're going to live, or if Pati's going to get more drugs at school, or if Calaca's going to come back and try to shoot me again?"

"Calaca's going to leave you alone," said Chuy. "I've already seen to that. And as for you, you're going to do what you do best, what you've always done your entire life: you're going to help other people instead of yourself. It's who you are." He took her hand and squeezed it gently. "I think that makes you the best person I know."

Marisa squeezed his hand back, feeling warmed by the words. And ominously frigid at the same time.

TWENTY-SIX

Another "friend of a patient" alert popped up in Marisa's djinni, as she walked slowly down to the hospital lobby, and she blinked on it absently. The halls were mostly quiet now, well lit but empty, with no one but a few errant visitors sleeping in chairs while they waited for morning. Marisa started reading, but stopped in surprise—it wasn't for Anja, but Francisca Maldonado. Marisa had been the one to check her in when she fainted, and she was still in the system as an auxiliary contact. She read the alert again, and found the key message: La Princesa had woken up.

Marisa looked at the bottom of the message, where it listed which of the patient's other friends were in the building. Marisa was the only one. She groaned, desperate to leave, but she couldn't bear to leave a brand-new coma survivor alone in the middle of the night. Even one as horrible as La Princesa. She turned around and walked back upstairs.

Franca looked up when she came into the room—a far, far nicer one than Chuy was in—but looked away in disgust when she recognized Marisa. Her voice was bitter. "Come to gloat?"

"I thought you might like some company."

"From a Carneseca?" asked Franca. She laughed, but it turned almost immediately to a cough. "I'd rather be alone."

Marisa clenched her fist, feeling her anger boil up. "I'm trying to be nice."

"Y luego?" asked Franca. "You say you feel sorry for me, and suddenly the feud is over and our families love each other and everything's good again?"

"We don't have to hate each other," said Marisa. "Our fathers do, but we don't even know why. Some car accident so old we don't even remember it? Can't we think for ourselves?"

"Some of us trust our fathers," said Franca. "If he hates you, he has a good reason; that's all I need to know."

Marisa let her anger boil over, snapping back with the worst thing she could think of: "Do you know what your father's been involved in? A lot's happened while you were asleep."

"I'm watching the reports."

"Do they talk about the great Don Francisco?" Marisa shot back. "Do they talk about how he paid for the drug that almost killed you—for the VR system that let another man wear your body like a suit? Does that bother you at all, or will you just forgive everything, and go right back to him, and let him buy you presents and dress you like a doll and sell you to whichever other crime family he wants to make a deal with—"

"Get out," hissed Franca. There were tears in her eyes, and

Marisa felt suddenly guilty, but her anger was high and she didn't want to back down. She stood in the doorway, staring coldly at Franca, who stared right back. "Get out," she said again.

Marisa waited, just long enough to show that she was making her own decision to leave, then turned and took a step into the hall. Almost instantly Franca called her back.

"Marisa."

Marisa hesitated, confused. Franca's voice didn't sound right, almost like it had before, when Nils had used her to deliver his message. But that was impossible—the software was deleted, the hardware was destroyed—

—but Franca had been offline when the virus had destroyed itself, and the server had been destroyed before she'd come online again. She still had the software in her head.

But who was using it, if the hardware was gone?

"I have another message for you."

Marisa turned slowly, as scared as if she were talking to a ghost. Franca was sitting in the bed, unnaturally calm, watching her with that same disconcerting detachment of a Bluescreen puppet.

Marisa stayed in the hall, too spooked to get closer. "Nils?"

"Nils is dead," said Franca's voice. "One of many things I want to thank you for."

"I didn't kill him," said Marisa.

"But you facilitated it," said the stranger. "You were always the wild card in this plan, but you played your part perfectly. I'm in your debt."

"Who are you?"

Franca cocked her head to the side. "You don't know?"

Not Nils, thought Marisa. Not eLiza. Certainly not Lal, or Omar, or anyone else she'd seen at the warehouse. But who else knew about Bluescreen? Who else had talked to her, had given her information, had guided her along some path she'd thought she'd been choosing on her own—

The answer struck her like a thunderbolt. "Grendel."

"You never fail to impress me."

And then it clicked, like the final letter of a computer code that downloaded the whole picture into her brain, a code she'd been piecing together this whole time without realizing. "eLiza came to you with the Dolly Girls code, but you wanted it for yourself," said Marisa. "You told her how to use it, and let her and Nils and Lal field-test it for you—see what it could do, and what it couldn't. Where the gaps were. Then you tipped off the Foundation, and I could never figure out why, but it was because you needed someone to take the heat. You knew they'd want to make an example of it— to expose the evils of human augmentation—so you tipped them off and they hired you to clean up your own loose ends. You got to kill the field-testers, keep the tech for yourself, and pin the whole disaster on someone so willing to be your decoy that they think it's their own idea." It all seemed so clear now. "You wrote the attack virus."

"And then I told you what was going on," said Grendel, "and you obliged by cleaning up all the evidence the army of puppets couldn't."

"So why are you telling me this?" asked Marisa.

"Because I owed you," said Grendel. He paused, watching her.

"And because it's more fun when you're trying to stop me."

Marisa fixed Franca's eyes with a cold, steely glare. "If you think you want me as an enemy, you don't know me very well."

"Of course I know you, Mari," said Grendel. "I've known you since you were two years old."

Marisa's eyes went wide. Two years old. The car accident. The mystery that had changed her life forever—the focal point of every feud, every fight, every great, unanswered question of her life. "What do you know about—" she started, but Franca's eyes closed, and her head slumped over. A moment later she looked up again, and her eyes narrowed spitefully.

"I thought I told you to leave." La Princesa was back. Grendel had disappeared.

Marisa turned, shaken, and walked away. *Was Grendel an enemy, or an ally?* she wondered as she walked down the brightly lit hospital corridor.

"Maybe he's both," she whispered, "or at least maybe he thinks he is."

"Who you talking to?" asked Bao.

Marisa looked up, startled to see Bao leaning casually against the wall, but smiled when she recognized him. "I thought you went home."

Bao shrugged. "Figured I'd wait. You live closer to me than Sahara anyway."

They fell in step beside each other and walked out of the hospital into the warm Los Angeles night. Nulis flew overhead, as busy at midnight as they were at noon. The streetlights shone like stars.

"The world's a lot more dangerous than I thought it was," said Marisa.

"No me digas," said Bao, and laughed at Marisa's surprised look. "What? I live in Mirador, you don't think I've picked up any Spanish?"

"Not bad," said Marisa. "Now say 'Trienta y tres tramos de troncos trozaron tres tristes trozadores de troncos.'"

"Whoa," said Bao. "That's hard-core Spanish. I'm still playing on beginner."

They fell into a comfortable silence, and Marisa thought again about Grendel, and about the Foundation, and about Ti Xú Dāo and Don Francisco and the whole gigantic world full of people she couldn't trust. People she was afraid of. Even Anja's father, and the vast collection of corporate interests he represented, slowly and cheerfully bleeding the rest of the population dry. That was the world she lived in, but it wasn't the world she wanted.

Maybe it was time somebody changed it.

"You know what else?" she asked.

"What?"

"I think we're a lot more dangerous than the world thought we were."

Bao smiled. "What are you planning?"

Marisa smiled back.

ACKNOWLEDGMENTS

We live in a world where cars can talk to refrigerators, and a robot on Mars sends messages to a supercomputer I keep in my pocket, and yet despite all of this I never fully realized how much technology had changed the world until I read a story about a professional video-game player getting an athletic visa to travel to a tournament. Video games are sports now. I don't know why, but that's what finally did it for me. The online world has subsumed the physical one. We live in the future.

This book is the first of what I hope will be a very long series, combining three of my favorite things in life: reading, games, and Mexican food. Even more than that, though, this series is about disruption: technologies and ideas that change the way we live our lives, sometimes for the better and sometimes much, much worse, but always looking forward and striving for something new. Disruption asks us hard but necessary questions: Why is my society/government/world/life the way it is? Do I like it that way? What would be a better way, and how do I make that happen? Or maybe we simply ask: What happens if I do *this*? And then live with the consequences. Writing a book about the future forced me to look at every different branch of science I could think of—programming and engineering and biology and fuel and robotics and genetics and so many more, but the most important one is the social science: How do we react when things change? And the corollary to that, if we're smart enough to think about it: How can we change things so that we get the reaction we want?

In the process of asking those questions I had some really amazing conversations with people much smarter than I am; some of them, though I'm certain I'm leaving some out, are Steve Diamond, Claudia Gray, Josiah Happel, Michael Happel, Mary Robinette Kowal, Gama Martinez, Guadalupe Garcia McCall, Rebecca McKinney, Patrick Miller, Ben Olsen, Maija-Liisa Phipps, Alexander Robinson, Brandon Sanderson, Eric Sumner, Howard Tayler, Natalie Whipple, and Stacy Whitman. Some of them I approached with specific questions, and others might be wondering why they're included here, but their ideas and friendship were invaluable, and I couldn't have written this book without them. Further thanks must be given to my agent, Sara Crowe; my editor, Jordan Brown; and of course my wife and children. They're the best.

Turn the page to read an excerpt from
the next book in the Mirador series

ONES AND ZEROES

ONE

Mari, where are you? We're about to get swarmed!
Marisa Carneseca grimaced and blinked on the message. **I'll be there as soon as I can,** she sent. **Give me a minute.**

"A minute"? her father sent back. **Our livelihood is failing, with our home itself hanging in the balance, and you need "a minute"?**

Yes, Marisa sent back. **I'm almost done, and then I'll be right there.** She rolled her eyes, then immediately regretted it—the djinni interface could compensate for involuntary eye movement, but a dramatic gesture like an eye roll—and Marisa's eye roll had been as dramatic as she could make it—was as disastrous as a fumbled swipe on a touch screen. Apps and icons swirled across her vision, seeming to scatter to every corner of the swanky cafe she was sitting in. She blinked rapidly on each of them, bringing them back into place. The most important was the list of lunch orders: everyone who placed an order at the Solipsis Cafe left a digital trail, and she had camped on the cafe's network to route all of those orders through her djinni—a supercomputer implanted directly into her brain. Lunch orders ticked by, one every few seconds, on a list that her djinni projected directly onto her eye implants. The list seemed to float in the air in front of her, though of course no one else could see it.

Which was handy, because spying on someone else's network was very illegal.

Marisa found the conversation with her father and pulled it back into the center of her vision. An angry message flashed at the end of it, waiting for a response. **It's the lunch rush, morena,** he'd sent her. **We can't do this without you.**

I know it's lunch, she sent back. **Why do you think I'm here?**

Because . . . you don't want to help with lunch?

Marisa controlled her eye roll this time, instead closing her eyes and clenching her fist in frustration. It was so like her father to put ellipses in a message—she could practically hear his voice pausing in the middle the sentence.

She opened her eyes again and looked down at the cafe table in front of her, and the salad sitting on it. She already felt guilty for being here—her family really did need her for the lunch rush at San Juanito, their family restaurant—and now she felt even more guilty for buying a salad. She hadn't wanted to, but the cafe wouldn't let her stay otherwise. She looked at the wall beside her—right on the other side of it, barely three feet away, the Solipsis Cafe server sat on a desk, oblivious to her infiltration. A direct hack would have been too easy to detect, which was why she needed to be so close—she wasn't logged in to their network, she was literally just reading the wireless signals as they flew through it. She glanced at the order list again, hoping the one she needed would pop up before her father went apoplectic. Still nothing. At least her father hadn't looked up her location yet—

You're downtown? her father sent her. **You'll never make it back in time!**

Marisa looked at the ceiling, shaking her head. GPS locaters were part of the parental controls her parents had enabled when they'd purchased her djinni in the first place—just like they had with all of her siblings. Marisa had circumvented most of the parental controls years ago, but she had to be careful about the really obvious ones, like location, where it was way too easy to be caught in a lie. And their punishment would be swift and merciless—they'd even turned her djinni off once, leaving her completely disconnected from everything. She shivered again at the memory of it. Someday she'd be able to pay for her own service plan, and then she could do whatever she wanted, but she was nowhere near being able to afford that now.

She could barely afford this salad.

Not only are you downtown, sent her father, **you're at the Solipsis Cafe!**

I know, she sent back.

Their salads cost ten yuan! We can't afford sixty-dollar lunches!

I know!

Did you use my account to pay for this?

Papi—

You come home right now, muchacha.

And waste this salad? she shot back. **It cost me sixty dollars!**

He didn't respond for a few seconds, and Marisa knew he was probably ranting out loud at whoever was close enough to hear him—her mother, certainly, and any of her siblings already roped into a shift at San Juanito. Which would be all of them, she thought, because only Problem Child Marisa would be terrible enough to run off during the lunch rush on a Saturday. She sneered at her uneaten salad, then speared a pepper with her fork and shoved it petulantly in her mouth. Her eyes went wide in surprise.

"Santa vaca, that's delicious," she said out loud, then immediately looked around to see if anyone had heard her. Most of the other diners were staring blankly into space, reading or watching things on their djinnis, but one man in a business suit eyed her strangely. Marisa turned back to her salad, wishing she could curl up and disappear.

Another message popped up in her djinni, from Sahara this time—Marisa's best friend and VR gaming teammate. **Where are you?**

Hell, Marisa sent back.

No, I already looked there, sent Sahara. She lived above the restaurant, renting the apartment from Marisa's parents, which made it easy for her to pop in and out. **Your dad's practically spitting nails.**

Careful, sent Marisa. **Pop in too often and he'll make you wait tables.**

Wouldn't be the first time he's tried, sent Sahara.

Your ID hasn't moved, sent Marisa's father. **Why aren't you moving? You're supposed to be on the train coming home RIGHT NOW. Or was I not clear?**

Marisa closed his message and looked back at the scrolling list of lunch orders. **I'm downtown,** she sent to Sahara. She took another bite of her salad. **This is the most expensive stakeout I've ever done, but holy crap is it delicious.**

Solipsis? asked Sahara.

Of course.

I've never eaten there.

A waiter nuli hovered nearby—basically just a watercooler with four rotor blades and a sensor. It pointed this sensor at Marisa's glass, decided she needed a refill, and dispensed a squirt of cold water before flying on to the next table.

I'm eating the roast pepper salad, sent Marisa, taking another bite. **The peppers are okay—honestly Dad's are better—but the salad dressing is amazing.**

How amazing can it be? sent Sahara. **It's salad dressing.**

Marisa picked up the little plastic cup the dressing had come in and dribbled more of it onto her vegetables. **It's like a baby koala saw its mother for the first time, and its tears of joy dripped down through a rainbow, and angels kissed every drop before laying them gently on my salad.**

That's the most unsanitary description of food I've ever heard, sent Sahara.

Trust me, sent Marisa, **eat here once and you'll want koala tears in everything you eat forever.**

Moving on, said Sahara. **You think you'll find him?**

Marisa said nothing, staring at the list of orders. "Him" in this case referred to Grendel, a hacker from the darkest corners of the net. He was a criminal, and a dangerous one, though Marisa's interest was more personal. She looked at her left arm—completely mechanical from the shoulder down. She'd lost it in a car accident when she was two years old, and the cause of that accident—they were virtually unheard of now that cars were self-driving—was only one of the unanswered questions about that day. The even bigger mystery was why she'd been in that particular car at all—the car of Zenaida de Maldonado, the wife of the biggest crime boss in Los Angeles. She'd had two of her sons and Marisa strapped in the back. Why had Marisa been there? Why had Zenaida turned off the autopilot? And when Zenaida died in that accident, why did her husband blame Marisa's father?

Marisa had never met anyone who claimed to know the truth about that day fifteen years ago—except Grendel. She and her friends had tangled with him a few months ago, and Marisa had been hunting him ever since, finally tracking him to an IP address. It was the only lead she had, and if she was going to follow it any further she needed to be here, right now, watching these lunch orders.

Another popped up. And another one.

But not the one she needed.

You gonna be ready for practice tonight? sent Sahara.

Should be, Marisa sent back absently. **If Papi doesn't cut off my Overworld privileges for missing work today.**

You're the heart of the team, sent Sahara, which wasn't

really true, but it was nice of her to say. Marisa smiled but never took her eyes off the order list. Another message flashed from her father, but she closed it without reading.

I want to try a new strategy tonight, sent Sahara. **Double Jungle. Keep you on the top, pretending to defend Anja, while she goes down to help Fang power through the sewers and hit the enemy vault, swift and fierce.**

I've read about some European teams trying that, wrote Marisa, **but they're always trying crazy—**

She stopped in mid-sentence, sending the message without thinking and focusing all her attention on the list of orders. One had just come in from KT Sigan.

I know it sounds crazy, sent Sahara, **but you never know what's going to work until you try it.**

I've got one, Marisa sent back. She blinked on the order and pulled up the details.

Nice, sent Sahara.

It didn't matter who the order had come from, only that it was an employee of KT Sigan. Sigan was one of the largest telecom companies in the world, providing internet service to millions of people around the world—including the IP address Marisa had linked to Grendel. If she could get inside their system, she could find out who he was, and where he was, not just online but in the real world. It would be the biggest break she'd had yet in her hunt for him. But hacking an international telecom was no simple matter, and dangerous to boot, so Marisa had started with the cafe: their cybersecurity was way lower, and if you were patient, you could get all kinds of information.

Such as the security code of a Sigan employee ordering lunch.

Marisa read the details of the order: it had come from someone named Pablo Nakamoto, who'd requested a chicken Caesar salad, and listed the delivery address as Port 9, on the third floor of the KT Sigan building. Somewhere in the back of the cafe's kitchen a chef was tossing together a salad, and filling up a little cup of salad dressing, and packing it all in a plastic box, and then a delivery nuli would zoom across the street and up to Port 9, where Pablo Nakamoto would take it and eat in his cubicle. Hidden behind the order was the good stuff: his financial information, which was encrypted, and the server path his request had followed to get here, which wasn't. Marisa followed this path backward to the source, finding not only his ID but the security code the server had used to process it. It was just a couple of numbers—a long string of ones and zeroes—but it was enough. Marisa could use it to log in to KT Sigan's system, masquerading as Nakamoto, and find everything she needed.

Another red icon popped up in her vision: her father was calling again.

Marisa clenched her teeth, staring at the security info, desperate to follow it . . . but saved the information to a note file and closed her cafe connection. The Sigan server would still be there later that night, but her family needed her now. She boxed up her salad, taking a last lick of the delectable dressing, and ran out the door.

TWO

Marisa collapsed on her bed, exhausted. For most of Marisa's life they'd lived in the apartment above their restaurant, where Sahara lived now, but a few years ago they'd managed to save enough money to buy a bigger house a mile or so away, and Marisa had gotten her own room for the first time in her life. Lying in that room now, bone tired from a long day waiting tables, she wondered how much longer she'd get to keep it. Both their home and their restaurant were in the Los Angeles neighborhood of Mirador, and Mirador was falling apart. Her family had done what they could—they'd cut expenses, they'd dropped luxuries—but it just wasn't enough anymore. A restaurant only made money if people paid to eat there, and day after day more people in Mirador were becoming too poor to go to restaurants. Power was free, for the most part—every building in the city was covered with solar trees—but essential utilities like water and internet were getting more expensive, and meanwhile everyone seemed to be losing their jobs to nulis. The only reason San Juanito had human waiters was because Marisa's parents had four kids they could use as free labor, and even then the restaurant was close to going under.

Marisa kicked off her shoes and rubbed her feet and calves, trying to massage the soreness out of them before she fell asleep. How much longer would they be able to keep this house? she wondered. How much longer would Marisa be in this room? She let go of her legs and fell back on the bed, staring at the ceiling. Bao, one of her closest friends, helped support his family by skimming microtransactions from tourists in Hollywood—the brave new world of high-tech pickpocketing. Was that Marisa's future? Her friend Anja, on the other hand, was the daughter of one of the richest men in LA. Marisa knew that *that* wasn't her future.

It was 2050. Los Angelenos had nearly limitless technology, and still most of them were struggling. Why wasn't the world more fair?

She watched the ceiling until it grew too blurry to see, and woke up to bright rays of sunlight stabbing through the gaps in her curtains.

"Wake up, Mari!" shouted her mother. "Church in an hour!"

Marisa squeezed her eyes shut and moved her shoulders in slow, painful patterns, trying to work out the kinks. It took her a minute to realize that it was already morning—the night had passed in a blink, and she didn't think she'd moved a millimeter from where she'd fallen the night before. Her legs were still dangling off the side of the bed, and as she moved them, needles of pain shot from knee to heel. She groaned, too tired to be angry, and rolled over on her side, curling into a fetal position.

Marisa's mother, Guadalupe, opened her door with a hurried flourish. "Come on, chulita, up and at 'em. Why are you wearing jeans? It's Sunday, mija, we need to go to church."

Marisa pushed herself to a sitting position, squinted against the light, and pointed at her San Juanito T-shirt with both hands.

"You fell asleep in your clothes!" said Guadalupe, bustling into the room and throwing open Marisa's closet. She was a large woman, with hair that hovered somewhere between blond and yellow. A laundry nuli rolled in after her, prowling for errant clothes, and Marisa wasn't able to lunge for her favorite shirt in time—the nuli grabbed it with a rubber-tipped claw and stuffed it into a basket for transport to the washing machine. Marisa groaned and fell back on the bed, covering her eyes with her arm. "I tell you this every week, Mari," her mother continued, sorting through the clothes in her closet, "but you don't have a single dress you can wear to church. Just because there's a band there doesn't make it a nightclub."

"I can wear the green one," said Marisa from under her arm.

"You can't wear the green one," said Guadalupe. "It goes halfway up your thighs. You can wear the blue one."

"I hate the blue one."

"Then stop spending your money on trashy dresses," said Guadalupe. "Nobody goes to church to look at your butt."

"I can think of three people off the top of my head," said Marisa.

"Sure," said Guadalupe, dropping the blue dress and a pair of black shoes on the bed. "But those aren't the kind of people you want looking at your butt. Now get up."

Marisa grumbled again, but she had to admit her mom had a point. Omar Maldonado, in particular, could stab himself to death with a wire hanger for all she cared. "What time is it?"

"You have a computer in your head," said Guadalupe, bustling back toward the hallway. "You'll figure it out. Now get in the shower fast before Pati gets there, or you won't have any hot water."

Marisa sighed in the sudden quiet, as her mom's blustering admonitions moved next door to her sister's room. She enjoyed the peace for a moment, contemplating for one glorious second the unspeakable joy of going back to sleep again, but then she rubbed her eyes, grabbed her dress, and headed for the shower. She made it there just two steps before Pati, and locked the door while the angry twelve-year-old rattled the handle.

"Let me in!" Pati whined. "I can pee while you shower."

"I'll be fast," called Marisa.

"Will you let me out first?" asked a male voice, and Marisa shrieked and spun around. Sandro, her sixteen-year-old brother, was combing his hair in the mirror—already showered and dressed. Because of course he was.

"Ugh," said Marisa, opening the door again. "Get out!"

"Thanks," said Sandro, smiling as he left.

"Thanks!" said Pati, and rushed in as Sandro walked out. Pati closed the door behind herself and started stripping down. "Morning, Mari, what's up?"

"For the love of . . ." Marisa shook her head, closing her eyes, then stepped into the shower and closed the curtain behind her.

"Can't I get a second of privacy?"

"You're wearing your clothes in the shower," Pati called out.

"I know," Marisa growled. "Just . . . don't follow me in *here*, or I'll upload every virus on the internet into your skull."

"I found a virus yesterday," said Pati cheerfully. "I tried to catch it, like you do, but I think I had my program set up wrong because the virus got into my active memory and I had to spend all afternoon cleaning out my djinni. And I need your help with my homework, because we're trying to learn binary and it doesn't make any sense—teacher said that two equals ten, and that two doesn't even exist, and it's the dumbest thing I've ever heard and I need you to explain it all to me—"

Marisa tuned her out, undressing and showering while the girl babbled on without hardly pausing for breath. When she turned off the water Pati was still going strong, extolling the virtues of some new antivirus package she'd just found online, and Marisa wrapped her towel around herself while they switched places. Pati's excited monologue continued from the shower stall, and Marisa stared at herself in the mirror—her hair was a twisted black bird's nest with fading red tips. Time to dye it again, or maybe try another color. Except that dye cost money, and she still had half a bottle of red. Red it was, then, but not this morning. She'd stay faded for another day. She dried herself and put her clothes on, sneering at the stupid blue dress, then retreated toward her bedroom to try to untangle her hair.

"Hey, Mari," said Gabi, her other little sister. Whereas Pati was a roiling singularity of energy, fourteen-year-old Gabi was practically a ghost—not because people ignored her, but because she tended to ignore everyone else. She drifted down the hallway with barely a wave, wearing a cream top and a black skirt with just enough bounce to look like a ballerina's. Gabi's ballet classes had been one of the more recent luxuries to face the budget chopping block, and ever since then she'd started looking for every opportunity to passive-aggressively remind the entire family what a tyrannical, life-destroying decision that had been. Now that Marisa looked a little more closely, she could swear that Gabi's entire outfit was a dance costume from one of last year's performances. Gabi went out of sight down the stairs, and Marisa went back to her room to find her makeup.

She didn't even think about the KT Sigan login information until her mother made another sweep of the house, dragging everyone downstairs to leave.

"Vámonos!" called Guadalupe, pushing everyone outside. Marisa ran the brush through her hair one last time before grabbing her shoes, hopping from one foot to the other as she tried to put them on in the middle of her mother's relentless drive toward the front door. She blinked open the notepad where she'd saved the security info, cursing herself for falling asleep so early last night, but before she could do anything with the data she was outside, blinking in the hot California sunlight, and her father was gathering them all with his loud, bombastic voice.

"Line up, Carnesecas!" he bellowed cheerfully. "Miran, que lindos!"

Good morning, sent Sahara.

No time, Marisa sent back, sweeping the message away with a blink. **Church.**

"Late night?" asked Sandro, falling into step beside Marisa. The church was at least a mile away, and they couldn't afford an autocab, so they walked.

Ooh, sent Sahara. **Have fun.**

"No," said Marisa, trying to keep track of all her conversations at once. "I fell asleep as soon as we got home."

"Maybe there was a sedative in that pricey salad," said Sandro.

"Cállate," said Marisa. She focused on her Sigan security notes, hoping to use the walk for something productive, and almost immediately tripped on a broken slab of sidewalk. "Madre de—"

"Ay, que fea," said her abuela, catching her right arm and steadying her before she fell. "That's a mouth, not a gutter." Guadalupe's mother had lived with them ever since the move to the larger house, and church was one of the only times she left it.

"I'm amazed she heard you," Sandro whispered.

Marisa waited for her abue to snap at Sandro for disrespect—they didn't call her la Bruja for nothing—but of course she only heard Marisa's breach of courtesy, not Sandro's. Of course. Marisa shook her head, considered trying to parse the data, but closed the notepad and blinked it away. She'd already scratched the toe of her shoe, and her abue was gripping her arm like a nuli with a broken claw. She'd have to resign herself to a morning with the family before she had a chance to break into Sigan's network. She leaned against her abuela's arm and sighed.

"Ay, abuelita," she said. "It's been one of those days."

"You've only been awake for an hour," said her abuela.

"One of those weeks, then," said Marisa. She looked at the

scratch on her shoe. "One of those lives, maybe."

"Why do you always wear the blue dress?" asked her abuela. "If I had your butt, I'd wear the green one."

Marisa smiled for the first time all morning. "I love you, Abue."

The seven of them made their way to church, already sweating in their stiff, uncomfortable clothes: Marisa, her siblings, her mother, her abuela, and at the head of them all her father, Carlo Magno Carneseca. The only one missing was her older brother, Chuy, but he was estranged from everyone in the family but Marisa herself, and even their relationship was strained. He'd left their home years ago, and lived today with his girlfriend and their year-old son. At times like this Marisa missed him even more than usual, but as long as Chuy insisted on running with a gang—La Sesenta, the most dangerous in Mirador—their father would never allow him back again. Chuy was probably too proud to come back anyway.

Men were idiots.

Is Omar going to be there? sent Sahara.

At church? asked Marisa. **Probably.**

If you slip the priest a few extra yuan will he damn him to hell?

Marisa smirked. **You think Omar needs help getting into hell?**

I just want to cover all my bases, sent Sahara.

Stop talking about Omar, Marisa sent back. **I'm going to church, I need to think reverent thoughts.**

What's up, my sexy bitches? sent Anja. Her message

popped up in the corner of Marisa's vision, automatically merging with Sahara's to create a single conversation.

Shh, Sahara chastised. **Marisa's trying to be reverent.**

Sorry, sent Anja. **What's up, my reverent bitches?**

I'm seriously going to just close this conversation and block you both, sent Marisa.

But then you'll miss my news, sent Anja. **It is both great and momentous.**

Aren't those the same thing? sent Marisa.

Marisa has news too, sent Sahara.

Yeah? sent Anja.

I found a Sigan security code, sent Marisa.

Tol, sent Anja. She and her father had moved here from Germany a year ago, and she used almost as much German as Marisa used Spanish. That word, Marisa knew, meant "cool," but that was pretty much the limit of Marisa's German. **What'd you find when you went in?**

I haven't yet, sent Marisa.

Then stop wasting time in church, sent Sahara. **Let's find Grendel!**

That's big news, sent Anja. **My news is bigger.**

Marisa laughed. **How am I possibly supposed to think about Jesus with you two chatbots babbling at me like this?**

Fine, then, sent Anja. **I'm calling a meeting. As soon as Fang and Jaya wake up, we shall convene our most sacred order of the Cherry Dogs.**

You want the team to meet in Overworld? asked Marisa.

So let it be coded, said Anja, **in the great central processor in the sky.**

She's either making fun of you, sent Sahara, **or this is really big news. She only talks churchy when it's serious.**

The seriousest, said Anja. **That's a stupid word, by the way.**

It's not a word, sent Sahara.

English is just stupid in general, sent Anja.

Blame Sahara, sent Marisa. **Yo soy Mexicana.**

"We're here," said Sandro, nudging Marisa subtly with his elbow. She refocused her eyes on the real world, and saw the big yellow church looming in front of them. Most of Mirador was right on the poverty line, if not well below it, but the Maldonados knew when to throw money at community projects, and the church they'd built was a massive tribute to both God and themselves, in relatively equal parts. Her eye caught a row of black autocars rolling up to the curb—two Dynasty Falcons, by the look of them, flanking a long, sleek Futura Sovereign. That could mean only one thing.

Gotta go, sent Marisa. **Don Francisco's here.**

From the *New York Times* bestselling author of *Partials*

Don't miss the second book in the Mirador series!

JOIN THE

Epic Reads

COMMUNITY

THE ULTIMATE YA DESTINATION

◄ DISCOVER ►
your next favorite read

◄ MEET ►
new authors to love

◄ WIN ►
free books

◄ SHARE ►
infographics, playlists, quizzes, and more

◄ WATCH ►
the latest videos